I0750350

THE FINAL DAYS

A NOVEL

by

WAYNE LANTER

Twiss Hill Press
Freeburg, Illinois

Twiss Hill Press
P. O. Box 122
Freeburg, Illinois 62243

ISBN 13: 978-0-9838412-1-0
ISBN 10: 0983841217
LCCN: 2013930602

Second edition

Cover by Donna Biffar

Twiss Hill Press
P.O. Box 122
Freeburg, Illinois

For Nathan and Joshua

- no father on this earth ever loved
or ever will love his son(s) more profoundly
- e e cummings

THE FINAL DAYS

A NOVEL

Chapter I

After his last class Friday John Carter came out of Jefferson Hall into a gathering snow. He circled the quad past the student union and paused a few moments to examine the circulars on the kiosk that divided the walkway. He scanned the offerings, the usual manifestos, rock concerts and poetry clubs, students looking for a ride home at Christmas, a notice *The Bulldog Bark*, the Barker State daily newspaper, needed workers.

One flier, lifted by the wind, caught his eye. A dull black, pulp-paper scrap, torn halfway down, with a small red dragon stamped in the lower left corner. The dragon he noted was not the open-winged symbol of Wales, but a crouching, slithering oriental variety.

He had seen the dragon on walls around campus, in dozens of places, probably with a rubber stamp. Beneath the dragon was always the accompanying statement, "We owe it to the Red Dragon."

No doubt an ad or announcement for a cyberspace game. He pulled the circular from the kiosk, stuffed it in his pocket and proceeded toward his office in Temperly Hall.

In spite of the temperature, the snow was peaceful and welcome. Few things enlivened Carter's imagination as the shift in seasons and changes in scenery it could produce. He especially admired the severity of winter.

Inside Temperly he shook off the snow and decided against the elevator. Why not? He felt good and took to the solitude of the wide darkened stairway of the old building, pulling himself along the smooth balustrade to the first landing. The blowing snow picked at the high-arched windows shadowing the stairwell with a late afternoon gloom.

He tried to adjust his eyes.

"I suppose the weather's as foul as it appears from in here?"

The voice came from the landing above him, and when he looked up, blinking in the dull light, he could see the dark form, then the more detailed image of the old man.

"Good afternoon, Professor," Carter said.

The man hovered above him on the landing at mid-flight, tottering, balanced on the cane in his right hand, the ballast of a battered leather briefcase hanging from his left.

Professor Laertes, the ancient, bent Doctor Joshua Laertes, doyen of Barker State classic and antiquities studies.

Laertes scowled.

Carter waited.

"Snow," Carter said. "Wet snow."

Once a tall, thin man, Carter guessed, he had bent with age into a hump-shouldered stance. He had outlived most of his colleagues, as well as a host of younger ones. At seventy-nine he seemed nearly immortal.

Laertes fascinated Carter. Academically he had continued, persisted Carter would have said, beyond anyone's expectation. His was more than dedication, more than a man doing a job, even a job in which he was intently interested. He was an artifact, an ancient remnant-of-mind of the cultures he studied, what he studied, what he did.

Ten years before he had won a Pulitzer, before that a Guggenheim. His bibliography resembled the tablature of the Athenian dead in the Peloponnesian War. With respect and diffidence Barker acolytes referred to him as The Ur.

This day he wore a brown long-coat over a threadbare tweed jacket, brown shirt and wide black tie. Parted at the middle, his coarse gray hair fell loosely to either side. His eyes, harbored in the refuge of thick bushy brows, stared out of a thin, wrinkled and pitted face.

He stared at Carter.

"How deep is it?" he asked.

"Not too bad," Carter said. "An inch or so."

With his cane he pointed to the snow on Carter's coat and pants.

"Not bad, huh?"

"Not if you're careful," Carter said.

He inched closer to Carter and leaned forward on his cane.

"You know I have to walk two blocks in this. They took my parking place. They tell me now there's a proposal to charge us five hundred dollars a year for parking space. Did you know that?"

He waved his cane in the general direction.

"Hell, it'd be cheaper to take a cab. For twenty-five years I parked behind the cafeteria and no one said anything. Everybody got along. Now they tow my car away. Twice this month, and gave me a ticket.

"The first time I thought it was a mistake. Just goes to show what I know. Cost me thirty dollars to get it back."

"Who did that?"

"Who? Who do you think?"

He raised his cane and pointed to the top of the stairs.

"Up there. Those are crazy men, John. And don't be fooled. It's not about parking. They don't give a tinker's damn about where I park my car. You know what they want. They want me out. And not because of my age. They can't even count that high. It's money. They want my salary."

A notorious gambler, Laertes developed a system for blackjack and because of it had been barred from the tables at Vegas. He played the stock market with equal acumen, over the years parlaying seemingly worthless securities into a fortune of several million. As he pointed out, he was not dependent on the largess of the Barker State coffers.

"Fifty thousand dollars," Laertes said, "to hire a couple part-timers. A hand-full of those assembly-line half-wits. You know what they call those groveling simpletons? Adjunct faculty. Did you ever hear of such nonsense? Adjunct to what? Scholarship?

"And for all of this I walk two blocks to get here and another two to get out."

He readjusted his grip on the briefcase.

"Well, if they want me out, I may just give them what they want," he said. "I'm too old to waste time on fools. Hell, I'd do better spending my time on the golf course."

Until he developed arthritis Laertes reigned as one of Lancaster's better country-club golfers. He regularly won tournaments and once wagered and won fifteen hundred dollars playing and beating an opponent by walking backwards through eighteen holes.

He tapped the cane on the plank floor fathoming the warp and wear of the boards before trusting them with his weight, then smiled at Carter.

"One thing about hanging around as long as I have, it gives you a limited perspective on the future."

But it was the past not Laertes' future that buzzed the Barker State rumor mills. He had been married five times, sired a child for each of the wives, for at least two other women, and had been over the years labeled the necessary although not efficient cause of any number of un-couplings and divorces. Unlike Aquinas he had survived a stabbing by a jealous husband. As the luck of legend and nature had it, at seventy-nine he remained not only among the living, but unrepentant.

He laughed, bent over the cane, pleased Carter thought, with his observation.

Somber again, he admonished Carter. "Be careful, John, they've even taken to tampering with my schedule. Have you seen your spring schedule?"

"No," Carter said. "I have had the same one now for seven years."

"Seven years? I suppose you know what kind of luck that can bring? If I were you, I'd check on it. They've closed two of my seminars. No one can register. Two or three days before classes begin, they'll open them again. But no one will be interested. A few of the graduate students who need me. They'll be the only ones. Nobody else. Then Crowly will come around with his nonsense that I'm too old and no one's interested in my classes.

"Contumacy. Mendacity and contumacy."

Carter watched him grumbling to the bottom, then turned to the stairs.

The fourth-floor landing opened into the long ornate hall with a high flat pressed-copper-skin ceiling and a half-dozen dangling less-than-bright white porcelain globes.

Carter's heart hammered from the climb. He dropped his books onto a chair near the door and bent over, hands on his knees to catch his breath.

The hall was deserted, except for the cardboard cutouts of the secretaries moving silently at the near end in the glass case of the office of the Academic Corporate Vice Chancellor for Instruction.

Carter stopped outside Morgana Carmichal's office and tapped on the frame. No answer. He glanced at the corkboard on the door. No messages. Would she have gone without locking up? Unlikely, he decided.

He withdrew up the hall, between the long flat glass-top cases of fossils, the worn wooden floor of the old building complaining beneath his feet, and slipped into the sanctuary of the small office he shared with Mason Oldam.

Even with the large windows on the corner walls and sub-freezing weather, the room had overheated.

His watch showed four-twenty. He tapped the crystal, then checked the wall clock. He'd wait another hour or so, clean up the details on his desk and give the storm, if it was a storm, time to develop.

Again he thought of Laertes' complaints. There were always complaints at the university, injustices, inconveniences. Contumacy, Laertes called it.

Outside the snow showered down in heavy white sheets. He would wait for the streetlights to come on, then make his way down the several untracked virgin blocks to Murphy's. This satisfied him. The disruption of routines in a world closed down, shrouded from sight and sound.

Privacy, he thought. Given the choice, he'd choose solitude, the insular life, monastic, even one snowbound and bone-chilled. He thought of it as privacy. In the chill of late afternoon, the soft, blank, concealing white of deepening snow represented him well.

The day had dimmed noticeably and the apparition of his reflection hung a short distance behind the glass in a half-light image. The reflection avoided more than it showed of the creases and crevasses of his face, his white hair, the extra pounds he carried over the ledge of his belt.

He took the dragon flier from his pocket and tacked it to the bulletin-board opposite his desk, partially covering Dewey's somber face.

He turned to survey the cluttered board. He had decorated the large bulletin-board with handbills for university events, political cartoons and the portraits and drawings of philosophers.

Mill, Kant, Hume, Locke, Stumpf, Husserl.

He had a particular fondness for Hume, and had half-a-dozen pictures of the Edinburgh sage along the top of the board.

There were several yellowed newspaper photos of his early days in Chicago, marching with Martin Luther King against the Vietnam War, and a picture of him as a ten-year-old carrying a picket sign with his father in a Southern Illinois mine strike.

He leaned over the desk to consult the poster sized calendar, the block of months he had picked up in the University bookstore for three dollars.

His eyes dropped along the months to December and the date. Friday, December first. The date of the first tracking snow would give the number of tracking snows there would be that winter. Who had said that? His grandfather, who else?

But now to the mundane, a quiz waiting his evaluation. He shuffled through the papers. Lost on the second paper in a welter of abstractions and illogic, looking for a foothold, he awoke to a muffled tapping behind him.

Turning partially in his chair, he looked over his glasses, a bit surprised anyone might still be in the building.

"Yes?" he said, expecting Morgana.

"Professor Carter, could we speak to you for a moment? We were just passing and thought, well, we were wondering if you would help us."

The voice he recognized, or thought at least he had heard before, but could not immediately associate with the face in the doorway. Then he saw the second girl, the other of the "we," and quickly calculated an approximation of semester, class—the seventh row, probably near the back—before a sea of years, faces and classes washed over him.

The girl who had spoken to him was tall and lean with large brown eyes and high cheek bones, thin lips, a soft olive complexion, without makeup, and a rather long nose, altogether a bit horse-faced. Her hair, the same color as her eyes, hung straight, clean and carefully combed nearly to her hips. She wore a work-shirt only a shade darker than her levis. Her sneakers and imitation sheepskin coat were both worn and scarred.

He said, "Yes," again, to buy time, to recall her name—if he was right about the voice and face.

"Yes," he said, "can I help you?"

"We don't want to be a bother, to impose or anything like that, but we were wondering. We're both in Dr. Johnson's ethics class. Do you know Dr. Johnson?"

"I know him," he said, hesitantly, then prepared for the vague, exploratory, veiled insinuation.

Here we go again, he thought. No doubt a complaint about Carl Johnson.

What would it be this time? He knew the list. What did she find offensive about Johnson? His character, his personality, his cynical intelligence, his irreverence? How about his male lover? Young females generally found that hard to accept.

Student attempts to cull favors by gossiping about other instructors nettled Carter. The good-professor bad-professor routine ranked very near the top of student dementia. Too often he had seen the results. More than once, he had been a target.

There had been rumors of late about Carl. For more than a year, his attendance had been spotty. He was sick a good bit of the time, and even when he showed up, he did not look well.

"You're having trouble in ethics?"

"Yes," the girl with the familiar voice said, moving past her friend into the room. "Dr. Johnson doesn't explain things very well."

He was about to ask, what might be the size and thrust of her concerns with Johnson, perusing a rather suggestive list of crudities, but let it pass. He leaned back, elbows propped on the arms of the chair, holding a pencil by its ends between the tips of his index fingers. He looked at the girl, then back to the pencil, then to the girl again. Following his suggestion, she fixed her eyes on the pencil, staring at it, and when it disappeared, stood frozen for a moment, mouth open, eyes focused on the space between his fingers.

A soft, disbelieving smile crossed her face, as if she had been tricked, but enjoyed the deceit. "How did you do that?" she said.

"What is it you don't understand?"

"What'd you do with the pencil?"

"It's not what I did with the pencil," Carter said. "The real questions concerns what you think you saw.

"Now, if you have a question about philosophy, maybe I can help. If not, I have work to do."

The girl tilted her head slightly and smiled again.

"I don't believe you did that."

"Philosophy," Carter said. "What about it?"

The girl shook her head, as if to remove the image of the missing pencil, took a deep breath and began again.

"I was in your class, last year," she said, "you might remember me. And you made it seem so easy. Dr. Johnson, well, you know how he is."

"As a matter of fact," Carter said, turning back to his desk, "I have never been in Carl Johnson's classroom. If you need help with Dr. Johnson, I suggest you talk to him and resolve your difficulties there."

When he again looked at the girl, she had retreated and stood facing him, her books held tightly to her chest.

Still, he could not recall her name.

Her eyes filled with tears and her bottom lip quivered almost imperceptibly. He expected she might burst into sobs, or bolt and make a run for it. The other girl had backed out of the doorway into the hall.

"Now," he said a bit more kindly, "what is it you are asking about ethics?"

The girl shook her head, then turned to the darkened window.

"I can't" she said, her voice breaking, and added, "God, you don't have to be cruel."

"Cruelty," he said calmly, "has to do with demeaning other people."

"I didn't mean anything by it. I didn't know Johnson was your friend."

"It doesn't have to do with friendship," Carter said. "But if you didn't mean it, then you shouldn't have said it."

His voice was sharp again. He did not enjoy feeling badly for what other people did. A whiff of deception hung on the room.

"I'm sorry," she said, shaking her head and joined her friend in the hall. "Thank you, anyway." Her voice wavered, but without recrimination.

He could hear them walk away and heard the other girl say something about "the bastard."

He pushed the papers on his desk away and leaned toward the window. The streetlights were coming on, glowing in the diffusion of the falling snow, the poles draped with the hangings of Christmas. He half expected to see the girls on the street, in the circle of light beneath one of the poles, and pressed closer to the glass for a better view of the front of the building. The street, the walk and steps were deserted. Tire tracks trailed up the hill, angling off to the side where cars had slipped trying to make the grade.

The pleasantries of the evening had already dissipated. Annoyed with himself he decided to abandon the papers and head for Murphy's. He locked the office and rode the elevator down, nodding to the cleaning lady in the foyer as he passed.

Facing the elements, the wind and snow, he felt better. The contours of the landscape were already buried, hidden from the eye, the sharp corners of an intruding world made round and soft and quietly pleasant. Renoir's softness, a smooth flowing world.

Several years earlier he had given up driving on campus, walking whenever possible. He preferred the smells of the out-of-doors, of spring and fall, the sound and force of wind swirling leaves through yards, the severity of the August sun.

Even in the bleak bitter cold, he held his ground.

Walking tempered the problem of transition, of having been one place and too quickly arriving at another. The time it took to walk the six blocks from his house to Murphy's, or from Murphy's to Temperly, kept him in balance with time and space.

Carter suspected if the truth were known, why his 1964 vintage Pontiac Bonneville remained unused, sometimes for months, it would have had to do with his shrinking sense of a manageable environment.

Even in snowstorms, especially in heavy snow he was relieved not to have a machine to shepherd. Going up the hill, he could feel the stir of biting air pressed to his legs, the snow over the tops of his shoes and wet on his socks.

Between the large elms, the snow showered down, and walking with his head bowed against the wind, he very nearly ran into the girl.

"I thought you might come this way," she said, "so I waited."

He squinted at her, shielding his eyes from the blowing snow, wondering now who exactly she was, and puzzled by her presence. No doubt she'd come to even the score? No doubt.

"It must be important," he said.

"It is," she said, with something of a smile.

"It is important. Can I walk with you?"

He did not answer, but shuffled away in the snow and she ran to catch up and fell in at his side.

"I want to apologize for the way I behaved back there," she said. "That's not like me. I'm a lot better than that."

"Okay," he said, "so you're better. Now what?"

"Well, I just wanted to tell you."

They walked along then for a short time without speaking until the girl broke the silence.

"You do know me, don't you?"

"No," Carter said, "I don't. You could be anyone of a thousand people, old or young, deaf or dumb."

"You know," the girl said, walking sideways ahead of him and bending to see his face. "You know, you are a bastard."

"Because I don't know you?"

"No. Because I made you feel bad back there. I didn't expect you to be so abrupt. You were always so kind in class. God. You caught me off guard, and my reaction caught you off guard, made you do something you didn't want to do, and now you're trying to get even with me. So you won't admit that you remember me."

"That wasn't what you asked," Carter said. "You asked if I knew who you were. I don't. You said you were in my class. When? And why should I remember you, anyway?"

"Where are you going?" the girl asked.

"What do you mean, 'where are you going?' It's none of your business where I'm going."

The girl smiled and pulled her collar up.

"You are a bastard," she said playfully, nodding as if it were self-evident but she had only just come to believe it. "Where are you going?"

When he did not answer she took his arm. "Would you feel better if I told you my name?"

"At the moment, it isn't your name that's bothering me?"

"What then?"

She was holding to his arm with both hands as if she thought he might escape.

"The least you could do is offer to buy me a beer or some such civil thing. I promise I won't hold a grudge."

Carter came in the side door of Murphy's with the girl trailing and stepped around out of the flow of patrons and waitresses. The two stools against the wall at the end of the bar provided, if nothing more, at least the appearance of privacy. He took off his overcoat, shook it out and laid it over the bar, slid onto a stool and ran his hands through his wet hair.

The girl dropped her purse on the floor, then opened her coat inside-out and hung it over the stool. She twisted around to face him, her hands folded in her lap.

"Well," she said, "here we are. Now what?"

"Two beers," Carter told the bartender, then without looking at her, "and don't tell me you don't drink beer."

"No, no. Beer's fine," she said, he thought a bit smugly. "After all I suggested it."

The booths in the back were partially filled with early diners and at the far end of the bar, to one side near the front door, three hundred pound Seamus Murphy, in levis, a tee shirt and white apron, armed with a bottle of Blue Ribbon and a spatula, worked over the spit of an open grill. Occasionally he stepped back to watch the TV that hung from the ceiling in the corner above him.

The noise from the TV mingled with the voices of customers and the smell of Murphy's cheeseburgers in the muted light and warmth, settled on Carter. He finished his beer quickly, then ordered another.

"You need to relax," she said, her voice softly audible over the noise.

"I know," he said, conciliatorily. "But it gets to be a rather grand pain-in-the-ass."

"Do you come here often?"

He nodded, and held his glass out to the bartender.

"Occasionally."

"One of these days I'll have to take you to Giuseppe's," she said. "I think you'd like it."

"Giuseppe's," Carter said.

"Well, it's nice. It's Italian. It has more atmosphere than this."

"And I'm supposed to like that?"

"People usually do."

"I've been to Giuseppe's. I didn't like it."

He caught himself, smiling, amused. Sometimes, he thought, sometimes.

"Look," he said, "I'm sorry about the crap back in the office. But once in a while it piles up, and I don't handle it very well."

The girl raised her glass to him.

"Neither of us has had a good day," she said. "But right now, it is improving. By the way, what did you do with the pencil? Will you tell me?"

"Maybe I should take you up on your offer?"

She smiled a broad, intrigued smile.

"God, which one is that?"

"Your name," he said, "for now, just your name."

"Caroline Connors. Vivien Caroline Connors."

Carter thought about it for a moment, but could not remember the name.

"Well, Vivien Caroline, what brings you out in the night chasing around after old, worn-out men? And don't tell me you want to talk about ethics."

"We could," she said with a bit more seriousness than he expected. "And another thing. It's Mrs."

"Mrs. Connors the student."

Carter held his glass up and examined it for finger prints.

"How the hell old are you anyway?"

"Twenty-two."

"Twenty-two and married."

"For five years. And two children. Chris is five and Susan three."

"You got started early."

"I've always been in a rush. I still am."

"Out of father's house into husband's pit," Carter said. "Jesus, don't you people ever get tired of living clichés?"

"In this case it went from uncle to husband. Mom dumped me off at my grandmother's, and when she died, they sent me to my aunt and uncle."

"Where's your father?"

"He was killed in Vietnam."

"And now you're back in school?"

The girl nodded. "Boy, am I. This may be the hardest thing I've ever done. Well, it's really tough, with two kids."

"And a husband who doesn't want to foot the bill in money or time."

"You got it," she said, "he's not been very supportive or kind about the whole thing."

"Why should he be? He bought one thing, and now you're making him pay for another. He's buying you a ticket out of the house, and probably out of his life. The man would have to be fool not to see that."

"But it doesn't have to be that way. I really love him. I really do. You know what it means to love someone and not want to live with them?" She shook her head. "Shit," she said. "Here we go with gruesome topics. I didn't want to get into this."

"Why not? It's as good as anything. Better than talking about the chances for world peace?"

"I know, but you'll think I'm just a sappy hausfrau out to get revenge on an evil husband. But that's not it.

"Could I have another beer?"

Carter ordered two more beers and poked through the pocket of his overcoat for the last of a pack of Marlboros. He had wanted to give up cigarettes, but had never found a way to drink and not smoke. He lit one, took several puffs, then laid it in the ash tray. When it was sufficiently burned down, he rubbed it into his palm, took another from the pack and crumpled the cellophane and paper into an invisible ball, and lit the cigarette.

"John," the girl said, her voice raised with just the slightest reproach. "Don't do that. What are you doing?"

"It beats using the waste can," Carter said.

"And what did you do with the pencil?"

"It was a cigarette," Carter said.

"When I was in your office, you had a pencil between your fingers. What did you do with the pencil?"

"What did I do with a pencil you thought you saw, would be a better question," Carter said.

"But you had a pencil. A yellow pencil you were holding just like this." She held up her fingers several inches apart.

"There is no pencil there," Carter said. "What did you do with it?"

She drew away slightly, and regarded him for a moment.

"You're not going to tell me about the pencil, about how you did that."

"There's nothing to tell," Carter said.

"I know. Pencils and cigarettes, lit cigarettes and cigarette packages disappear all the time. Just, poof. Nothing."

"That's the way the universe operates," Carter said. "Now you see it, now you don't. Or better yet, now you don't see it. Tell me about your marriage."

"Well," she said quietly, "I'm not out to get even with anybody."

"But you're looking for a better deal," he told the girl. "You got what you wanted five years ago, and now you want something else."

"Needed," the girl said. "Needed then, and now I need more. I really feel terrible about the whole thing. I feel like a perfect shit. That man has been kind to me beyond belief. He loves those kids, and here I am messing things up for everybody."

"Then don't," Carter said. "It's still your choice. No one's twisting your arm."

"I wish. I wish I could say 'this is what I want and this is what I'm going to do.' But I don't know what I want. God, I'm twenty-two years old, I've spent the last five years of my life changing diapers and wiping noses, and just outside there's this big world I don't know anything about, a world I've never even seen."

"And in the order of things not seen, where's husband and kiddies at this moment?"

"At work. He's a janitor at the Washington Grade School over on Addison. He works from four to twelve. The kids are with their grandparents."

Her hands were thin with long slender fingers she used gracefully when she talked. She seemed a good bit older than twenty-two, and prettier than he thought. Her nose was thin, very nearly aquiline, her cheekbones high, eyebrows plucked and penciled in.

"Why'd you get married so early?"

"I had to."

"You got pregnant."

She nodded.

"That was intentional. I planned it."

"Then you didn't have to get married."

"It was the only way to get away from my uncle."

"Uncle or father, it's all the same."

"Not quite. You see, my uncle started with me when I was nine. My aunt worked nights, and I was always home alone with him, and, well, one thing led to another, and I guess he felt if he had to feed me he should get something out of it."

"Namely banging his nine-year-old niece."

"Yeah. Then my older brother came to live with us and he found out about it, and for the next six years I had to put up with both of them."

"Meanwhile, auntie looked the other way."

"I told her about it, once. About my uncle getting in bed with me. I was about eleven or twelve then, and she hit me. Told me if I knew what was good for me I'd keep my mouth shut. If I didn't, she said, if I wanted to start trouble, then I could look for another place to live. Which I did. But it took me five years to get it done."

"That makes sense. You keep the old man serviced and he won't bother her. So everybody's happy. Except you. Makes sense."

"Yeah. Like you say, for everybody but me.

"God," the girl said, looking at Carter carefully, "I don't know why I'm telling you this. You're surprised, aren't you? You think I'm crazy."

"Surprised? That uncles jump their nieces? I don't know. You seem to have survived it."

"It took me a long time to get over the hang ups. But I made it pretty well."

"A long time?"

"Ten years? I started messing around with the neighborhood boys when I was ten. Hell, if I was going to be pushed into it at home, I thought I might as well do it once in a while when I wanted to."

"From what I hear it happens a good bit more frequently than people think," Carter said.

"I can believe that," the girl said.

"So what do you want to know about ethics?"

She smiled.

"That does seem funny, now. I mean, after all I've told you, wanting to talk about ethics. You probably think I'm the last person in the world who should be talking about ethics."

"The good dwells within us, my dear," Carter said. "And, then, evil, too."

"What do you think of Dr. Johnson?"

"Carl Johnson," Carter said. "Oh, Carl's all right, if you don't make too much out of what he says, or the way he looks. Carl Johnson is a pig and a saint. It depends only on the day and your mood."

"He's really strange. Every other word that comes out of that man's mouth is about sex."

"That bothers you."

"No, it doesn't bother me so much, but it does seem unusual for a college teacher, specially an ethics teacher."

"The domain, dear girl, of moral philosophy is not, I am pleased to say, limited to Sunday-school classes and prim and proper old ladies. There's a good bit more to it. It even has to do with, heaven forbid, the pleasures of the body."

"But there's more to life than sex. Sex is only part of it."

"So much for the obvious. But if you're looking for examples that's one most students can relate to. And if it's bizarre enough it might even keep the back row awake. Some might call it moral turpitude," Carter said and pushed his empty glass away.

"They'd do damn near anything to make sex a moral issue. Take sex out of the world, say out of religion, and what would you have? Have you ever read the Bible? A society based on the Bible. Sex, booze and violence. A crazy, arbitrary, mad god. No wonder those loonies ended up lost in the wilderness. No wonder every nut in the world wants to be a prophet or a martyr."

"What does that mean?"

"Absolutely nothing," Carter said. "But silly complaints from foolish girls cause good people trouble."

"John, I'm not out to cause trouble."

"I know," Carter said, "but three years ago in a rather naive bit of politics, the Faculty Senate of this esteemed institution, the one I work for, wanted to clarify a disagreement and asked for a definition of what the administration would consider cause for dismissal on grounds of 'moral turpitude.' With typical bureaucratic overkill, the kind you get from fifth graders, the reply listed everything from drinking in public to traffic violations, a statement sufficiently broad and absurd enough to attract the attention of the newspapers and inspire a series of articles on the ethics of Barker professor-student relationships.

"As luck would have it, several months later Anselm Nolan, a lowly, and to the press, an inconsequential history professor, fell into a seamy little mine-field of a divorce with a wife who possessed an uncommon flair for revenge, and who realized a presently hot item with the press might serve her purposes.

"And this is the best part. For the thirteen years she had kept a meticulous record of Anselm's dalliances. Every smile and touch, every word of kindness was a listed matter of suspicion. She offered the newspaper the information as an example of the problem on university campuses in general, and at this university in particular. Moreover, she persuaded the last of Anselm's paramours, a graduate student twenty years his junior to come forth with a rather soppy story about how her affair with Anselm had affected her psychologically and ruined her chances of ever becoming a first-rate historian.

"As it was, Anselm's old lady should have been the historian. With her memory for detail and her flair for dramatics, she could have launched Ivan-the-Terrible as a Russian fourteen-year-plan for population control.

"So the newspapers howled 'moral turpitude,' then printed a complete confession by the girl. We had all run into her on different occasions and to the last figured she was a bit batty. However, the furor went howling for several months, with accusations and threats, along with intimations of lawsuits. But, in the end, no one could agree on the perimeters or nature of moral turpitude.

"Carl, your old friend, had it right. He defined moral turpitude. It was as good as anything I heard.

"'I'll tell you what moral turpitude is,' he said. 'If I get caught in bed with your wife, that's funny. If you get caught in bed with my wife, well, that's annoying. But if either of us get caught in bed with a dead man, sir, that's moral turpitude.'"

Funny or annoying and humorous, Carter thought. Hell the dead wouldn't object.

"I didn't mean to start rumors about anyone," the girl said. "And Johnson's not my friend. I don't even like him.

"What happened to Nolan?"

"Who knows," Carter said. "Maybe he went into business with an uncle. He'd have been a fool to go back in the classroom. Maybe he's dealing drugs. If you're going to have people hacking at you, why not get something for it?"

"But I am glad you let me come with you. I was hoping you'd be free tonight. That's what I came in to ask you."

"In the office?"

"Yes. To ask if we could go out for a beer."

"When did you decide that?"

"Last year. God. I did everything I could to get you to notice me in class."

"By notice you mean take you out for a beer."

"Yeah. That would have been nice."

"And since it didn't happen, you decided to come in and ask me out?"

"It wasn't easy. That's why I brought Ruth along. John, whether you know it or not, you do intimidate people. Students talk about you. Even when you're nice you scare them to death. I've been sitting around for months trying to get up enough courage to come and ask you. That's why I was so upset when you got angry. I thought, 'Oh, hell, there it goes, I blew it.' Then I thought, 'Well, too bad about the grouchy old bastard. He wants to be that way, I'm still going to ask him.'"

"What happened to your friend?"

"She thinks I'm crazy."

"Maybe you are."

"Maybe."

"That brings us to the present. Now what?"

"The snow has stopped. We could go out and play in the snow."

"And then?"

"My feet are wet. I need to warm up. How about you? We could go to Ruth's. She lives just a few minutes from here. She won't be home tonight. What do you think?"

"Let's have another beer," Carter said. "Then you go on to your friend's house or home and get your feet dry."

"Mmmm. It would be a nice way to end the evening. We could have fun."

"In the snow?"

"Yeah," she said. "That too."

"Not tonight," Carter said.

"When?" the girl said. "This was really nice, John. Are you busy tomorrow? We could rendezvous here."

"Why should we? Why should I?"

"You don't want to?"

"That's not the question. My question is why should you want to do that? Why should I want to?"

"Meet me and I'll tell you."

"You could tell me now."

"Well, if you're going to leave, I'd rather wait. We should save something for next time."

"I stop in here a couple times a week," Carter said. "If you're around, you can tell me."

Chapter II

The following morning Carter found a note from Katherine Marie on the kitchen table. "Left a little early because of the weather. Back late Sunday. Love, K."

She would be away for the weekend. Something about Chicago and a convention. Traveling ice-packed highways. She'll probably end up-side-down in a ditch outside Litchfield.

He sat at the small kitchen table sipping coffee, looking out on the all-white, overly bright day, thinking about the girl. He had left her outside Murphy's with less than a promise to see her again. She had taken his reticence well enough, kidding him about what his wife would say if he wasn't home on time. Then she had gone off.

Back to hubby and kids, the conjugal duties of the female, he thought, whatever the hell that means.

With a second cup of coffee he proceeded to the living-room that served the large house as den, office and library. Three walls were covered from floor to ceiling with books, the fourth held a large fireplace and oak mantle. After sorting through Friday's mail he finished his coffee, then poked around in the ashes and started a fire.

The girl's aura, her voice and scent, hung at the edge, printed on the chilled, bright white-light of the morning.

He wondered what a female of twenty-two might see in him. What might bring her out on a winter night to track him down and propose a liaison? Adding to her resume. No doubt.

The university was rife with couplings, as it had always been. The intimacy of classroom instruction, tampering with the inner workings of the most sensitive and vulnerable tissues of the mind and soul often stimulated tension and sexual suggestion.

Otherwise, sex as a gift to sweeten the judgment of the classroom adjudicator. How about adventure? Carter suspected for female students taking their male teachers to bed, there were as many motives as there were hook-ups. In one case he had heard a Barker State coed took as her task for the semester, not only the rigors of academic excellence, accumulating an A average in her four courses, but the added homework of bedding her four male instructors at least five times each before final week.

Of course there was always cooing and ahhing and ass-wiggling. A number of times Carter's ego had been soothingly stroked, pleasantly so, by female flattery and perceptions, perceptions so unlike his own.

"Dr. Carter you are the most macho teacher I've ever had."

What is macho? Carter didn't know. He had never supposed himself to be particularly masculine or overly supplied with testosterone.

"Dr. Carter," a perky, attractive coed had crooned to him, quietly one day as they crossed the quad, "I just love your voice. You remind me of Richard Burton and Johnny Cash. You look more like Cash, but you sound so much like Burton. Did anyone ever tell you that?"

What did Cash look like? A face and, probably, a soul aged, furrowed and scarred with a history of self-abuse and hope?

But Carter had been flattered with the Burton comparison. He tried to recall the last time a woman, young or otherwise had approached him with more than a compliment and came to an autumn afternoon several years before when a knock on the classroom door interrupted a lecture on Aristotle. The source of the tap, he discovered to be a former student, a young woman. When he came into the hall, she quickly slipped a note with a phone number into his hand.

"Call me. The sooner the better. It's important," she said.

He did call, but on further consideration decided not to pursue the option.

That was the last time a female student, present or former, had made her interests known to him. It was the last time he had entertained the idea of acquiescing to such an encouragement. Maybe, he thought, I should have taken Mrs. Connors up on her suggestion. Certainly she's attractive, and personably so.

However it was, his fascination and counsel divided, and he lost heart in the inquiry. Although the offer was enticing and unusual, and the adolescent of his soul was pleased with the girl's attention, the old man of experience remained skeptical. Back we go to Hume, he assumed, the scramble of light and sight. Talking to the girl had been enjoyable, and he'd leave it at that.

An hour later, however, he was still drifting through the bits and pieces of the conversation when the phone rang. The voice he recognized immediately, although he was not sure why or how.

"Thought I'd call and apologize for dumping on you last night," she said. "That's not me."

"It's all right," he said, his voice shaded now with a patina of skepticism, now annoyed. Her candor left Carter a bit unsettled.

"Did you dry out and get warm?"

"Finally. But it took a long time," she said. "I could have used help."

When he did not respond, she continued.

"What are you doing tonight?" she said.

"Whatever it is, I'll enjoy it."

"Did you think about tonight?"

"No," Carter said, "not tonight."

The girl did not answer immediately. Then she said, "John, you trying to be a bastard again?"

"I'm busy," Carter said, "until ten or so."

"And after that?"

"There is no life after," he said.

"We could meet at Murphy's."

"I'd rather not," Carter said.

Again she did not respond, and he continued.

"Last night was pleasant. You shouldn't think it has anything to do with my schedule tonight," he said, hoping to sound credible.

"I was wondering about that," she said.

Her voice did not offer even a slight detectable shift in tone. It was as if she had not heard him. As if she were talking to herself and did not hear him when he spoke.

"We could meet after class, Monday," Carter said, trying to remember his Monday afternoon schedule.

"Well, I'd rather not," she said, "but if it's the best you can do. I mean, it seems such a waste."

"How about tomorrow afternoon?" he said, and left it at that.

That evening he planned to attend a faculty senate Christmas party.

In early October the notice had come in the campus mail and he had scratched out a check for ten dollars to the senate secretary. He had kept the date open, held in abeyance should he, when the time arrived, not feel up to it.

Now he decided he would go.

Then, too, he wasn't really sure what the girl was up to. Maybe she, too, was celebrity- or professor-humping. Maybe she had designated him as celebrity of the week.

Although he had encountered any number of bloated egos at Barker, Carter had never thought of the faculty as celebrities. In truth? The professorate? Carter was often reminded of Carl Johnson's definition. "Sheep in sheep's clothing bleating at the wind."

Of course there were baseball annies, and rock-band groupies making plaster-casts of Jagger's prick. When male academic celebrities came to campus, grad-school females queued up for the privilege of giving the visiting all-star a romp in the sack. You just never knew but that a fond remembrance might one day provide an appointment.

Baylor Henry, a nationally renowned economist from Yale, who spent one semester at Barker, confessed quite openly to Carter that any number of female students had showed up at his apartment.

"And they didn't come to talk about the GNP."

Carter surmised a good bit of political, big money sex was celebrity- or novelty-balling, with a monetary kicker. Celeb and novelty liaisons, he imagined, were driven mostly by curiosity and/or boredom and often limited to one-night-stands, simply adding knots to the G string or hanging beaver pelts on the wall.

Carter couldn't recall immediately when he might have been the celeb singled-out and tracked, but a number of times he had been taken in with revenge or counterbalance sex. The "I owe the sonofabitch one," or "I've got one coming" scheme appearing in the night intent on evening the score with a spouse or lover.

Occasionally, and not unusually, it came from familiar sources. After a few nights of amorous activity with a long-time friend, the friend apprised him of her motives.

"I'm using you," she said. "Did you know that?"

"Everybody's using everybody all the time," Carter had said.

"You were my best and safest alternative to get even with him."

Carter had let it go, pleased to be of service and satisfied at the very least she had found a use for him.

Among the list, in Carter's estimation the blackmail strain was particularly odious. It amounted to little more than an insidious branch of prostitution, sex for material benefits, although it was not usually as dangerous as the Iago category.

Iago-fucking was devised solely to encourage the physical assault of one human by another. Often it took a masochistic bent, designed to entice the old man into a savagery of domestic mayhem. Often females used it to direct their keeper's wrath toward another male. The plenary variety was contrived to do both.

In its more historical and deadly form, since the males of the species were enormously fond of kicking hell out of each other, occasionally one would end dead and the other incarcerated and the dissimulator shed of both. Then following a brief period of moaning the perpetrating seductress would go off with another and start over.

Several categories had a softer, more humane touch. For Carter friendship- or favor-fucking was one of these. Without malice, and with something of good will, FF could be a generous and humane pastime. And not without merit. In practice, he had known trysts of the favor variety to develop into extended relationships of mutual respect.

Once in a time or two lust could be a decent ingredient in the mix, the chemistry of attraction triggering a sexual encounter. Sex just for the hell of it. Sex for fun. Maybe.

As he aged, Carter thought less and less of this. Most sex was by design, opportunistic and hardly an end in itself.

Where he fit into this with the girl, he didn't know.

At eight-fifteen Carter left the house for the brisk walk along the river to the University Assembly Center, a renovated three-story brick Steamboat Gothic farmhouse the university had acquired in a land acquisition. The house set on a knoll in a woods, bordered on two sides by a crook in the river. The surrounding lands had been sold off or plastered with the black scabs of parking lots and tennis courts.

Carter cut through the woods and came up in the snow on the side of the house away from the road and the parking lot in the rear. Already the first-floor was filled with music, voices and laughter. He circled to the back porch, knocked the snow off his shoes, then let himself in. After depositing his overcoat on a chair in the foyer he proceeded to the living-room and what appeared to be the main body of twenty or thirty early arrivals.

The carpeted large main-room, which had once served as a ballroom, was lined with stainless-steel pipe and canvas chairs. A large brown conference table decorated with a Christmas-candle center-piece crowded one corner. The walls were hung with abstract modern art provided by Barker State artists and farm memorabilia junk. At the center of the long outside wall a fire burned in the marble-mantled fireplace. A green Christmas wreath with a red ribbon hung above the mantle.

Of the people Carter expected to see he recognized Timo Clark and Kerm Soliski in a far corner near the table of hors d'oeuvres.

Timo was a Nigerian lecturer of African literature, a tall thin woman with light brown skin of a richly blended shade unlike anything Carter had ever seen. She was tall, with slender hips and well formed, finely sculpted breasts that fell from her long neck and soft shoulders in a full, ample slope and supported by the extravagant lower full-crescent of the breasts themselves.

She was, to Carter's estimation, between thirty-five and forty-five, although for ego's sake, Carter set her nearer to forty-five.

Her body was strong and well-conditioned, firm, as if her daily routines might have included an eternalizing activity.

Her face was thin with wide soft eyes and a prominent brow. She wore her hair closely cropped, and for this occasion, a low cut, shear purple-silk dress that blended, in Carter's senses, magically with the mood of her resplendent skin, a dress that without the impediments of under-garments, moved when she moved, as she moved.

One of her parents was an Anglican missionary, the other Nigerian. "That's what comes of missionaries going to Africa," Carter was fond of thinking. "A damn decent trade for the natives having had to put up with Christian proselytizing."

Timo had come to America as a teenager, attended Princeton and Yale, and spent a good bit of time in Europe.

At a more visceral level she was sculpted of a mix of sensual gestures, both personal and female. It was in the way she held herself, the way she stood, her manners. When she smiled she smiled a full, beautiful smile.

She was a complex rife of perception and intelligence fashioned wonderfully to hold the attracted right there, at arm's length, beguiled and sedated, the way a snake hypnotizes a bird. When she spoke she spoke so softly Carter always ended leaning toward her as if he had a major hearing deficiency. His slightly tilted, bent stance did nothing to alter the habit. Simply enough she used soft speech to quiet the world and bring it to her. A damn effective tool, Carter appreciated, that added a bit of attractive mystery to the already visually enigmatic.

Although she had been at Barker for five years, they had met only three years before, very nearly to the day, in December when Carter volunteered to represent the philosophy department on the Inter Scholastic Discipline Coordination Committee. Usually he viewed committee work as worthless, since whatever could be agreed upon would be impenetrably general and without significance, and in the end the administration already knew what course it would take, committee or no committee. But since he had volunteered he felt obligated to appear. Then, too, it was the easiest way to keep informed about what was not happening and the unreason for it.

Seated at the table the first day, Carter surveyed the participants for familiar faces. Many of them he recognized from past hassles, people who always showed up supporting the administration scam of the day.

After the meeting was called to order, introductions were made, mostly as a formality or for the benefit of the initiates.

During a quick survey Carter noted the several faces with which he was not familiar, assigning each a personality and status their appearance suggested. As always for good or bad, in every case he was wrong. But nowhere had he been more errant than in his first-impression of Timo Clark.

Not only did he misread the terms of her origins, class and education. She was far better schooled than most of the Barker State pretenders, but even after she spoke, giving substance to her startling visual appearance, Carter did not know what that would afford.

Several meetings later when Carter reminded the committee the primary purpose of a university education was to prepare citizens, two business school representatives announced that in their opinion people did not become prosperous by way of citizenship.

"Contrary to your idealizing, the vast majority of people would rather have material wealth than good citizenship. In truth it makes no difference what people believe or think, as long as they have money to spend and goods to buy."

This bit of social observation came from Raymond Arnold, the same professor who had a few years earlier told Carter there was really no need to conserve world oil deposits since by the time the present supply was used up new ones would have developed.

During the early weeks of committee work Timo had remained beyond the polemics. But that day while other committee members gazed in to space or doodled on their note pads, she came in on Carter's behalf.

"While the American business mentality suggests Americans are a majority of some kind," she said, "Professor Carter speaks for the majority of the people in the world. People in countries without stable governments or citizens educated well enough to form good governments would not agree that material wealth is most important. Without educated citizens, material wealth is, at best, precarious and ephemeral."

Carter didn't say more, but sat back and watched and listened.

"It is very American," Timo said, "to imagine people think only of money. I doubt if Americans spend as much time thinking about money as the media and money changers would have us believe. There are things other than money people hold more precious. And as Professor Carter has stated, it is the university's task to provide an education to develop and support these principles.

"Maybe it would be a good idea for the spoiled American minority of the world to give up their childish fantasies and join the human community."

The committee's response was not to respond at all but to continue as if nothing had been said.

Thinking about it later, Carter viewed Timo's support as pleasantly professional, laced with the possibility of personal elements. But that wasn't the end of it.

At lunch one day Carter had locked horns with Willis Crabtree, director of the Black Studies division about the need for "Black Studies." Timo was at the table and in passing Crabtree referred to her as "African sister Clark."

Calmly, but with annoyance, Timo reminded him that she was not his "sister," and was only vaguely, as she put it, African.

"I'm Nigerian," she said. "You're American, and certainly not my brother. And although we may have a good bit in common as humans, it has nothing to do with the shade of our skins. That is not a significant determinant of human classification or relationships."

It was a so-far-so-obvious statement the bureaucrats never understood.

After the committee completed its work the following March, Carter ran into Timo at off times, in the cafeteria, at faculty gatherings. Several times she even came to his office, albeit to see Mason, but he had an opportunity to talk to her.

She was one of the few women with whom his fascination was blind, nearly total, and he judged almost adolescent. In her presence, he stumbled, a small, awkward boy, and had to caution himself not to overact, aping tricks or making silly remarks to get her attention.

In the end, however, he did not know a mind he better trusted, a temperament he appreciated more. Carter often told philosophy classes that "Humans have to be wise to be good," and with Timo in mind he would have added, "One must be wise to be good, but must also be wise to be beautiful."

Although he had had a number of opportunities, Carter did not approach Timo. His reluctance was dyed in the dread of having misread the signals. He could well have been wrong a second time. With Timo, the man of action as a fool held Carter at bay. With others he did not care. With her he would not risk becoming another assuming fool.

Now she posed beneath a large portrait of a Barker State honorable, a recently retired Chancellor, with her back to the wall, talking to Kerm Soliski. And again, John Carter the prey, caught himself wondering what it would be to share a bed with her.

Soliski had a bushy head of gray and brown hair, a short gray beard and round wire glasses. He wore a faded green sweatshirt, paint-smeared baggy corduroy pants and Adidas running shoes. He was a good six inches shorter than Timo and just then they reminded Carter of a couple of Doonesbury characters, a svelte, chic, black female and a fuzzy-haired, shabby, short, and less than physically attractive male looking up to his mistress.

When Carter came in, Kerm nodded to him.

"Merry Christmas, John."

"I suppose so," Carter said.

Although he was American, from Iowa City, Soliski had recently come to Barker from Europe where he had spent ten years as a student and as a teacher. He had paintings in the Tate, the MoMA. Several of the swank New York galleries showed him regularly.

"Why here," Carter had asked once about his residence at Barker, "why not New York? Isn't that where the action is?"

"It's nice out here in the woods," Soliski said. "If I could get any farther away, I'd be there. I don't need the distractions. I like it here."

"And how are you Ms. Clark?" Carter said.

"Oh, I am doing very well Dr. Carter, and you?"

Her formality amused Carter. He had never heard her speak quite so carefully and for just a moment sensed she might be toying with him.

"I'm fine," he said.

"And please. You should call me Timo," she said. "Ms. Clark sounds stuffy. Like a Boston matron or huffy old woman."

"How about Doctor Carter? Isn't that formal?"

"Oh, but you see it is proper for mere instructors to respect their esteemed elders."

As he leaned closer to hear her, Carter caught just the faintest scent of her hair, the fragrance of her clothing and skin.

When he understood what she said, Carter laughed. Kerm bent over laughing.

"Okay, then, what's new?" Carter said.

"Well, I guess you heard the news," Kerm said. "Actually, I'm not sure it's news. More like rumors."

"Hey, I'm always good for a rumor," Carter said. "The more salacious the better."

"I guess it came out yesterday. They're going to terminate thirty or thirty-five faculty positions."

"From which departments?" Carter said.

"Across the board. Have you heard about it?"

"Kerm, I'd be the last to hear. What brought this on?"

"Who knows? They say the education budget has to be cut. The board claims they need the money for construction. The site plan calls for Newton Hall to come down and new mall built on the land. They want to make Barker self-funding."

"Endowments aren't enough."

"You hear rumors all the time," Timo said. "But I believe this."

"Yes," Kerm said. "Apparently a list has already been made up."

"By lottery, I suppose," Carter said. "When it comes to the administration, I'm as much a cynic as anyone. But this does seem a bit far-fetched."

"Well, everybody's talking about it."

"Have you seen the list?" Carter said.

"No," Kerm said, "but Daly and the AAUP council have."

Carter watched Kerm, then Timo.

"You trust Daly? I'd agree with Timo. But usually Daly's not reliable."

"He is this time," Kerm said.

"But Kermit," Timo said, "you will believe anything."

Timo held a drink in her right hand. Her left hand and arm, her long, slender brown arm with its exquisite hand of delicate fingers, hung motionless at her side.

What would the artist do with that? Carter wondered. How would Kerm paint that arm and hand, the shadows and shades of the lift of her breast and the wonderful angle of her shoulders? And the colors? The purple cloth and the brown of her skin that wasn't exactly brown, or chocolate, or nutmeg or cinnamon or copper or anything else Carter could name.

After the visual delight of Timo's skin, white skin, or beige or tan or mauve, or whatever it was, seemed as anemic and without luster as chalk-water.

What could art add to the sensuality, to the contours of an already nearly perfect female form?

Carter mused on the sensual enticement of undressing her slowly, one small fold of material at a time, unveiling her luxurious skin, her long, exquisite fingers touching him as the words of her soft voice caressed him. While he would have welcomed her attention, he understood, grudgingly so, that many of the males at the party entertained the same fancy.

Carter shook free of the image and excused himself and headed for the kitchen in search of alcohol. In the kitchen drinkers had collected around the bottles and mixes on the counter and the island oasis of a large chopping block table.

Harry Gotsch, an English department cipher, stationed in the back doorway blocking the possibility of escape, elaborated the merits of a story he had recently published. A large, round-shouldered man with a sagging, flabby face, his thin and wispy hair hung over the eye-slits in the pudding of flesh padding his cheek and jowl bones. He appeared, even in photos, to be perpetually hung-over, and from what Carter knew of his habits, he probably was. Gotsch kept a bottle in the desk drawer in his office and frequently fortified himself between classes. At times his classroom behavior bordered on the erratic, always on the erotic.

Carl Johnson referred to Gotsch as "CNN," because, as Carl observed, "although he has nothing new to say, he does broadcast twenty-four hours a day."

Carter had last seen Gotsch at the Christmas party the previous year, and Gotsch had been in precisely the same position, doing very much the same thing then. So he fits in doorways, Carter thought.

Gotsch looked up when Carter came in, then returned to his audience of what appeared to Carter to be six or seven graduate students and a somebody-instructor Carter remembered from the psychology department.

"The best part," Gotsch said," was when old John's wife catches him peeing in her flower bed. She's mad at him. Thinks he's trying to get even with her for what she said about his sister. She knows he's been drinking again and makes up her mind to find his bottle of whiskey and pee in it.

"I got this idea from a story I heard about a baseball player who wasn't getting to play. When the manager sent him out to get coffee, the kid would pee in it. Did this three or four times. Finally the manager's drinking the coffee, he's got this disgusted look on his face, he turns to the kid and shakes his head and says, 'you know, the reason you never get to play, is not only do you look like shit out there, but you're so bad when you touch coffee it tastes like piss.'"

Carter poured a double, amused with the story, speculating mildly on the origins and contents of the bottle he had just emptied.

An hour later the rooms had filled, and rattled with the clatter of late arrivals. Carter, dipped in the bliss of a substantial quantity of bourbon, had settled on a couch in the living-room beneath the haze of cigarette smoke and noise next to Charles Lessiack.

Carter had known Lessiack for only a few years, but had, when they met several years before, an immediate and natural affinity for the man, an attraction that had grown with fondness each time they again met.

A small man with a blond crew cut, Lessiack's blue eyes seemed always wide open and his face about to register a delighted smile. He had at thirty-five gained an international reputation in particle physics with a publishing record as good as any at Barker, and maybe as good as anybody in the country.

A second couple had joined Kerm and Timo, and after a few minutes Kerm broke away and rotated toward Carter's end of the couch.

"I suppose you two know each other," Carter said, then turned back to Lessiack while Soliski seated himself on a footstool across from them. "And what's the latest madness of the scientific revolution," Carter said, watching Lessiack's face.

"Synthetic revulsion," a voice behind Carter said.

Lessiack grinned.

"Would you say it's madness?"

"Isn't physics where they keep the mad scientists?"

"We artists are supposed to be the crazies," Soliski said. "I mean, where did Vincent's van go?"

"It was probably car jacked," Carter ventured.

"No, no. It took an unheard of, eerie short cut through the sound to the hospital."

"Creation is madness," a voice above and behind said, the voice of Betty Sutter, a short stocky woman with a square head, thin brown hair and marble-gray eyes. She, too, resided in the department of physics, although Carter was not exactly sure of her status or position, and had, more than once, wondered why or by what turn scientist with her features had come to the physics lab. How did Billings Learned Hand become a legendary jurist? Or Booker T. Washington an educator and writer?

"The world according to synthetic design," she said. "The book of creation is not Genesis but synthesis."

"You think you're up to it?" Carter said.

"Well, someone has to do it," Lessiack said in his boyish way, as if he had set about a task as reasonable and minor as sweeping the kitchen floor. "We're always trying to come up with new models."

"I know what you mean," Soliski said. "We have that problem in the art department. In fact the newer the better. I mean no older than twenty or twenty-one. Although I'd hope yours are no better clothed than ours."

"Tinker Toys and Silly Putty," Sutter said and began singing, 'It's a Barnum and Bailey world, fictional as it can be, but it won't be make believe if you build a model for me.'"

"By the way," Carter said to Lessiack, "congratulations. I see you just had another article in *Physics Today.*"

Carter said this without anything of animosity or envy, although he was immediately piqued that he had been neglectful and should have done more, written more, contributed more—an impulse followed quickly by the Pyrrhic realization that it did not matter anyway.

Lessiack smiled, his eyes wide.

"Did you enjoy it?"

"What I could translate. Philosophers get a bad rap for obscurity, but we're nothing compared to you people."

"Do you think so?" Lessiack said. "My wife will be glad to hear that. She thinks I'm too obvious."

Pieces of it came easily. Carter knew about quarks and bosons, although other parts remained baffling, unclear. Several times his curiosity had taken him to Lessiack's articles in *Physics Today.* He pondered the articles off and on for several days then dropped the copies into a folder and slipped the folder into his desk file-drawer.

Soliski lit a cigarette and dropped the burnt match into the ashtray. Carter watched the smoke rise and hang on the air. The first concord of alcohol hung a serene haze on Carter's vision. If the distortion of the source was unknown, at the moment the entropy of the receiver was becoming increasingly certain.

Carter shook off the thought.

"Was Schrödinger's cat Siamese or a Tabby? Do cats have pedigrees?" Kerm said.

"They forgot to put him in the box," Sutter said, then laughed at the joke.

"Hell, I had a wife once who had fourteen cats in her apartment," Carter said. "If had known the physics department needed a couple . . ."

"Which is only a little better than the cat in the hat," Sutter said.

"How about the woman with the hat?" Soliski said.

They laughed.

"All the way back to Matisse?" Carter said.

"Or across to Matisse."

Lessiack lifted his hand as if, indeed, it might contain a beam of light, and the mirage of Timo's soft image floated on Carter's horizon near the large Christmas tree. She was talking to Councia Brown from the English Department. Councia was Afro American several shades darker than Timo and wore a white dress that contrasted dramatically with her skin.

In color and culture they came from the extremes of the African spectrum. Timo a native of the sub-Sahara, with a clean sense of her immediate ancestry, had grown up as a member of a racial and cultural majority. Councia was an American, with all of the anguish and misgivings of the appellation.

As a small girl she had suffered the sexual abuse of an alcoholic father, seen a brother she loved felled by street violence, and watched her mother beaten into a passivity, broken finally by the responsibility of too many children, too much work and too little appreciation.

Behind them the Christmas tree blinked in a standard selection of reds, whites and greens. Timo held her head back slightly, as people wearing contact lenses often do.

Carter didn't have far to travel to imagine Timo in the fine hues, the warm colors of a well composed oil on canvas.

"It's a matter in time" Sutter said.

She leaned over the back of the couch with her head hung between them like a small, pale, friendly gargoyle.

Carter tracked the path of Soliski's eyes repeatedly returning to Sutter and wondered when the square head with grey eyes would end up in a painting, maybe in a corner, behind a tree, in a graveyard of electronic tombstones, on a bronze in a museum hallway. Maybe a white marble head in a long hallway emblazoned with laser shafts of sunlight.

"Matter at its base is thought," Sutter said. "Thinking makes it so."

"In the beginning was the word," Carter said, "and the word was made flesh?"

"Ah, flesh, sacred flesh," Kerm said. "The hell with love. Give me lust."

"And we dwelt among it," Sutter said. "We dwell among the lust of dust." She laughed again, a harsh delighted cackle.

"Then an electron might say 'Before Abraham, I am.'"

"No," Lessiack said, "'Before atom, I am.'"

Timo came to reclaim Kerm and the conversation broke up. Lessiack left a little after eleven-thirty. By then a dozen or so arm-linked and swaying impromptu carolers were performing before the fireplace. A crock of Glug had materialized on the kitchen stove and several of the songsters brandished mugs that splashed as they swayed.

Left for the moment to his own devices, and the fog of the conversation, Carter advanced unsteadily though predictably toward the kitchen for a refill. He had in mind to relocate Timo and Kerm, one, the other, or both, aware after a brief search that they were not likely to be together, and then that they had no doubt already gone their joint or separate ways.

Off the kitchen in a darkened room, a former sewing- or sun-room which now housed a collection of Phasmatropes, Daedaleums and other early historical visual devices an anonymous donor had bequeathed the University, Gotsch and his following had gathered to watch, 'What Santa Got For Christmas,' an archival 16mm hardcore sortie of a plump but well-staffed Santa mounting a bit more than his legendary sleigh and rooftops. While his shabby coursers, reindeers resembling a reign of tattered goats looked on, giving free reign to his prominent north-pole pastime, Santa frolicked and cavorted in a sleigh-full-of-toys with a lively, nimble nymph. The sub-plot featured Santa's helpers, a couple of Snow White-variety dwarfs, entertaining no other than the unfrocked Snow White herself.

Carter watched from the doorway for a moment and was a little surprised to discover Timo had not gone but was on the couch with Gotsch, and had apparently been there for some time. The sweet smell of cannabis hung on the air, and Carter counted at least three joints circulating among the company.

Predictably the film provided an improbable montage of loosely related dalliances, moving from Santa's sleigh to the fair maid's living-room where the activities proceeded among a scattering of gifts beneath a thin and haggard Christmas tree, with Santa astride the writhing white fleshed nymph.

Not yet sated with the vision of Santa's prodding, Gotsch rewound the film, running it backwards, then forward and back again, then again, so without a directional or spatial point of reference, Santa proceeded to undo and redo what he had done. Carter nodded. Time's arrow of Skinter Klaus' prick could fly in either direction with equal veracity. At least on celluloid it could.

"And momma told me Santa would come only once a year," a female voice said.

"That's because he has popcorn balls."

"Momma lied," another said.

"I saw momma kissing Santa Claus. Maybe that was the reason."

Gotsch slapped his leg.

"There it is," he shouted. "Goddam, he just did it again. Santa's hauling ashes."

He flipped the projector into reverse, then played it again, in slow motion.

"The moment of truth. Hemingway's moment of truth, seeing the white bone in the sunlight," Gotsch said. "Damn old killer Claus laying pipe. Getting the job done."

Everyone laughed, including Timo. Assuming the obvious and a bit disappointed, Carter went off to the kitchen in search of a drink.

By midnight the porn club had slipped away. The last of the whiskey gone, Carter rummaged through the cabinets above and beneath the counter hoping to uncover a secreted bottle, set aside or overlooked. All that was left was the small crock of glug warmed on the stove.

Contrary to Kerm's belief, nothing more had been mentioned about the proposed layoffs. Probably more of Daly's nonsense, puffing up his image by claiming jobs were endangered, but he had saved them.

Satisfied, finally, that Ma Barker's cupboards were bare, Carter considered the glug. The thick Swedish laxative of prune juice and sugar was too sweet for his taste, but he ladled out a cup and headed back toward the living-room to join what was left of the party.

At the far end of the hall a man stepped out of the bathroom and disappeared into the foyer. Gotsch, Carter thought, a bit surprised. He had assumed Gotsch and Timo had gone off together which was enough to engender small pangs of disappointment.

When the outside door closed, Carter decided it hadn't been Gotsch. The light in the hall was dim, the man had been moving away with his back to Carter, not to mention what the evening of drink had done to Carter's vision. So it wasn't Gotsch. Who then? He didn't know.

He was back to thinking about Timo. About the pleasant possibilities and why it should bother him that she might have gone off with Gotsch.

He wondered what it might be like to be instructed by the sensual, the beautiful. Just then he wanted to hear what she had to say about the proposed layoffs. He suspected her attitudes might shift if there was no one to hear.

But he didn't know. Timo was difficult to anticipate. When he considered approaching her, he wasn't certain exactly how to do it. He knew absolutely nothing of her preferences, and even less of what she might think of him.

He was never sure when or how to respond to her, as a colleague or as a friend, an acquaintance. He couldn't read it in her face or hear it in the intonations of her speech, although it was, in his mind, a superb, beautiful face, and a beguiling voice. Not wanting to alienate her with a suggestion she might misunderstand, he stayed at a distance. This night, it had been a disappointed distance.

In the living-room the carolers had drifted into disarray, the bits and pieces of the ribald and risqué. They were singing something Carter could not decipher to the tune of "God Rest Ye Merry Gentlemen," about the untoward relationship of Rudolph and Mrs. Claus.

Still, the embers glowed in the fireplace, and using a peanut and three metal egg poaching cups he had taken from a kitchen counter drawer, when the last song was done, as much to entertain those left who had gathered in attendance as to kill off the small remainder of the night, Carter set out the mystification and ballyhoo sleight-of-hand of a shell-game.

A hell of a way to kill boredom, he thought. Ah, yes, Plato—everything as idea-thinking. When people don't have anything to think about, they feel they have to do something, maybe the first thing they come across. Then they have something to think about. What did Aquinas say? "That which is first in thought is last in act."

Carter would have added, "and then thought about, and talked about, gossiped about."

Or something from Valery. "Sometimes I think: sometimes I am."

"Here," Carter said, pushing the poaching cups in small circles over the polished surface of the table, "here we have God the Father, God the Son, and God the Holy Ghost. Now you see it, now you don't. Three peas in one pod. Hidden and unknowable forever."

Chapter III

A bit past three on Sunday Carter left the house, stopped briefly at Mikel's Bookstore, then walked down the four blocks to Murphy's. The snow had melted leaving patches on the shaded side of buildings. The wind whipped in gusts, the temperature still well below freezing. The sun hung bright and white on the distant sky.

Two patrons sat at the bar and several students were camped out around the pool table. Vivien had arrived minutes earlier and he found her in a booth near the back wall. On his way in, sliding past the pool players, Carter lifted the cue ball from the table, palmed it, then rotated the sphere, setting it on the tips of the fingers of his right hand, teed up for everyone to see. The pool players stood, momentarily fixed, a little startled at the interruption, curious but hesitant, waiting expectantly, before one complained in a whining little boy's voice.

"C'mon, Doc, you're messing up our game."

Carter held the ball out over the table beneath the plastic Tiffany shade, deliberately, and passed his right hand over the ball. Then slowly, and with great care, extracted a pale-blue silk kerchief from the ball.

The boy who had complained, laughed self-consciously, his face fixed in a brittle grin. The other player shook his head and tapped the butt of his pool cue on the floor and began hooting.

"All right. Let's hear it for Doc."

"Doc, Doc, Doc, Doc," they chanted in a low grumble.

Holding the kerchief by the corner with the thumb and index finger of his left hand, Carter again palmed the ball before setting it where it had been on the table.

Vivien watched the performance, then raised her hand and motioned to Carter.

"You'll have to show me how to do that," she said as he slipped into the booth.

"Here," he said handing her the kerchief. "For the lady."

"Can you do that in the bright light of day as well?"

"Illusion prospers," Carter said, "wherever the mind imagines and supposes."

"It's dark here," she said. "Maybe it's what is not seen, rather than imagined."

"Dark, dank places," Carter said. "My ancestors came from the back of the cave. Ah, along the River Tywy?"

Other than the pool players and the men at the bar there was a couple in a booth on the far wall across from the bar.

Chairs had been stacked on the tables in the backroom and Sam Perrin was sweeping around them, quietly without much of purpose.

Sam had gray hair and a deeply creased face. A thin man in his late sixties, within the last year he had lost much of his vigor and presence. He had been cleaning up for Murphy for as long as Carter could remember.

Working at odd jobs over the years Sam bartered his way to a comfortable livelihood, refusing money, collecting whatever he had coming in food and drink and services.

"What you pay in tax, I save," he told Carter. "Uncle Sam don't know me. No tax. No social security. I never registered for the draft. I do not buy with my name on anything. I do not sign my name to paper. Not once."

He lived in a single room above Murphy's in exchange for working in the bar, and did not own a car.

Otherwise, what he did not need he avoided. He eschewed medical care—except when he could trade for work as a part-time janitor in a clinic downtown, or for cleaning the yards and doing small household repairs for several of the doctors he knew from the clinic.

Then in his mid-sixties, he had no birth certificate, he found not only did the government not know who he was, or that he was, but by a gradual process of time and attrition, the identity he had concealed from the authorities also alluded him.

He could not remember the day of the week, not even to mark it on the calendar, nor the direction to follow or the destination if he arrived.

"Sam Perrin's a stowaway," Murphy told Carter. "There's no record of him anywhere, not even a birth certificate."

The previous spring when he lost most of his odd jobs Murphy took him in and provided him with food, clothing and shelter in exchange for what little work Sam could still do.

After he finished sweeping he'd spend the rest of the afternoon in a back booth, drink a glass of beer or two and watch television or read the paper, holding the pages up straight out at arms-length, scanning from front to back, over and over. If a noise or voice caught his attention, he'd look up, blank-eyed, then drift back to the paper. By seven o'clock he'd be asleep, his head on his folded arms on the table.

During a lull, a break in the crowd, when he could get away from the grill, Murphy would shake Sam awake, raise him and lead him upstairs. There he'd deposit him on the couch, make sure the television was on, and lock the door as he left.

Carter stepped around Sam, removed his coat and hung it over the back of the booth. The girl had a magazine spread on the table. When Carter came in she had been bent over reading with her face several inches from the page.

"You'll go blind trying to read in here," he said.

She looked up and smiled.

"Thank you, father." Then frowned and said, "John, that's from masturbating, not from reading."

"Are you a master baiter?"

She scoffed.

"In all your wisdom, you wouldn't happen to know anything about cancer, would you?"

"Like what?"

"What are the chances of getting it if it's in your family?"

"You got the wrong doctor," Carter said.

"You wouldn't by any chance have a cure up your sleeve?"

Her inquiries were matter of fact and playful, Carter thought, without alarm or concern.

"Who do you know that has cancer?"

"My sister. What's more disturbing, my twin sister."

"You have a twin sister?"

"Yes. She stayed with my mom after dad was killed. But she's been living here in Lancaster for the last few years."

"And a brother?"

"An older brother."

"I see," Carter said. "And when did you find out she had cancer?"

"Oh, about two years ago. But now it's getting worse."

"Which means."

"I don't know. Do you believe in doctors?"

"When I'm sick."

"Do you trust them?"

"What did they say?"

"They said she had two months to live."

"When was that?"

"Two months ago."

"So you're waiting and hoping it isn't true."

"She's in the hospital again. They took her in last night."

"Well, I wouldn't worry about getting cancer just because of a sister."

"But it does run in families."

"That's what the article says? What is that?"

"The *AMA Journal*. I got it from the med-school. But the article doesn't say. And I can't make any sense out of the formulas and numbers, anyway."

Carter ordered a pitcher of beer and knocked a cigarette out of the pack he had picked up on the way in.

"Death's the same for genius and idiot," he said.

Simply put, Carter had seen too much. His parents, within a year, the unbelievable statistic of six department members in eighteen months, Katherine Marie's brother.

At his mother's bedside, alone, late, the night she died, he had listened to her labored breathing, listened to the whisper of life in her body as it struggled toward one more dawn.

He had been seated between the bed and the window looking out over the vast black, moon filled, dark winter fields of corn-stalk stubbles poked through the spotted snow cover, the black earth looking as if it had been charred by a devastating incendiary event of unimaginable proportions.

At the time he was not thinking about her, but about why he was there, what he was about keeping this strange vigil of limited time, when all else of what he knew of her was gone.

Then he was drawn back, startled and drawn in by the sudden silence of her no longer breathing. And he held his breath, then, feeling the surge of her presence, the blood rush of her memory, her voice, her gestures, above the bed, over her empty unmoved, breathless body, he rose without thought, not daring to breath for fear of disturbing the air, compelled by something of awe, and opened the window to the sharp, frigid night.

But it had ended. Nothing dramatic. Nothing alarming. Just quietly, nothing. Life done. Life gone.

He sat with the body for a few minutes without alarm, certain she was dead, then walked to the nursing station at the far end of the hall and told the nurse that "I think Mrs. Carter in Room 217 has died."

The quiet changed him.

He filled their glasses and lit a cigarette. The girl folded the magazine and stuffed it into her purse.

"Have you ever been around anyone who had cancer?" she said.

Carter took a drag off the cigarette, pulling the smoke deep into his lungs before setting it in the ashtray.

"It's tough," he said, hearing the unusual sound of his words and wondering what he would have felt at twenty-two listening to someone tell him "it's tough" to have a family member dying of cancer.

He could have told her about the scare Katherine Marie had with a breast tumor ten years earlier, but thought better of it.

The episode had actually amounted to little, except for the week waiting for the reprieve of the pathologist's report. Katherine Marie had steeled herself for the worst, convinced she was dying, not at a date in the indistinct future, but now, within the next months or possibly even the next weeks or days.

The day the doctor discovered the tumor, the conviction of her imminent and immediate demise struck her suddenly and with the force of a virulent fever. Home from the hospital she dropped onto the living-room couch nearly comatose with disbelief. She went without food or drink for the next three days, after which she rose, or as Carter believed and had said, was resurrected, not yet resigned fully, but prepared to face the certainty as if it (the tumor which embodied the full realization of her mortality) were a burdensome, ill-natured lover, to whom she would be forced to submit.

Finally, Carter believed, she accepted the intruder and his terms, and assented to his will and the changes demanded of her remaining life, as fact. In a way that was not entirely her own, that surprised Carter, she came to him for consolation and comfort, wanting him to hold her for hours at a time, to talk to her to relieve as she said, "the excruciating silence" ringing in her head.

Carter had responded, he hoped, as any person might respond to the desperation and despair of another, talking as he did to what he imagined lay at the bottom of her fears, not because he could relieve them, or even assuage the pain of loss to which the experience had exposed her, but because the words themselves, properly directed, as words often can, served to insulate her from what she already believed.

The day they received the biopsy report, she brought home a bottle of Burgundy and sat the entire evening into the early hours of morning by the fire, staring into the flames, in silence. And Carter sat with her, talking quietly as he had done the previous week, caressing her neck and shoulders, holding her again when she cried, feeling for both of them the gratitude that she had for just a moment having slipped the executioner.

The episode sunk deep into Carter, his affection for this woman, his partner and companion of nearly twenty years that he hardly knew, his own feeble attempts to preserve life, to stay the inevitable by the magic of words, the sounds humans make about their loves and fears.

Not only did the episode provide him with an appreciation of the affection one human can have for another, but he was struck with regret that too often such affection would come only at critical times.

He would have carried forward the connection he believed they had made, mentioned to Katherine Marie on several occasions the needs humans have for one another, then watched her turn away.

Within days she dismissed and minimized the travail of her anguish, as clearly Carter did not, as if he had not been there, as if nothing had been said, no connections made. For this he was truly sorry.

Vivien watched Carter closely.

"People die of all kinds of things," Carter said. "At first it's the disease, the particulars of what killed them that horrifies us. Then, after a while, you realize there are a million killers hanging around and they look pretty much the same. The dead are dead and worrying about how they died doesn't help us."

Her eyes hadn't left him the entire time and were now moist. "You're saying she's dead."

"Is it cancer for sure?"

"Yes. That's what the doctors say."

"How many?"

"Three."

"Where?"

"University Hospital. Two there and then at the Medical Group downtown."

"They all say the same thing?"

"Yes. They say six months."

She reached for her purse. She was crying now and tears fell off her cheeks. Carter reached for her hand.

"Maybe it's not that bad," he said. "Maybe they can treat it."

She shook her head.

"That's a lie, John Carter." She looked at him. Her eyes were red. "No. That's not true. You wouldn't let me pull that crap on you."

Her rebuff startled Carter.

"Unless you didn't notice, little girl, I was trying to be kind."

"John, don't do that. I'm not a little girl. I'm not your goddam daughter or some other weeping inferior. And I did notice."

Carter smiled.

"I can see this is going to be a good night."

"Your problem is you expect too much of people. You expect them to be honest and kind, and life just isn't that way. Then when things turn out different from what you expect, you get mad and think telling the truth will make everything work out."

"I suppose that's the truth."

"It is," she said, catching her breath and trying to smile.

"Which isn't going to help anything," Carter said.

"Look. Okay, I'm over it. But Christ. And why am I always bawling around you? You're right. I am an inferior weepy female."

"Otherwise you seldom cry."

"I never cry. And I have good reason. God knows I have reasons."

Her voice was laced with a tint of bravado.

"I'm not being solicitous when I say I'm sorry about your sister."

"I know. But I want somebody, anybody to tell me it will be all right. That everything will work out. Then when they do, I get pissed because I'm lying to myself and they're lying to me, and I'm trying to believe the lie and want the truth to be better, and, well, shit. What are you going to do?"

"You can agree with Rollo May. 'Death is just one goddam absurd stinking horror.'"

"But what do you think about it?"

"Don't think about things you can't change? Just drink, eat, screw and be merry?"

"And pull silk scarves out of pool balls. There has to be more to it than that?"

"More than the appetites? Because you want more? Because we've been given, it seems to me rather sadistically, appetites and ravenous desires? That, my dear, is insufficient in reason or hope."

"But you have a great deal of hope."

"Not that kind."

"You have hope. I've watched you in class. If you were sick you'd want to get better."

"Or die," Carter said.

"But you'd want something anyway."

Sitting with his back to the bar, Carter watched Sam circling the tables, rotating toward them.

When he paused again on his broom, Carter leaned out of the booth toward the old man.

"I'll bet you even money they get that sonofabitch Hitler before the year is out."

Sam bent slowly and gave Carter a straight look, then smiled. He stepped around behind the broom as if it were a microphone.

"Did you see the news?" Sam said. "Ninety thousand men on the beach in France."

"What did the Germans do?"

Sam bent over and laughed. He twisted sideways and pointed toward the backdoor as if pointing around a corner.

"They run all the way to the trees. Them Heines run so fast it take three people just to see it. One to say 'here they come,' one to say 'there they is, 'and another to say 'there they go.'"

Sam straightened up and looked at Carter sideways. He had not shaved in several days and sunlight gave a silver glint to his graying beard. He lowered his eyes to the pack of cigarettes Carter had laid on the table, then looked at Carter.

Carter shook out three cigarettes and handed them to Sam. He snapped the lighter open and was about to give Sam a light when Murphy appeared at the table.

"Doc, I wish you wouldn't do that," Murphy said. "Not unless you want to sit and watch him and make sure he smokes the whole thing. And it ain't that I care about him smoking. I don't. That ain't the problem. He can't do himself no more damage than's already done. Hell man's got too few pleasures to give up any. The problem with Sam ain't smoking, it's what he don't smoke but lets burn. He'll light one, put it down and forget it and light another. They're all over the place. Five, six at a time.

"Couple days ago he set fire to the couch upstairs and damn near burn the place down. Lit one and forgot it. Lit another and the first one burned down off the ashtray onto the couch. We were lucky to catch it."

Sam waited expectantly and Carter wondered if he knew what he was feeling, if he could remember the cause for the intuition. When he saw Carter what did he think or feel or intuit? What sensation or emotion took him?

Murphy held out his hand and Sam gave him two of the cigarettes.

"Let him smoke that one," Murphy said. "Just don't give him any extras to carry upstairs."

Carter lit the cigarette for Sam then took a small box from his coat pocket.

"Maybe this'll take his mind off smoking," Carter said.

Sam looked at the box, at Carter, then back to the box.

"Here," Carter said, and opened it and took out the small red and yellow plastic figure he had picked up in the bookstore.

"Like this," Carter said. He pushed the arms around and fashioned an airplane, then redesigned the plane into a car.

Sam put the cigarette in his mouth, took the toy and held it out, looking at it, squinting in the smoke, then looped his left arm over the broom handle to free his other hand and work with the toy. He backed into the open space between the tables, carrying the gift in both hands, dragging the broom with the handle beneath his arm.

Vivien studied Carter.

"What was that about?"

"I don't know. We were just talking about the war."

"He thinks there's a war. What war?"

"World War Two."

"In the fifties?"

"The forties. Forty-four to be exact."

"But he thinks it was just yesterday."

"Why not," Carter said. "That's all that's left. If you can't remember you can't think. Locke understood we are what we remember ourselves to be. If you can't think—well, what the hell is there?"

"He's like a little kid. Why did you give him that?"

"So he can play with it," Carter said. "Nothing to remember. All you have to do is push the parts around."

She looked at Carter carefully.

"You bought that just for him, didn't you? I mean, you always carry transformer toys around with you?"

"It'll keep him occupied—for a while," Carter said. "That may be long enough."

She reached across the table and laid her hand on Carter's arm.

"John, that was wonderful."

She looked around for Sam who had slipped into a booth behind the jukebox and was bent over working on the toy.

"Have you ever known anyone who died and came back to life?" she said.

"You mean Sam?"

"No, I mean really dead."

"The Kubler-Ross stuff."

"Who's that?"

"She wrote several books about life after death. Just a rehash of religious fantasy. Life after death. All that crap."

The girl sat up straight and ran her fingers through her hair.

"John, the whole world can't be wrong. My god, people everywhere believe in life after death. They can't all be wrong."

"Look," he said, "that doesn't change the facts. The mortgage comes due, you can't pay, and you're out on your ass. Now, even though you don't have the money, and it takes money to find another place, even if you do find one, it's a sure bet you won't be in the house of the senses or mind you're in now."

"Why not?"

"Tell me about your life before you were born."

"How would I know that?'

"Precisely," Carter said. "Nothing to see with, nothing to hear or think with. What do you think has happened to Sam? He's living in another place at another time. He's not here. You want to talk about Sam's soul?

Where is it? Looks to me as if it's already gone off in part."

The girl looked away, silent for a moment, then shook her head.

"Let's not talk about it. This scares me. I'm scared."

"What's your sister's name?"

"Mary Ann."

"Mary Ann what? Is she married."

Vivien shook her head.

"Mary Ann Walters, and no, she's not married. Why do you want to know about my sister?"

"Walters. Your maiden name?"

"Nope. That came from mom's third husband."

"How's your mother taking it?"

"She doesn't know," the girl said.

"She doesn't know her daughter is dying of cancer?"

"No. We haven't told her."

"We? You and your sister?"

"Yes."

"Why not?"

"We didn't want to hurt her. There isn't anything she can do."

"It never occurred to you she might want to know?"

"No. I don't think so. You don't know my mother. I mean, she's not like you. You talk about these things. But people don't talk about dying. They don't even want to think about it."

"But I'd think courtesy alone would require she be kept informed about the health of her children."

She shook her head, emphatically.

"No. You can't just go around telling people their children are dying. Especially people who don't want to hear about it."

"You mean your mother wouldn't want to know her daughter is dying?"

"No, it's not that."

"How does your sister feel about it?"

"About dying?"

"No. About not telling your mother."

"Well, she hasn't said anything. But she's always been secretive. Even when we were kids. You could never tell what she was thinking or what she had been doing."

"And she's not married?"

"No. Not Mary Ann. She's not the marrying kind."

"The marrying kind? What kind is that?"

"I don't know. She doesn't have any men friends. She doesn't have one man friend that I know of. And for certain she's never been in bed with a man.

"She told me once she wanted to marry Gomez from *The Adams Family* because he was nice, doting, rich and only turned-on by French, and she didn't know a word of French."

"No men friends means no male sexual friends."

"That's what I was trying to say."

"A good bit different from her twin, wouldn't you say?"

Vivien smiled and nodded.

"I would. What would you say?"

"And you haven't told anyone about this? You haven't told your aunt and uncle?"

"God, no. Talk about a disaster. Listen, if my uncle ever learns about this, he'll find a way to work it to his advantage. Anyway, Jinx hates him. She won't even talk to him."

"Jinx? Your sister?"

"That's what everyone calls her. She knows what I went through when I was living there. I think that had a lot to do with the way she feels about men."

"How old were you when you father died?"

"Eight. We were living in Omaha. Mom's part Cherokee. She's got relatives there."

"And she's still in Omaha."

"No. She's in Cheyenne. She's married again—twice since dad died. Her husband's a rodeo rider or something. They travel a lot."

"Maybe your father's death had to do with the way your sister feels about men. Losing a parent can be a pretty traumatic thing for an eight-year-old. Has she ever talked about it?"

"No. Not that. I don't think so."

"Maybe that's why you're hanging around with me. Trying to get back the father you lost or never had."

The girl ran her tongue over her lips, and considered this for a moment. When she spoke she spoke slowly and in a whisper.

"God, do you really think so? It sounds absolutely decadent. Licentious, and all that. God, making love to daddy. Wow!"

"Necrophilia," Carter said.

"What's that?"

"Love of death or of the dead."

While the observation had been less than profound, he suspected her playful reaction to the suggestion would not necessarily end the matter.

He poured what remained in the pitcher into his glass. With his index finger he made a pile of the tobacco shards that had fallen on the table.

"Where did you ever get a name like Jinx?"

"No," she said, "that's my sister's nickname. She's called Jinx."

Carter emptied his glass and stood and slipped on his coat.

"You're leaving," the girl said.

"Aren't you?"

"You're going to abandon me again on the corner, aren't you?"

"What do you think?" Carter said.

"I think," she said, lifting her arms over her head and stretching, "I think Ruth is at work, and won't be home until late. What do you think?"

Chapter IV

The four-story colonial brick box of Temperly Hall stood at the southwest end of the quad, an unostentatious bank of classrooms and offices, one of the three campus buildings dating back to the University's beginning as Barker Teachers College.

The nine small rooms at the distant end of the fourth-floor of its "H" shaped hall served as offices for the fourteen members of the philosophy faculty, two each to an office, a lunchroom that doubled for meetings and conferences, and another designated as a work-space for the ever growing number of part-time faculty the university employed.

At the near end the suite of the Academic Corporate Vice Chancellor for Instruction looked out onto the quad and the Long Walk to the far end of the university grounds and the chancellor's residence. These rooms had served as classrooms for fifty years. When the college became a university they were taken over for administrative office space.

By a twist of architecture and circumstance, Temperly had only a single stairway and one elevator, and both opened at the top to the doors of the vice-chancellor's suite. A peculiar irony, Carter thought.

"And you can't forget," he told himself Monday morning, again, as he passed. "They won't let you. The gaudy, garish glitter of advertising and public relations. The education managers."

A Yankee Trader mentality. Twentieth Century American education fallen victim to a peculiar mix of pragmatism and manifest destiny. Names emblazoned on the door. Advertising, executive suites, large cars, excessive salaries financed with money pulled from the guts of educational programs.

His office door was opened several inches and Carter found Morgana and Mason bunched in the corner, huddled over a desk with filled ashtrays and empty coffee cups. He was about to ask what time they had arrived, and then imagined Mason no doubt wanted to hear more about the manuscript, wanted Carter to elaborate on the brief criticism he had offered after reading it Sunday.

"Have you heard?" Mason asked.

"Heard what?"

"He hasn't heard," Morgana said with a dramatic insinuation that Carter had been deprived of privileged information. "My god, he hasn't heard."

She put her hand on Mason's arm.

"You want to tell him?"

"I know," Carter said. "They've lowered the entrance requirement to financial inheritance and two blips on an EEG."

"It's not a comic matter," Morgana instructed. "Mason was in Crowly's office this morning talking to the secretaries."

"Yesterday, about three in the afternoon," Mason said, "Crowly called her at home and told her to be in the office by four-thirty. He needed a letter typed. She said he has done that before so he can get it out by eight in the morning. But this time it wasn't just a letter."

"Who's she?"

"Janice Watkins."

Carter shook his head.

"How many times have I told you to stay away from executive secretaries?"

"Carter, dammit, don't you want to hear what she said?"

"Not especially," Carter said. "She's the VC's secretary and she's not going to give you anything straight. It's gossip, or a rumor they want you to spread. How often do you have to get caught in that before you see what they're doing?"

Morgana stood and held up her hands palms out toward Carter.

"Okay, so you see through the scam. Okay. So you alone have the blessing of divine insight and can read Crowly's whims and thoughts, which I must admit may be the same thing. But let me ask you this; what if, just this once, this time, what if it's true?"

"What if what is true?"

Morgana gestured to Mason with feigned disbelief.

"Do you hear the man? Do you hear what I hear?"

Morgana was a small and bone-thin, given to smoking cartons of True cigarettes in a long holder and sipping an ever present cup of coffee. She wore flimsy silk or satin bright colored dresses, mostly of brown and maroon embossed with strands of beads and necklaces, black stockings and, always, spike heels.

"I suppose you remember the time you came sailing in here with your nose bent out of shape because Crowly had changed the summer schedule?" Carter said.

"That was different."

"Or the time you felt Crowly had sidestepped the textbook committee?"

"That wasn't the same thing."

"Sounds pretty much the same to me."

"Dammit Carter, this is serious. I'll admit sometimes I've jumped the gun. But Crowly's such a sneak you have to be on your toes. He pulls one of his shitty stunts, without talking to anyone, and it takes us weeks or months to catch on. And by then it's too late. So I've been a little premature, so what? If I'd had good information, we could have saved a lot of stress and trouble."

"Precisely my point," Carter said.

"There are four letters," Mason said.

"Four people in this department are getting letters of termination," Morgana added.

"Letters of termination to be executed next semester. Six weeks from today," Mason said.

"I know," Carter said.

"Carter, you don't know. Nobody knows just yet."

"It's all over campus," Carter said. "There was even some small talk about it at the Senate party Saturday night."

"Then it's true."

"Not necessarily."

"Carter, people are going to lose their jobs. And I do not give a damn if you believe the rumors or even if you started them. This is serious."

"Who? Who are they going to dismiss?" Carter said.

"That we don't know."

Morgana held her hand up as if she were taking an oath. Again seated on the desk, and using her cigarette and holder for a baton, she poked at the air.

"His Excellency, Our Liege, Lord Crowly will assign the warrants for execution later," she announced.

"They're out to rape this university," she said. "First they do away with academic deans. Then they neuter the Faculty Senate. Now they're trying to dismantle the departments. And all the while assigning themselves exorbitant salaries for the good work done."

"That's what power breeds," Carter said. "Pillage, rape and plunder."

"It will probably be the four junior members," Mason said.

Mason's voice was weak and unsteady. Seated with his back to the window, the yellow of the morning sun glowed on his thin red hair. His eyes looked very tired.

Dollars and cents, Carter thought. Nobody wants to be out on the street looking for gainful employment. But the essence of working with the material world, growing wheat, mining coal, academics do not encounter, and it colors and slants their vision. Wheat crops fail, the roof falls in the best of mines. Measurable events. No rationalizations.

"That would be Astroski, Talmar, Wright and Sheffeld," Morgana said.

"Not Talmar," Carter said. "He came over from History. Hell, he's been here longer than the gods."

"Then who?" Mason said.

"I don't know." Carter dropped his books on his desk and scanned the top for notes and messages, memos, anything out of the ordinary.

"Your guess is as good as mine. What makes you think they'll go by seniority?"

"They have to," Morgana said. "According to Faculty Senate rules on hiring and retrenchment they have to go by seniority. They can't go against that."

Although he often gave them the benefit of the doubt, Carter thought the education managers didn't know really what they were doing, what the results of their mindlessness would be.

"They can do any silly thing they want," Carter said. "That's what everybody conveniently ignores."

"They'd never get away with it," Morgana said.

"And who, dear lady, who will stop them?"

"The faculty would rebel. The trustees. The academic community. How about AAUP?"

"Look," Carter said, "this faculty does not possess even the slightest capability of understanding what is and what is not in its best interest. It most certainly does not harbor a hidden inclination to protect itself. Give them a loaded gun and they'd shoot themselves in the head.

"It's a matter of collusion," Carter said. "The academic community, and the AAUP, are sycophants in the habit of licking and kissing the hands of their masters, and in some cases their tormentors, fawning for honors and positions and pats on the head. People don't want to be accused of biting the hand that feeds them. Especially if they are among the few that are well fed. I mean, how would you like to be told you are sinful, disloyal and without gratitude?"

"But there must be someone who can help," Mason said. "You make it sound so, well, I don't know. So hopeless. There must be something that can be done."

Carter sat down, aware only then that the knot of the conversation had crawled into his bowels. Now he wanted to think, had to think. He did not trust the information. It was too easy, too cut and dried. Doubtless, Crowly wanted something, intended to do something, but he wouldn't be fool enough to be this obvious.

Then again maybe he would. Long ago Carter had recognized the difficulty of under thinking people like Crowly. Not only did they live without decency or good sense, but they were dense. There had to be more to it. If for no reason other than that they identified devious, though often pointless, games as good management strategy. Ossification and complication as a habit of mind.

"This isn't all of it," Carter said. "They tell you one thing and intend to do another."

"Well we know what they want," Morgana said. "They want to replace full-time faculty with graduate students and part-timers. Do you realize this department has lost seven members in two years? We are at this moment seven minds less than we were twenty-four months ago. Eight, if you count Tonello. Six people have died or Baker left for greener pastures."

"I know the numbers," Carter said. "But there's got to be more to it than we're getting."

Mason faced away looking out to Market Street. Carter had seen this before.

"I wouldn't imagine there's much to worry about right now," Carter said. "We've been through a good bit more than this."

When Mason joined the Barker faculty, a newly ordained PhD, Carter had helped him over the rough spots.

Possibly because of their office assignment they had over a few years become confidants and close friends. Taking solace in Carter's tutelage Mason came to depend on Carter, as he said, "In a way I have not depended on anyone in my entire life."

He had invited Carter and Katherine Marie to his wedding, then extended a second invitation personally because he did not want Carter to think the first was merely pro forma.

Mason's wife Ardyth, was a small, plain, intelligent woman that Carter liked, but had never really gotten to know. She was friendly enough, a good hostess to Mason's friends, but lived, Carter thought, like a small, timid but strong animal sheltered in the seclusion of a burrow or hollow tree behind large, thick glasses that made her eyes appear round and blurred. She seemed on the outside a comparable image of what Carter imagined Mason looked like inside.

From what Carter could tell she disdained makeup, or anything that might be interpreted as tampering with her appearance. She wore her hair tied back and seemed to have an unlimited supply of faded house dresses. She had matriculated from a small girl's school in the East, with a PhD in psychology for which she had not yet found a use at Barker. As many with advanced degrees without positions, who for whatever reasons stay in university towns, she worked at the odds-and-ends, the spin-off, the academic flotsam and jetsam she could pick up to keep herself busy and to supplement their income.

Part of the employment difficulty, Carter supposed, though no one ever mentioned it, came from Ardyth's speech problems. Born with a speech defect, she had gone through extensive and expensive therapy and had managed to correct the difficulty to something very nearly normal. In doing so she had taken on a stilted idiolect, and spoke with a staccato, pronounced formal syntax.

She reminded Carter of an eight-year-old, standing in a tastefully furnished sitting-room, hands behind her back, grimacing and trying to articulate the syllables of perfect speech for a towering, stern and demanding and unrelenting elder.

Not infrequently Carter saw her coming and going about the campus, mysteriously he thought, without a hat, hair tied back, wrapped tightly in a worn coat, leaning against the wind, her perennial white socks slipped down into her thin black shoes.

The alliance of Ardyth Spencer-Whitehall and Mason Oldam, from what Carter could determine was a rather proper and staid affair of rules and conventions, supported by a massive misinterpretation of motives. However it was, when their first child, a boy they named Carter Mason Oldam, was born Mason asked Carter to stand-up for the child at baptism.

The ritual of pouring water on an infant to drive out the stain of inherited sin was just offbeat and primeval enough to appeal to Carter's sense of circus and stage, a reenactment of a cave-like savage ceremony shaking a gourd at evil, at man's tormentor.

That was thirteen years ago. There had not been a second child.

The role of godfather amused Carter. He took it as a novelty, bringing young Carter Mason gifts on his birthday and at Christmas. In subsequent years the novelty grew into family as Carter's academic connections with Mason senior deepened.

Mason proved to be a talented teacher and writer, and Carter took up the role of advisor, editor and critic for Mason's work. He consulted journals on their interest in Mason's proposed ideas. He wrote letters to philosophy seminars and conventions suggesting topics he knew Mason could handle and provided the directors with Mason's name and qualifications.

Carter collected Mason's publications and the reviews of his essays and articles, kept them in a folder in his desk and often used them in class.

"These are examples," he was fond of telling students, "of what a good mind can do when it's given an opportunity to explore the problems."

Once when Ardyth was ill and the Oldam household funds depleted, Carter wrote Mason a check for three thousand dollars with the gratuity that it could be repaid "whenever it is convenient."

When young Mason needed orthodontic work, Carter paid the two thousand dollar fee, this time without a suggestion for repayment. Since most things of value are not self-supporting, Carter saw the expenditures as his part in keeping the scholarship afloat.

"I'd guess," Carter told Mason after Morgana had gone, "that nobody is going to lose a job over this. These clowns get caught in their own propaganda. They beat the drum about the quality of education at Barker, about which they know absolutely nothing, but having done that, they can't easily reduce our numbers. Especially when we are already so few. If they cut faculty to save money, they'd have trouble justifying a salary increase for themselves."

Even before he finished, he was sorry he had said it. He could not tell immediately what effect the words had on Mason, but he found the lie a bit unsettling. Crowly would not be guided by logic. There was no way to predict what he would or would not do. Certainly it would have nothing to do with the quality of the institution he commanded.

Several years earlier, two weeks into the fall semester when Philosophy Professor Margaret Coleman died, Carter discovered Crowly had replaced her with several part-time instructors,. One had been in Carter's summer seminar on Hume the year before. On two occasions, while chatting with him about his studies Carter had found the man in a lie listing the classes he had completed, and another time, a bit closer to home, discovered he had lifted a substantial part of a paper on Berkeley's *Treatise on the Principles of Human Knowledge* from another student. The irony of the theft, the sentiment of dishonesty, had not been lost on Carter, and when the man's name came up Carter decided to look into the matter. A quick check of transcripts revealed Carter's suspicions to be well-founded. Not only had he not distinguished himself academically, but he had completed only two graduate-level courses.

Assuming an oversight, a bureaucratic foul-up in the screening process, Carter sent Department Chairman, William Norman a memo detailing his findings, confident Norman would correct the situation. Carter expected an immediate response. After three weeks he requested an appointment with Norman then waited another two weeks to get a hearing.

"Did you have a chance to look at my memo?" Carter said.

"Yes. And as a matter of fact I was a little surprised you went to the trouble."

"Trouble?"

"Well, this is a matter for the department chair and not something you should concern yourself with. The people we hire are well qualified, in fact, many of them are over-qualified."

Carter left the meeting telling himself he should have expected as much knowing the lineage of Norman's pedigree.

When Crowly became Vice Chancellor Carter did not question Crowly's qualifications. Simply there was no reason to. He had passed the Major Administration Selection Committee. Then too the university often employed administrators with a good bit less than perfect credentials. While poorly qualified administrators did not often improve the university, usually they did not cause serious damage. There seemed to be nothing better to do than live with them.

Carter viewed Crowly's appointment with good will and collegiality and made an appointment to speak with him.

At six-three, and nearly two hundred fifty pounds, Crowly reminded Carter of large red potato. He had played football at New Mexico State, received a degree in physical education, and a Masters in Educational Administration. He came to Barker as a clerk in the registrar's office, enrolled in classes two nights a week and within a year received a PhD in Education. The following year he was made assistant registrar, a year later Vice Chancellor of Instruction.

Carter congratulated him on the appointment, discussed briefly the kinds of problems he had seen at Barker in his years there that Crowly might have to face and wished him the best.

Crowly seemed personable enough, even candid, and admitted to Carter that he was a bit surprised he had gotten the job.

"What I really expected to be doing at this time in my life was working a dirt farm in New Mexico. That's what I was trained for."

Again Carter wished him well, and later encouraged other faculty to stop in and talk with Crowly about their problems.

What Carter did not realize at the time was that Crowly had been hired or promoted to Vice Chancellor for the purpose of restructuring the university. He had presented himself to Chancellor Remcheck and Board President Shindel as the man for the job and they had agreed to give him full rein.

A week after taking over he initiated a new system for selecting department heads. Within a month, using the imprimatur of the Faculty Senate, he devised a system of nomination and appointment. He sent out a memo requesting departments to submit nominations. He received three from philosophy—Talmar, Norman and Bennett, and declared immediately the Talmar and Bennett nominations were invalid since those filing the nomination had not responded within the allotted time.

The next day he appointed Norman.

This caused a stir, but in truth, nobody cared. In Carter's estimation the job was a pain-in-the-ass, without benefit to anyone but the administration and only with privileges Crowly would grant. Carter half expected that Talmar and Bennett were not much offended by the double-dealing.

That the senate concurred in Crowly's tactics, did not surprise Carter. Under Remcheck the senate already had been effectively reduced to a debating society, without the authority or the will to represent the faculty in any real way.

Rumor had it that at Crowly's insistence Norman nominated himself. The day following his discussion with Norman, Carter brought his conversation with Norman to Crowly's attention, expecting what, he wasn't sure. But more than simply passing over the matter, Crowly took Carter's interest in the situation as a personal attack.

"That's an administration prerogative to hire instructors as we see fit," Crowly said.

"Passing on the credentials of an instructor is the task of the Faculty Hiring Committee," Carter said as pleasantly as he could.

"Not on part-time instructors."

"But it's a full-time position."

"We've decide to eliminate that position and open three part-time positions instead."

"Whatever you've done, it doesn't make him qualified. The man is not qualified to go into a college classroom as an instructor in philosophy. And you're saying it won't make it so."

"Mr. Carter, you don't seem to understand," Crowly said. "We do make it so. The administration decides who is and who is not qualified. If we want to put instructors in the classroom solely on the basis of whether or not they can count to ten, we will. The law states quite clearly that the trustees of this institution shall hire administrators who shall in turn hire qualified people to provide instruction."

Carter's contempt for Crowly had not yet become vindictive.

Of course there were rumors, tales, sightings of Crowly and his secretaries at the local watering holes. With some mischief and amusement Carter kept a mental list of promotions, the gifts within Crowly's benefaction handed out to the females who shared their beds with him. That a female wanted to screw her way to a slightly better position with a pay raise, Carter did not find objectionable. Their sexual availability was not Crowly's fault.

On the other hand, Crowly's reduction of academic policies to legal norms had startled Carter, then angered him, and he had reminded Crowly about administrators getting degrees with a Wheaties box top and a quarter and not knowing the difference between legitimate and bogus educational pursuits.

"You know Carter, I took you for an intelligent man," Crowly had said. "But now I'm not so sure. You've been around long enough to know that occasionally we have to take unusual steps just to survive. It's our job to keep this place going. And you're not making it any easier. We need cooperation from our faculty, not criticism. Why don't you forget this nonsense and join the team and get with the game plan?"

At a faculty reception, earlier in the year, Carter had heard Crowly joking about his success in a high school algebra class.

"The football coach was the teacher," Crowly said. "He had the whole team in class and he'd code the answers with football plays. Christ. Otherwise, I'd never have made it."

"To begin with, you don't have the competence to pass on my intelligence," Carter said. "And if you mean by team that you're the coach and you're going to give me the algebra answers, no thanks. If that's your idea of a game plan, you're going to get your ass kicked. I don't need answers. Anyway, not yours."

After that Crowly had not spoken to him, even when they passed in the hall. He'd look away, check his watch and try to avoid Carter's gaze.

It was not something Carter enjoyed, but there was nothing he could do about it.

"Hell, half the country is out of work," Carter told Mason, only half kidding. "There are other things to do besides teaching.

"Anyway, if what you heard is correct and if they go by seniority, which they may do, you're not at the bottom of the pile, by a long shot. If they don't, be positive and look at the absurd side. There's only a thirty percent chance you'll be one of the four, out of a job, family uprooted and the sixteen years of your life and profession down the drain—as a reward for having given enthusiasm, intelligence and good will to your job."

"I don't know," Mason said. "I know what you're saying. If something happened I'd get along. I know that. But it's depressing. I've worked hard here. As hard as anyone. I've taken on classes at a moment's notice and struggled through one day at a time, just a page up, worked on committees. God, you name it. And when it's all done what do I get? Come to find out these people don't want me around. They want to get rid of me."

"It's a fast-food, bowling-shirt culture," Carter said. "Democracy in action, and reductionism. If you can't give everyone two cars and three TVs with enough ready cash on hand to make idiots into geniuses, because you are mass-minded and cannot think too well, you do the cheapest thing. You drop everyone into the cesspool, find the lowest common-denominator and make sure the brightest and best have no more than two cars and three TVs. In other words, you kill Ivan's goat. But the price is high."

The story was the same coming from colleagues at Michigan State and Georgia, Penn and Penn State. Every dog has its fleas, Carter thought, rationalizing in large part, although some are a little harder to scratch than others.

"You know," he told Mason, "when I was in London I spent the better part of a week in the British Museum. Several days alone looking at the Greek Archaic period display.

"The amazing part of the exhibit is not so much the beauty of the craftsmanship of the vessels, the pots and dishes. It's not even the fact that the styles of the vessels are so similar. What's amazing is that the museum has gathered so many pieces.

"Most times, it seems, when we hear or use the word civilization we don't fully comprehend what the words mean. But if there is an absolute in life, it isn't religion or art or philosophy, or even government. It's culture. Kant believed culture was the closest thing we have to an absolute.

"The glass cases at the British, row on row, contain the remnants of a style, a way of thinking, of doing and living pervasive to a people. So much so in fact that they could not think in any other way or be another way. If the remnants of an ethos that long ago are that numerous, in that splendid condition, and the British is by no means the only collection of Archaic Greek pottery in the world, then how much over how long a period had there been?

"The totality of the thinking and living habits represented behind the glass of those cases is culture. It's a warning that educators and artists in the culture had better guide and create it well as it goes—since cultural wrong turns are as absolute and as damaging as right turns are beneficial.

"This isn't to say the Archaic period led to the Golden Age or Classical period, although it probably did. I'm talking about the pervasiveness of the visions and assumptions, the customs and practices a culture contains.

"You're sounding like Hegel," Mason said.

"I hope not. I'm not talking about the mystical or spiritual. Maybe an almost absolute realism."

Mason smiled for the first time.

"Almost absolute?" he said. "You're going to have trouble explaining that."

"I know," Carter said.

"More subjective reporting," Mason said.

"Yeah," Carter said. "Our task, the task of the university, is to give practical direction to provide vision and humanity and depth. And, you know, that's precisely what is not happening here at Barker. The task, as sacred as it is, has been superseded by a pop, common mentality, the lowest common-denominator—hustling dollars.

"And another thing," he told Mason, "this failing is not the sole enterprise of a few half-assed administrators. It's a hell of a lot bigger than that. Nearly everybody has a hand in it. These places are fiefdoms. Baronies with serfs—a class system as doomed as the time in history they represents.

"When you object, or call attention to the misdirection, even the faculty look at you as if you're mad. And by god, when you get down to it, maybe we are. Maybe we should cash in our chips and let the dogs have the rancid meat. Maybe the past is not important or the animal too sick to save for the future."

"But then why are we doing this?"

"Yeah," Carter said, "I don't know. Maybe we should get out. Maybe we should."

Chapter V

Saturday afternoon Katherine Marie and two office associates took over the dining-room. Carter did not know the women beyond a brief and sliding introduction just after they arrived, the kind Katherine used as a warning for him to stay out of the way. They spread cosmetic ads on the large table, then hovered over the layouts.

When he entered the room, Katherine Marie watched him suspiciously. He rounded the table. She regarded him with apprehension.

"Carter," she said, "Carter, don't, don't do it."

"Don't? Don't what?"

"Whatever you're thinking. Don't do it."

"I was going to get a beer," he said. "Is that innocuous enough?"

"I don't believe you," she said. "Carter, I know you and I don't believe you."

Carter feigned indignation.

"Just the proper stuff of good marriages," he said, then addressed the smaller of the visitors, a wrinkled mid-forties edition, with fierce, dull-black hair and large splotches of eye-shadow.

"Would you distrust one who brought you gifts?" he said, bowing, holding out a rose he had pulled from the air.

"Remember, a single rose means I love you," Carter said, a dusting of sarcasm on his voice.

Katherine Marie reached across the table and lifted the flower from Carter's hand and dropped it into a vase on a small table near the door.

"Don't touch it," she said to the woman, "it'll give you warts. That's the only gift you'll get from him."

"Which is slightly better than syphilis or fallen arches," Carter said.

"Carter," Katherine Marie said. "Really, John, that's enough."

Several times more Carter ambled through to the kitchen, then retreated to watch from the doorway.

The women chatted softly and ignored him, a resurrection of traditional group habits. Women clinging to other women, peer bonding. Carter thought it was a good idea. Friendship was always a good idea. From the vantage of the kitchen door, listening to what they said, how they said it, Carter could not immediately determine who was in charge.

When he retreated, their presence and the patter of their voices on the air drifted after Carter into the living-room. Drifted after him, pursued him through the living-room to the front hall. The sounds of their presence left him rootless, rootless, without a place to hang out beyond earshot.

Exiled in my own house, Carter thought. Disenfranchised.

His impulse-response to the occupation was to leave and spend the afternoon outdoors, in the office or at Murphy's. That none of the possibilities offered any real attraction annoyed him even more.

Near mid-afternoon Carter returned to the dining-room.

"Is anyone going to want food?" Carter said. "I could order out. How about Chinese?"

"John, just leave us alone," Katherine Marie said. "I know you mean well, but we are not hungry. Anyway, we're going out later. Believe it or not we can take care of ourselves."

Carter retreated to the living-room and caught sight of the mailman on the porch stairs and heard the lid on the mail slot thump shut. In the hall he could feel ripples of frigid air stirring beneath the door. He gathered up the delivery then sorted through the bills, brochures, book ads, two requests from the Heart Fund, another from MS. At the bottom of the stack was a white envelope with no return. It was addressed to "Carter/1413 College Street." He tore it open and unfolded the note-book-paper page and read the very nearly illegible script.

> Dear John,
>
> The kids are in bed for the night and I was sitting here thinking about you. I am very glad I had the courage to bother you about going out for beer. Being around you has been good for me. And not many things have been of late.
>
> It is times like this I need you around. It would be good to talk to you right now. So much of what you say makes sense. It helps me when I get lost in feeling sorry for my-self, or thinking I'm the only person in the world who has problems.

Carter glanced at the date. Thursday, probably Thursday night. He continued reading.

> I've done a great deal of thinking since the last time we were together. (I hope you don't mind hearing all this.) I really do want out of this marriage. I'm even serious about giving him the kids. It would probably be better for everyone.
>
> Anyway, we can talk about all this later. I'll try to call you sometime Saturday. If not, maybe Sunday.
>
> Lottsa love,
> Vivien

Carter folded the letter and shoved it in his back pocket. Jesus, they never give up. It's genetic. Carved in stone. No matter what is stated or unsaid.

He dropped the mail on the hall table and went to the kitchen looking for food.

By six o'clock he had switched to bourbon and was drunk, slouched down in front of the TV, comatose, rounding off the edges of an otherwise vacant afternoon, staring at the waning minutes of an uninspired Notre Dame-Boston College football game.

A little after three Katherine had gone off with her business sisters for a drink with the warning (promise) she might not be back until late.

In spite of her threat promise Vivien hadn't called, which meant her Thursday night urge of the moment had passed, or she had been unable to get free, or to a phone, which came to the same thing. She'll call tomorrow, Carter thought, and tried to concentrate, to pull his mind through the whiskey haze long enough to remember what in fact he had planned for the day. He still had several hours of library work in preparation for class Monday, and needed time to proofread a manuscript for Mason. Ten pages, an hour, two, to do it well.

The fire had burned down to a bed of bright red coals. Carter poked at it carefully, then laid on several logs. Drifting in the balm and haze of inebriation, he settled onto the couch, stretched out intent upon thinking further about the girl.

He was aware of a phone ringing, somewhere, several times before he could reach for it. Again the fire glowed in the distance, a pale pink and red dying star on the far side of the universe of the dark room. When he found the phone he dropped the hand piece and for a moment could not locate it in the dark.

"Hello," he said pulling the instrument toward him. "Hello."

The voice was barely audible, quivering and weak.

"John, is that you?"

"Yes," Carter said, thinking for a second it was Katherine Marie.

"Where are you?"

"Is that you?" the voice said again.

"Yes. Who is this?"

"Just a minute," the voice said, and he could hear shuffling, then the deep hum and drone of a discussion shrouded by a hand over the mouth piece.

"John, are you there?"

Carter did not answer, now, and attempted to focus his blurred vision on the glowing coals in the fireplace.

"Okay," he said finally, "what's this about?"

"John, this is Vivien. I have to see you. It's urgent."

Her voice sounded only slightly improved, and Carter waited for her to continue.

"It is urgent," she said. "Can you get away?"

"What time is it?"

"I don't know. Ten. Maybe eleven."

Carter pushed himself up and fumbled for the lamp on the end table.

"Look, it's late and I'm not in the best of shape. How about tomorrow?"

Again her voice was strained and frail and nearly to the point of breaking.

"John, please?"

"Jesus, you pick good times."

His desire to see her had diminished with the dark of sleep and the late hour, and the weather.

"You do everything in the middle of the night?"

The phone was silent. Then she said, "Can you make it in twenty minutes?"

"At least tell me what's going on. If I'm coming out in the cold."

"The sonofabitch beat me up," she said, her voice breaking. "I'll tell you about it later. At Murphy's."

Carter hung up the phone and sat staring at the window, the shadows of the bare branches of winter's trees moving over the dull, dim milk-white glow the streetlight threw onto the frozen glass.

"You wanted a break in the routine," Carter chided himself as he pulled on his coat. "Well, here we go. Half drunk, tired, out in the middle of the frozen night because a scatter-brained female gets the shit knocked out of her.

Sometime, he thought, Carter, you're going to have to reconsider seriously the terrain of your own sanity.

The cutting edge of the December night did nothing to allay his skepticism about the advisability of going out. The sky was clear, however, clean and clear, for which he was thankful. A globe of a waning gibbous moon hung high brightening the night. The streets were noticeably deserted and considering the hour, even on a Saturday night, a relatively sizeable crowd occupied Murphy's. Carter squeezed in and passed through unobtrusively on his way to the booths in the back where he assumed he would find the girl.

He surveyed the faces several times before returning to the bar. He located the clock above the large aquarium behind the bar. He subtracted ten minutes, then decided she had probably not yet arrived. He slipped onto an empty stool, and not because he wanted or needed a drink, but because he could not feel comfortable sitting at a bar with nothing in front of him, he ordered a beer.

For Saturday night the patrons seemed strangely sedated, a good bit less boisterous and invigorated than their Friday counterparts.

Everybody's tired, Carter thought. Burnt out with the length of the semester.

The beer tasted particularly bitter, and his head was still hazy from his afternoon indulgence.

"Christ, Carter, why do you do that?" he said under his breath.

He considered one day he would take the cure, cast off the habit, become a closet temperance-leaguer. He had not yet considered AA. The time would come, though on his terms, without a crowd of therapy groupies, without baring his breast-bone before witnesses, it would come alone in the dark of his own tired and beaten skin.

Drinking, however, had not yet caused him problems of health, or profession. Maybe that was what he needed. A sign. A small hint of the impending end well on its way, approaching, indeed. Maybe his health would begin, slowly, to trouble him, then fail.

Maybe there would be a sign. Maybe he would lose interest in drinking and, then too, maybe in females. No longer find them attractive. He had heard of that happening. Maybe on a spring day coming along the quad, the air filled with sunlight and the fragrance of tulip trees, the women, their winter wraps discarded and the pleasant flesh of arms and legs, thighs and breasts open to view, maybe he would not see the women, or in seeing feel nothing.

Maybe. But not just yet.

He surveyed the crowd, looking for the girl, and satisfied she was not there settled in to wait.

Sunday afternoon they had walked to Ruth's apartment on the west side of the campus, a new complex with an open view of the skyfull Illinois prairie to the northwest, the pale, pink disk of sun hung over the white fields.

Carter had been just the slightest bit anxious. The girl seemed less so, although she continued to talk as they walked the short blocks to the apartment, as if to keep the spell, the momentum alive.

Not so much that Carter doubted himself, why he should have been there with her just then, how he knew the afternoon would end, though at times performance could be precarious.

On numerous occasions he had wandered into liaisons oozing with the sap of ulterior motives. The first time passion-driven, exhilarating as it might be, was nevertheless awkward. They would need to become acquainted sexually, just as they had become verbally conversant. For Carter familiarity bred trust and trust brought comfort.

So what did he remember now of the afternoon?

Her voice, that would be the first thing, the sound of her voice, the timbre, the intonation, and her smile. Her voice and smile as they walked.

He remembered putting his hand on the small of her back going up the steps to the second-floor, touching her intimately for the first time, surprised at how solid her body was. He led her by the hand to the bedroom and slipped her blouse up over her head, quickly undressed himself and fell back onto the bed pulling the sheet over him.

She kneeled beside him running her fingers, then her lips and tongue over his chest and neck, along the heavy muscles of his thighs.

Her breasts were perfectly formed, ample, high and firm, round and yet prominent.

"I suppose you have a month or two to waste?" he said. "Once we get started, we may not want to quit."

She laughed a smug little girl's laugh.

"And that covers a lot of ground."

"It's what is uncovered, not covered that counts."

She kissed him, lying by his side.

"Let's not wait," she said. "We've already waited too long."

Carter had always been apprehensive about moments like this. Positioning. He felt awkward. It seemed presumptuous. What if she changed her mind while he was getting arranged?

Then she pulled him gently on top of her, holding his face in her hands, her mouth pressed to his.

She was warm and eager, soft, her nest wet, spread and opened to him, his gentle searching stroke, moving easily with a steady, coaxing encouragement.

"My god," she whispered, her breath against his neck, "Talk to me. Tell me how you feel."

"Wonderful," he said, kissing her half closed eyes with his open lips.

Even though the apartment was neutral ground—or so she said—he was vaguely uneasy. In a sense she was too eager, too compliant, too much in a rush which added to his discomfort.

"Tell me when you cum," she said, "and I'll cum with you."

"Not yet," he said, rising over her, holding, then beginning again, down and into her, deeply, softly, his thighs pressed against hers.

"Tell me, tell me," she whispered. "Oh Christ, tell me."

He did and she wrapped her arms around him, holding them together until the last irregular, exhausted thrust before he left her.

For a very long time they lay together silently in the warm room, perspiring as the last shadows of the day spread across the ceiling, the walls, high in the corner above the mirror over the dresser. They were long, faded shadows, curled, shaded one on the other, bordering the light of a sun vanishing from the sight of one spinning world going into another.

She lay with her cheek to his chest, her hand open on his thigh.

"And you, my dear?" Carter said

She whispered, "That's the most incredible feeling. You know, there's something crazy about me. Jesus, when you cum in me, I go off like popcorn. It feels like something opens inside and turns everything loose. I can almost start just by talking about it."

She sat up next to him and he ran his fingers over the rise of her breasts, to the nipples, then cupped them in his hands.

Her body was wonderfully compact, thin and strong, and just then he was renewed by the vision, the touch of the tips of his fingers on her skin. The touch, the texture of her skin stayed with him at least as clearly as the sound of her voice.

So this is it, Carter thought. Desire spent, flesh on flesh designed by nature to lead us around.

She was silent for a long while. Then the room was dark.

"The darkness steals your youth," he said. "I can't tell how old you are."

She leaned toward him and grinned.

"I am very old," she said, speaking slowly, her voice cracking.

Sobered only a bit from his intoxication Carter could feel the gnawing of the unsettled and incomplete, the not totally satisfied.

"We still have unfinished business," he said.

"God, I hope so."

She leaned over and kissed him on the cheek, her long hair falling across his chest.

"Now, you have to tell me why you came to my office last week?"

"John, at this moment, that should be obvious."

"A rhetorical question, maybe. But why?"

"That could be a long story."

"I'll listen."

She smiled.

"You're sweet. Very nice."

"No I'm not. I'm a grouchy old bastard, remember. And I don't have any other redeeming qualities."

She clicked her tongue.

"My poor, poor man."

"Tell me your story."

She leaned down and kissed him again, then ran her lips up to his ear.

"Just a minute. I'll be right back."

She picked up a white, thigh-length robe off a bedside chair and slipped it on. Then he could hear her in the kitchen, probably in the refrigerator. She returned with a bottle of wine and two glasses and sat cross-legged on the end of the bed.

"This may be a long story," she said. "Where do you want me to begin? I was in your intro class last year."

"Which explains nothing."

"It explains everything. After class I'd go home and for hours I'd hear you talking."

She lifted her head and tilted it as if she might find what she would say printed on the ceiling.

"Your voice. I love to listen to you. Even when you're impatient. And your mouth. Watching the words form, the way the words sound when they fit together in my head.

"I'd wake up at night listening to you. Your words are in my brain like the lyrics of a song I hear and then keep replaying all night.

"And all day I'd have to listen to your voice. And feel your eyes watching me. It's not easy. Having you in my head like that.

"One day I came up to the desk before class and asked you how many absences I had, and you looked at me and, honest to god, I felt like I was naked, like you could see right through me, like you had just undressed me right there.

"That was a very disturbing class. Everything you said that day sounded like sex. I sat in the back of the room and leaned against the wall with my eyes closed. You probably thought I was sleeping. But I wasn't."

"And there's still the age thing."

"John, you'd be surprised how women feel about older men. I've never hung around much with people my own age. Most of the people in my life are older. And if skin color or hair and eyes or height are not considered, why should age be?

"Maybe I'm attracted to people who intimidate me. I always think you know things about me that I don't know. And it scares me.

"You know how you have a certain feeling and then you see something or somebody that fits the feeling. I close my eyes and think of someone I'd want to screw, then when I look you fit just what I imagined. And I'll tell you, that feels good, so good.

"This is like a dream. I never expected it to happen."

"Dreams are dreams," Carter said, "until they come true, then they're plans."

"Do you think I'm acting a little strange?"

"Don't you always act this way?"

"No. I really don't. My heart hasn't stopped pounding since we got here. I just don't believe you're here. I've been in this room hundreds of times and you've never been here. Now you are."

"You've been here with other men."

"No. With Ruth or friends. Alone. But, god, you're here now."

An hour later they had relocated to the living-room, Carter fallen into an large overstuffed chair, Vivien across from him on the couch leaning forward, her elbows on her knees. The wine had softened her face, her warm and now relaxed face. For the moment a tension had quieted in her.

Coming into the apartment Carter had surveyed the room and the titles shelved in the bookcase near the door. One section was devoted to poetry, as far as he could tell, seventeenth century and modern.

"Ruth reads a lot of poetry," he said.

"Yes. Don't you?"

"Not as much as I once did."

"Doesn't everyone read poetry."

"Who do you read?" he said.

"Oh, I don't know. You mean living? Today?"

Carter nodded.

"That's okay. Living," he said.

"Have you ever heard of Mary Oliver?"

"Yes. As a matter of fact I have. I once had a cousin of hers in class."

"And you? Who do you read?" she said.

He did not answer immediately.

"Actually, it isn't a matter of favorites," he said." I remember a poem, lines, words, ideas, feelings—but not who wrote it.

"Probably Bill Stafford, Phillip Larkin."

He pulled himself up from the chair and crossed the room to the bookcase, took down a volume of Oliver's poems and returned to the chair. In the early darkness he paged through the sparse offerings.

"I've not seen this particular book," he said, then aware of her presence, her closeness.

Standing barefooted next to the chair her head was only a little above his. She set her wine glass on the end table next to his and crawled onto his lap like a small child.

"Will you read to me?" she said, and he could smell the sweet wine breath of her words, the warm insistence of her soft breasts pressed to him.

"What would you like?"

She looped her arms around him and laid her head on his shoulder, her mouth, her moist lips touching his neck.

"Your voice. Anything."

And in the quiet with the girl on his lap, he read aloud from the slender book.

When he finished she sat up and looked at him.

"You asked me what I was doing here. I've never been around a man who read poetry. Who really carried about people. Is it possible to be a man without beating on people or lying about everything you do? John, this is really new for me."

Near seven he woke to the dim, strange apartment with Vivien still on his lap, sleeping, her scent heavy in his head.

So be it, Carter, he thought.

And because the time had not yet come when he no longer had an interest in the night and its possibilities and promises, he went back to searching the faces at Murphy's for a face he knew, hoping the girl was there and that he had missed her.

He decided he'd wait another fifteen minutes. If she had been knocked around, she'd need to talk, need him to help her pick up the pieces. She'd need consolation, someone to say that no one has the right to beat on another person.

Carter had never reconciled the cataloguing of domestic violence as a normal component of human connections. The belief that might makes right was an obscenity.

Several times he walked into the backroom, hoping she had come in the side door and might be there.

And when he was sure she was not, he rotated back to the bar.

Although her call had sounded urgent, she had been coherent and communicative and he could not easily imagine if she had been badly injured

The idea of someone beating her gnawed at him and he wanted very badly just then to see her, to assure himself she was all right. The uncertainty of her condition and his immediate inability to locate her, to inquire about her, intensified his protective impulses.

It crossed his mind he might find her number in the phone directory, but he decided against it. If he found the number and if he called, and if she answered, even if she was home alone, what would he say?

Twenty minutes later he gave in to the obvious. He drained the last of a second beer, ordered another for the road, slipped the full glass carefully bottom down into his overcoat pocket, and exited by way of the side door.

A block from Murphy's in the alley behind the McDonald's two men, students he guessed, leaned into a dumpster, rummaging the food that had been dumped there an hour or so earlier. Wisps of steam rose around them on the piercing night air. When he stopped at the alley entrance, they straightened up and watched him.

"It's tough to get the coffee grounds off the Big Macs," a student told him, explaining the scavenging practice. "But when you don't have any money, it's that or go hungry. And the food's good."

Scholars, Carter imagined, forced to feed on the wastes of the trash society. Future scholars. The practice of trickle-down economics.

Leaving them to their recycling he continued home along the path he had come, only mildly perturbed with having been stood up, and satisfied he had found something worthwhile in the night.

That he was not alarmed by Vivien's failure to appear surprised him. But at least at the moment, late as it was, and in the history of his experience, her failure to show did not seem unnatural.

That's what fist-fights'll get you, he thought. Pretty ladies do not like to go about with their lips puffed and swollen.

If she had been beaten up, and if "the sonofabitch" she had referred to as her attacker was her husband, Carter could not help but muse over what exactly had caused the altercation. Had she informed him that she was in fact leaving, that he could have the kids, etc., etc. Or had he caught her screwing around. Carter wondered if his name had come up. Maybe she used him as a whip, and got whipped for it.

"Little girls," he told himself, "do foolish things."

He chuckled.

"Indeed."

Then told himself something else.

"Old men do too."

He had been stood up before. Her reason for not showing, was to his mind, a good reason, good precisely because he assumed it had been necessary. And he was always a sucker for a good reason.

Regardless, he could not find now even a nominal twinge of rancor for either of them. His connection with the girl did not include protection. People should not beat on other people. That was true. But people do a lot of things they are not supposed to do.

When he came in Katherine Marie was in bed asleep, and he took his pillow down to the living-room couch and rolled up in two wool afghans.

It was good to be home.

He liked this house—his digs. Shortly after they occupied the house he came to think of it as a refuge, a warm and stable and serene port. In other houses he had been comfortable, found them functional and convenient, but these rooms had a wonderful, intimate feeling.

The acoustics were very good. Sound did not carry, but seemed to slide along the walls, or lie down about the floor and furniture like a large soft cat. Even the sharpest noises were muffled or modulated and carried along with an extended purr.

In spite of the large room with high ceilings, the lighting was superb. The size and arrangement of windows and interior doors kept even the more secluded corners of halls and alcoves well lighted.

The fire had gone out. The wind whistled in the chimney, whining against the bricks. Carter found the loneliness of the sound soothing. Then, attempting to recall what he had decided finally about Sunday, what he had set up with Mason when he had called in the afternoon, Carter fell asleep.

Chapter VI

On the way to the cafeteria Carter stopped at Morgana's office. He knocked on the partially opened door, then stuck his head in. She was seated with her back to him, talking with a young man Carter assumed to be a student. She leaned back and looked over her shoulder, then held up a long, thin finger with a long polished black fingernail.

"Be with you in a minute," she said in a throaty voice affected by too many years of too many cigarettes.

Three packs a day for thirty years. Carter did a rough tabulation. Six hundred fifty some-odd thousand. Jesus Christ. He shook his head. The number alone is enough to do you in. No wonder we burn out.

For mid-morning the hall was unusually quiet. Carter propped himself against the wall to wait, and gave his attention to the glass display cases of fossils that lined the hall.

For decades the cases had been distributed among the four floors and halls of Temperly, giving the old building a bit of museum atmosphere. Three years before, Lamar Landeau, Dean of Humanities, decided to implement a more positive utilization of space productivity and dismantled the display placards and charts and crowded the cases onto the fourth-floor to make room for electronic video game machines on the other three floors.

Carter leaned over the case and a moment later found his face in the glass, a pale yellow moon of a ceiling light shining weakly over him. A few of the fossils he could identify, the majority he could not. The memory of the decision to dismantle the displays still rankled him and he pulled away, feeling the sacred or very nearly sacred had been violated.

The boy exited the office and nodded as he passed. Carter could hear Morgana shuffling about.

"It's coffee time," he said.

She came into the hall, slinging the long strap of her purse over her shoulder.

"It sure as hell is," she said.

A not too robust woman in the beginning, she had withered substantially. Right before his eyes. She had shrunk down to a minimum of sinew wrapped in a wrinkled sheath of loose skin.

Her years had not been without turmoil and ordeal and looking out at a mostly disapproving world, from that particular cage had, Carter knew well, deeply biased her.

She had been thrice married to husbands as different as three men might be. The common strain, if there was one, rested in her belief that each had attempted to take over her life.

"I don't know where the nonsense comes from," she told Carter in an unusual bit of self-analysis. "But they looked good until breakfast. I mean, they weren't evil people or anything. It wasn't that simple. They thought I needed guidance. And it wasn't any specific thing. I mean, they wanted to help me by changing my life, when I was damn near as content with it as anyone could be.

"Hell, maybe it's me. Do I invite that in men? You think I'm giving off confusing signals? Telling men I want them to take care of me when what I really want is for people to stay the hell out of my way?"

On the elevator she rummaged through her purse and pulled out a folded paper and handed it to Carter.

"Read this," she said in an I-told-you-so tone.

"Where'd you get this?"

"Good agents never reveal their sources."

"A copy then?"

"Yes. But we know now who's going to get letters."

"Who?"

"Oldam, Winslow, Baker and Fisk."

Carter paused, considering the names.

"You know that doesn't make sense," Morgana said.

"So. Since when did sense matter?" Carter said.

"There doesn't seem to be any common-denominator," Morgana said. "At least none we can determine."

Carter shook his head.

"That violates seniority."

"And tenure."

"I still don't believe it," Carter said. "They've got something else in mind. If you asked Crowly for the time, just as a matter of principle, at four o'clock he'd tell you it was five to or five after. That's a cardinal rule."

"These will be in the mail, certified mail tomorrow."

"Have you talked to anyone? Who else knows about this?"

"Only Carl Johnson. We thought we'd wait until Crowly had notified the next of kin."

"Meaning what?"

"Well, I don't know. Dammit, Carter, this is a letter-edged-in-black. Those people haven't any real chance of getting another job. This is the black hand, the kiss of death.

"This morning after class, Carl and I went through this department and over to Psychology and History to see if there was anything, even a semblance of conscience or integrity floating around. And you know what we got?"

"Yep."

"Nothing. Absolutely nothing. All anybody would say is 'sorry, I don't want to get involved.'"

"Have you talked to Daly?"

"Well, maybe we should. The AAUP will have to handle this."

"And handle it they will. They'll stand around and whimper. Remember the last job-action they directed. Don't wear your mortar board and tassels to graduation."

Carter laughed.

"Honest to god, that's pathetic."

"But this is serious, Carter."

"It is serious, always," he said, with a slightly mocking manner, then refocused on the names, and Mason.

"Let me talk to Mason about this."

"You could just wait until he receives it in the mail."

"Do you think that would be decent?"

"No."

"If the shoe were on the other foot, how would you want it handled?"

"No. You're right. Will you see him this afternoon."

"He has a morning schedule. I'll stop in on the way home and talk to him. If someone doesn't get there first."

"Should I give this to Daly?"

"I would," Carter said, "but don't be surprised if he already has it. If, in fact, he has not had it for some time."

Morgana looked surprised.

"You think so?"

"Not necessarily. But it is possible."

The cafeteria was crowded and they past the line to the coffee urns.

"Make mine black," Morgana said. "I'll get a table."

Already, in his mind, Carter was stationed on the couch in the living-room of Mason's small but tastefully furnished house. Ardyth perched on the edge of her well-worn French Provincial chair, her large eyes fixed irrevocably on Carter, waited with suspended suspicion, a twinge of apprehension. Mason hovered about, indistinct, the soft velour of his presence absorbing Carter's words.

Be direct, Carter counseled, and also decided to be as fair as he could. Mason was aware of Carter's sympathies and prejudices. There would be no reason to go over that, except to reinforce Mason's understanding, and Ardyth's. Carter would have to try to explain that they were dealing with a madness that operated without cause or reason, with a lunatic glee in the virulence of its malice.

People could not live without hope, and Carter wondered now where Mason would find it. Where, for that matter, anyone dangling on the frayed threads of impermanence might find it.

On occasion, poking at the assumptions of his students, as well as his own, he would ask just that question. Why do you get out of bed this morning? Why do you come to class? And why bother?

The answers were seldom well crafted or thought out, though occasionally humorous.

"I had to get up to pee, so I thought I'd stay up."

"You can only spend so much time on your back."

"It was a mistake."

"If there had been someone worthwhile with me, I wouldn't have."

Unless he could turn Mason's mind, refocus his visions, he would no doubt fall into the vacuum of hope gone. Knowing Mason Carter also knew that would have to be addressed, eventually, if not this afternoon.

It was a bleak prospect that had seeped into the profession, which had rotted the roots. Hustling the fast buck of mass-education markets, the easy learning schemes with fast degrees had done its part, but undermining the future of the professorate was even more destructive. Carter had seen it around him, slicing at the veracity, at the heart of the university.

And what would he say? What would John Carter say about that. The impulse came over him to simply forget the entire thing and leave Mason to his own devices, which would be the reality of the situation, at any rate.

What would he say?

Well, he would suggest the obvious. The job was a pain-in-the-ass, not worth doing if the effort was not rewarded with more than an insufficient salary and Crowly with his teeth in your neck. And the argument so often offered up that these conditions were just a part of life was to Carter's thinking the kind of cosmetic tripe small minds dump on the trail to cover the stench of their own inadequacies.

He was angry again. Not for himself, now, but for Mason and his vulnerabilities, and because he could not help or protect him.

Then he was angry for being upset. Wasn't this what he had expected from the beginning?

Carter poured out two cups of coffee. Waiting at the cash register, William Norman came up behind him.

"How are you today, John?"

"Fine," Carter said. "And you?"

"Oh, well enough. Just trying to get into the spirit of things."

The specter of Norman at his back made Carter uncomfortable and he twisted to face him.

Norman's white hair was meticulously trimmed. He wore clear, round glasses without frames and a gold neck chain attached to ear-pieces. As always the collar of his powder-blue shirt looked more nearly sculpted than starched. From the little Carter knew of haberdasher habits and costs, his suit was quite expensive. By comparison, even without looking, Carter felt shabby and threadbare.

Norman was a leading proponent of what Carter called the "wardrobe faculty." People who spent exorbitant sums on stylish clothing, a life style and form without substance.

That's about as far as they got.

One night at a party at Norman's house Carter wandered into a room that served as a library and study and haphazardly pulled down a book, then another, and was truly surprised to discover that the ending publication dates of the books on the three shelves coincided exactly with the year Norman received his doctorate in Education Administration.

For most years of Carter's tenure at Barker, department chairs were a matter of pride and esteem. Senior members, full professors selected by department vote rotated two-year terms. The chair had always served with the advice and consent of the department, and was seldom if ever questioned by the deans. These were matters of academic complicity in which differences of opinion were compromised if not without debate, still agreed to. In his experience there had been a very real attempt to accommodate academic concerns. But wasn't that the idea of the university? To promote academic quality? Looking back, those days now appeared both idyllic and naive.

The break had been abrupt. Two weeks after the board appointed Remcheck Chancellor, philosophy chair Colin Belmont, who had served only six months of his two year term, was sacked, and Crowly inserted Norman in Belmont's place. The fuss was general. Accusations and protests were voiced. But the flap ended where it began. It was a flap and nothing more. Even those who protested most vociferously, after a brief time sulked off to their cells.

Carter listened to Norman's whimper, wondering why he had even bothered to acknowledge him. Without saying more he paid for the coffee and located the table. Mason was with Morgana.

"If I'd known you were here," Carter said.

Mason raised his hand.

"No, no. That's all right. I've had too much coffee this morning."

Through the large window behind Morgana, Carter could see out along the quadrangle. It was snowing again. He took out a cigarette, puffed it up to a bright glow and blew the smoke into the air.

Morgana refused to acknowledge Carter's "stunts," as she called them, and ignored him now.

"Did you enjoy your little tête-à-tête with boss Norman?"

"Have you heard any more about the dismissals?" Mason said.

Carter had laid the cigarettes on the table and Mason took one from the pack.

Usually he did not smoke, and Carter watched him cautiously, then lit the cigarette for him. Masons hands shook and he blew out a small novice puff of smoke.

"We don't have a full list as of yet," Carter said, watching Morgana.

"You know," Carter continued, "when my first marriage fell apart, even though it was probably a good thing, since the relationship was shot, I still felt as if I was headed into a black-hole. The feeling must have come from knowing that I had to make a change. Even though I knew the change would be good for me.

"Maybe we should try to see this nonsense like that. It's not what we want, or what should be done, and even though we didn't ask for it, we can change our lives—and we will."

Mason shook his head.

"I've done everything they asked," he said. "I've worked hard for this university, and I don't see how they can just throw it away."

"From your record here," Carter said, "you'd have a good chance at another school."

"Moving would mean uprooting the family, selling the house."

He paused, holding the cigarette out, his hands still shaking, and watched the smoke rise in small waves.

"But we have tenure rules," Mason said, finally. "How can they break the rules?"

Mason stuffed out the cigarette and stood.

"You have a nine o'clock?" Carter said.

Mason nodded and picked up his brief case.

"I'll see you at noon," Carter said.

Mason disappeared into the hall and Morgana faced Carter.

"He's having a bad time. He's not in very good shape," she said.

"Yeah. And I'm not sure how to get him out of it."

"You want him out of it?"

"Well, it sure'n hell isn't doing him any good to worry it to death. What I told him about his chances at another school is true. With his publications and vita, and age, he's a helluva lot more employable than either of us."

"My mother always said that the only thing she wanted out of life was to die before any of her children," Morgana said.

"Is she going to get her wish?"

"If I can hang on a little longer, she may."

"It's that bad?"

Morgana looked hard at Carter.

"For Christ sake, John, we worry about him too much. There are things parents can't do. Especially surrogates."

"You think I should back off a little."

"You know, we could be the Holy Family," Morgana said.

"You want to be the Virgin Mary?"

"Might as well. I've tried everything else," she said. "Anyway you should have had a couple kids of your own."

"It's really a shame," Carter said. "Mason is so goddam talented, both as a teacher and a writer. And as a philosopher. It's just a shame this has to happen to him, of all people. It's what pisses you off about working in a dump like this."

"Spoken like a true father."

"Where are yours now?"

"Ah, Michael's in Paris working for AT&T, becoming, as his brother says, a capitalist ass-hole, and Thomas is practicing medicine in Cincinnati."

"American medical doctors are not·capitalist?"

Morgana laughed.

"Not according to them."

"And you don't have a need to mother Mason," Carter said.

"Oh, once you've started, mothering that is, you might as well go on with it."

Carter was about to return to the paradox of attempting to teach values and virtues in an institution run by people without any, when Vivien came out of the line on the far side of the room. She was carrying a food tray and a bundle of books, and he could not discern immediately if she was alone. She had braided her hair on one side and wore a large pair of bug-eyed sunglasses.

"Someone you're waiting for?" Morgana said, following the direction of his gaze.

"No. Just a student I was supposed to talk to the other day."

The other night, he said to himself. He had not heard from her Sunday, and although he was only slightly curious about the reasons for the encounter, the reasons she had reported, he had wondered about the extent of the damage. Were the glasses a tell-tale sign? Had she gotten both eyes blackened? Had somebody tried to "punch her lights out?"

The peculiarity of that idiom intrigued Carter. The eyes as lights, pictured-portal passages to the source, to an interior animism. A nearly animal attempt to attack the source, the mythic ethereal wellspring of spirit. "An eye for an eye," or in this case two black eyes for a fist. Retaliation, maybe, though not without attempting to rearrange or redirect a vision.

Carter went flipping, teasing back through the pages, the dust and grit to Plato's we see what we see, and there can be no error in that, to Apollo's nimble cavorting as "the viewer of the heavens," full circle to the great-eye of female fertility through which men enter the world, and to which they are bound to return, to enter and reenter.

And then, the brutal, harsh realities, the bubbling, infantile arrogance and incredible fantastic belief that you could and would actually want to level a physical assault on the world of the soul, with the attendant attempt to give aid and comfort to the outrage by covering the evidence. When the swinging is done, Carter thought, at heart we're all eyebeaters. Or possibly not.

"Morgana Mary," he said, coffee and cigarette in hand. "I hate to leave good company, but I do need to talk to that young woman. If I don't get a chance before then, on the way home I'll stop at Mason's and check on him. If you hear any more, give me a call. If I come across anything, I'll call you."

Morgana nodded gravely.

"Remember," she said, as much for instruction as jest, "good lovers are always a proper blend of father and lover. Be generous."

Chapter VII

The afternoon was bitterly cold. The snow dwindled to a scatter of flakes on a gusty wind. Carter left Temperly after his two o'clock class and walked the six blocks to Ruth's apartment to meet Vivien.

A helluva time to come down with something, he thought, wondering how much the strain of the morning had to do with it. In a pretense of mind over matter he decided to ignore the symptoms.

The girl had, indeed, gotten knocked around. In the bright light of the cafeteria her wounds were obvious. Beneath the blue-brown glasses her left eye and cheek were marked with swirls of red-purple bruises and broken blood vessels. Her bottom lip was still puffed and the rim of her chin was marked with an ugly contusion. She was, when Carter approached the incident, evasive about the dispute, although she seemed unruffled by it.

"What are you going to do?" Carter said.

"Now?"

"No. About people beating on you?"

"What can I do? Nothing, I suppose."

Her response did not surprise him. He had seen it before in other women, the terrible calm in face of a very real and present danger. It was as if they truly did not see the danger, or possibly saw it as permissible, a treatment they deserved and if dangerous, only mildly so.

"You make it sound like a conventional bit of marital commerce," he said. "But you know it'll happen again."

"Yes," she said, calmly, "but he didn't mean anything by it."

"I suppose not."

"You can suppose whatever you choose," she said.

"You've been hanging around me too long. You're starting to sound like me."

"Is that bad?"

"I don't know."

"Well, it wasn't intentional. Didn't you ever get pissed-off and just do something you really didn't intend to do?"

"Yeah. I know. But have you looked in a mirror lately? Your face isn't exactly a tribute to unintentionally."

"Look, he intended to do it. That's not what I meant."

"What did you mean, then?"

"John, don't be that way. Hell, I don't know. I mean, it isn't that big of a deal."

"Okay," Carter said, "you call me in the middle of the night saying you've been maimed, violated and I don't know what else. So I get my tired and worn ass up, go tracking out into the dark prepared to offer salvation and solace, and you don't even bother to show up. Now you tell me it was no big deal. Hey, I don't mind that you didn't show up, but Christ there must be something of reason in it. At least tell me you enjoyed it."

"It's a long story," she said. "Let's say there would have had even more trouble if I had tried to go out. After our little ruckus he left the house. I thought he was gone for the night. That's when I called you. Then he came back. That's all there was to it."

He wondered what had been added to the story in the last few days. Had the trouble resurfaced? Would she bring it with her?

When he came to the apartment he knocked and then tried the knob. The door opened and he stepped into the living-room and closed it quietly behind him.

He heard someone moving about in the bedroom and then heard her voice.

"Is that you, John?"

"Yes," he said. "Who else at this hour?"

She giggled then said, "I'll be just a moment."

It was the second time he had been in the apartment, and his memory of the place was spotty. The long outside wall of the living-room on either side of a large window had been papered with posters, peace signs and a rash of paintings crafted, in the considered judgment of Carter's eye, by less than an artistic hand. The room was otherwise a jumble and scatter of overstuffed furniture, bookcases and books. Two Chianti bottles with candles poked in the mouths were on an end table near the couch, and several stacks of magazines had been piled near the bedroom door.

He circled the room, examining the paintings, then instinctively drifted toward the window. He had not met Ruth, and had seen her only once, that day with Vivien in the hall outside his office. He thought he had seen her another time at Murphy's, but because of the poor light and too much to drink he could not be sure. The condition of the room, however, the apartment, what he could see of the bedroom, the books, posters, paintings, would not have fit Vivien. Certainly she was a visitor here. The paintings, if they were Ruth's, reflected a nurtured artistic interest, the endless hours of practice pointed at competence, if a small and unpolished talent. The names in the corners of the canvases Carter made out as Ruth, scratched over what looked like Lassiter.

When Vivien came into the room he was looking out over the woods behind the complex.

"You always stand at windows?"

"The higher the better. It feeds my megalomania. Although, I must admit, I'm seldom sovereign whether I survey it or not."

She laughed a deep, pleased laugh. A comfortable womanly laugh. The edge that had been there in the morning when they talked, the edge he only now realized had been there, was gone from her voice.

She was barefooted and wore a large gray sweatshirt that came to mid-thigh. In the soft light her wounds seemed less serious, less damaging when she smiled, and Carter was again impressed with how tall she was.

She put her hand on his shoulder and leaned up and kissed him on the cheek.

"How about a beer?"

"Sounds good."

She appeared from the kitchen with two beers, but stopped in the doorway.

"Before we go any farther, I want you to know that I'm sorry about Saturday night. I also want you to know that after this, I'm through telling you I'm sorry. This is the last time. The absolute last time."

Carter laughed and reached for the beer.

"Mrs. Vivien Connors, my dear, that is bullshit. Tomorrow, the next day, or next week, you'll do some other fool thing and come back saying you're sorry."

"John. Damn you," she said, "I know. But at least you could humor me."

"You didn't sound very contrite this morning."

"I wasn't. I was scared. I went to your office and when you weren't there, I thought maybe you'd be in the cafeteria. That place gives me the shivers. I never go there. And you were with that woman."

"Morgana."

"Who is she?"

"She teaches philosophy."

She handed him the beer and stared at him as if she was trying to remember the name.

"That's not your wife?"

"Yes," Carter said. "That most certainly is not my wife."

"Then I knew you were pissed at me and when you came over to the table I didn't want to go into another of those wet-eyed episodes. I just knew you were going to give me shit about not showing up."

"Well, people trying to solve their problems with violence is truly barbaric."

Her face lit up.

"Do you think so? God it sounds absolutely decadent," she said with a slightly taunting tone. "Haven't you ever wanted to live dangerously? I mean, live with the unexpected?"

She sat on the couch and propped her feet on the stack of magazines on the coffee table. Her legs were straight and very well formed, her feet thin with high, well curved arches and long toes. Carter did not often find women's feet especially attractive. And he was not sure why or what prompted his newly founded appreciation. The sweat-shirt had lifted above her thighs, and she held out her hand to him.

"Professor Carter, you are wasting good time with silly conversation."

Carter dropped onto the couch beside her and ran his hand beneath the soft cloth of the old sweatshirt along the cool, smooth skin of her back.

"And now, John, what do you think we should do now?"

Outside the wind had picked up, blowing snow and shaking the building. The luminous hands on the small clock on the bedside table showed seven-ten. Carter propped himself up on an elbow to see the clock. The room was icy and Vivien was face down, possibly sleeping, beneath the soft bulk of the eiderdown. Her face was toward him, deep in the pillow with her hair swirled in a pile so the glow of the streetlamp gave the nape of her neck a soft luminescence. Carter leaned down and touched his lips behind her ear, but she did not move.

"Are you awake?" he said, and when she did not answer, added, "It's after seven. I have to go."

She looped her left arm over his chest and pulled herself toward him.

"You don't have to go. You don't have any place to go. Anyway, if you go, you'll just have to come back. So why go?"

"I have to visit a friend."

"You're already visiting a friend. Don't be greedy."

"Do you think there's hot water? There certainly doesn't seem to be any heat. What'd they do, turn off the heat?"

She sat up, then laid her head on his chest.

"Visit your friend tomorrow. Stay with me."

Her breasts and face were warm against his skin, and Carter pulled the eiderdown over them again. He'd have to call, to see if Mason would be home. And then, well, then—for the first time he was aware of how uncomfortable he was with what he had to do.

"I'd rather stay," he said, "much rather."

"Good. Then it's settled. We'll stay right here for the rest of the night."

"By the way, when do you expect Ruth?"

"I don't know. But it's not a problem. She doesn't mind sleeping on the couch."

"Don't you have to be home?"

"Nope. Not tonight."

"Then, when?"

"Not tonight," Vivien said.

"And my dear, what will you get for that?'

"A wonderful night with you."

"That's not what I meant," Carter said.

"But it is what I meant."

"Where's the phone?'

"Over there."

She pointed to the dresser on the far side of the room and snapped on the lamp on her side of the bed as Carter slipped out onto the frigid floor.

"You know what?" she said watching him cross the room. "You've got a sexy ass."

"And, at this moment, a cold one."

He found the phone and lifted it and pulled the cord free from behind the dresser.

"Will it reach to the bed?"

"It should. Who are you calling?"

"My wife."

"Your wife? Why your wife?"

"I'm going to tell her about you."

"Tell her about me? You're out of your mind."

"No I'm not. She'll get a kick out of this."

"Who are you calling?"

He dialed the number, then waited.

"She'd like to meet you. She got pissed at me the other day and said 'I'd like to meet anyone who would put up with you for even five minutes.' So, you qualify, and I thought I'd give her a chance."

The line was busy and Carter listened for a few seconds to the pulse beating on the other end. The girl watched him closely now, in the diffuse light, not sure what exactly he had in mind, what he was doing. Then she put her mouth to his ear.

"What will you tell her? How we made love? How we did it?"

"Yeah," Carter said. "She likes details."

"Would she like to watch?"

"Would you enjoy that?" Carter said.

"Maybe we should get the whips and chains out."

Carter replaced the receiver and set the phone on the floor.

"The line's busy."

"Then you'll have to stay. You don't have any reason to go now."

"I'll have to call later. She'll be disappointed that she missed you."

"Carter? Who did you call?"

"Just a friend."

She pushed herself up and got out of bed.

"I have to go potty. Don't go away."

"See if there's any hot water."

Carter watched her, this time, the sensual half-shadowed silhouette of her legs, the firm buttocks and sculpted back. A strange and delightful feast of graceful movements, the scent of female fragrance.

Maybe you could write an article. A book of essays. To begin how about "A Critique of Prurient Seasons?" And how would you begin? With the leading question, of course.

Is there nothing in you, Carter, beyond your appetites? Nothing of moral fiber and sinew to withstand the assault of your sense and their attendant pleasures?

And the answer.

Jesus, no.

Bentham had it right. Jeremy dead the many years, sitting, still, at the door of the London University Museum of Natural History, his mummified head set on the floor between his feet, replaced with a plastic model, voting, too, at meetings of the Royal academy, voting "present."

The low murmur of voices filtered in from the living-room and Carter sat up. He hadn't heard the doorbell. Somebody with a key. Probably Ruth. If not, who? The voice sounded male. Christ! Now what? The stalking male syndrome? The outraged husband. Vivien's old man in hot pursuit, hell-bent on revenge, vengeance or satisfaction, but mayhem nonetheless. Determined to reclaim what was his. Retake lost ground. Make himself known and felt. Righteous in his now justified indignation at having exposed the deception. An outpouring of excessive testosterone and Doubled-Y chromosomes customized and supported by stupidity. Now come looking for an adversary to expiate his rage. Well, here we go, Carter thought. The saga of the jealous husband.

In his philandering Carter had avoided, on occasion just barely, the rage of betrayed husbands and boy-friends.

He sat motionless, listening. The voices a bare mumble, but a measured and even mumble.

What would he say?

First things first. He located his pants. How in the hell can you defend yourself stark naked? The plausibility of "this is not what you think it is" would be a little hard to maintain. He had one foot in when he heard the door close and Vivien came in from the living-room.

"Who's there?" he said, tentatively.

"Nobody. Not now."

Her voice was calm and pliant, and for a moment he wanted to take her word for it.

"Who was there?"

"Oh, just a friend of Ruth's."

"A friend? You were in the bathroom."

"I was. I went into the living-room for a cigarette. There was someone at the door."

"A friend? Who?"

"No one you know."

She jumped on the bed and rolled over and forced her mouth against his ear.

"God, Carter," she said in a throaty whisper, "let's fuck."

"Male or female?

"Male. Carter, come on. It's nothing. Ruth has weird friends. They show up at strange times."

Just then the lilt of music drifted in from the other room. Carter watched her face.

"What's that?"

"You like it?"

"What is it?"

"Under African Skies." She recited the lines with the song, "After the dream of falling and calling your name out."

The realization that followed annoyed Carter.

One day (night) in the waning moon of his first marriage one of his wife's future lovers (a supposed lover—since he didn't know, and did not want to know) actually appeared at Carter's door asking his permission to fuck her—or at least to try.

The incident struck Carter as so bizarre that he was surprised several years later when he could not remember the man's face or name. But he did remember the question.

"Is it all right with you if . . .?"

And the answer.

"What she does, is her business," Carter had said. "I suggest you ask her."

Then he added, "I've never been able to account for what goes on between my own legs, and I'm sure'n hell not going to try to account for what goes on between hers."

"It's my favorite song," Vivien said.

She settled in beside him and curled up. Now she was chilled and pressed against him.

"Jesus," she said shivering. "You're right. This place is freezing."

The insulation of the music quelled Carter's annoyance a bit. The soft flesh of her breasts, his lips touching the firm smooth skin of her neck, pulled him back.

"You know," he told her, "I was just thinking. You're a perfect lover for me."

"Do you think so?"

"Well, you can care about someone and not be comfortable with them in bed. It takes a while to get to know each other. Sometimes it never happens."

"Do you care?"

"For you?"

"Yes."

"It's nice to be around someone who wants you around."

"What about your wife? Doesn't she want you around?"

"Oh, hell," Carter said. "That thing has pretty much died of its own weight. When we started off I needed her and I supposed she needed me. I needed help getting my life in order and she needed the respectability of marriage. Marriage gave her a certain amount of prestige. My position at the university did that.

"I really did care for her. Yeah, I still do. But people grow and go in different directions. She reads a lot and has good taste, and I depended on that. I trusted her judgment, even when I shouldn't have.

"But the whole thing has fallen into disrepair. It's dying of neglect and we're both guilty."

"I think I know what you mean."

Her face was quizzical.

"By the way, there's hot water. What do you want with hot water?"

"I was considering taking a shower."

"That's weird. Why would you get out of a warm bed to take a shower in a freezing apartment? You're strange."

"Haven't you ever heard of cleanliness?"

"What did I do? I thought you liked my smell?"

"I do," he said. "But that's not all of it."

She pushed herself up and looked at him.

"Did I get you dirty? When did you fall in the mud?"

"Just because I asked about hot water?"

"John, the word is not cleanliness. It's compulsiveness. You're compulsive."

"To change the subject a bit," Carter said, "you haven't said anything recently about your sister. How is she?"

She stiffened with the question, but did not answer, then rolled away and put her hands behind her head. She was staring at the ceiling.

"I'd rather not talk about it. Not now, anyway."

Carter lay back and dropped his hand to the phone. At least they could agree on that this day, the impulse to avoid talking about unpleasant matters. He thought about it for a moment. No. It wasn't self-deception. No, he was not out to deceive. But he was not up to slopping through the dung, either.

He dialed the phone, then, rehearsing his lines, picking over what he would suggest to Mason to ease the shock, to slake the disgust caught in his own throat.

Again the line was busy and he replaced the receiver and sat for a moment silently staring at the small TV on the chest across the room.

She watched him.

"What are you looking at? What are you doing?"

"Turning on the television," he said, settling again on the pillow stacked against the headboard, a small glow spreading over the screen.

Chapter VIII

Carter had one class Tuesday, a two hour 500 graduate ethics seminar and another two hours in the office. The semester had slipped into its last weeks and he reminded himself, once more, to encourage his students to complete their work as soon as they could. Even so it seemed unlikely all of them would finish on time.

In spite of admonitions in the beginning to be prepared for long hours of work with meager results, and to take deadlines seriously, three times in the last six weeks he had been asked to grant an extension. Two, he was satisfied, did not have time to complete the assignment.

Working in pairs, they were required to produce a piece of original research from a list of several philosophic problems he had assigned, and to report their findings in a paper to be shared with the seminar. To the difficulty of the task Carter had added the burden of unusually early due dates, dates he fully intended to renegotiate.

The reasons for the third postponement he did not know. The girl showed up in his office the Friday before and said she had been ill and had not seen her workmate for over a week (a male student with whom she had asked to be matched, and, Carter assumed, was probably mated) and so would not be prepared for the discussion.

She was pretty by most standards, with dark, deep set haggard eyes and a soft, worn, almost beaten demeanor. Her shoulders were rounded and she seemed unable to lift her arms, even to gesture, as if she had already walked a very long way beneath the weight of filial or female fidelity.

It was more than illness, and Carter granted her what he considered a generous clemency. That was, however, the last he saw of either of them, and from it concluded they had probably gone,
no doubt separately, to other more immediate and necessary considerations.

"The focus of this seminar," Carter told the assemblage, "has shifted from philosophy to psychology. The question is now whether or not you are dedicated and professional enough to fulfill the requirements of the course. I do not expect anyone to be his brother's keeper. The character of a group, a class, still resides in the question of individual responsibility. You all have a substantial number of academic campaigns behind you. I suggest you tighten your belts and make an attempt to behave as veterans."

He asked if anyone had need of assistance, and when no one responded, adjourned the seminar. Halfway to the office he was aware that he was being followed by two students, males, who he decided had probably picked up his scent when he crossed their path. Gauging the distance from their voices, they trailed along behind the length of the hall. They've imprinted on me, Carter thought. Christ, the chicks following the chicken hawk. He did not acknowledge their presence, entered the office and dropped his books on the desk, mindful immediately of Mason's absence.

"Professor Carter," one said, "do you have a minute?"

"Do you ever knock before you charge in?"

The youth was a good bit shorter than Carter, with rat-colored hair pushed to the side, and a sallow and badly scarred and pimpled complexion.

When he wasn't speaking the boy's lips did not close and his teeth were exposed so he seemed always to be grinning. As if it were a welcome to which he need not respond, he ignored Carter's question, and squinting intently through his small glasses, circled to the far side of the desk.

"This is the third time this semester that we haven't had class," the boy said.

Carter looked at him, then to the other.

"That's a statement worthy of graduate intelligence. So you can count to three."

"Well, we don't think it's fair or honest not to have class. You're being paid to teach and you're not."

Carter ran through a list of responses, then reconsidered.

"So you're an authority on teaching, are you? But more to the point, an authority on my teaching. And I suppose, that within your infinite wisdom and the sure knowledge of how and why things operate, you also know why we've had three postponements this semester?"

"No sir, but that's not important."

"Not important? Because you don't think it is?"

"No sir. It's not my job to know that. But we want you to hold class."

"With what? Partially completed research? Half-baked unexamined or prepared ideas?" Carter leaned toward the boy who did not back up. "I'll bet you'd like that. It would probably coincide with everything else you do."

The other boy had taken up a position beside his friend. "We paid money to learn and we're not learning," he said.

A flush of anger pushed into Carter's chest.

"We were talking about teaching. Now you've change it to learning. Has it ever occurred to you that just possibly one has nothing to do with the other?" he said. "From what I've seen and heard here, it is my considered opinion, that whether we have class or not, you would learn very little. Has either of you ever taken a seminar before?"

"Yes, sir. Two."

"Where? In day care?"

"No, sir."

"Well, in seminars the participants learn from doing research and by sharing in the research others do. If anyone has failed, it's your fellow classmates, and you, for not having either the sense or the common decency to think through your disjointed impulses before you act on them."

While he spoke Carter tried to remember their names. Underclassmen, no doubt, allowed in over their heads. Another of Crowly's consumer policies to put more bodies in the classroom. So the uncomprehending and the dumb shall enter with the rest.

When the boy mentioned missing class, Carter had opened his grade book and while they talked had gone down the list of names and dates.

Surprisingly, there were few absences, but two, for two students, Coates and Wilson, coincided not only with one another, but were marked for classes the previous two days the seminar had met by schedule in the library.

At the request of several students Carter had taken the seminar to a library conference room to help those in the seminar who were not yet comfortably familiar with the library's computer research anomalies.

"Are you graduate students?"

"No, sir."

"Then what?"

"I'm a senior."

"And you?'

"A senior."

"In a graduate seminar?"

"Yes, sir."

"Honors, then?"

"No, sir."

"Then how in the holy name of hell did you get in?"

"We applied for it."

"Meaning what."

"There was this sign in the Student Union that said we could get graduate credit while we were still undergraduates. And we signed up."

"I suppose you two have your research and your paper completed."

"Not yet," the second of the two said. "It isn't due until next week."

"You're working together?"

"Yes."

"Correct me if I wrong," he said, "but I believe it's Mr. Wilson and Mr. Coates."

"Yes, sir."

"Well, Messieurs Wilson and Coates, do either of you ever talk to other persons in the seminar?"

Coates shook his head.

"Why should we?"

"Well, I don't know," Carter said. "Maybe you could find out what's going on when you're not there. You know, contrary to your immediate impressions, when you're absent, the world does go on. The days you're complaining about not having class, we were in the library. And had you been present at the previous class, or had the good sense to check with me or others in the seminar, you wouldn't be here now with your whining. This is not a grade school.

"Now, my schedule shows you're due to make a presentation Thursday of final week, or nine days from today. But suppose just to facilitate learning, not wanting to burden the seminar any more than we have to with rampant unlearning, suppose you two have your paper ready this Thursday, so we can have class."

They both backed away, and Carter was reminded of an old vaudevillian dance team doing a two-step shuffle.

"But that's not fair," the one with rodent teeth protested. "That's not the schedule you gave us."

"The schedule has just changed," Carter said, "at your request. Oh, yes, and another thing. Either you are prepared this Thursday or you can both drop the class."

They did not move, now, but stood staring at him. Carter waited a full thirty seconds before speaking, and then to be done with the matter entirely.

"Gentlemen, you have a two hour presentation due in exactly two days. Now, I suggest you get busy with your work and not waste any more of my time or yours."

Coates, Carter remembered, was the one with the glasses and teeth. Now he squirmed and shifted toward the door.

"Why would you want to do that?" he said. "I mean, we shouldn't be punished because other people don't do their work."

"I didn't think this was punishment," Carter said. "You won't be punished because others don't do their work, but rewarded for doing your work. You said you want to learn. Since you two are Barker State's resident authorities on learning and classroom procedure, you should be grateful for the opportunity. But do remember, if you get an F, it will be because you didn't do your work."

Wilson looked at Carter, shaking his head. .

"You did that because we complained about class."

"I try to help my students whenever I can," Carter said. He nodded to the door and ushered them out, not without reluctance on their part, then fell into the chair, propped his elbows on the desk and cradled his head in his hands.

Jesus, he thought, no wonder I drink. Stumbling around on the edge of chaos, lost in the jungle of the irrational. Where do they come from? Who are they. We want you to learn us better.

A general student attitude about education. "All you have to do is watch, complain and occasionally change the program."

Television. The university reduced to the sensibilities of the tube. Entertainers, entertaining by giving awards to entertainers. Students demanding A's because they paid their admission.

Junk bond education.

If there were rules for integrity in education even remotely reflective of what the SEC tries to enforce, the Barker board of trustees, administration and half the faculty would have been under indictment for fraud.

Ads in the student Union for quick graduate credit. The rubber stamp of success. He reached for the phone, then reconsidered.

Initially he supposed there had been a mistake. How did it happen? Crowly. Now he was not so sure. Crowly did it. Those two are not even in Honors and they're allowed to enroll in a 500 seminar.

Again he went over the realization, the bare-bones of the skeleton pushing up through the dust. How many others were there? How many of these cretins in other graduate seminars? The unschooled and untrained dumped off where they should not be. He had never before had the need to examine or inquire of his students about their class status. Wasn't that a matter for admissions? For the department and admissions? And what about department chairman Norman? What was his place in this?

"Crowly," he said to himself. "Crowly and Norman, beefing up enrollment to make themselves look good. They've changed the rules again."

And, again, this thing with Mason.

The previous evening he had stopped at Mason's on the way home. He had searched for the exact words, the wording.

"New rules. Mason," he had said, "we're playing by new rules. This isn't the university we knew ten, or for that matter, three years ago. We can't live on those assumptions. And we can't depend on anyone to use rational academic sense as a guideline for decisions."

Mason was standing at the fireplace, dressed in a tan sport-coat and a dark vest-sweater. Ardyth hung out discreetly in the kitchen at the end of the hall, waiting busily, sensing that Carter's visit was portentous.

"This is just rumor," Carter had said in an attempt at something more than truth. "But from the looks of things it's a relatively healthy rumor and Morgana and I thought you should hear it from us as soon as possible."

Mason's face hardened, and Carter knew he already understood what was coming.

"Of course there's nothing final in what they are doing. Daly's been in contact with the AAUP national office. They don't think it will stick."

"How many are there?'

"Four. You were right about that."

Mason's hands were shaking, Carter assumed from anger. His face was very white. When he tried to speak his voice cracked.

"Who?" Mason croaked, then swallowed.

"Winslow, Fisk, Baker and you."

"Why me?'

"No reason at all. Unreason," Carter said. "Whim, and the heavy weight of unreason."

Mason tried to smile then sat on the couch near the fireplace. It was not anger, Carter decided, that had him, but the fear and depression he had seen that morning in the cafeteria.

"There'll have to be a hearing," Carter said. "Regardless of their pretenses, there'll have to be a hearing."

The clock on the mantle showed eight-forty-five. There was a strong temptation to continue, to go on talking to burn off energy, anxiety, when there was actually nothing more to say. There was to Carter's mind nothing more he could say. He sat back, allowing a disappointing silence to drift over the room.

Conjecture, assumption, surmise, what have you, nothing could fathom the Crowlys, hell-bent on power and a fast buck. They were aliens to Carter, and to people like Mason. Sad though dangerous mental dwarfs from a foreign landscape who would willingly, gleefully, maim and destroy for money. Hired assassins.

Mason had taken it harder than Carter imagined he would. People could find relief, catharsis, a transformation, or emotional shift when fears became reality. Then there would be a new flash of hope. During the Nazi occupation of Paris residents were heard to say "Thank God they're here, now we can live in hope instead of fear." Still, in Carter's lexicon, a rationalized consolation.

But not so with Mason. Already he was locked in a deep depression, had been since Carter arrived, and sat at the far end of the couch staring at the floor as if it had lodged in his mind and was now confined, imprisoned by the perimeters of what he had just heard. Carter sensed that Mason had expected the news, had in a way almost counted on it.

For short time they sat with the chill, beneath the welcome blanket of silence. When Carter looked up next, Ardyth had appeared apparition-like at Mason's side. She sat next to Mason and put her arm around his shoulder. He tilted slightly toward her into a frail pieta.

"Is it true, John Carter," Ardyth said, "Mason will be without employment?"

Carter nodded.

"That's what it looks like now. The best information we have says there will be four of the philosophy department terminated. But that is not final, by any means."

"And Mason Oldam is one of them."

Ardyth spoke very precisely, articulating each word.

"Yes," Carter said. "That's what we think."

"I see."

She nodded sternly and the firelight reflected in her glasses, a glare of small flames that obscured her eyes.

"Is there anything to be done about it?"

"I don't think so," Carter said. "A year ago or so, I would have given you a different answer. But then things were different. Today, I don't know."

"And who is responsible for this?"

Carter shrugged.

"Crowly, I suppose, but he's probably just following orders. There's no way to know for sure. Maybe Crowly wants to save money to make himself look good. But it's coming down from the top."

"Yes. I have heard about that horrible man."

Carter neglected to tell them that a hearing would insure next to nothing. Smart lawyers could make dumb arguments sound plausible, even admirable.

The source of Mason's situation and unqualified students enrolled in graduate seminars, the academic slide of the university were intimately linked in Carter's mind.

It had to do with Remcheck and Crowly.

Now Crowly was at it again. He had circumvented or ignored departmental admissions requirements.

Carter picked up the phone and dialed Carl Johnson's extension. Johnson had served on the admissions committee. Possibly he had heard about the change.

"We are aware that unqualified students have slipped through," Johnson said. "No doubt Crowly taking advantage of the loopholes. It is most clearly a case of avarice and unremitting administrative decay. Nothing rots the mind as quickly as working in administration."

Johnson sounded as if he was reading from a prepared text, as if he had had the conversation before.

"Of course," he continued, "to choose administration as a livelihood, one must already be well down the way to dementia. We will pose the question at our next meeting and deal with it."

But in truth nothing would be done.

Carter consulted Mason's schedule and found he had been due an hour before. Maybe he wouldn't come in at all. Carter dialed the department secretary and asked if Mason had called in sick.

"Isn't he here?" she asked.

"He may be," Carter said. "I just got in."

When he called Ardyth answered the phone. Carter detected a bit of strain in her voice, then decided he was being overly sensitive. After a polite greeting he asked to speak with Mason.

"He's not here, John," Ardyth said. "He left for school several hours ago. You will find him there."

"Yes. I'll do that," Carter said, and decided not to mention that Mason had not yet arrived.

"By the way, how did it go last night, after I left?"

She was silent for ten seconds or so, Carter calculated, no doubt trying to judge just how much she should tell and how she wanted to tell it.

"Not well," she said finally. "Mason did not sleep."

"Did you talk to him?"

"No," she said. "I tried. But you know how he is at times like this."

Carter knew.

On two occasions he had seen Mason shaken, then broken sufficiently to require hospitalization. The process, the procession of events leading to the breakdown had been almost imperceptible and Carter had caught onto it quite late, and then only because of several offbeat, uncharacteristic shifts in Mason's behavior.

Mason had folded up the first time during exam week of the spring semester of his sixth year at Barker. For several weeks Carter noted his proclivity for prolonged silence, even when others were around. He would break off, sometimes in mid-sentence and simply vanish into himself, disappear, most likely to avoid what went on around him. This Carter did not fault. He's burned out, he thought, burned out like the rest of us and just trying to make a stand to the end.

When he was alone in the office Mason developed the habit of locking the door from the inside. He would not answer the phone and seemed truly frightened by what its ringing would require—who the caller might be. He crossed streets oblivious of streetlights and traffic, and puzzled painfully at times trying to recognize people he knew well.

The Monday morning that final week Carter found him sitting on the floor of the office. The thin pages of a philosophy text which had been ripped from the book and wadded up were scattered about the floor, a batch of small, dirty, irregular snowballs.

He had apparently spent the night in the office, although no one knew that for certain, and Mason, even when he was once again on track, could not remember anything about the episode or how long he had been there.

When Carter spoke to him, he would not or could not speak, and it was then Carter realized a malady more than malaise had him by the throat.

Unable to elicit anything of a response Carter called Ardyth and together they took him to the university hospital.

The second break had been less severe, although just as debilitating. That time Ardyth had seen it coming, the withdrawal and unresponsiveness, the failure to keep appointments and to meet classes. She called Carter and asked him to encourage Mason to admit himself to the hospital before his condition worsened. After several conversations, Mason did just that.

That was two years ago. Since then Mason had pretty well held his own, although Carter had never gotten a handle on what it was exactly that troubled him and why he had come apart.

"Psychic wear and tear," his psychiatrist, Dr. Goldenstein told Carter. "It's the attrition of daily life, of living the way we do that does in certain kinds of personalities. We used to think that trauma related incidents cause psychotic breaks. And that does happen. But more often we see people who have difficulty just shouldering the normal, everyday strains of modern life. They get under more than they can carry and finally need a break. So they shut off emotionally and crawl inside themselves."

It was a neat little account which explained absolutely nothing. I could have read that in a newspaper, Carter told himself. People break down because people break down. People aren't cloth. Wear and tear my ass. Those clowns get paid two hundred thousand a year for telling you that people break down.

Now it appeared Mason was again missing in action and Carter tried to think of where, if he was AWOL, where he might go. Jesus, if he had anything of decent male vices and habits like chasing females or drinking he'd be easy to track. But Mason did not drink, and to Carter's knowledge had never strayed in the direction of another female, anywhere beyond Ardyth's gaze.

He would try the hospital. Maybe Goldenstein had seen him. Possibly Mason sensed his imminent slippage again into the dolor of psychic defeat and had made a run for it.

Carter poked through the university directory for Goldenstein's name, then dialed the number. A secretary answered and said the doctor would not be in until three and that she had not seen Mason.

"Have you tried the hospital? He could have gone there without notifying Dr. Goldenstein. I can give you the number."

Carter took the number and thanked her, then called admissions at the hospital.

"Could you tell me if you have admitted Mason Oldam today?"

The girl left the phone for several minutes then told him that "During the last forty-eight hours no one named Mason Oldam has been admitted."

"I was only curious about today," Carter said.

"No. Not today. We don't show anyone by that name."

"He would have been Dr. Goldenstein's patient."

"Even so," the girl said, "he would have had to come through here. It's hospital policy. All patients are admitted here."

Carter thanked her, replaced the phone and checked Mason's schedule again. Had he gone to class without stopping at the office? Occasionally he did that.

Carter took his coat and headed out of Temperly across the quad to Palmer Hall. He kept the room number in mind, 12B. He had not been scheduled in Palmer for several years and wondered now if the renovations of the previous summer had changed anything.

He checked his watch. Mason was down for a twelve o'clock class and it was twelve-thirty. Tuesday noon classes ran until one-twenty.

Carter pulled up his coat-collar and hurried along the Quad, still holding on to the outside hope that Mason had made it into 12B, prepared to carry on and see the day through.

The noon air was raw and clear, the sky a faded blue. Christmas wreaths hung from the ornate lamps along the quad. In spite of the urgency of his search, Carter couldn't help but feel the levity of the season.

He walked quickly across the quad and reached Palmer breathing heavily. He paused inside the door, chiding himself. A goddam loon, running around loose. Too much bourbon and too many cigarettes. His head was light coming into the warm building. He imagined12B would be in the basement and he slid down onto the top step to catch his breath.

A perfect candidate for a heart attack, he thought. He could see the headlines in *The Bulldog Bark*, "Philosophy Professor John Carter Found Dead on the Steps of Palmer Hall."

Found dead. Deceased, expired, having given up the last breath racing to class. Racing time.

The ignominy of it, dying an obscure, worthless death in a plagued department of a mediocre school in the middle of nowhere. Even Shakespeare would have trouble writing that epithet.

And so? Now what?

A contingent of three students passed him on the stairs, and one, a girl, stopped to see if he was okay.

"Are you sick?" she said.

Carter breathed deeply and tried to smile.

"And if I am my dear, may my health be served by one as lovely as you."

They laughed.

The girl blushed.

"I didn't expect that," she said.

She stood for a moment smiling at him, pleased with the compliment.

"I thank you, again, for your consideration."

She held her books tightly to her chest, her eyes fixed on him. Her round face was cherubic and pink.

"If she'd do that for a stranger," one of her male companions said, "think of what she'd do for a friend."

"Or for money," the other added.

The girl ignored the remarks.

"You are okay?" she said to Carter, looking at him intently.

"Yes," Carter said, annoyed with the remarks. "And it is kind of you."

"She enjoys old men," the first remarked.

"Anything over thirty."

"Anything under eighty."

Without more she rejoined her companions and they exited by the door Carter had just entered.

Slowly Carter pulled himself up and dropped down the few steps into the labyrinthine passages of the basement. The walls were glazed black-red brick, over-fired and burned dull, crumbling in spots. The ceiling was a mass of pipes, small water pipes and large heat ducks wrapped in asbestos to transport hot air from the furnaces and boilers of the netherworld up into the world of man.

The passage was lighted by three small yellowish bulbs dangling from single cords. Carter checked a door, then another, but could not find a matching number or a sequence to the numbers. The first was 101, the second 201.

Then he reclassified the hall in terms of 01, expecting the third door would be labeled 301. It was not. It was 14C.

Carter stood staring at the lettering, staying for the moment the impulse to return to the steps and begin again.

There was absolutely no sense to it. Renovation? Christ. Who devised this? He peered off into the murky recess of the tunnel, not sure now where it would take him. He found the next door and could barely make out the faded black letters. MEN. It's probably a broom closet. He tried the handle. The door was locked.

Four doors farther on, 9C, 11D, 12C and 209 he came to the end of the hall. A rumble in the pipes complained of his presence. He stepped around the corner into an even darker passage and nearly ran into a janitor at work sweeping the concrete floor.

"You wouldn't by any chance happen to know where I can find room 12B?"

The old man leaned on his broom as if the answer would require a good bit of contemplation and might take time and conversation to find. He was old, very old, and had a massive head, with deeply wrinkled leathery skin and long unkempt, matted white hair. His eyes were bloodshot, a condition with which Carter could sympathize, and, as closely as Carter could determine in the shadows, seemed not to be focused as they normally might. A cackling laugh crawled out of his throat and he twisted to look behind him.

"You can't get there from here," he said. "At least not the way you're going."

"Then I shall try another," Carter said, half in jest. "By the way, who's the clown that numbered the doors?"

"They numbered as they come; they come numbered as they was," the old man said, taking a plug of tobacco from the pocket of his bibbed overalls. He spat on the floor, then chewed off a piece and pushed it into his cheek.

The hall had a damp, putrid musk about it Carter had not noticed at first. Maybe it was the old man. The smell seemed to be drifting down from the darkness, a mixture of sweeping compound and stale water and of someone who hadn't bathed recently. It was the smell of something definitely dead.

"I'm a philosophy professor," Carter said. "I'm looking for a friend of mine. He's in room 12B."

The old man looked about him as if the spirit of Carter's friend might be there on the air with them.

"The halls of higher learning is filled with the friends of philosophy," he said. "Philosophy, she is the golden way of life that say how we know about death."

He grinned a broken wrack of tobacco stained teeth and his off- cast eyes seemed to search about Carter.

"What philosophies you have? You know Anaxagoras? Heraclitus?"

"Yes," Carter said. "More than I need."

"It's tell you what to do and how you be kind in life?"

"Yeah," Carter said. "It tells about that—if you pay attention and listen closely."

"I see."

The old man nodded as if assenting to the truth of the proposition. He backed away from Carter and pushed his broom off down the hall toward the smells and the darkness. A few steps on he stopped and cocked his head, listening for Carter's footsteps.

"Is a long way to find your friend," he said.

Carter followed him, by several steps, then closer, along the passages, through the boiler room and into another part of the building, or into a part of another building Carter had never before seen.

"There," he said, waving a hand toward a door partially hidden behind a stack of chairs. "There 12B."

Carter thanked him.

The room was empty.

Chapter IX

Carter came out of Palmer on the street side. He had intended to return to the office, but changed his mind. It had gone too fast, too quickly. He needed time to think.

Of habit he headed for Murphy's, along the business district, the shops and fast food dives of the aptly named Money Street. Large plastic green wreathes and red electric candles hung from the lamp posts. Shop were filled with Christmas decorations. Shekel Drive.

Beyond his aversion for the shops, the hucksters that opened them and then went out of business with the regularity of a pulse beat, he stopped to survey the junk. T-shirts, jackets, sweatshirts in the blue and gold of Barker State. The most widely displayed and frequent use of the school logo, to decorate junk. Mugs and steins, knickknacks and curios.

Half of the displays were of large stuffed animals, simple creatures, baleful and gaunt, set in a country snow scene. A dwarf Santa commanding an ornate sleigh, and a leopard, a lion and an unidentifiable creature that looked like something from *Sesame Street*.

Maybe the great She Wolf of the North impersonating the bulldog Barker Bill. Here was the spirit of the university. And what was that? Tenacity? Gripping or staying power? Endurance? Or just plan canine stupidity? How about a relish for sniffing assholes?

Carter shuffled along the edge of a dark wood, indeed, on a dark afternoon, the torch burning low.

And anyway, what had happened to Mason?

And what about the girl? The thing with Vivien had not yet settled with any satisfaction in his mind. Determined to go on with it, for a while at least, he still found the connection disquieting.

He could not rid himself of her scent, the images it brought to mind. Not that he tried, but it was there, bothersome and at times acutely so. Why? He didn't know exactly. Was he getting caught in the web of his senses? In the pleasure of the liaison? Well, maybe? But what else is there to get caught in?

He checked his watch. Murphy's would be occupied by the business crowd, and he wasn't up to that. He steered south off Money to Journalli Avenue. A block farther on, he pushed passed the purple cinder-block walls and through the large burned and scarred wooden door into the upper circle of the Moon Crater Lounge.

The bar was an amphitheater of levels furnished with rock-formation tables and folding canvas stools. American flags sat stiffly on thin vertical shafts protruding from the rocks. Faceless men in spacesuits, or spacesuits without men, were painted on the walls circling the arena. Each level supported a watering service station of bars, bartenders and moon-maiden waitresses. The lower level served only beer, another wine, the third, hard alcohol, the level Carter had dubbed "the down of the dedicated drinkers."

The distinction between tiers was only occasionally observed and seldom noticeable. Waitresses and patrons migrated freely from level to level. A plastic canopy painted with the celestial phenomena of asteroids, stars, circled by star cruisers and illuminated by an enormous moon with mirrors mounted in its craters, hung high over the dance-floor.

From nine until two, four nights a week bikini-clad disco-dancers in glass dematerialization booths lining the dance-floor worked to the music. A less than weightless rock band-of-the-day played from a space-station stage suspended from the cable light-beams of the distant plastic and painted stars.

When the music played, the great yellow moon rotated slowly, counterclockwise, bathed in the soft rays of a host of purple and red spotlights. Not as reflective as its celestial counterpart shining back the light it received, this one, from the source of technology within, cast small beams onto the distant walls and the firmament above.

Carter dropped down to the second-ledge bar and picked up a beer. The afternoon crowd was sparse. A repair crew had lowered the moon and opened the side exposing the tangled wire-gutting and nerve-clusters of its dark interior. The large black boxes of speakers set around the top of the theater blasted out music unmistakably rock, but otherwise, to Carter, indistinct and unidentifiable. At the far side of the dance-floor, under the appraising eye of the Crater's manager, four young, well equipped females in halters and shorts worked with the music. Condemned, alone forever, to dance in their cases, Carter mused, their glass coffins.

Even before he settled into a seat, a man at the bar, a former student whose face Carter recognized, came over and without invitation set his beer down and staked out a claim to a chunk of Carter's rock.

"How are you today, Doc?" he said, smiling a bit triumphantly, Carter thought, prepared for the assault of the success story of the month.

What would it be this time? I took your modern philosophy class five years ago, Professor, and it helped me so much. I just sold a million dollars of Chewy Goo dog food. Now my wife is pregnant and all it's because of you.

"Do you remember me?"

"If you've done something worth remembering, I probably do," Carter said.

"Well, no, not really. But teachers remember their students."

"Yes," Carter said. "The better ones, we remember, sometimes."

"I was in your ethics class three years ago."

"I recognized your face." Carter said. "What's your name?"

"Mark Whitfield."

For the sake of conversation Carter was about to ask the obvious of what, where and why now of Whitfield's present, when Whitfield stood and stared across the amphitheater, then waved and beckoned. Whoever it was, Carter could not see clearly.

"Minus Factor," Whitfield said. "What unbelievable luck seeing him here."

"Where?" Carter said.

"Over there, Doc," Whitfield said. "Jeees, he plays for the Pats."

"Yes," Carter said, "I've heard that."

Factor's was a name and face Carter could easily remember. For the duration of four months, three days a week for four months his senior year during the spring semester, Factor had occupied one of Carter's classes.

He was enormous. Six-nine, two hundred ninety pounds, and as sports writers frequently noted, constructed of muscle, fiber and bone, and little else. He was also black, so black that in the sunlight his skin had the blue-glint of a well-blued gun barrel, a feature that had crawled unbidden into Carter's unconscious, and kicked around the best of his humanitarian impulses. Factor's appearance, and his attitudes and behavior, were inherently disturbing for Carter and he had never been able to set it right.

Physically, from the first day to the last, Factor inhabited the back of the room, sat in the center chair of the last row, with his back to the wall, surrounded by no one, nothing, as if the wall was the end of the universe and beyond him there was nothing, and nothing that could safely or comfortably approach him. He sat there with the regal elegance of an African chief, enormous, very black and totally composed, of a self-assuredness Carter found both unnerving and distressing. And as luck would have it, he did it three days a week, fifty minutes a day. To Carter's dismay he did not miss one minute of one class the entire semester.

Factor's physical appearance and presence served to further aggravate the irritations his attitudes and homespun naturalistic answers and queries caused Carter. For no matter, the system, the philosopher under scrutiny, (this was a survey course for seniors) in response to Carter's questions Factor seemed always to slice precisely and quickly to the core of the proposition. He did so with an animal energy and glee that startled, then disturbed Carter when he found that simply to set the record, the discussion even, required of him the same invariant zeal.

To Carter's question to the class of how they proposed to deal with their own deaths, Factor answered that in his estimation, Carter and others, were making too much of it. Their desire to be god-like, a white man's affliction, was really at the bottom of it.

Carter had reminded him that there was little proof to support the proposition that thinking was a matter of race. Although at times attitudes could be cast in black and white terms, not thinking about something had never been as advantageous to man as thinking about it had.

"Mr. Factor, if man had not inquired of the conditions and phenomena which confront him, if he had, as you suggest, accepted it without examination, we should still be in the dark ages. We should still be calling spirits down out of the trees to heal our sick and give up our dead without the slightest inquiry into the disease or forces that made them dead."

For his part, Factor said, he saw no reason whatsoever to think about it. Death was there, it would surely happen, and that was as it should be. Further, individual, personal death, he advised, was just a physical fact, a fact that marked the end of life and with which we could not deal until it occurred, and with which we would be incapable of dealing once it had occurred.

With annoyance, as well as duty, Carter skipped the equivocation and tried to bring the class into the discussion. Drumming up a detailed consideration of death was difficult at any time, and the black-sun of Factor's smile shining arrogantly from the back row did not make the task easier.

"Mr. Factor, if we take your advice and not examine and catalogue, order and arrange our findings, how would you set out then to communicate with other human beings, to explain, say, what a cow looks like if you have never seen a cow? Say, to a blind man?" Carter had asked. "Would you say it had four legs like an elephant? Or a long nose like an anteater?"

“I would say," Factor had responded, "that for blind people a cow is only worth the milk, meat or transportation or work they get from it. And what it look like don't mean no more than what it sound or smell like."

Now, he came round the circle moving with the grace and flow of a huge black cat. The beer glass he carried was smothered in the expanse of his large left hand. He extended his right to Carter.

"Doctor J.C," he said, offering Carter a huge hand to shake. "Surprised to see you here. Didn't know professors come to places like this."

"You'd be surprised where you'll find us," Carter said.

"I might at that," Factor said. "Mind if I join you?"

Whitfield circled to the far side of Factor like a small white-dwarf satellite.

"Jeees," he said, "thought you were playing for the Patriots."

"That's right," Factor said.

"Well, what you doing here? I mean, don't you have practice and films to watch?"

"My old man died," Factor said. "Goin home for the funeral. Jus stop to visit."

"I saw that in the paper," Carter said. "I'm sorry."

"J.C., how you been?" Factor said, pulling two of the small canvas stools together for a seat.

"As well as can be expected," Carter said.

The Sunday before Carter had watched Factor and the Pats play the Jets. With Factor playing one of his better games, spending most of his afternoon in the New York backfield, the Pats came away with a 31-28 win.

When Factor sat down Carter realized again just how big he was. Factor's head was larger than any head Carter had seen. Not only was it large, but the shape of an egg. He had shaved his head so it resembled a large black egg. A long gold earring hung to his shoulder from an ear nearly as big as Carter's hand. A clutter of fine gold chains were wound about the stump of his massive neck and his sleeveless shirt was unbuttoned halfway down exposing the expanse of his megatherian torso. His eyes were as black as his skin, with no pupils, so that even when he looked directly at something he appeared not to be focused on a point, but gazing into the distances, regarding a multitude of areas and objects.

It's been a bad day for eyes, Carter thought, flashing back through the tangled events of the lost hours.

Carter had had athletes in class before. Most he observed were not very bright—about the run of the mill of the population. And that was as it should be, since most had done little on their own beyond collecting the benefits bestowed by the gifts of exceptional physical talent. But not infrequently people collect on natural talents. In the performing arts as in sports, training could hardly substitute for what nature left out.

The problem, Carter had observed, came when the beneficiaries of natural physical gifts were compensated materially beyond good sense for their gifts and came to view the compensation as a symbol of their moral worth, instead of for what it really was.

Carter had seen that kind of physical ability and its attendant moral assumptions often enough. But he had not come across the combination of physical prowess and mental agility and acumen that he found in Factor. This, Carter imagined, was the best of what humans could be given.

To have a mind every bit as quick and strong and agile as the body was a gift few humans could claim. When he imagined a son he might have, this is what Carter imagined, what every prospective parent had in mind.

In the last weeks of Factor's senior year, even while he was listed to go number one in the NFL draft, he had showed up at Carter's office one afternoon with an edition of Achebe's *Things Fall Apart* in hand.

"I was thinking bout this," he said, holding out the dog-eared paperback.

"It's an excellent piece of work," Carter had said.

"I need to talk about it," Factor said.

"Then you've come to the right place."

Factor sat at the end of Carter's desk and listened as Carter talked about Achebe, about Africa and what Achebe was trying to cut through in European attitudes about Africa. He watched Carter closely, stopping him occasionally to question or to clarify what he had heard. Carter, trying to give the ideas a frame of reference for him, was touched by Factor's intense interest, the perspicacity of his questions.

In the afternoon's proceedings Factor grew increasingly reticent and calm and fell finally to silence. When Carter paused, after a prolonged interlude, Factor stood abruptly and held out his massive hand.

"Thank you, Doctor J.C.," he said. "I'll think about what you say. Could we do this again?"

"That would be a good idea," Carter had said.

Twice a week Factor showed up in Carter's office after class, once during final week, to talk about what he was reading.

Carter prepared a list of several hundred books for him, rekindling his own interest in African philosophy.

"What will you do when you're through with football?" he asked Factor the last times they were together.

Factor looked at him out of the black-sun glare of his eyes as if he were deep within himself, deeper than Carter could then see.

"Maybe I be a doctor like J.C." he said, Carter considered, not altogether in jest.

"You have the mind for it," Carter said.

"But I ain't done that good in school."

"You have in my class. Take my word for it, if you really want to, you can. Play football until you're done with it. There'll still be time for other things—if you want them."

"You tellen me I could do what you do?."

"Yes. You could. You're already a good student. You simply have to apply it in the right ways."

"Why you think nobody never told me that before? My old man always said I was no good. Good for nothing he say."

"Whatever his reasons," Carter said, "it isn't true."

Carter did not see Factor again that summer.

He had gone first in the draft to New England. And with a vicarious fatherly pride Carter tracked him through the sport pages and TV reports.

The following summer he read that Factor's mother had died in Chicago. Carter was between spring and summer school, so he extricated the Bonneville from the garage, put it on the highway and lumbered north, up 55 to Chicago, the Southside and the True Light Baptist church.

It was a hot, soot-peppered Chicago day. Because of the large crowd at the church Carter had to park several blocks away. He walked the sidewalk among the trash, uncomfortably, feeling that even on a city sidewalk he was trespassing, the only white face in sight, aware again of what it was to be black in a dominant white society.

He did not see Maurice immediately, but checked the address again, to be sure, then slipped into the church and found a seat near the aisle in the last pew.

The service lasted a little less than an hour, with testimonials and amens, the small church filled with hymns from a robed and swaying choir.

Before the ceremony ended Carter exited and waited outside. During the service he had spotted Factor near the front and assumed he would be one of the last out.

Moments later the funeral director, a small neatly dressed man in white shirt and bowtie pushed back the church doors then opened the hearse. When he saw Carter he stood staring as if Carter was something he would rather not have seen.

The coffin appeared carried by six men. While not as tall as Factor, they were every bit as large. Several were without coats. Their enormous arms and thick necks and huge chests bulging in white short sleeved shirts in the bright sunlight.

Linebackers, Carter thought. Certainly linemen. And names came immediately to mind. Big Daddy Lipscomb. Too Tall Jones. Mean Joe Green. Lawrence Taylor.

As Factor exited the church Carter caught his arm.

"Just stopped by to pay my respects," Carter said.

Factor looked down at him, surprised, quizzically, amused and pleased with Carter's presence.

"Doctor J.C., what you doin here? You ain't come all the way here just for the service?"

"Yeah," Carter said. "Just wanted to stop in to pay my respects and say I'm sorry about your mother."

Factor did not say anything more. By then two women, probably Factor's sisters, joined them.

"Mothers are special people," Carter said.

"Amen to that," one of the women said.

"Come on Moe," the other said tugging at Factor's arm. "We gotta go. We gonna be late to the cemetery."

Factor took Carter's hand, shook it, but did not say anything.

"You go on," Carter said. "Next time you're in Lancaster stop in and say hello. I'll be thinking about you."

Driving home he was not sure going to the funeral had been a good idea. He had intruded on a private ceremony, a very private and almost secret rite. But he had done it, and that was that. He had done what he thought was fitting, and you have to do that once in a while.

Now Factor's father had died. At least the old man had seen his son succeed in the early stages of an NFL career. There had to be a modicum of good in that.

"It's tough losing those you care about," Carter said. "I was sorry I didn't get to see your father at your mother's funeral."

"That ain't your fault," Factor said. "He wasn't there. He laid up drunk somewhere. Nobody could help that."

"It's still tough," Carter said.

"Just as good this way," Factor said. "All that man did was drink and hate people."

"I saw you against the Jets last week," Whitfield said. "That was some catch you made in the fourth quarter. Some catch."

Factor looked at him as if he was not sure what the statement meant.

"Luck," he said. "I'm a linebacker. I get paid to catch people not balls. Luck."

"That was your fourth interception of the year," Whitfield said. "You're leading the league for linebackers in interceptions."

"Yeah," Factor said. "Now ain't that somethin."

But he was interested in Carter.

"Surprised to see you here."

"I could say the same thing," Carter said, although it wouldn't be too hard to find you in a crowd."

"What you say? I thought all us people looked alike," Factor said, and smiled, that wide, arrogant smile.

"That's true," Carter said, "they do. They have two eyes, two ears, a nose and a mouth."

Factor leaned back and roared with delight, as if he were a small child and someone had tickled him.

"They gots big feets and kinky hair," he said.

"Sounds like my Irish grandmother," Carter said. "Did you have an Irish grandmother?"

Factor held up a large hand with the fingers extended. "Five Irish grandmothers. And four African grandfathers."

Whitfield had settled on the opposite side of the rock from Carter and Factor and sat staring at them, his face screwed up in bewilderment.

"What's it like playing for a pro football team?" he said. "I mean, in front of all those people?"

When Factor held up his hand, his arm and his hand, it was the longest arm Carter had ever seen on a human being. And not only was it long, but the muscles, the stretch of fibers from wrist to shoulder were bundled in an extraordinary braid of layers bound tightly by a network of prominent, handsome veins. The arm uncoiled like a cobra charmed into standing, its head of a hand spread and weaving on the air.

Factor ignored Whitfield's question and pulled a ten dollar bill from the vest pocket of his shirt.

"Here," he said to Whitfield. "Why don't you see if you can get more beer?"

Obediently Whitfield took the money and made off in the direction of the bar.

"Still teachin philosophy?" Factor asked Carter.

"Still teaching philosophy."

Factor nodded.

"That must be some nice job. Nobody to bother you, pressing always behind trying to take away your job."

"I wish that were true," Carter said.

"What you say?" Factor drew back, upright. "Now. They don't do that. You mean they want to bring in other teachers and get rid of you? What they say? You ain't good enough?"

"Something like that," Carter said. "It's a long story. A long political story."

"Then why you stay? I mean, go another place. I ain't never seen a man like you in school. I tell everybody and they say the same thing. They say, why Doc J.C., he's one damn good teacher. Why you stay? What keep you here? It say you should stay?"

"Jobs are hard to find for fifty-five-year-old philosophy teachers," Carter said.

"Then you try this other thing. Why not try another thing? I mean, there a coach at New England. He never coach before in his life. He is fifty years old and decides he gonna quit selling real estate and become a coach. That eight years ago. And damn if he don't. He's one good coach."

"Just like that, they hired him?"

"I don't know where he got a job. But he only what say, now, fifty-eight or nine."

Whitfield reappeared with a pitcher of beer and laid the change on the rock in front of Factor.

"You never did tell me what it feels like playing in front of all those people," Whitfield said.

"Like walking down the street with no clothes on," Factor said. "Everybody see your shortcomings."

Now it was Carter who laughed, a response that pleased Factor into feigned irritation with Whitfield.

"What your name, white boy?" Factor said.

"Whitfield, Mark Whitfield. We were brothers at Phi Lambda Chi. We were in the same house."

Factor leaned back and cocked his head.

"The same house you say? That so? But you ain't never look like a brother," he said disparagingly and coiled the tentacle of his great right arm around Carter encompassing him.

"J.C. here, a brother. Irish-African brother, he got four grandmothers and five grandfathers."

Carter poured another beer. The soft atmosphere of the afternoon had taken hold and he wondered when he again ventured out what he would tell Ardyth? Guess what, lady, your old man just flipped out again? If that was so. Maybe she already knew? Maybe it wasn't true.

The crew closed up the moon, raised it again to the firmament, waiting to see if it needed further attention. The music shifted to a series of slow semi-ballads, still nothing Carter recognized, and he leaned back, pleased with Factor's praise.

The idea, the intrigue of finding a new academic home, a different school, lifted Carter. In earlier years he anticipated changes, and had need or circumstances required, would have jumped at it.

Of late, however, the waters had quieted, the tide stilled and those at port had shown little willingness to cut loose in favor of even the shortest voyage.

The moon rotated slowly, lights and mirrors shining. A large Santa with a sleigh full of toys and reindeers circled the moon. Carter was drawn back to the vision of himself as a traveler in an ancient and future arena.

"There are good things about teaching," Carter told Factor. "Even here at Barker. I suppose I've chosen to be here."

The suggestion that he might bear the guilt of opportunity missed annoyed Carter.

"You know that list you give me? All them books? Well, I read em. Ever last one.

"You know, you help a lot of folk around here," Factor said.

"And how many did I miss?" Carter shook his head. He laughed and held up his beer glass. "Their rolls are legion."

Factor looked away from Carter, then stood.

"You gonna be around here?" he said to Carter.

"Why not?" Carter said. "It's as good as any other place."

Factor nodded approval. "Good. I be back."

Carter sipped on his beer, feeling the warm soothing fingers of the alcohol. Again he remembered Mason, but the anesthetic of the beer made it seem less urgent. He had been too concerned. Overreacted to Mason's absence.

Whitfield tailed away after Factor to the far side of the crater and Carter could barely make them out. Then he did not see Whitfield at all. Maybe he reached escape velocity. Maybe he fell off the moon. Maybe just this once, for Whitfield, gravity had failed.

Two cigarettes later, Factor reappeared at Carter's rock, accompanied by two young women. Both were dressed in brightly colored loose blouses, full pants-skirts tied up to show the inside of a leg, and spike heels. One was small and petite, the other taller, full-bodied.

"These ladies want join us," Factor said. "They say we must be prosperous type men."

When they were seated, he introduced the women. Tracy and Shirlene.

"Are you students at Barker?" Carter asked.

The women giggled. Shirlene, the taller of the two, pointed at Factor.

"Minus, what you tell that man?"

Factor leaned closer to Carter.

"That one there need somebody take care of her. She think you can do that."

His voice had a chiding, slightly patronizing flavor. He lifted his glass to the women.

"Here to Professor Carter who still be teachin when this old man have his legs wore down from chasin people who try not to get caught. You be here forever."

"That's a fair sentence," Carter said, filling his glass.

An hour and two pitchers of beer later, Factor guided them out of the Moon Crater. It was snowing again.

With the women already in the car, Factor put his hand on Carter's shoulder.

"J.C., you need help out these ladies have a party?"

"No, no," Carter said, pleased with the suggestion. "You go on. You can take care of things. You don't need me.

"I'll see you on Sunday. Where will you be?"

"Pittsburgh," Factor said. "Saturday. You gonna watch?"

"I try to," Carter said. "I've seen three of your games so far this year."

Factor smiled.

"I send you tickets for the Superbowl. One for you and your woman."

"Yeah? You do that?

"Next time you get in town give me a call," Carter said. "We'll have a beer."

"Yeah," Factor said, "I do that."

Chapter X

"Carter?" Katherine Marie called from the top of the stairs. Carter closed the door and stood for a moment absorbing the warm air. "Carter," she said, "pick up the phone. It's for you."

Carter unbuttoned his coat, slipped it off and hooked it on the hall-tree. A pile of mail covered the small table with the phone. The Seth Thomas above the table set against the green striped and flocked wall-paper showed seven-forty-two.

"It's Ardyth Oldam," Katherine said impatiently, as if Carter should have known. "This is the fourth time she's phoned."

Carter took the instrument gingerly, reluctantly, now expecting, guessing Mason had, indeed, gone astray. He waited for Katherine to replace the upstairs receiver, although he wasn't sure what difference it made if Katherine Marie knew of Mason's problems, what she should have or could have known.

Ardyth sounded composed, almost cheerful, and for a moment, Carter hoped he had been mistaken about Mason.

"I know where Mason is," she said, and Carter wondered if she meant, "Mason is safe and well."

"Is he okay?" Carter said.

"Yes," Ardyth said. "But he is not well."

"Where is he?"

"That is why I called, John Carter."

"Why?"

"I will need you to go with me to get Mason."

Carter's mind was blank. Why did she need him to go along to get Mason? He flipped back to the Monday morning, the eerie, spooked morning he found Mason sitting on the floor of the office, among the crumpled pages of Locke's *An Essay Concerning Human Understanding.* Or was it Hume's *Treatise*? Carter couldn't remember.

"I will meet you in five minutes," Ardyth said, "if you will help me."

"Yes," Carter said. "I'll be ready."

He hung up the phone and stood staring at himself in the hall mirror.

"What was that about?" Katherine Marie said.

"I don't know," Carter said.

"Well, it must be important. The woman called four times. The phone's been ringing all evening."

Katherine Marie was wrapped in a housecoat and had come halfway down the stairs. She stood with her hands on the rail, towering over Carter, looking down on him with what he imagined as less than compassion. Hanging over him, he would have said, hanging over him with foreboding.

Another of her stances. He wondered who she was now. In twenty years he had not yet come to appreciate the art and grace of her multiple and varied poses.

"I'm sorry she disturbed your evening," he said.

"Mason Oldam's had another breakdown?" she guessed, and Carter nodded, pulling on his coat, going to the door.

"Something like that."

"Will you be back soon?"

She had not broken her pose, but her voice carried the intimation that she was about to be abandoned and that it was his fault.

"Yes," he said. "I have abandoned you for a sick friend."

"That's not what I asked."

"If Mason's dead, I'll be back soon. If he's only maimed, it will take a little longer. If he's lost only part of his marbles, etc., etc. How do I know?"

Outside Carter stationed himself behind the corner pillar of the concrete rail and porch support. The evening had darkened into a fine mist of wintry rain that hung about the street lamps. The wet streets glistened with a thin coat of what would soon enough become ice.

Carter wrapped his wool scarf more tightly about his neck and thought for a moment of going back for a hat. Surely they wouldn't be out in the rain. Where the hell was Mason, anyway? Where had he gone?

He heard the car turn the corner and saw the headlights of Ardyth's blue Volkswagen. By the time she arrived he had made it to the curb.

"That was quick," he said, squeezing into the small machine, pulling the door shut.

When he spoke Ardyth did not turn or answer. She held to the wheel with both hands. Her face was somber, stoic.

She, too, had worn a scarf, and suddenly Carter realized in the years he had known her and Mason, he had never before been alone with her, not even for a short time. She had always been Mason's wife, half of the Oldams, whatever that was, but not separate and individual.

Seeing her like this, in a totally new way, fascinated Carter. The dashlights reflected off her glasses so he could not see her eyes, and although her features were a bit thin and pointed, maybe pinched, she appeared beautifully composed. The vision set his senses on edge. For just a brief few seconds he was no longer dealing with Mason's wife, but, now, in a way he had not before, with a very devoted and attractive woman.

"You know where Mason is?" he said.

"Yes," she said. "I don't think he met his classes today."

"I didn't see him," Carter said. "I checked, but I'm not sure."

"No. He did not meet them."

"Was he home this afternoon?'

"No."

"Are we merely looking for Mason, or do you know where he is?"

"Oh, no," Ardyth said. "I know where we will find him. When he did not come home by four-thirty and it began to rain, I knew where he would be."

Carter nodded but did not press the inquiry. Her explanation sounded plausible enough. Then he realized she had omitted several items.

"How?" Carter said. "Somebody saw him."

"No. It is not difficult to know where he is."

Okay, Carter conceded, guesses and intuition, riding into the eternity of a very dark and long night. Something Ardyth divined about Mason's wanderings guided her now.

Maybe he had been wrong about Mason and Ardyth's connections. Maybe they had a telepathic kinship of kindness that transcended the physical and social. Maybe they were aliens, one mind in two bodies, halved as the brain is halved, independent, and yet holding together a world of perception and thought.

Small globs of ice formed on the wiper blades and they slowed so each pass looked to be the last. Without hesitation or indecision, Ardyth drove straight away toward the edge of town, then circled back along a one-way street.

"Our destination's a secret?" Carter said.

She tilted her head a little toward him, keeping her eyes on the road.

"I am sorry, John Carter. I have been thinking about the weather and hoping Mason has not been out in the rain too long. I think he will be at the Koto Gardens. Do you know the Koto Gardens?"

"No," but that doesn't say much. There are several thousand places around here that I don't know anything about."

"Mason likes it there very much. When the weather permits he goes to the gardens on afternoons to read. I think he will be there."

"What is it?"

"Have you seen the Japanese garden in San Francisco?"

"Yes," Carter said, "several years ago."

"It is like that."

Two years before, during a crisp week in October Carter had ridden a Greyhound across the prairies and Rockies into California and the foothills to San Francisco, ostensibly to attend the American Philosophical Association convention, but also to visit a former lover. The woman, Myra Whitely, with whom he had consorted regularly for several years, a medical researcher, had relocated to San Francisco State two years before that.

Struggling with what Carter characterized as the onset of the inevitability of her thirty-second birthday, hoping to deny it, she decided Carter was not only too old for her, but definitely the wrong kind of man.

"Jees, what am I doing," she told Carter, "wasting my life hopping in bed with a fifty-year-old goy? What will I tell my mother?"

Carter, wondering what a thirty-two-year-old might be worried about telling her mother, said that while in San Francisco he hoped to visit with her, and did not have much interest in staying in a hotel and wondered further if she could offer him shelter for the few days he was in town.

"That's really out of the question," she said.

So he took up residence in a downtown hotel, and two days later ran into her, in a Japanese Garden on the bay, as far as he knew by accident, although he had a strong suspicion she had located him at the hotel and in her crazy, indecisive and confused inability to decide whether she wanted to talk to him or not, had followed him.

They talked for several hours over cups of warm Saki and went later in the afternoon to the No Name bar in Sausalito and then fell into a comfortable bed. The following morning she said she would drive him back to the city, but would not see him again.

"This is the most disgusting thing I've ever done."

"Jesus Christ, Myra," Carter said, "how can screwing someone you've been screwing for five years, be disgusting. Frequency and duration alone would grant respectability."

"Like two dogs. We're like dogs. There was never any love between us. We don't care for each other."

"I didn't come to San Francisco just to see you," Carter said, "but I wouldn't have come if you hadn't been here."

"But Jesus Christ, Carter, it's been two whole, long goddam years."

"So?"

"But, I mean, you're a stranger. It's like I'm fucking somebody I don't even know. And there's also the problem I could get pregnant. What would you do then?"

"You didn't enjoy last night?"

"That was last night. I could just throw-up every time I think about it."

After two more days, saddened and demoralized he had his fill of the convention and caught a plane home.

A warm and generous few days with someone for whom he held an extreme fondness had been made bitter and rancorous. He had not gotten back to the coast, and the interlude hung as a warning sign on his memories of Japanese gardens.

Ardyth drove through the entrance to the Koto Gardens, a narrow tree lined drive made sinister by the darkness and the weather. She stopped in the miniature parking area and shut off the lights and engine. They sat in the dark, the quiet and the dark, listening to the purr of sleet falling on the roof.

Ardyth unbuckled her seat belt and reached into the back for an umbrella.

"We will need this," she said.

Carter got out and waited while she came around to his side.

"How big is this place?"

"It is quite big," Ardyth said.

There were several small foot-lights along the walk leading into the gardens, but otherwise the darkness was nearly total. Carter could make out the forms of small buildings, but nothing distinct.

"Would it help if we left the car lights on?"

Ardyth took a flashlight from her coat pocket and handed Carter the umbrella.

"You carry this. I will take the light."

Then with Carter trying to approximate her stride and pace and at the same time follow the light, they crossed the lot onto the chat walk, over a small rail-less planked bridge to the center of the garden and the open Shinto pagoda.

"The Japanese have a wonderful sense of nature," Ardyth said. "I feel it when I come here."

Carter was not sure about the nature thing, but at the moment he did not find either the weather or the setting inspirational.

"Mason Oldam would bring me here often before we were married," Ardyth said, as if the practice was more definitely past tense than language would permit.

The warmth of her voice cut the darkness clearly, and Carter realized she must have had a detailed map of the garden in her head. Each turn in the path, each step, each stone, carried a fond embrace or caress of memory. Was it possible that she could navigate the entire garden without guidance or direction. No doubt the light she carried was for the convenience of his blindness, alone.

They came to the steps on the near side of the pagoda and Carter slipped on the newly formed ice and nearly fell. He regained his balance and was about to ask Ardyth where they might find Mason when she directed the beam away from the path onto the rocks of what Carter, for lack of a better word, would have called a grotto.

"He will be there," Ardyth said, and another forty feet on, abreast the rock face of the enclosure, on a stone bench, sitting rigidly upright, a thin coat of ice on his hair and sport coat, they found Mason Oldam. Ardyth handed Carter the flashlight and stepped onto the grass to Mason's side.

The glass-like follicles of ice and grass blades crunched beneath her feet. She bent over him as if she was about to investigate the fragrance of a lovely flower, and ran the open palm of her left hand over his cheek and mouth, wiping the water away.

"We will go home," she said quietly.

Carter stepped in behind her holding the umbrella over them, and without shining the light directly on Mason's face, he could see Mason had recognized Ardyth's voice. He lifted his head and said something Carter could not decipher.

"John Carter," Ardyth said, and Carter assumed she was speaking to him. "It is John Carter," she said again and Mason nodded as if he understood.

She looped her arm under his and lifted gently, and to Carter's surprise Mason stood. He stood for a moment with Carter shining the light on the walk for him to see and holding the umbrella over them, and Ardyth looking up at him, as if they were servants or attendants, and he, Mason, the master, leading the journey, having come to a crossroads on an inclement night, to an unfamiliar crossing which offered choices he had not yet considered. Mason's arms hung limply at his sides and his legs shook and were unsteady.

Without speaking Carter took Mason's free arm. Holding the light and umbrella in one hand, the other gripped firmly to Mason, he helped Ardyth guide Mason onto the path toward the pagoda. The sleet was heavier then, the pin-like points of ice picking at them, the ground more treacherous. Shuffling across the narrow bridge behind Mason and Ardyth, on the slope of planks, taking small sliding steps, straining to keep the umbrella over Mason, Carter slipped, lost his balance and fell from the low bridge into the two-foot-deep moat that ran around the park.

For a moment he felt nothing, heard only the after-splash of his fall, amazed by the swiftness of his imbalance, and angry with himself for his carelessness.

"Fuck," he said, immediately sorry for saying it and wondered if Ardyth had heard him.

Ardyth paused on the path with Mason. "John Carter, are you all right?" she said.

"I just fell in the water. I think I lost the flashlight."

The shock of the icy water on his legs and back shook him. Hurriedly trying to extricate himself from the moat he slipped and fell again onto his hands and knees, spun like a pig-on-a-spit, now thoroughly soaked on all sides.

He found the handle of the umbrella and wadded out of the water, the crunch of the ice-coated grass welcoming him back to land.

"I lost your flashlight," he said.

The instrument glowed an impossible distance of seven or eight feet out in the moat, its opaque spirit beaming along the bottom, obscured and warped by the translucence of the water.

"It does not matter," Ardyth said.

Soaked and numbed, Carter helped Ardyth get Mason into the back seat of the Volkswagen. Already his wet trousers had stiffened and he shifted his mind to the living-room at home, the fire and a glass of J. W. Dant.

Ardyth drove into town quickly but carefully with Carter holding to the dash handle with both hands and Mason sitting boldly erect in the rear seat, his eyes dark and vacant as the night.

"Sunday morning," Mason said, and Ardyth leaned back to listen.

"What about Sunday morning?" she said.

"Sunday morning," Mason said again. Then twenty seconds later said, "Yes, that's it. I believe that's it."

Chapter XI

Carter came in and climbed the stairs to the bath off the master bedroom. From the steps he caught a glimpse of Katherine Marie in the living-room huddled on the couch in front of the fire. Positioning, Carter thought. Plumped down where he could not avoid her.

Her habits of avoidance and confrontation, while unspoken had over the years become obvious and predictable. Carter marveled at her talent for moving silently about the house, invisibly, when she chose, and at her skill for finding a spot where one human being living in intimate proximity to another would not think to look.

Most nights, when Carter retired early, she'd find something of interest or necessity, usually a movie or left-over office task to occupy an hour or so. Nights when it appeared he might stay up a little longer than usual she had an extraordinary capacity for disappearing. Then, finally, going to bed he'd find her, where she had not been before, wrapped in the cocoon of blanket, supposedly asleep, her back to his side of the bed.

For days, sometimes, she circled him as if he were a repellant magnetic field, unless, of course she wanted something. Then her positioning took nearly the opposite tact.

Tonight, possessed of his favorite, or at least frequent, seat before the fire, she no doubt wanted something. What? Maybe, she intend to carry on their earlier encounter, wanting a chance for rectification, to set the record straight, but by way of what? Explanation? Twisted words? Proffering the obfuscation of shadows to the scattered ideas she had earlier intended, to cover what had gone wrong in the exchange. Among her other habits, she seldom knew when to rest her case, when exhausted words could no longer serve.

He closed the bathroom door to hold in the heat, skinned out of his wet clothes and stood shivering, waiting for the tub to fill. With the water nearing the overflow drain, he settled in, slipping down until he was submerged. He breathed deeply and closed his eyes, needing badly, now, to think and to thaw his chilled bones.

Twenty minutes later he extricated himself from the wrap of warm water. He dressed and dropped his wet clothes down the laundry chute before going to the living-room for a drink.

"We're having an ice storm," Katherine Marie announced, "they say it could go on all night. I don't know what I'll do if I can't get to the office."

Carter dropped several ice cubes into a tumbler and poured out a supply of bourbon, then settled into the big chair closest to the fire. His back and arm ached where he had landed against the bridge when he fell and the chill still had not left him.

"You'll probably do what everyone else does," he said.

"I'm sorry about Mason, whatever it is," Katherine said.

"It's not the kind of thing sympathy will help," Carter said.

She looked at him appraisingly, then with a mild suspicion.

"What happened to you?"

"I fell in a puddle of ice-water."

"At least you didn't dive in."

She faced him more directly and laid her head on the back of the couch.

"John, have you considered seeing a doctor?"

"A doctor? Jesus. I'm not sick. It's just a chill. The water is freezing."

"But you're always falling. Maybe it's your inner-ear. It could be infected. Maybe you have a virus. It could be a lot of things."

Carter sipped the bourbon, the alcohol warming him. Her suggestion annoyed him precisely because she could have been right.

"Where'd you get your MD?"

"Actually, I've known several people who have had inner-ear infections that caused them to lose their balance."

"Well, you're right about part of it," Carter said. "I'm certainly unbalanced. A near perfect product of the modern story. An inferior product.

Man stumbling around in a darkened and fallen state."

"That's not what people think."

"Sure it is. What is original sin about? I'm a perfect example of defective humanity."

"But nobody believes that any more. About God punishing us. I mean that's nonsense."

"Yeah, I know," Carter said, the humor of the episode catching him. "Any damn fool who'd go out tramping around in the wind and sleet has to be slightly demented. He'd probably think nothing of swimming in ice water."

Katherine Marie's face softened, then became emotionless. For the moment, at least, she wanted to talk about something else.

"Will Mason be all right?"

"I don't know," Carter said. "Probably not."

"Do you know what's wrong?"

"Sure. He's suffering from the same thing that's got us all," Carter said. "He's just a little more afflicted than the rest. Just another example of defective humanity. It's terminal."

"I don't suppose you want to talk about it?"

"I don't have anything to tell," Carter said. "Gossip won't do anyone any good. Not Mason, or anybody else."

"I am sorry about this evening. I didn't mean to sound cryptic."

"Is that what it was?"

"Well, yes, something like that."

The bath and bourbon, the fire blazing, now, had warmed Carter. For the first time in several days, he felt comfortable and at ease.

"I had lunch at the Optimist Club today," Katherine Marie said. "Your Chancellor spoke. The Rotary, the Chamber of Commerce, even people from the Lions were there."

She had on a soft maroon housecoat, was barefooted with her heels set on a pillow on an antique ottoman with carved legs Carter had salvaged from a post-exam junk heap in front of an old house on Van Buren Street.

She held a small glass of wine aloft in her left hand slightly at an angle, her elbow propped on her right hand. Her robe had come unwrapped a bit about her thighs, opened enough to offer a glimpse of firelight on soft female flesh, and Carter was again appraised of her subtle beauty.

At sixty her body was still well-formed and solid and she was as lovely to him as she had been those twenty years ago when he married her.

"Carl Johnson was there. He was representing the Symphony Society."

She sat for a moment looking at the wine glass.

"John, that man is—well, what should I say? He's what? Well, he's queer. That's the only way to put it."

"Queer? Why is he queer?"

"John, Carl Johnson's sexual preferences are obvious to everyone."

"What? Dogs, cats, chickens, monkeys?" Carter chuckled.

"You know what I mean."

"I know Carl has his quirks. But his sexual habits seem situated in the normal range. I mean he prefers humans."

"You mean men."

"Yes. But men are human.

"Carl is beyond quirks. He's evil. I know gays and they're different. But my god. You know what he did?

"We were having lunch and he told Mary Fellner that women should have their vaginas sewn up.

"Good lord, did you ever hear anything so crude and ridiculous?"

Carter did not respond immediately.

"Yeah," he said finally, "Carl does go off once in a while. But a good bit of what he says is for effect. Shock effect. He shocked you, didn't he? He makes a habit of saying what no one else would think, and certainly wouldn't say. It's sort of the naughty little boy syndrome.

"Then, too, keep in mind that not too many years ago there were females in this town, a hyper-hetero group, who went public with a proposition that the state legislature pass a law to emasculate homosexual males—even when the males hadn't used their equipment for anything more than elimination and decoration, or with each other.

"It was almost comic. As if they were competing for males. Maybe a shortage of potent, breeding studs. As if given a choice all males might choose the gay-life and leave Harriet Hetero without any breeding possibilities."

"But still, he could have said it in a more acceptable way."

"And no one would have heard him.

"By the way, speaking of the prosaic, what did the good Chancellor Remcheck have to say that might warm the heart of an old scholar and reprobate?"

"Oh, he talked about the university's expansion. It's quite impressive. Exciting. They have construction planned for the spring."

"I'll be damned. Christopher Wren in Lancaster. Who'd a guessed it?"

"They're going to tear down the old science building."

"The old science building?" Carter said. "That's what they said?"

"Yes. Chancellor Remcheck."

Carter lifted his glass and watched the distorted flames bend through the ice and liquid. The old science building.

"Do you have any idea what that building is? What it represents?"

"Well, it's old."

"That sounds like Remcheck. Is that what he said?"

"He said the land is too valuable not to be used in a more productive way. They're going to build a complex for campus stores, a mall, with stores and classrooms. We may get to handle the ad accounts for several of the shops."

"We?"

"Carol and I."

"I don't suppose anyone bothered to remind him that he's destroying one of the two remaining best examples of Jeffersonian architecture in the Mississippi Valley? Or point out that Barker has hundreds of square acres of parking lots and tennis courts they could convert."

"But the location is perfect."

"Well, Newton Hall, the old science building as you gingerly put it, is the first building of its kind west of the Alleghenies. The first building constructed on this campus and the place where a significant part of the developmental work on the atomic bomb was done. Did you know that?"

Katherine Marie shook her head.

"Do you think Remcheck or Shindel know that?"

She watched the fire, staring at the flames, the tip of her tongue touched to the edge of her glass.

"Of course they don't," Carter said. "There's more history in the walls of that building than in the minds of all those dummies."

Carter circled the room to the liquor cabinet for a refill. The snap of sleet picked rhythmically at the windowpanes. Light from the corner streetlamp played off the ice that had already gathered on the wide concrete porch balustrade.

"On the other hand, the irony is absolutely superior. Imagine a destructive misfit like Remcheck out to take down a building that served so prominently in the development of the atomic industry. And not even know what he's doing. And certainly not caring."

"Do you really think they are all dummies?"

"Of course," Carter said, then laughed. "What did you expect me to say? Cunning, conniving dummies. And that's why they're dangerous."

Carter took Katherine's glass and filled it from the bottle on top of the liquor cabinet.

"It may be a religious difference," he said. "And philosophical, in a sort of broad, amorphous sense. We simply view the world differently. Ruskin believed art was moral. And he was right; everything we do is moral.

It reflects our tastes and our tastes reflect our choices for the world.

"Certain people choose to contribute, others to take," Carter said.

"I would have thought building a university was contributing?"

"Shops and classrooms do not necessarily a university make."

Carter handed Katherine the glass and stood behind her. He ran his hand along the open fold of the robe up to her neck.

"Carter, why do you have to be angry all the time? I know you don't care for Remcheck, but that's no reason to attack everything the man does. Aren't you supposed to mellow or something? I mean, you are fifty-five."

It was an old argument. Whenever Remcheck's name came up, Carter felt the knife go in. And as time passed he responded more infrequently with reason and more often to the pain.

The plans for university expansion over the grave of Newton Hall's foundation were not new. Carter had known of the scheme for six months, but had not yet succumbed to the idea. It had to do with Remcheck and his "new look" image for the university.

"Look," Carter told Katherine Marie, "when I talk to you, understand that I am in large talking to myself."

Carter stood staring into the fire.

"But it is the kind of thing you'd expect from pig-farmers and real-estate salesmen. The kind of thing Barker's board of trustees would think of as sound, productive educational development."

Carter, and the other members of the Major Administrative Selection Committee, two since deceased and three now gone on to other jobs, had seen it coming, when instead of Remcheck, after a national search the committee recommended a candidate they characterized as "eminently qualified." In spite of the recommendation, led by the President of the Board William Shindel, a pork-farmer-become-politician, the trustees chose Remcheck, because according to Shindel, Remcheck had "outstanding experience that qualified him and would assure his success at Barker."

Before coming to the university as a public relations agent Remcheck had served in Vietnam as a Marine Corps platoon leader and later as a liaison officer in intelligence attached to the CIA. According to Shindel, commanding a unit in Vietnam qualified Remcheck for the presidency, since what the university needed most was more discipline and a harder look at the real world. Shindel told the press, God had instructed him to choose Remcheck.

After that there was not a great deal of discussion. Carter and the committee publicly questioned Shindel's sanity, and Remcheck, sporting a shaved head and perpetual Marine Corps grin, was appointed Chancellor at the next meeting of trustees.

As the first order of business, he effected what he called "needed measures of economic austerity," froze and later cut the budgets by one-third of the departments that had been represented, quite incidentally, on the Major Appointments Committee. By edict he expanded the boundaries of student housing to include a nine acre mobile home park bordering the university's west side, a park Shindel owned.

"Anyone crazy enough to go public with a confession that God is talking to him, is not inviting rational dialogue," Carter had told Morgana. "He's a flake."

Several months later Crowly came on as another of Remcheck's "new look" enhancements. They had served together in Vietnam, in an intelligence operation, in a unit whose purposes, operations and numbers had been mostly classified.

Late in the war, or at least rumor had it that late in the war, they developed a penchant for disposing of uncooperative captive Cong informants from helicopters a thousand feet up over the Mekong Delta. Whether the dead men had jumped or fallen was not known, although it was suggested prisoners, manacled as they were, may have willing taken to the practicalities of open air and gravity, rather than face Remcheck and Crowly's promises of evisceration if they did not talk.

In an era of body-counts and war by attrition the Marine Corps brass pretty much disregarded Remcheck's unorthodox methods. Finally, however, after the unit had expanded its operations to Saigon street-girls, an investigation was pressed by several members of the Senate Armed Forces Committee.

When the scope of the activities surfaced, Remcheck and Crowly came within a breath of being put to Courts-martial. The general command threatened a full investigation if the practice was not abandoned, and relocated Remcheck to a desk job in Saigon.

What more there was, Carter didn't know. He knew this much only from student rumors and gossip, "the rap on the chancellor and his buddies," as one student had put it.

Crowly's rise under Remcheck led Carter to conclude there was probably more than a little truth to the rap. Tales seeping out of the penthouse, stories of Remcheck or Crowly standing guard outside closed office doors while the other entertained a secretary, added to Carter's suspicions. He wondered from what door, which floor, for old time's sake in a reenactment of rituals of camaraderie, one night a secretary might fall.

"Everyone thinks it's a good idea," Katherine Marie said.

"Everyone?" Carter said. "Not everyone. There are those among us who do not condone this. It's what Morgana said. They are out to rape the university."

"I don't know what she'd know about it," Katherine Marie said.

"Oh, she'd know as much about it as any other intelligent, observant person."

"Well, she's as bad as Carl Johnson. She probably gets that from hanging around him. Anyway, she's not my kind of woman. Everybody knows about her. Fag-hags are not very attractive people."

"Homosexuals are gays," Carter said, "not fags. And I think Morgana would be amused to hear you call her a hag. She's ten years your junior. What do you think she'd have to say about you? Though you're right about one thing. She is definitely not your kind of woman.

"That stuff about queers and fag-hags is ridiculous. That kind of thinking went out thirty years ago. Morgana and Carl are friends and your pejoratives won't sully that."

"Well, Chancellor Remcheck's plans for the university are progressive, John. And you can't stand in the way of progress."

"Progress?"

"We have to replace the old with the new. That's the way it works."

"For some people. Societies do not replace anything, unless somebody can make money off it. Especially not this society. Remember greed is a very old vice. So be careful what cultural context you put it in.

"What we have here, is a rampant epidemic of historical naiveté, or ignorance. Tearing down Newton Hall is an architectural equivalent to Hitler burning books. Maybe even worse. There's always a chance a copy of a book will survive. There's no copy of Newton Hall. And once it is down, all you have left is pictures. I suppose you could burn the pictures, too.

"This entire country has cultural Alzheimer's. Americans can't even remember what they destroy, much less why they have mindlessly obliterated much of their past."

"John, we know that," Katherine Marie said. "We know where we've been. It doesn't do any good to go over it again and again. You can't worship the past. What's dead is dead."

"And what's not, soon will be. Instead of putting the money back into the school in educational terms, it's going to be handed over to the construction people to erect shoddy cinder-block edifices with a half-life of ten years."

"You're making too much of it," Katherine Marie said. "There's nothing wrong with people making money. I mean, no matter what you think, these are not evil people. Anyway, we can't change it. We don't make these decisions, they do."

"Yeah, I know. They have an edifice-complex, Carter said. "Which is strangely akin to screwing the motherland."

Succinctly put, he thought. Do not question the king. Roll with it and collect whatever filters down. No matter where we begin it comes back to the same thing.

The room had warmed considerably and added to Carter's discomfort. Abandoning the conversation, he took his drink to the front door. A heavy coating of ice laced the storm door. The trees sparkled in the streetlight, bending beneath the weight of the sleet become ice.

Carter opened the door intending to go out to the porch and mingle with the ornate glitter and gleam, the iced fireflies and sparklers in the trees. Then he decided not to hazard it. The pain in his shoulder and back, the aching muscles of his legs and arms had been tolerably relieved by the doubles of bourbon. Better to remain a healthy passive observer than to risk further wounds by participating.

Shivering in the solitude he retreated to the more disturbing concerns about Mason. He'd call Ardyth at ten-thirty. He would give her time to determine what, if anything, might need to be done. Ruminating on Mason's plight and the distasteful twists of the Barker conversation, Carter advanced on the liquor cabinet to refurbish his drink.

Now, Remcheck was on his mind. No, not on his mind, but deep inside him as if a stake had been driven into his bowels.

Until Katherine Marie mentioned him, Carter had forgotten about the grinning-goat and the disdain he had for the man and what he represented.

But in the end, his alienation did not come from the nonsense of Katherine Marie's opinions. What others believed or didn't believe, did not disturb him. For that was as it should be. But knowing the follies and foibles of human reason, and the effects of ill-planned adventures, adopted and pushed forward without examination, for financial gain and prestige—and knowing people, large numbers of people, would be injured irreparably by these easy decisions, saddened Carter.

But that was his life. He had sought, at times diligently, in ways, no matter how small, to eradicate by instruction, to find a remedy for blind arrogance, the reduction of life to whim, to the stupidity of avarice and greed and hatred, and was now again sorely reminded how he had failed. If this was a measure, his failure was colossal and ongoing. And not only his. The entire educational enterprise, the traditions had failed, and he felt that, too, was his. The ideal blown and lifted on an evil wind. And it wasn't the infantile crap of I should have done better. But the sting of clear-cut failure. Not having been well enough prepared or armed or competent or political enough. Failure. Defeat.

Was it enough for a life to gather to itself accolades for the pretenses of good done and wealth that feeds on the hunger, disease and ignorance of others? If for the many it was. For Carter, clearly, it was not. Failure and the question of how to proceed in the face of a diminishing spirit lay like malignant tumors at the root of John Carter's dilemma.

"I didn't mean to get you off onto university politics," Katherine Marie told Carter. "There's another matter we need to talk about.

Chapter XII

Carter woke shortly before eight and lay staring at the ceiling trying to remember how he had gotten to bed. As usual he had drunk too much, remembered talking to Ardyth, then tracked through the pieces of the last hours of consciousness, reassembling a pleasant memory of a prolonged romp on the rug before the fire with Katherine Marie.

Recounting the evening and night, he took inventory of the damage, of his condition. His arm and the back of his ribcage on the left side were painfully sore, as was his right elbow. The cough he had courted for several days had dropped into his chest. His ribs hurt when he coughed, but other than a nagging bronchitis, he did not feel ill.

He had spoken to Ardyth and inquired about Mason. For the most she sounded optimistic. After sleeping several hours Mason had eaten and seemed a good bit more coherent than when they found him.

"John Carter, I have found the letter you spoke of. I did not know it had arrived. Mason Oldam received it early in the morning when I was out."

Carter asked if she had been in touch with Dr. Goldenstein and she said she had not, but planned to contact him.

"I'll call you tomorrow afternoon," he had told her and left it at that.

Carter propped himself up on a sore elbow and looked out along College Street. Power and telephone lines were down, huge tree limbs cluttered the entire block and at the corner the wooden light-pole had snapped under the weight of the wires and hung at a forty-five degree angle over the street, an enormous walking stick caught in the web of an even larger spider.

The clock-radio beside the bed was blank. He switched to battery power and dialed down to the weather station.

The forecast called for rain and freezing temperatures. A large part of the city was already without electricity and telephone services. The university had been closed.

Carter could hear tree limbs snapping and falling along the street and farther away down the block in the neighborhood yards.

Katherine Marie came in from the bathroom, already dressed.

"I'm going to try to make it to the office," she said, "it doesn't look too bad."

"World War Three," Carter said. "While we slept, they had World War Three. Devastation and ruin. Massive retaliation in the form of an ice storm. The explosions soaked up the heat. The temperature outside is absolute zero and dropping every hour."

She backed away from the mirror and watched him.

"You've been reading too much again, John."

"There will be no work today," Carter said. "The office is closed. The power is off and the computers are blank-eyed and silent. Why don't you come back to bed?"

"There's always work," she said. "My desk is stacked with work."

"Ah, ha," Carter said, "you are off to a rendezvous with your lover. I know what you're doing."

He waved a finger in the air.

"Who will it be today? The short, fat fruit vendor with the long nose, who smells of garlic and Old Spice, or the young, handsome sommelier with a withered arm?"

"John, I wish you wouldn't say things like that."

"Ah, caught in the truth," he said.

"That is not the truth."

"I see," Carter said. "A female lover. So that's it. All these years and her husband never suspected."

Katherine Marie did not answer but disappeared into the bathroom. Moments later she stood at the end of the bed, putting an earring in place.

"The truth is," she said, "that within a year I am going to be the best PR person in this town. And a year after that I'm going to have my own agency. And a little ice and rain are not going to interfere with that. I'm tired of people looking down on me."

"I'll put money into that," Carter said. "If I can help. I think you should."

"Even though we never talk about it," Katherine Marie said.

"But we do," Carter said. "We talked about it last night. Or don't you remember?"

"And I don't intend missing work just because of an ice storm."

"Well, you may not miss work," Carter said, "but I'll miss you."

She left the room and a few minutes later he heard the front door close. He was never sure how much was real and what she did for affect. Hundreds of times, in hundreds of ways he had tried to convince her that she was too stuffy.

It had not always been this way, he reminded himself. In the beginning they had been good companions as well as lovers. She had been a comforting relief to the turmoil of his first marriage.

And then by degrees it had drifted.

Jesus. It could have been so much better. It had been so much better. They almost connected.

Carter rolled over in a tepid bed looking for the warm side of the pillow. What is the word for the warm side of the pillow in a cold room in the middle of winter?

Although he had thought about it great deal, Carter could not pinpoint the exact juncture at which the marriage had gone awry. While he held to a practiced tolerance for allowing people their own space and thing, in this case Katherine Marie, the sap had gone out of it. Even within the freedom of coming and going and no children they had been unable to endure the abrasive rub of academy and marketplace, and neither sex nor companionship could encourage and maintain the affection—or the deepening of affection, love.

In the detritus of tedium and humdrum, of too often passing at the door, the almost unnoticed friction of opposite directions, they had lost their cohesiveness. Now they slid past one another too easily and too quickly to bond.

He rose almost on impulse and padded across the chilled floor to the bathroom to find his dull, barely visible reflection in the large mirror.

The ache of marital misalliance he could confront and address later in the day, at Murphy's, if Seamus had means of lighting the signs.

The pain he located, newly surfaced floated on the awareness of the severity of Mason's affliction. The mystery of the human mind gone to hell, popped over to the dark side. The awareness that Mason might not ever again be whole numbed Carter.

He shaved in the grey light from the bathroom window and dressed, and wondered if any of the university facilities were open. Maybe the decision had been only to cancel classes. He tried the bedroom phone. The line was dead, so he went to the kitchen, the idea or plan forming in his head to walk over to the library.

Katherine Marie had made coffee in an old pot they kept for just such times as these. He lit the fire, waited several minutes and poured out a cup. He was sitting looking out at the ice-encased large elm nearest the kitchen's west side, thinking about what he might do, when Vivien's face appeared at the glass of the backdoor. She smiled and waved and Carter took a few seconds adjusting to the context of her face, here, at his door.

Viewed against the background, the surroundings of his office, the halls at Temperly, Murphy's, Ruth's apartment she fit, especially at Ruth's, but not here. He opened the door and stood looking at her. Her eyes were no longer swollen and showed only the slightest traces of damage. A small streak of blue shaded the bridge of her nose. One eyelid was tinted with a faint pink-red shadow.

"Good morning," she said. "I just happened by and thought I'd stop to say hello."

"Hello," Carter said. "Hello."

"You sound like a parrot."

"I am a parrot. A surprised parrot."

"Can I come in, or must I remain forever outside your door?"

"No, no," Carter said. "Come on in."

He closed the door behind her and awkwardly reclaimed his coffee from the table.

"What the hell are you doing here?"

"I told you, I was just going by and so I stopped to see you."

"That's not right," Carter said. "Nobody in their right mind would be out today. Then again, maybe you would."

"I like winter weather."

"Why did you stop here?"

"To see you."

"But I'm not the only one who lives here."

"Does your roommate object to your friends? You wanted her to meet me."

"Well, at least she doesn't knock the shit out of me."

"You might be surprised about what she would do."

"I might," Carter said.

"Anyway, I saw her leave."

"You saw her leave. Half-an-hour ago. How long have you been out there?"

"All night. I'm the great ice-witch."

She widened her eyes and featured a maniacal grin, holding her hands in the air with her fingers hooked into claws.

"How about a cup of coffee?"

"No. Remember? I don't drink coffee. Anyway, it would melt the ice. Ice-witches have ice in their veins."

"And in their wombs."

"Do you think so? What would Carter's experience tell him about that?"

"Is it cold out?"

"Very."

"I was just headed for the library to see if it was open."

"It is cold. But not too bad."

Carter emptied his coffee into the sink.

"I'll get my coat."

"And a hat, if you have one. Otherwise your head will freeze. You're not as young as you once were."

"And you're a shithead," Carter said.

The sky was a deep gray and the rain a fine mist. Carter navigated carefully across the ice, taking small steps, with Vivien holding to his arm.

"Who in god's name is guiding whom?" he said.

"Some places are better than others. The best place is in the middle of the street, away from the power lines and tree limbs."

The broken branches and limbs lying in the street were sculpted there, ice-encased with the beautiful, smooth swept lines of exquisite glass. The gray of the day hung in the fine threads of the stems of the wilted wintered leaves and the wet blackened wood as if it had been carved down from a superior stone and polished revealing more and more of its interior, layer by layer as it was worked. The gray-red cobblestones of College Street were glazed over into an extended pattern of rounded and broken, sparkling gems.

The devastation was more complete than Carter had surmised. Whole trees had toppled, simply gone down stiff-legged, uprooted and popped out of the ground. Several had consented to drop considerately into the open spaces of driveways, along sidewalks, away from secondary buildings. Several had fallen like members of a regiment taken by the same fusillade, spinning down onto the remains of its comrades. Quite improbably, two tilted into each other, into the arms of the other, leaning precariously, unable to stand, unable to fall, offering support neither could supply for itself.

Others had not sought open spaces, but succumbing to the extended years of angled growth and gravity went down onto the roofs of houses, shearing off porches and demolishing automobiles.

"The savage violence of nature's pruning," Carter said. "Nature's way of getting rid of the dead-wood."

They picked their way along the street, slowly and with great difficulty, around and over the debris, making little progress for the effort and time it took. Carter looked ahead, and as far as he could see, the scene was the same, and he wondered how Katherine Marie had vanished so quickly, how she had so adeptly navigated the devastation. Then he struck on the notion that maybe she had not, and that while seeking passage, circling the massive mushroom stump of the roots of a fallen tree, they might find her, so to speak among the ruins. Maybe she, too, had fallen.

The soft mist had intensified, washing the ice clean and making it impossible to secure anything of a foothold or footing. For an hour they pulled themselves along, laughing and slipping, balanced and holding to one another, to the debris, to the door handles of cars. Twice Carter slipped, the second time twisting his right knee beneath him, then stood for a time catching his breath, allowing the pain to drain out of the strained joint and his injured rib, and looked back toward his house along the route they had come.

The eight blocks represented a journey far out of proportion to the distance as it was set in his mind, to the time retracing his steps would take, and he decided, nonetheless, he would not return.

"Jesus," he said, "I'm getting beaten up. Last night I dammed near killed myself falling into the moat at Koto Gardens. Now this."

"What were you doing at Koto?"

"You might say I'd gone there to see a friend."

"But there's nothing there. Koto's been closed for two months. I don't know about you. And you think I'm strange."

"You are strange."

"You want to go back?"

"No, I do not want to go back. Believe it or not, I'm having fun."

"We could go back for a wheelchair."

Carter stopped, then tried to take a deep breath.

"Why don't you knock off those silly jokes about age. There's nothing humorous about age or sex. The only thing even vaguely humorous, is that people are afraid of sex and age and have to hide their fears with jokes."

"You don't make jokes about sex?"

"Seldom."

"Not about ice in wombs?"

"That wasn't a joke. I was serious."

"Well, either way, I'm sorry."

"Another apology."

Vivien smiled.

"Yeah. I lied."

She wore an old imitation sheepskin coat and a green and white wool-knit cap. Her hair was braided and pulled to the side, an elegance he remembered of his mother a very long time ago. Her face had a hardy, hail quality of Bergson's élan vital, and now of cheer.

"Why are we doing this?" he said.

"I don't know. You wanted to go to the library."

For the next several blocks the path was less difficult. Power crews were clearing away the debris. They had started at the university, working out from the center into the outlying areas.

"Imagine," Carter told her, "seeing the size of this, what it must have been for the explorers stumbling onto the Mississippi River. Imagine what they must have felt. What they thought, seeing something that big, that they had never seen before. It would have to change your whole perception of life, how you appraised what you had seen before. Nothing would ever be the same."

The stores along Money Street apparently had power and were already opened. The merchants had salted the sidewalks and from there the footing made walking easier. A scattering of students populated the street, a few going to jobs, others no doubt out enjoying the unusual sense of the day.

"Why are we going to the library?"

"I thought I'd take you a place you'd never been before."

"John, that is not funny. Why don't you knock off those silly jokes about students?"

Moments later they broke out of the passage between the chem-labs and Palmer Hall onto the ice-garden magnificence of the quad. Here the trees had not broken or fallen, but stood, miraculously glass-blown, huge and stately without having suffered the slightest damage. The bushes along the walks were shrouded with white snow-like ice, row on row, trimmed by the flowing force of the rain running and freezing over the tightly knit branches. Even the ground beneath the trees was without debris.

"This is utterly impressive," Carter said. "Absolutely lavish."

"Carter this is spooky. I mean, it looks like it was planned. Why haven't the limbs broken off the trees?"

"The mind and methods of modern technology and husbandry, my dear. That's what the caretakers of this splendid institution get paid for. They've got everything trimmed down to good health. Not like the rest of us, floundering in our stool."

"This looks like Alice in Wonderland."

"Through the Looking-glass," Carter said.

"Did you see Dr. Zhivago? Remember the ice-palace? Where they went. What's his name?"

"Who?"

"The doctor?"

"Yuri Zhivago."

"What was his wife's name."

"Tonya."

"No, no. The other one."

"He didn't have two wives."

"Carter. The other woman."

"Lura."

"God, I loved that movie."

They crossed the quad to Hawthorne, beneath the canopy of trees, limbs hung heavily with their glaze of ice, nearly finger to finger. It was raining again, the mist falling on the limbs, spraying, falling and gathering again. They climbed the two flights of icy stairs to the main door and stood looking back down onto the quad.

"A scene out of National Geographic," Carter said.

"I wish I had a picture of this. I should have brought my camera," Vivien said. "It's beautiful"

"I was in Chicago in the late sixties when they had a huge snow storm," Carter said. "It snowed twenty-nine inches in ten hours, then another thirteen inches the next day. The transit authority tried to keep the buses running as long as they could, but finally the snow got too deep and they stalled, and before it was over there was a line of buses on Western Avenue as far as you could see. I didn't know there were that many buses in Chicago."

The library was not open. Through the glass doors Carter could see to the main desk and the night-light and the clock on the wall. Behind the desk the doors to the librarians' offices were closed and the aisles leading into the stacks were empty. The clock showed eleven-fifteen.

"It doesn't look as if the power has been off here," Carter said. "The clocks are still on time."

"But we can't get in. Do you think everything is closed?"

"C'mon," Carter said.

He took her hand and moved along the portico to the walk leading to the dock area in the rear. There they descended a small stairway behind a dumpster to a three-quarter-size door at the bottom. He locked both hands tightly on the knob, then pulled and lifted and the door popped open.

"My private entrance," he said. "That's a little trick I learned from

Waldus Paul, the former Arts and Science dean. Waldus believed the library was the citadel of the university and the only refuge we have against the Philistines and everyone should have a private entrance."

"What's that?"

"What?"

"The Philistines."

"Eyeless in Gaza, at the mill with slaves, under the Philistine's yoke."

"Gaza? Where's that?"

"Have you ever read the Bible?"

"No. Should I?"

"The land of Canaan," Carter said. "A peculiar bit of Israelite provincialism."

"Isn't there an alarm to keep people from getting in?"

"Not if the door is opened. Only if it's forced or broken into."

The door led into a darkened passage with a dim, red exit-light at the end of a long tunnel-like hall. Beyond the sign they emerged into a room of carts and packing crates and the accompanying support paraphernalia for storage.

"Where are we going?" Vivien asked.

"You'll see," Carter told her.

At the top of a stairway Carter pushed through a heavy leather covered swinging door and they came into the library's large main room. The tiles of the floor glowed in the leaden light of the gray day outside, and looking up, they could only barely make out the separate colors of the stained-glass portholes at the top of the rotunda.

"I've never seen anything like this before," Vivien said. "It's breathtaking."

She slipped out of her coat and dropped it to the floor and walked away from Carter in a series of graceful, well-practiced swirls. She circled between the tables and came back to Carter.

"That's very impressive," Carter said. "I didn't know you were a dancer. Though I should have guessed."

"How could you have known?"

"From your legs. Your legs look like dancers' legs."

"Did you like that?"

"Yes. I did. Nicely done."

"It's a little difficult in these shoes, but god, it's lovely in here. It's a museum. A big church.

"A cathedral," Carter said.

"You know, I've been in here dozens of times and I've never looked up. When there are people around, well, I mean, it's different."

"You should see the Long Room of the library at Trinity College in Dublin. Or the library at Oxford."

"Carter," she said, speaking very softly, in a whisper, "is there anyone else here? I mean, are we alone?"

"I would suppose so," Carter said. "Unless a librarian happens to be here. And that wouldn't surprise me."

"Carter, this is scary. What if we're being watched?"

"We are watched. Even when they're not here the librarians know what is happening to their books. The books have voices like the harp in 'Jack and the Beanstalk' and talk to the librarians and tell them everything. Each librarian has three heads like a troll. One to see, one to hear and one to speak."

"You mean like the three monkeys? See-no-evil, hear-no-evil, speak-no-evil?"

"Yeah. The heads think the books belong to them and sometimes they fight over them, and what the books say. The heads do not want people to handle the books or read them. They're very protective.

"Then there's the Cyclops eye of the great idle-mind focused on us, following our every step. Like a cosmic TV camera."

He paused and tilted his head.

"If you listen closely, you can hear him breathing. You can hear his eye squeak as it rotates in its socket."

"Carter, don't. You're giving me the shivers."

"Listen to this," Carter said. "Be very quiet and just listen."

They stood motionless, silent and motionless, and Carter raised his hand and snapped his fingers. Then he did it again.

"What do you hear?"

"It echoes, six or seven times."

"No," Carter said, "Not a mere six or seven times, but it echoes infinitely, reverberating as the spirits of the walls each listen to the sound before passing it on to the next so he can listen to it. The sound drifts out of our hearing, but the walls keep it, even something as small as a snapping sound, they will keep."

"The walls must be filled with sound."

"Yes," Carter said, "and thought. They are thinking, too."

Over the wooden bookcases along the inner wall to the side of the main desk were two of the four paintings the university had on loan from the Ivan Albright collection at the Chicago Art Institute.

Carter had not before seen any of these particular Albright works. The canvas nearest the desk, the first of the two in the main room, was Into the World Came a Soul Called Ida.

Poor Ida. Forlorn and perplexed Ida, in decayed corpulence.

"God, that is awful," Vivien said. "Why would they want to have pictures like that in here?"

"No, my dear," Carter said, "you mean full of awe. And they want, as you say, 'pictures like that' in here because people come here to see, to view and to appreciate works of art."

"That's not art."

The intensity of her opinion amused Carter.

"And upon what fine and learned base do you set that idea? Why do they bother you?"

"I don't like it. Who wants to look at a picture of a fat old woman?"

Carter had the remembered that the woman was not old, but in fact quite young.

"She's not old," Carter said. "That's what artists see in everyone. This artist, anyway. We're born corrupt. Well almost. Remember what Twain said? 'I was born humble, but it didn't last.'"

"I'll never look like that. I'll kill myself first."

The painting, Flesh, a substantial counterpart, hung next to Ida, and Carter passed over it quickly.

"Come on," he said, "look at this."

He pointed to the arched doorways leading to the south wing and the law library. LEX and JUS were carved into the stone work above the arches.

He put his hand on Vivien's head.

"Now my darling young woman, which will you choose, the law of man or the law of the gods, who in their infinite wisdom and divine hindsight, can make no mistake?"

"Oh, man," she said reverently, mocking the venerable tone of his voice. "Men are more fun in bed. Gods never have any fun."

"And I, not yet having been in bed with a god or a goddess," Carter said, "honoring the fortitude and pure guts of rebellion, shall cast my lot with the underworld, and with the hosts of other fools before me, aspiring to the status of the gods, I will choose Gods."

On the other side they met and she wrapped her arms around his neck.

"Now that we are legally bound," she said, "you'll just have to stay with me."

"Twenty years," Carter said. "It's all you get. That's all I get."

"Seventy years, and then seventy more."

"C'mon," Carter said, and they ran, Vivien running and Carter limping along in a trot on his bruised knee a bit behind, through the south-wing to the elevator at the end of the hall.

"Carter, where are you taking me?"

"For a ride," he said. "Hasn't anyone ever taken you for a ride?"

"Jesus, have they. But I'm not sure we're talking about the same thing."

"We are."

Carter's leg pained him now, aching, so when he walked he did so with difficulty.

"But the electricity is off. The elevators won't work."

"Oh, you of little faith. What you say may be true. Possibly, the electricity is off. More than likely the university has a backup system for essential items, such as elevators and other places where people might be stranded."

They boarded the elevator and Carter pushed the buttons and the door closed.

"Into the shadow of the valley of the depths of hell, rode the six hundred," he said. "We're going to the third-level."

"What's there?"

"Books. Books. And books."

"What kinds of books?"

"Books for to read, written by bodiless faces on old decayed photos with names beneath them."

"John, you're not making any sense."

"Oh, yes I am."

"And what will you do once you are there?"

He looped his arm around her neck.

"Have you ever been had in a library?"

"In the basement of a library? No, I don't think so. Once in the bandroom in high school by a biology teacher, but not in a library."

"How about on an elevator? And my dear, do you feel the world shake, the bottom falling out?"

They disembarked at the third-level into the ranks of book stacks lined in long rows of a crescent shaped room. Just inside the elevator door Carter located the card-catalogue. He pulled open the middle drawer and, squinting in the faint light, began paging through the cards.

"What are you looking for?"

"Spirits," Carter said. "Voices. The voices of the dead. They speak to me in tongues. To give me guidance."

"Are you lost?"

"Very much so," Carter said. "There are all kinds of stories of people trying to commune with the dead by living in libraries. I mean literally living here. Sleeping in the stacks, never venturing past the stairway door. There are those who come in with the compulsion to read everything in the library, and set out systematically, beginning at book one of row one to read every book in the entire building."

She walked to the rail of the balcony.

"I would have sworn we were going down. How did we get up here?"

"Would you have preferred to drop into the crypt of the trolls, where they keep the bodies of the children they feed on? Have you seen the *Phantom of the Opera*? The ghoul who haunted the opera and played the organ when no one was around? Actually, he lived in a sewer."

"Jesus," she said, "where do you get those gruesome stories?"

She hunched up her shoulders.

"This is really a creepy place. I mean, with no lights and nobody around."

She gasped. She was staring past him at the wall, her mouth open, her eyes locked on the large painting hung over the card catalogue.

"My god, that's even worse than the other one. Where did those come from?" she said, averting her eyes and covering them with her hand.

"That's part of the same collection," he said. "Have you read *The Picture of Dorian Gray*?"

"No," she said weakly.

She was standing behind him, pressed closely and holding his arm, her face against his shoulder.

"Look at the cat's eyes. The slick Egyptian cat's eyes," Carter said.

"Who is that?"

"Dorian Gray. A character from Oscar Wilde's novel."

"From a story?"

"A novel."

"Then he's not real. I mean, he didn't live."

"Oh, he lived all right. He still does."

"But not real flesh and blood."

"Maybe even better."

She was silent for a while, staring at the picture.

"Carter, this is spooky. Let's go. I mean, can't you do this tomorrow?"

"This shouldn't take too long," Carter said.

She did not answer and he resumed his search for several minutes before he sensed she was no longer there and drew his attention back to the room. He could not see her and assumed she had drifted off on her own, to examine the stacks. He called to her softly.

"Vivien," he said, and reverted to the card-file, and then added, "well, it may take a little longer than I thought."

When she did not answer, he finished copying the call-letters and pushed the drawer closed. He walked along the ends of the rows crossing the room, expecting to find her simply shopping or reading. The last row he followed the length of the room and stood with his hands on his hips, silently, listening to the sounds of the building and the wind and rain at the skylight. To his left an arched passage led around the interior of the dome to the next room.

The seven rooms of the third-level were set in a circle, opening on the rotunda, with short, rounded Romanesque arched tunnels between them. Several of the small exterior rooms of the tunnels had been converted into individual rest-rooms and Carter stopped midway to listen again.

The heating pipes in the old building gurgled and banged and he heard a heavy wheezing or hissing, as if someone was having difficulty breathing.

"Vivien," he said, and the breathing abated, then, in several seconds, began again.

The humor of the prank, if it was a prank, did not please Carter. His coat was damp from the long walk in the rain, damp and uncomfortable, and his leg and back pained him, further aggravated by the hard tile floors. He was thinking about retreat, retreat and refuge, Murphy's to be exact.

He had located the call-numbers on the books and tramped into the second room, poking through the shelves, running down the letters, when a door slamming, or what sounded like a door slamming, echoed up into the rotunda.

He assumed it had come from below, but decided it could have just as easily originated on any of the levels surrounding the dome and dropped down and echoed up to the balcony.

The silent aftershock of the sound rang in his ears, the no-sound of the senses pulsating displaced only finally in the wind beyond the building's stone walls.

Carter retraced his steps to the end of the row and the heavy marble balustrade and carefully and slowly leaned out over the rail to view the lower areas of the rotunda. He could not see into the darkened passages of the east-wing, and could detect neither motion nor sound.

The second-level was also without life, and he was about to return to his search when out of the corner of his eye he caught a glint of movement on the third-level in the room directly opposite him.

Vivien, he guessed, hoped.

No doubt she had gone to the restroom, which could also account for the door slamming, and was now circling the third-level.

Who else could it have been? The library staff. Unlikely, but possible. In the years of his off-hours prowling in the library he had never encountered anyone. Not staff. Not janitors. No one. Not only was the library a citadel, but in large part a morgue.

He retreated, then, from the railing into the stacks and located the general area of the books he had chosen, using his cigarette-lighter to better see the letters and titles.

The three volumes he wanted were on the same shelf, and with the books tucked beneath his overcoat, pausing several times to listen, he worked his way back to the elevator. He bowed courteously to Dorian Gray, to the splendid, cluttered magnificence of decay, and rode the machine down, its cables and wheels whirring and bumping to the main floor.

He expected Vivien to appear at any moment and decided to wait for her at the circulation desk. There, however, he found her, sitting on the floor with her back to the wall, her arms wrapped around her legs, knees beneath her chin, waiting for him. Her face appeared drawn and tired, her eyes dark and distant, and when she looked up and smiled her smile was almost a grin, a snarl.

"You look worse than the woman in the picture," he said.

"I don't feel so hot, either."

"Are you ready to go?"

She rose without saying more and followed him down to the tunnel and again outside to the early afternoon and the ice and continuing rain.

"How did you get down?" Carter said. "I didn't hear the elevator."

"I took the stairs."

"You made the noise, the door slamming?"

"No," she said, "that wasn't me."

"Which stairway?"

"By the elevator."

Carter remembered Dorian Gray's eyes, the surprised, anguished pop-eyes, looking as if cockroaches had eaten out the pupils. And the hands. His hands stained with blood that seemed to have leaked out of the pours of his skin. Bright red blood, and the lips and the mouth of a partially decomposed corpse. But mostly he remembered the eyes, and the flicker of movement across the expanse of the rotunda's dome in the fifth room.

"Shall we go to Murphy's?" he said, congratulating himself, despite his pained leg, for the unbelievable length of having eluded Cerberus one more time.

"No," she said. "Not today."

Chapter XIII

Thursday the rain ended a little before midnight, and an accompanying sudden rise in temperature melted the ice. The morning sky to the west shown clear behind the front, promising another chilled day.

Debris from the storm lay in piles along College Street pushed to either side by large frontend loaders and the ground was wet and very black, as if it had been scorched by a firestorm.

Carter retrieved the morning paper from the porch, then went to the kitchen and filled the coffeemaker. An uncomfortable chill hung on the kitchen and he sat at the table to wait out the machine's hissing and burping.

Outside the library Vivien had left him, and immediately and true to course he navigated alone and with less than dead-reckoning and full-sail over the ice to Murphy's. There he commandeered a back booth and ordered a beer and dipped into the books he had taken from the library.

Functional Disorders and Human Psychosis.

He had hoped to familiarize himself with Mason's problems, or at least to see if he could form a better understanding of what might be the problem.

It was just that sort of thing. That sort of habit. When pressed Carter grabbed a book. In the beginning the impulse rose and peaked on a sincere, almost absolutistic wave. A belief in knowing. "In the beginning was the Word . . ." A pure intent out of which he expected an answer to wash over the unorganized debris of experience. Knowing made sense out of the sensible.

But he had not gone past a few pages. He no longer had patience for quasi-scientific explanations and psychiatric abstractions. The complex lost itself in a maze.

On several occasions, he had been tempted to talk to Goldenstein, and he thought he might still. Of course Goldenstein would tell him nothing.

Probably Goldenstein had not leveled with Ardyth, and certainly not with Mason, about the severity of Mason's possession.

He paged through the paper, skipping over the international news, and settled on the sports page. A large picture of Minus Factor in his Patriots uniform filled the upper right side of the page.

"Minus 'Yardage' Factor Biggest Reason For Patriots' Success," Carter read. He skimmed the story, the battery of figures, and then the gossip, who said what, why, and, who cares? Carter made a mental note to watch the Patriots' game on Saturday. He checked the time. Noon EST. Eleven. Against the Steelers in Pittsburgh.

By eight he had drained the coffeepot and read the paper twice. In a third time scavenging he picked over *Dear Abby*, two recipes for Christmas bread and his horoscope for the day.

Carter was a Virgo. Katherine Marie a Gemini. He wondered about the girl. He'd have to ask her.

A rumbling overhead announced a Gemini afoot, and to avoid the inevitability of morning verbal amenities he decided to escape.

The transformation of iced-walks to concrete made the morning passage more sure-footed. Carter was invigorated with the newly realized grip of his shoes to the concrete, to mother earth.

The campus streets were adrift with a scatter of students moving in and out of breakfast spots, to work, going late to eight o'clock classes. Enlivened by the chilled air, though a bit dizzy from the lack of sleep, he threaded his way through the small bunches of pedestrians.

Food, he counseled, teased by the pleasant aromas spread on the air by the exhaust fans of the grills he passed. I need food.

At Temperly he took the elevator to the basement cafeteria and ran into Morgana and Carl Johnson huddled in the hall outside the door.

"Carter, am I ever glad to see you," Morgana said. "Have you been upstairs yet?"

Carter shook his head and gave immediate play to conjecture, from the tone of her voice aware something unpleasant had taken place. Mason? Had it been Mason? And what this time? What had he done this time?

"Security has the hall cordoned off," Morgana said.

"My god, Carter, it is majestic," Carl said. "The brown-shirts are up there prancing about with superlative officiousness. A collection of Nazi marionettes. Never have I seen them so pleased with having something to do. How would you feel if your sole mission in life was to keep people from writing nasty marks on the wall or chasing pot-smokers and guarding the pissoir?"

Morgana read the question on Carter's face.

"Somebody painted the glass doors of Crowly's office with blood."

"With blood?"

"That's right. With blood symbols."

"Of what?"

"Arabic characters," Carl said. "Superb designs, a splendid graffiti calling down curses from the gods, speaking to the corrupted soul of that beastly man and all the people like him."

Carter thought for a moment of what it might mean, the foolishness of the stunt; the ludicrousness of the stunt and Carl's infantile excitement—

a child at the circus. Carl's bright orange silk neckerchief and pale-green sport-coat waved like festival flags. Had he dressed for the occasion?

"Why Arabic?" Carter asked.

"Why not? They could have done it in Chinese. The mystery of the Far East," Carl said.

"They? Who in the hell is they?"

"They," Carl said lifting his chin, "they are the oppressed, the downtrodden, those crazed with fear and deprivation."

His voice rose dramatically, several octaves, just then alive with the fantasy of the vandalism.

"So they painted Crowly's office with blood. With human blood?"

"Goat's blood," Johnson said. "Goats' blood for goats."

Morgana lit a cigarette and rotated opposite Johnson.

"Carl, enough," she said. "That's more than enough. You'll have those idiots believing you did it."

"But darling Mary, don't you see, I did," Carl protested. "Every human of decent spirit is joined wherever a blow is struck at tyranny, whenever it happens."

But there was another story, another narrative and scenario. The students who delivered the Vietnam rap on Remcheck and Crowly had in passing added another chapter, an episode Carter, at the time, deemed apocalyptic. Who had they pissed-off enough to merit retaliation?

During Remcheck's early days at Barker, there were other rumors of Remcheck recruiting faculty and administrators for a quasi-undercover internal university intelligence agency whose members would be afforded additional salary increments and release time for reporting to Remcheck on the behavior and attitudes of dissident faculty and staff. Notably, only a few of those approached had been truly offended by the plan, although most had the good sense to refuse the offer. But Carter did not know, and could not easily calculate, how many had agreed to serve or who Remcheck and Crowly had prodded into retaliating?

"How do you know it's goat's blood?"

"I heard the Chief of Security talking to Crowly. He said it was goat's blood."

How the hell does goat's blood look? Carter thought. Maybe they found the body.

"Well, I'm sure they can clean it up," he said. "I'm going to have breakfast."

"John, this is Vesuvius. The rumble and lava of doom. Perdition. While the natives sleep."

"For whom?" Carter said. "Anyway, Carl, I'm not snoring, I'm hungry.

And this is not World War Three."

"But it is. This is Luther's *99 Thesis* on the Cathedral door, the most exciting thing that's happened around here in ten years."

"By the way," Carter said, "in a more mundane groove, do you have a student name Vivien Connors?"

Carl shook his head slowly, "No, I don't think so," he said, "no, not that I can recall. Is she visible? I mean she's not an alien? Or a cellophane cut-out?"

"She's in your ethics class."

"As vague and obscure as an ethical principle, then," Carl said.

"Well, maybe."

Carter replayed Carl's description of the fourth-floor. Arabic gratuities in goat's blood. Maybe cave paintings in New York subways. Cave paintings among the litter and debris of a disposable society shedding its psychic filth as it passes.

After New York, Carter had been amazed by the tube in London, the tidy, well-lighted, almost joyful atmosphere of the trains and stations and the lack of graffiti—except in the sections of the city occupied by Iranians and Arabs. There posters had been ripped from the walls, obscenities in English and slogans in Arabic spray painted on the stairway walls.

Who in the hell would want to paint Crowly's office with blood? Maybe Crowly did it. He could blame it on the faculty. There was any number of people he could scapegoat. Maybe he had used scapegoat's blood.

Carter took his place in the cafeteria line and ordered eggs and sausage, toast and black coffee. He was not usually in the breakfast habit. Food before noon weighed on him. But just now he'd take the chance to settle the imbalance he suffered from lack of sleep, to quiet the discomfort in his arms and hands.

On the fourth-floor Carter exited the elevator and slipped into the corridor among the crowd that had gathered to witness the vandalism. Security personnel had stretched a thin nylon cord from the doorknob of a storage room across the hall to a stanchion set between the vice chancellor's office and the elevator. A guard stood at each end of the cord.

The rent a cops have arrived. Carter was amused. Carl had called them "Nazi marionettes."

Outside the cordon a group of secretaries and clerks from admission and accounting milled about. They had picked up word of the spectacle and converged to marvel at the suggestion of violence.

Goats' blood? It looked to Carter like red paint. Where did Johnson get that stuff? Goats' blood. And Arabic symbols. Closer to the Jell-O-dipped finger wanderings of a four-year-old.

The black letters on the door to Crowly's office had been scarred and scraped, the glass scratched as if someone had taken a knife and attempted to obliterate the names. Several of the large white ceiling-globes along the hall had been smashed. The tops of two of the glass fossil-cases nearest Crowly's office were shattered, and again, as if someone had struck them with a fist or other blunt instrument. Pictures had been taken from the walls and lay scattered about, the glass broken, the frames twisted. A path of paint trailed away along the floor toward Carter's office.

Carter shrugged, taking care to step over the red splotches of scapegoat's blood that had run into the grooves of the shrunken, worn wooden planking.

A letter had been tacked to the corkboard on his office door. He took it off and glanced at the name, then read it.

> Dear faculty member,
>
> There is an eight-year-old child in Lancaster who has been on dialysis all his life and whose family is no longer able to pay for this treatment.
>
> A program has been set up whereby the child will be granted an hour of dialysis for every empty cigarette pack collected. In this case, an hour of dialysis equates to another day for the child, since he requires only an hour of treatment per day. Would you please announce this program to your students? If you would be willing to hold on to empty packs that you collect, I will come to your office and pick them up.
>
> The deadline for the program is December 27th.
>
> Contact me if you require any further information. Let me know when and if you have any empty packs for me.
>
> Thanks for your time.
>
> Robert Smedlbach
> Department of Psychology
> Barker State University

He slipped the key into the lock and snapped it open. He pulled out the bottom drawer of his desk, retrieved a cartoon of Marlboros and shook out the packs onto the desk. Seven. He stripped off the cellophane, tore open the top, and dropped the loose cigarettes into the drawer. He placed the flattened packs in a campus mail envelope, addressed it and went to the hall and dropped it in the campus basket.

Seven days he thought. Jesus. A cigarette pack for a day of life. Cheap enough. What is the price of a human life? How else could we measure our value? The R.J. Reynolds' scale of value.

The warm air of the small room, the overly warm air, made breathing difficult. He went to the window, intending to open it, then stopped to appraise, then reappraise the contents, the familiar arrangements of desk, chair, cabinet as he knew them. They now appeared in the proportion of distances and places, in relation to other objects in the room, not as they should have been, not as he remembered them. The jade plant on the bookcase, succulent and gem-like, was now set and standing farther from the wall, say, by an inch or two, an inch or two farther in the approximation of range perception would allow. A stack of three books at the top of the desk, lay blatantly at an angle with the corner. His habit was nearly compulsive to absent-mindedly align the corners of objects, ashtrays and books, napkins, place mats in restaurants.

Again he surveyed the room, once with a cursory sweep, and then more carefully and found a dozen or so additional items had been repositioned, or appeared to him to have been moved, as if a small gentle quake had shaken the room. Then he suspected someone had taken the room apart and attempted to reconstruct it and had not quite got it right.

Had the large drawer of his desk been open a quarter of an inch, as he now tried to remember? The desk chair he ritualistically pushed to the desk each day as a final finishing act before leaving, was now a foot from where it should have been. Had he inadvertently moved the chair to get to the drawer?

Was it Mason? Mason in a mild, wild, but well-tempered fit, as he had the morning he sat on the floor tearing pages from books, unable to bring himself to anything akin to violent demonstration?

Even though classes had reconvened Thursday following the ice storm, he had not seen Mason. That in itself was not unusual. Their Tuesday-Thursday schedules did not match—Carter had morning classes, Mason afternoon. Carter had put off calling Ardyth.

What about the cleaning ladies? It was not their habit to leave anything of themselves when they withdrew.

Carter picked up the phone, dialed an outside line, then held the instrument out at arms-length, regarding it as if it were contaminated. Bugged? But why? Why would anyone want to bug his phone? The rush and panic of his own paranoia amused him. He shook his head, then put the instrument down and decided to call Mason from the pay-phone outside the cafeteria in the basement.

He could not detect anything unusual about Mason's desk, could not tell if it had been disturbed—which, he decided, proved nothing.

Someone had been in the room and had pushed things around. But why? And better yet, who?

With his foot he pushed the chair farther away from the desk, as if it might be infested with vermin, then sat down.

For a very long while Carter sat at the desk hoping to accustom himself to the idea. He sat with the chair tilted back, feet on the desk, his hands hooked behind his head. What had the invader surmised, looking at this strange private place?

The impulse surged through him and he reached for the phone. He'd check with Crowly's secretary and ask if Mason had called. Had he said anything. Did he say . . . what?

No. That wouldn't work. He replaced the receiver and stood for a moment with his hand on the instrument. What if there was something in Mason's absence? Did Crowly know about that?

He could still hear voices in the hall, people milling about, chatting in hushed but excited tones. The muttering of the voices of hidden faces.

The clock above Mason's desk showed nine-fifty and Carter gathered up his grade-book, notes and text, and left the office with the door open and picked his way through the sightseers, along the fossil cases toward his classroom. At the intersection of the halls he nodded a quiet good-morning to the philosophy department secretary, Susan Griffin. She smiled and acknowledged the greeting, conspiratorially, he thought.

Before entering the classroom he paused to gather his thoughts. Today he did not feel up to lecturing, to explaining . . . what? Aristotle's Golden Mean? What would he ask? If Aristotle tried to examine man in terms of need, then what do we need to survive, to remain human? And what then?

Waiting for the late arrivals, as a divertissement, he asked a girl in the front row if she had a quarter. While she picked through her purse he opened his red grade-book upside-down, and shook it to show those watching that it was empty. Then he closed the book and when she handed him the quarter, slipped the coin into the pages at the top of the book as if he were inserting it into a thin, toy-bank. Holding the book with the index-finger and thumb of his left hand, with his right, he withdrew from the bottom of the book a dollar bill and handed it to the girl.

"Small payment for your assistance," he said, shaking the book open once again, upside-down.

"Where did the quarter go?" the girl said.

"It's in the dollar bill. If you look closely, you'll see it."

She examined the bill, slowly, then looked at Carter.

"Is this real?"

"Of the transgressions for which I may be blamed," Carter said, "I am not a counterfeiter. It may be a crime to print money, but the law says nothing about changing it. Quite the contrary, the law supports usury and money changers."

Five minutes after the hour he began the role. Thirty-seven on the list, twenty-six accounted for. Seventy percent present, Carter calculated.

Crowly had conducted a survey compiling statistics on individual classes, detailing percentage-retention-rates as well as the percentage of A's, B's and C's awarded in each class. The blind-bastard of big-brother watched over the academic world through the myopic eye of the VC's office.

Then memos. "To: All faculty. The number of students not completing classes for which they register is costing the university tens of thousands of dollars, not only in money refunded, but in future tuition and fees not collected when these students do not register for additional classes."

Public institutions driven by profit.

"Last time," Carter told the class, "I asked you to consider what it is humans need to be human. What it is without which we cannot remain human." He paused, then added, "What humans need, not what they want. Need as opposed to want."

As usual the ranks fell silent and fixed. Carter had been amused that open questions often served as an anesthetic. Local and brief, but mind-numbing.

One girl, her pale angelic face shrouded in the hooded-habit of finely textured and well-trimmed and groomed hair, bowed her head and stared at the book on her desk.

Was Carter to assume she did not know even what needs she might have, or having lived so splendidly and without want she truly could not understand the question? It was akin to a *Doonesbury* cartoon.

A boy in the back of the room in the corner stretched his arms, then with both hands on top of his head, twisted to look out to the blank, gray sky of the not too bright day.

"Let's begin with the obvious," Carter said. "With physical needs. What physical needs do humans have?"

"Food," a voice offered, and Carter scanned the room for the volunteer. "Food, drink and sleep," Carter added. "We need food, sleep and drink, if we hope to stay alive."

"Good food," another voice offered. "And strong drink."

Carter laughed, alone, and nodded. "And how good? And how strong? Are you talking about a hamburger and coke at McDonalds? Is that good and strong enough? And how much?"

"Sex," a hesitant male voice offered.

"How important is sex?"

"Very important."

"In what way?"

"Without sex there wouldn't be marriage or families. There wouldn't be a human society."

"You're saying human society is made possible by sex?"

"Well, isn't that why people get married?"

"Maybe not. Sex doesn't necessarily mean reproduction—nor vice-versa, and then marriage is only one part of human relations. How about friendship?"

"If I had my choice," the boy said, and let the phrase hang there. The class approved.

"I suppose that's as far as it goes," Carter said.

The girl with the groomed hair looked up to Carter with eyes as clear as any he had seen and the innocence of that vision stopped him for a moment.

"Do you imagine sex as a primary drive?" he asked. "Can we live full human lives without sex? And if we can't, what do you say about clergy or monks or other people, male or female, who live celibate lives?"

"I'd say they are crazy," a boy in the second row whined.

"Which doesn't answer the question," Carter said. "The question is whether or not people can live full lives without being sexually active. And then, exactly how much food, drink, sleep and sex do humans need?"

"What do you mean by a full life?"

The woman who asked the question, Carter presumed to be a bit older. She wasn't dressed nearly as well as the younger females in the class, and seemed more relaxed. He thought her name was Carol.

"That," Carter said, "is precisely how the matter is hinged."

"Some people need more than others," the well-groomed girl said. "Some people are satisfied with very little. Other people are not."

"But is that need or want?"

Several hands went up. Carter pointed to a boy in the back of the room.

"Are you saying everybody has the same needs?" he wanted to know.

"Aristotle asked it in those terms," Carter said.

"That's socialism," the boy said. "It sounds like communism."

"Socialism and communism are not necessarily the same thing," Carter said.

"The only thing that's different about them is the spelling," the boy replied.

"Bumper-sticker thinking," Carter said. "Which isn't thinking at all. Anyway, we were talking about human needs, not politics."

"Let's go back to sex," the boy with the whining voice suggested.

"Okay, what do humans need to live a full life?"

"They certainly need more than the bare necessities," Carol said.

"You and Oscar Wilde. 'Give me the luxuries and I can dispense with the necessities.'"

The class laughed, a bit self-consciously, and then a spate of hands went up. Carter designated one.

"We need as much as we can get," the girl said. She had a thin face, and long brown hair and wore glasses. "I mean, you never know when you will need what you have saved."

"You mean hoarded?" Carter said.

"But if you don't get it, somebody else will and when you need it, it won't be there," she said. "And if people have never had much they don't know what they're missing. I mean, it's not like we took everything away from them. Why should we give money to people who won't ever have anything anyway?"

The class applauded approval.

"Well," Carter said to the girl, "I'm not sure who "they" are, but suppose we talk about you. How much do you spend each year on clothes?"

The girl smiled. "Not nearly enough."

"What's enough?"

"That depends on where I'm going. What I need clothes for."

"Then you don't wear clothes simply to keep warm?"

"Of course not."

"Some people do."

"If that's why they need clothes, then that fits their need. I need clothes for other things."

"The country club?"

"As a matter of fact, yes. I mean, you were asking about a full life. Some people need country clubs to live full lives."

Carter flipped through a handful of analogies to expose the equivocation, then rephrased his original suggestion.

"I doubt if Aristotle would agree with your contention that country clubs are a part of human needs, or that they make it possible for humans to live full lives. When he talked about human need he had something a bit more sophisticated in mind.

"It comes down to this: human need is what people need if they are to remain human, not what you perceive you need and others don't.

"Let's go at this another way," Carter said. "Let's ask ourselves what man is. Then maybe we can determine what he needs to live a full life."

Carol raised her hand. "Well, man is an animal," she said, as if the finality was in the obvious.

"Just an animal?" Carter asked. "A dog is an animal. Is man no different from a dog?"

"Some people are worse than dogs," the boy with the glasses said.

"How many of you have dogs?" Carter asked.

A dozen or so hands went up.

"Does your dog have needs? If so, what are they? If we can't say for sure what man is, maybe we can back into it and say what he is not. By definition man is not a dog. Why so?"

"Because he doesn't bark at sticks or pee on the rug," Carol said. The class laughed. Carter laughed.

"But then, again," Carol said. "Maybe I'm wrong."

"Yeah, Carter said. "Man has been known to do things a good bit more bizarre than that.

"Of course, your dog needs food, water and sleep, just as you do. All animals do."

On the blackboard, using his right index finger as a piece of chalk, he printed MAN, and a foot to the right DOG.

"Let's make a list. What do humans need to remain human, and what do dogs need to be dogs? Start with dogs."

"You've already given most of it," Carol said. "Food, drink sleep. How about love? Animals need love."

"Can an animal live without love?"

She shook her head.

"I don't think so. At least not when they are small."

"Do animals need art and music—in other words, culture? Or is that exclusively human, and if so what does it say about man?"

The girl stared at Carter, shaking her head.

"There are people who do not need music," she said. "It's not that important."

"You're talking about rock fans?"

A murmur ran through the class.

"Man is created in the image of God. Dogs aren't," the girl with glasses said.

"In other words God is made in your image, not a dog's."

"The Bible says man shall have dominion over animals."

Carter shook his head. It had to happen.

"That tells us absolutely nothing," Carter said. "It merely clouds the issue. We haven't the slightest proof for a God, and know even less about what He might be. Unless you're going to tell me you've been talking to Him.

"Look at it this way. Granting the Christian teaching on god as the infinitely perfect being, there is no determinative proposition or relation of comparison between god and the entire order of finite beings, including man, with his concepts and language.

"If god is truly infinite in a perfect and not a privative or undefined sense, he must remain unknown to and unknowable by us."

The boy in the corner abandoned his starless gaze and raised his hand.

"That country club thing, and this talk about God is a real pig mentality," he said. "It's the kind of crap you'd expect to hear in a dump like this. All this place has is money and privilege, and nothing of heart or spirit. Anyway, the whole idea has to do with luck. Good or bad. The luck of where you were born. People in India think they're lucky to be born there. The Chinese don't want to be American. They hate Americans. They intend to defeat us. There are a lot of people who are unlucky enough to live around country clubs and churches and don't think they need them. In fact, we don't need golf courses, swimming pools or churches. We need planes and tanks and missiles to keep the Chinese out."

The girl with the glasses blushed. An uneasy hiatus fell on the room, the inhabitants set sullenly in their rows, rank and file.

This was a new variety of groomed and indoctrinated hoarders and squanderers, conservative and regressive, greedy and hostile and, in a very serious way, dangerous.

These were people insulated, already in their nineteenth year, and earlier, from anything approaching a humane response to the larger community, and possessed, again, by training, of a cynicism calculated to encourage collecting monetary benefits and to indulge their most absurd and childlike whims.

Yet that was not entirely true. Carter rebuked himself when he said "these people." There were a few who wanted to understand, who looked into themselves. A few semester before one such lovely scamp who had fallen into his class from a beach in California took the time to complain to him, and to his appreciation, beautifully so. Usually she showed up in class, and often at Carter's office, dressed in skimpy skirts and low cut blouses offering an abundant soft-spread of flesh, which, as intended, piqued Carter's appreciation. When they met other than in his office or the classroom their infrequent meetings were chance and she greeted him with "Hey, Doctor Carter. What's happenin man."

Several times she had mentioned the difficulty of the class, and then in frustration dropped a note on his desk.

> Dr. Carter,
>
> I want to make a confession to you. Before my enrollment in this class, I made the assumption that ethics philosophy would be a simple class if I just used logic. I can clearly see now that this is my most difficult class. The material in this class isn't organized information like that of psychology or history, or even math. This subject requires a great deal of introspection. And that in itself is not that tough, but the reading material is what is troubling me. I find myself constantly fumbling through my dictionary in order to make sense of what I just read. I am unable to read an entire paragraph and understand what I just read! I just wanted to let you know that I am extremely frustrated. I do have to say that it has given me new insight and developed my perception of the world. I guess it's one of those "no pain, no gain," situations. I'm sure that this class is beneficial to my life, but god it's hard!
>
> Sincerely,
> Julie

Her candor touched Carter. Her candor and willingness to brave the difficulties of unknowing, to struggle clear of the impediments, and go on faith where he had asked them to go, he understood, spoke well for her—at least for her spirit. She was not by any means the brightest of his students that semester, not even smart. But he couldn't remember ever one more sincere.

When he remembered her, it was in the spring sun, the trees in bud and greening. He'd see her out on the quad in a miniskirt and halter, waving to him, and hear her yelling, "Hey, man, Doctor Carter."

The arrogance and confidence of student proclamations, the conviction of their announcements struck deep in Carter. At the end of the hour, for homework, he asked them to consider for discussion the role of beauty and aesthetics in the scheme of human needs, and left the room and walked back to his office.

The torment of the inhabitants was not even the traditional arguments of right- and left-wing, but now a quarrelsome hatred.

A note tacked to the corkboard on his door said Ardyth had called and wanted him to call her. He dropped his books and sat down to catch his breath, holding the note out before him with both arms stretched forward on top of the desk. Eleven o'clock and he felt as if he'd run five miles. He was tired, winded and tired, weary, he would say, an early and unhealthy fatigue in his arms and legs.

Momentarily he set the telephone note aside and sifted through the packet of mail the secretary had dropped on his desk. Brochures and fliers advertising new books, a copy of *The Philosophical Quarterly*, a notification of an increase in AAUP dues and a memo from Crowly directing him to appear for a meeting Monday afternoon at two o'clock.

Carter read through the brief text of the memo several times, noting that AAUP President, Andrew Daly and Lamar Landeau had both received a copy.

Landeau as Dean of the Humanities Division, occupied an office in the vice chancellor's complex and saw and spoke to Crowly daily, and Carter assumed the copy to Landeau was Crowly the bureaucrat leaving a paper-trail. More than likely Landeau, an administrators left over from the pre-Remcheck days, but still a Crowly and Remcheck associate, was a part of the plot, whatever it was.

Carter dialed Crowly's office, and when the secretary answered, asked about the memo.

"I'll need a copy of the agenda for the meeting," Carter said. "And who will be there."

"I don't have that information," the secretary said.

"Then let me talk to Crowly."

"I'm sorry, but Dr. Crowly is in conference."

"When will he be out?"

"I don't expect him until four-thirty or five."

"I suppose he's given up eating lunch."

"I don't know. He will be at lunch from twelve until two."

Carter hung up and sat for the next few minutes trying to imagine what Crowly might want.

Had it to do with Mason? Did Crowly want to know about Mason's problems? Was he concerned with the effect of the letter of dismissal on Mason?

No. Not Crowly. No, Crowly was no shepherd. Crowly the man was not much better. Either way, he was not thinking about Mason. This was about something else. But what? And why the formality of the memo?

And a copy to the president of the AAUP? Who knew what they were up to? Carter abandoned the inquiry. He promised to think about it later. Within the next day or so he'd corner Crowly for an explanation.

Before he could add to the idea a slight sound at the door, a soft tap claimed his attention.

"Come in," Carter said and Timo Clark push the door partly open.

She was dressed in a loose, brightly designed blouse and Nigerian lappa. She wore a wide, intricately braided head band and a pair of large horn-rimmed glasses.

Standing in the doorway although tall, she seemed diminutive.

"Do you have a moment?" she said, and Carter stood awkwardly, to hold open the door, to further welcome her.

"I have a moment," he said. "In fact, I have a whole bunch of moments."

Carter pulled the chair over from Mason's desk and motioned for Timo to be seated.

"This is a surprise," he said. "What are you doing in this part of the woods?"

"I was wondering if you would have time to talk to me."

"Well, lady, what do you think?"

"If I'm correct," she said, "I think you have had a bad day."

"Yeah," Carter said, "but at the end of the semester every day is a bad day. Although right now it's getting better."

Then he added, "How did you know that?"

"There is a belief in my tribe that when you are anointed, you can see evil and know where it will come." She smiled.

"Which tribe?"

"Fulani."

"And you're anointed?"

"Yes. You see, I have been told my contract for the spring will not be renewed. So, I am one of the select. Do you believe that?"

"Do I believe you are leaving?"

"Yes."

"But contracts are for two semesters."

"No. This fall I was given a single semester assignment."

"That's ridiculous. So they've denied you tenure."

"Yes. In a way."

"How? Your tenure committee?"

"Oh, they were quite agreeable."

"Agreeable?"

"I got very good reports. They will file a complaint."

"But regardless, you're out."

"Yes. I believe so."

"What you're saying is that in effect they've done away with tenure."

"Yes. But I suppose there's not much to do about it."

"I suppose not. You could take them to court."

Timo looked around the room, then focused on Carter.

"For a long time I've wanted to go home. Maybe this will be a good chance for that. I have been offered a position at the university in Lagos. Working with Professor Soyinka."

"The Nobel playwright."

Timo smiled and folded her hands and brought them up to her lips.

"Yes," she said, "I'm very excited. I met him in Paris last summer. And I also have an offer from the University of London."

The University of London. The few times he had been to England Carter had never gotten enough time in London. There was just too much. Too much to see, to do. Jesus. How was that for a fantasy. Teaching in London. A year or two among the Brits."

"But either way you're gone," he said

"Yes, it is for certain."

Carter had not expected this. No matter the transience of university life, he was never prepared for people to leave. What you should prepare for but do not, creeps up on you, he thought.

"How long have you been away?"

"Twenty years. No. Twenty-two years. Since I was sixteen."

"Many things have changed," he said.

"Yes. People change and so do their surroundings, that is the way it is. But I wanted you to know. You have been very helpful to me. And friendly. I want to thank you."

"I'm not sure what I've done," Carter said, "but if it was good, you deserved it. I'm extremely pleased for you."

The compliment sounded hollow, resonating with a good bit less sincerity than Carter intended and he hoped she did not think he was envious.

"Since I may not get another chance. Although we've not been really close, I'm sorry you're leaving. Even though we didn't see each other often—I always looked forward to the next time. You've been a valuable member of this faculty—a valuable and wonderful member, and I'll miss you.

"I don't know, maybe we should have been closer friends. And I'm sorry I didn't do anything about it. I should have."

"I know," she said. "I would have preferred that. But I think you were worried about other things. People worry about many items and do not get around to making the other things. I didn't know."

"I was," he said, "but that's over now. When will you be leaving?"

"Monday. I'm going to London first. I want to tell them personally that I will not be taking the appointment they offered me. Then after a week I'll go on to Frankfort and Lagos."

Carter wondered what he could say. Timo sat perfectly still at the end of the desk with her hands arranged and lying in her lap.

"Well, I'll miss you," Carter said. "But I already told you that."

She sat perfectly still as he had seen her do on a number of occasions, simply sharing her presence with another person as if she were sharing words, or caresses.

"Yes," Carter said finally. "You are anointed. You are among the select. But that doesn't have anything to do with Barker State and not getting a new contract. And hell, who knows, maybe one of these days I'll end up in Lagos. If so, I'll look for you. God knows it could happen."

Timo seemed to sense that he would not have more to say and rose slowly.

"I must go now," she said and extended her hand to Carter.

She took his hand and held it, cradled his hand in those long, thin, exquisite fingers he had so much admired and imagined. She held his hand for a short time, then excused herself, softly, quietly, and left the office, and he sat heavily in his chair trying to understand the conversation, to assimilate the reality of her leaving.

In her he found a wonderful human presence, and once considered even without sex Timo would have been a perfect companion.

So this is it. He berated himself for not having seized the opportunity, for his timidity, for allowing her to slip away without having made an attempt to know her better.

Not often did he regretted a connection left undone, but he did now. He regretted it, and painfully so.

When he came out of his office half-an-hour later the hall was vacant except for the maintenance men at work on tall ladders replacing the broken ceiling globes. He took the elevator down, checking if he had change for the phone, wondering what Ardyth might tell him.

Chapter XIV

In the dark of the December late afternoon and charred face of the weather wilted winter landscape, the river lay black and sullen. It lay quiet, almost immobile, a blank black passage without even the stir of a chilled breeze to give it life. It lay like a great flat slick-skinned serpent between the student union and the university medical complex, sliding on a nearly level plane without urgency, dispatched not by the fierce force of headwaters, but encouraged only by the slow imperceptible pull of rotation of earth to pass unobtrusively and without breath. On either side its banks rose sharply several feet before leveling off and lifting gently to long steep knolls that in turn buttressed the pilings of a single arched footbridge.

By five it was no longer possible to see more than several hundred feet from the bridge. The mercury lamps goose-necked from the railings over the water, and glowing in the gathering darkness, further shrouded the distant silence of water.

Most of the afternoon Carter had been walking. His sore knee ached, and he stood now, on the bridge watching the apparition- like shapes of people passing alone and in pairs or clusters, before vanishing into the darkness. Behind him, a thousand feet or so, where the water fell over the dam, the specter sliding hidden and sullen beneath the bridge splashed and roared alive.

He stood for a long time in the white circle from the vapor-lamps, then leaned over the rail to stare into the dark water. Several times he turned his back to the heavy, coarse balustrade, raised his eyes along the brick wall of the hospital and the long row of fifth-floor windows. He counted over seven, twice to be sure, then traced a trajectory down the wall to the sidewalk and the brick flowerboxes along the parking lot.

From where he stood in the darkness the windows were indistinguishable, bland, regimented architectural necessities, reoccurring with monotonous regularity along the full length of the wall.

A soft glow in the window, framed by drapes hanging open, a portal, a passage. From the window the previous night in the frenzy, the perfectly contained frenzy of dementia, Mason had taken flight to the rare and thin air of human failing—human desire stretched and frustrated and wounded—and plummeted to his death.

Carter had not yet got it through his head. Not the facts, the desultory bits and pieces he had gathered from Ardyth on the phone, and not the character of the act, an act of a man knowing he shall not survive, putting himself, for whatever reason, in the graceless jeopardy of nature's irrefutable conditions, falling quickly, freely, the sensation of flight assaulting his senses, falling quickly and surely, seeking respite, relief from his anguish and torment.

Carter tried to imagine a reconstructed minutiae of the image in the last seconds of the journey, seeing Mason again and again in a hospital gown, moving and fixed, at a distance, then telescoped and larger as if Carter could be both here and there, beside him, seeing Mason simultaneously from various angles moving and fixed as he approached the window, the now opened passage, raising himself, head lowered to avoid the sash, pausing in the progress of his exit, momentarily to consider something he had forgotten to remember, balanced, shifting his weight over the sill, for a brief, fixed moment, suspended before giving up what he could not recall to topple into free-flight of air and gravity, tumbling slightly, the hospital gown billowed in the eddies of air, the rush of the currents of breeze his body created roaring at his ears as he plummeted earthward.

Ardyth had said, "John Carter, Mason Oldam is dead. I do not yet understand how he died. They have said he fell from the fifth-floor at the hospital."

"When did it happen?" Carter asked, and when she said she did not know, he could not pursue the matter further, just then.

"This afternoon I will make arrangements for Mason Oldam. But I will be home after six o'clock."

Carter bowed again to the water, his elbows propped on the coarse concrete, the chill of the black winter late afternoon at his bare neck fingering the skin at the base of his skull. It had begun to snow, a steady, heavy drifting down of white through the shroud of the lamps hung over the river, a veil enveloping the river, the realization of Mason's going filling the air around him.

"Mason Oldam is dead," Ardyth's voice repeated to him.

"Jesus Christ," he told himself, and said "Jesus Christ," again, this time to Mason. "What did you do?"

His words dropped dead on the chilled air, and then in the shadows, in the improbable, somber chambers of his imagination, his vision, in the deep of the night he apprehended the specter of a single, silent boat on the river, poled by a man in a long coat and black boater, the water motionless, and a passenger in white crouched in the bow, holding to the gunnels, his face grim and stained with streaks of blood and dirt, the small cleansing rivulets of tears.

Carter ran along the bridge-rail, raised his hand, waved and tried to shout, but could not. Then he watched as the boat poled away up the river approaching the farthest bank.

Later, sitting in the Oldam living-room Carter would tell Ardyth about his vision.

"I saw Mason tonight," he told her, doubting his own sanity.

She nodded, condescendingly, he thought, tolerating the inappropriateness of his statement.

"Many times," she said, "when those we care about die, we see them. I too have heard his voice. I hear him, but he is not there."

Carter could not see beyond her glasses, and could not from her voice tell how well she was or was not taking Mason's death. He had come to pay his respects, to offer what help he could, and had been surprised she was alone.

The news of death usually brought out the long-necked birds of prey, to feed on the emotional carrion. He imagined the relatives, whoever they were, would be in town soon.

The living-room was warm and Carter realized just then he had been chilled for the last several hours. The furniture was arranged differently than he remembered and a number of expensive prints and at least two oil-originals he had not seen before hung on the walls. One, a soft focus of a nude young woman sleeping on a bed in a scatter of bed-clothing, caught his attention.

A small Christmas tree decorated with red and green ornaments and tinsel and small glass candle-bulbs stood in front of the double window. The lights were not on.

Ardyth sat in the big chair across from him on the opposite side of the coffee-table

"Mason Oldam did not want a funeral," she said. "We will have a memorial service for him next month. You will come, John Carter, and read an eulogy for him. Mason Oldam said John Carter would read an eulogy for him when he died."

Carter looked away. This wasn't what he had expected or wanted to hear. What else had Mason expected he might do? What could he have done to have avoided this night? He hadn't expected the impossibility of retractions, of providing solace when solace changes nothing. His voice faltered and broke, failing beneath the weight of the monumental futility, the leaded burden of the ineptitude of devotion and passion. And then Carter wept, and felt like a fool, weeping as he could not remember having before for anyone or anything.

Ardyth sat next to him on the couch, he wanted to believe, to share his sorrow, finding her grief in him, a grief that did not just now allow her the luxury of tears. Faced with the terrible reality of Mason's death, to avoid the storm, the small timid animal in her had withdrawn deeper into the burrow. She sat with her hands folded, head bowed, staring at the black pit of the empty fireplace.

"I will get us coffee," she said, finally, breaking their silence, and Carter thought her voice had softened. "Will you have coffee, John Carter?"

Not yet trusting himself to talk, Carter nodded.

"Buddy will be home shortly," Ardyth said.

"Does... does he know?" Carter asked, his breath catching.

"No," she said, and Carter read into the slow, even tone of the word, the pain and dread she must have had for the task of telling her son his father was dead.

Carter sipped the black coffee and felt better, still embarrassed he had come with the good-will-of-consolation and had himself needed to be consoled.

"How did it happen?" Carter asked, recovered somewhat.

"He fell from the roof of the hospital," Ardyth said.

"From the roof? How did he do that?"

"I do not know."

"Wasn't it the fifth-floor? Did he jump?"

"They have said he fell," Ardyth repeated.

"Does it make sense?"

She did not answer immediately, but straightened up, and the coffee cup and saucer she held clicked when she brought them together.

"Why would you ask?"

"I don't know. It's just the kind of question anyone would ask."

"What is it to make sense?"

"How does someone fall from the roof of a building when he's supposed to be under lock-and-key on the fifth-floor?"

"No, I do not think Mason would kill himself."

They heard the backdoor open and the boy come into the kitchen. Carter hadn't seen him in over a year, the thin, almost emaciated body, bone-thin torso and long arms with knobby elbows and wrists, in Carter's memory, a weasel of a youth, well stocked with tics that twisted his face behind the smudged glasses that obscured his eyes.

"Buddy," Ardyth said, "is that you."

"Yes it is," the boy said, in an almost perfect imitation of her voice.

"John Carter is here."

The boy did not answer, but came into the living-room. He carried a stack of books under one arm and placed them on the end-table near the Christmas tree. Within the year he had grown five or six inches and taken on the body of a small but nicely developed man. He no longer wore glasses and his eyes were an intriguing shade of hazel green. His hair was thick and softly textured with an auburn dusting of red and brown.

So it happens, Carter thought. The metamorphosis. The worm into the Monarch. They labor along, biding time and then—Poof!

"Do you remember John Carter?"

"Yes, I do, mother," Buddy said, and as an afterthought, a bit impulsively, thrust out his right hand. Carter took the hand, the soft boy's hand and shook it.

"It's good to see you again, Buddy," Carter said.

"Why haven't you visited us?" he said.

Carter had had no experience with people this age and size, and assumed from what he heard that such creatures were generally nothing if not a pain-in-the-ass. In his teen years he had been. Jesus. Obnoxious ingrate, rude, insolent—sometimes just mindlessly unkind.

He watched the boy closely trying to decide what it was about him that seemed so unusual. He was taller, his presence more imposing.

His manner was quiet and seemed to Carter that of a much older person. He had a natural, fluid ease, as if the air about him was cushioned, elastic and pliable. When they shook hands, he held Carter's gently in his, then nodded and smiled with a warm sincerity. He was attentive, as if indeed, he had wondered the entire year why Carter had not visited.

"You are always welcome here," he said. "Ardyth and Mason and I welcome you."

Carter had not had a son. It came to him most people do not have a son or sons, although it was beguiling to imagine what could have been. Yes, he had considered it. In fifteen years he'd be seventy. There was still time. That would push the clock a bit. And then there were no guarantees. Nothing to say he'd make it—or the child. Not to mention the need for a willing, fertile female. What about Vivien? He hadn't seen her since she left him at the library. No. The entire enterprise was fraught with risks.

The boy looked past Carter, around the room, then to Ardyth.

"Will father be home tonight?"

Ardyth put her hand over her mouth and said a stifled, muffled, "No, not tonight."

"But Dr. Goldenstein said Mason could come home today?"

"Yes," Ardyth answered. "That is what he said."

The boy seemed satisfied with this.

"I did not mean to intrude," he said to Carter, "but you will have to come and see us more often."

He reclaimed the books from the table beneath the picture, the quiet, soft print of the young woman, and exited into the front hall and the stairs to the second-floor.

When the boy left the room, the shock of Mason's absence, struck Carter anew. He could work it into his mind, finalize the fact, forget it for a moment, and then had to begin again.

Carter was still looking at the print of the girl. The sensual beauty of the form, of the warm contours of the woman's legs and breasts, her arm lifted over her head.

"That was Mason's favorite," Ardyth said. "Buddy painted it for him last year."

"It's beautiful," Carter said. "I can see why."

"Yes," Ardyth said. "He said Buddy should work seriously at his art."

"Will you be all right?" Carter asked.

Ardyth nodded.

"Yes. I think so. I cannot feel much presently. But I will have to be all right."

She walked with him to the front hall and waited while he slipped into his coat.

"If I can help, you will call me?"

"Yes."

"And if you hear anything about how it happened, I would like to know."

The melodic notes of a piano dropped down the stairs and Carter stopped again, hesitant, wondering what else he could say, what else there might be.

"That is Buddy playing," Ardyth said. "He will play all night if I do not interrupt him."

Carter assumed at first the music had come from a recording.

"I had better go," Carter said, no longer trusting himself.

"Thank you, John Carter, for visiting us," Ardyth said.

Without more Carter went out into the white darkness. Behind him the green Christmas wreath hung at the center of the door as black as night, and the haunting melancholy notes audible in the distance of the closed house trailed him down the empty steps to the street.

Apollo, Carter imagined, with a mix of grief and awe. Blessed by the gods. The rare gifts, a beautiful boy with rare gifts—and a timid, tough little woman, a woman Carter loved dearly, who would before the night was done, interrupt the rhapsody and try to explain to her son that his father was dead.

Carter tracked home the several dozen mid-December blocks to College Street and before going in stopped on the porch to knock the snow from his shoes and watch, the few moments, until the tracks he had left in passing on the sidewalk were no longer visible.

Just then Carter stumbled in the mist, the implication, or lack of it in Mason's death. He had read the books, done his homework, and had, he reasoned, a pretty thorough understanding of what death could mean to the living.

But now he was no longer sure.

He re-entered the sarcophagus and echo of the darkened house and built a fire and sat alone until near midnight, preferring then to be alone in the firelight of the dark living-room, rising only occasionally to replenish his supply of bourbon, or to prod the fireplace coals to life with another log.

Then it bottomed out. No matter the path, he came always, again, to the beginning. Clearly, death defied reason. This he knew well enough. But Mason's death rung with the additional contradictions of place and time. He wondered why, if what he heard of fact, what he had been told, why no one seemed bothered by the contradictions or at least the inconsistencies.

The wood in the box was seasoned, and when he laid the pieces on the fire, cleanly split chunks of oak, the bark cracked and fumed with a sweet smell. It flamed alive with yellow tongues licking into the hollow of the blackened flue and in the shifting shades of transformation the fleeting specter he again saw Mason's face.

Carter sat up straight and stared at the fire. And for a brief moment, he could imagine the agony, the terrible uncompromising agony Mason must have carried.

Finally, drunk and exhausted, he made his way to bed. Katherine Marie had not yet come in, from where he did not know, and he lay a few minutes in the dark listening to the downstairs hall clock count out twelve chimes, then passed quickly into a short, deep sleep.

At two-fifteen the wind woke him and he found Katherine Marie asleep, curled in a fetal position in the center of the bed with her back to him, her arms wrapped over her head. Fending off the wind and night spirits, he guessed, and wondered if she had heard about Mason. He wanted to tell her and raised his hand to wake her, but changed his mind and withdrew the hand and set it down softly on his chest. She would not take waking kindly. Prodded from sleep, she would have little patience with being disturbed despite the information and his reasons for wanting just then to tell her about it.

For the next three hours he lay in the darkness, passing in and out of a fitful half-sleep, tormented by the night sounds, his mind riddled with the anomalies and peculiarities of Mason's death.

Just before dawn, he remembered the clock striking five, but could not account for anything more. When he came to it was nine-ten and Katherine Marie had already departed. In just this way their comings and goings drifted from day to day.

He rolled to the far side of the bed and hung an arm out over the edge into the chilled air. He had found little of respite and reprieve in sleep, and his mouth burned with the brackish taste of time blunted and severed without recompense or requital.

A heavy, frozen, opaque glaze hung on the bedroom windows, and he knew, this day, too, there would be no break in the weather, no forgiveness for folly or the foolhardy. The sinister whine of the winter wind gathered in the eaves of the old house and lashed out whipping the bare trees.

His back and knee ached, a dull, obdurate pain that intensified whenever he moved, and for the first time in memory he was tired, truly too tired to get out of bed.

Half-an-hour later in the kitchen, he poured out a cup of coffee and spread the morning paper on the table. On the bottom of page one was a small article under a brief heading. "Philosophy Professor Found Dead." Found? The word struck Carter. Found. As if he had lain dormant, preserved in the bowels of a crevasse for an epoch or two. Found dead. But never found alive. The entire episode neutered, stripped of personal implications. The discretion of the press. What might they have said? Philosophy Professor Assassinated by "whom?" Professor Undone by "what?" Professor's Demise Traced to Abuse and Terminal Neglect.

He folded the paper and set it aside, then opened it and reread the article.

How had Mason gotten onto the roof? And why had he assumed Mason had jumped from a fifth-floor? And why the seventh window? Where had he collected that tidbit? From Ardyth. And where had she collected it? And what did Mason know? What was it that drove him? What impulse choreographed the final dance?

Carter rested at the table, when Mrs. Elmore, his north side neighbor, emerged from her backdoor onto the porch with a broom.

Ancient and durable, a twig of a woman, no more than five feet tall, with thin gray hair and an obstinate nature, she maintained a perverse belief in her own ability to do whatever she decided she wanted, and to survive doing it.

The years before, when Carter had taken up residence in the old house on College Street beside the Elmores, he considered her daft, having already given up to time the better part of her senses, a bit loony, certainly harmless, and had not expected her to last more than a few years. But she had lasted, and over the years Carter became acquainted with the strange invincible mettle that was hers, and had to revise his first estimations.

In the last few years she lost her husband, two children, a grandchild and God only knows how many friends. The parade to the graveyard lurched along steadily, if with stops and starts, and Carter remembered thinking, one day soon she's going to crack, just give up and call it quits.

But crack, she did not. Out of the passing of time and people she ossified into an indomitable shriveled and bedeviled Phoenix struggling to pull itself free from the ashes and dust of the consuming fires of failing flesh. Amazingly her flesh did not fail. It wrinkled and sagged and hardened and seemed to diminish, but it did not fail.

And out of the depths of what Carter not only did not know about her, but would not have guessed, while her countenance grew more grim with each passing, her posture more rigid and determined, she simply stood fast, hard and fast. And now, in a metaphor of what he did know of her, she had taken up arms, so to speak, and gone again on this morning into battle.

Scantily clad and bareheaded she came out of the kitchen with a broom as tall, if not taller than she was. With quick little defiant jerks she whacked at the snow, pushing it towards the edge of the porch, beating back the fine, white dust, fashioning for herself a small clearing. She worked steadily and had all but finished, near the top of the steps, when a swirling dust-devil of white powder marched across the yard and engulfed the porch. Caught in the cross currents of the wind, staggering precariously close to the edge, enshrouded by the blur, she vanished from Carter's view.

Carter emptied a half-cup of coffee into the sink and refilled the cup. When the phone rang, he let it ring a second time, watching Mrs. Elmore reappear and prepare to mount another attack. Reluctantly he picked up the phone, a little surprised to hear Katherine Marie's voice.

She had just heard about Mason.

"Does anyone know what happened?"

"I don't know," Carter said, "maybe somebody, somewhere."

After a brief pause she said, "John, you make that sound positively ominous."

"It is," Carter said. "The man is dead."

Again a pause. "I know how you feel about Mason," Katherine Marie said, "but being bitter won't help."

Another non sequitur for the litany, Carter thought.

For his part, he was not equipped with a prescriptive remedy for grief. Again Minus Factor came to mind, sitting with his back to the wall, grinning.

"You white folk make too much of dying."

Well, you goddam right. Somebody has to. Call it a reverence for life, or whatever you want. When someone disappears, it hurts and the pain is not easily or immediately dissipated.

"I'll be home by three," she said. "I want to stop and pick up a Christmas tree. Will you be all right until then?"

He guessed he would, replaced the receiver and decided he needed to get out of the house. He had been sitting alone for too long. He snapped off the coffee-maker then unplugged it.

In the hall the phone rang a second time, and he spent the next ten minutes assuring Morgana that everything would be done to help Ardyth.

"How is she taking it."

"From all indications, better than I am," Carter said.

"Then you've talked to her."

"Yes. Last night."

"I suppose she has a minister."

"A minister?"

"Yes. You know, Carter. Minister, as in church."

The likelihood had eluded Carter. Religion. He had expected relatives, but not the churchites. Morgana was right. The somber voices of blackcoats, the well-phrased euphemisms were certain to get into the act.

"Do you know how it happened?" Morgana wanted to know. "Carl said he heard it was suicide. He talked to Goldenstein, and apparently the police have it listed as a suicide."

"What else did Goldenstein say?"

"He said Mason had been badly depressed. But we knew that, didn't we?"

"Mason wouldn't kill himself," Carter said. "Depression is one thing, killing yourself something else. We get so accustomed to listening to the cheap-ass psychological nonsense, we get to believing that every time someone gets a hangnail he wants to knock himself off."

Carter had on his coat and was headed for the door when the phone rang a third time. He glanced at the hall clock, then picked up the receiver. This time it was Andrew Daly. Daly's voice was weak and flat, and although Carter did not find anything unusual in that, he did have difficulty understanding what Daly was saying and exactly why he had called.

Long ago Daly had fallen from the graces of Carter's respect. A little man, and not altogether intelligent, during his tenure as Barker State AAUP President, to solidify and promote his position and prestige, Daly had made a number of personal deals with the administration. Otherwise, his solutions to faculty problems were timid exercises intended to avoid offending anyone.

More than once Carter pointed out that because of people like Daly, neither the AAUP nor the Faculty Senate had any power at Barker. To Carter's mind, Daly typified the obeisance, the fumbling, groveling obeisance and timidity of the Barker State faculty, and the profession generally.

"I called to offer you condolences for the death of Mason Oldam."

"Why call me?" Carter said. "Did you call his wife?"

"Well, no, not yet. I called you because you and he were friends."

"What about his family?"

"We will send a delegation to visit them. And flowers."

For a moment Carter regretted his antagonism.

"It's not a very nice thing," Carter said. "We're all upset about it."

"I just wanted you to know you have our sympathy."

Just then Carter beheld himself in the hall mirror. Sympathy? His eyes were bloodshot and hung with heavy bags. He had not combed his hair and it stood on end and waved whenever he moved his head.

I don't need sympathy, Carter thought. And what about Ardyth and young Mason? Save some for him. Sell him the sympathy. A bit of sympathy to replace your old-man.

"By the way, while you're on the phone, as you should know Mr. Daly, I've been summoned to Crowly's office for a séance on Monday. You have any idea what he's got in mind?"

Daly's voice faltered.

"No," he said, "I didn't know. I wouldn't know what it could be."

From the tone of his voice, Carter knew Daly had called to tell him something but had changed his mind. When the time came he had come up short.

Carter hung up the phone and left the house, headed for Murphy's, the residue of the matter swirled about him as bitter as the morning wind.

In spite of the pain in his back and leg, the severity of the winter air, the raw beauty of the morning gave him new life. He was doubly anesthetized, stoned by the blow of Mason's death, the horror and brutality of death, and overwhelmed by the ominous mortal scaling of things bounded by the resolutions and protocol of nature. John Carter, walking a street on planet earth, in winter, thinking of a dead friend.

An accident, Carter believed, the whole thing is an accident, and nobody's attempt to give it order will do so.

The thin dry snow blowing across the walk in front of him, that followed and blew into his steps as he vacated them, the bitter winter air, were the bits and pieces of a magnificent paradox; the order of disorder.

How could order of any kind find its way out of disorder? Accident.

What had Professor Gould said?

"One in a trillion. A remote and thoroughly improbable accident."

"Try this," he proposed to a class one day. "Stand at the top of a five mile high ladder on a five thousand acre parking lot with the words of the Bible cut into individual letters of the alphabet in a basket and turn the basket upside down to drop the confetti of the letters onto the surface below. How many times would you have to do it before the characters would land arranged precisely in their original configuration, printed as they are in the Bible?"

Not only did the class not comprehend the enormity and significance of the suggestion, but in a perverse attempt to avoid tangling with the idea, they maneuvered the discussion into an inquisition for desecrating a sacred document. In feigned offense, brought on in part at least, Carter suspected, by the shock of just the slightest whiff of what the unyielding prospect of eternity, nothingness, the infinite and absolute meant to a finite mind of time and space, they drifted into a prosecution of why anyone would want to tamper with God's word.

"Which Bible?" a boy near the door wanted to know.

"Would it matter?" Carter had responded, slipping, giving the inquiry credibility.

"Of course," the boy said, "there's only one true Bible. The rest are fakes."

"You're avoiding the question," Carter said. "The possibility that existence as we know it, the presence of Homo sapiens in this universe, and in fact, in the material world, intelligence, awareness, the electrical impulses running through the atoms and molecules and cells and synapses of your brain may be an accident."

The class roared its approval, but immediately set out to explore what the punishment might be for questioning the Bible.

"You have to trust in the word of God," a girl said. "Otherwise, He will punish you. And once the word of God is written, man has no right to destroy it."

Finally, one of the brighter students, a girl Carter had come to depend upon for intelligent, if somewhat veiled observations, raised her hand.

"But there is order," she said, "order in the way the material world is connected. There are things such as gravity, which always work, and things like the speed of light which do not change."

Carter agreed, rather. "As far as we know," he said. "But what if these, too, are accidents?"

Thus, so, he took instruction from them. And filled with the wonder and mystery, the torn and worn muscles of his legs stretched and pulled, adrift without sextant or compass, with nothing of mean-time by which to fix his star, he tacked and veered toward Murphy's. He steered into the comfort and smoke-musk and stood for a moment stamping his feet warm before ordering a beer. His face burned from the wind, chaffed and red, and his lungs ached, but it was invigorating and simulating.

Silver loops of tinsel stretched the length of the long room further decorated with red crepe-paper bells. A scrawny, stunted, bush-like Christmas tree took up the end of the bar nearest the front booths. Smaller tinsel hoops hung from the tree, along with a couple of bare strands of lights and a random scattering of red and green ornaments. At the top, instead of a star or Santa Claus, some wag had set a green plastic frog with a bar-bell held over his head, his muscles bulging.

A straggle of early drinkers and pool-players populated the room and Murphy's hulk worked slowly at the far end of the bar rolling aluminum kegs of beer into the cooler. The voice-over of a TV sitcom rerun drifted through the smell of burned-out cigarettes and stale beer.

When Carter came in, Murphy stopped and wiped his hands on the great round of his apron and leaned on the bar as if he had been waiting for him.

"Hey, Doc," he said, "you know that teacher got killed?"

Carter sipped his beer and nodded.

"Yeah, he said, "you might say I knew 'that teacher.'"

"I was looking at his picture in the paper and wondered if I knew him. He ever come in here?"

Carter paid for his beer.

"I don't know. He could have—but to tell you truth, I doubt it."

"Well, I remember most of the teachers, and I think I saw him a couple times. I got a knack for faces, you know, but the guy I got in mind was older than that picture they had in the paper. The guy that come in here looked like he was scared. Had this real wrinkled face and eyes that were round like half-dollars. Like maybe somebody surprised him and he didn't know how to take it."

A smile crossed his large round face.

"I got a good memory for people's habits. You'd be surprised what you can tell just by watching people. There ain't much goes on here that I don't see and once I see it, hell, I got a memory like a goddam elephant."

And a body like one, Carter thought. A goddam elephant would like that body. Carter wondered how Murphy bathed, if he did, or if he had a keeper hose him down.

"He might have," Carter said, "he might have come in here on occasion".

A memory for people's habits? What kind of habits would Mason have had? What did Murphy know, if it was Mason? It was anyone's guess. Carter didn't know, but he did know Murphy's appetite for gossip outweighed even his consumption of drink and food.

A voracious, vicious gossip, most of what he said, even when he had nothing to report, especially when he had nothing to report, he laced with innuendo and intimations. And as always, he had an insidious, suggestive smile, which just now beamed down on Carter.

Murphy's behavior was another matter. The reputation of his personal habits had inspired stories that had over time become Barker State campus legend. The trail of his exploits, if committed to print, would have read like the script of a not too well contrived, but sleazy, comic soap-opera.

Of course Murphy took delight in repeating the details of his deeds, act and reaction, dressed in the embellishments gained with time, expanding each until the truth, the facts, or whatever, were obscured in the elaborations of the fictions.

Story to wit: a summer afternoon, in the bright-light of day, Murphy transported his three-hundred-pound-bulk up a ladder to the gabled roof of the house of a local politician, and after entering a dormer to the master bedroom, deposited the hoard of his undraped rolls of fat and flesh on the bed for the lady of the house to discover.

By his own admission, he was stoned at the time, and when she discovered him and commanded him to leave, he said he demanded to know what she was doing in his bedroom, and then sought her forgiveness for his condition, hastening to explain that despite her need, he was, just then, only slightly incapacitated, though still unable to serve her as had he been straight, he otherwise might have.

"She did not scream," the story unfolded, "but mulled the proposal for a moment, not only as if the idea might not be totally repugnant, but as if it very well may have fit her fancy.

"She said, 'Do I know you?' and when I said, 'That shouldn't come between us,' she said, 'I am not in the habit of going to bed with men I do not know.'"

When she demanded again that he leave her bed and bedroom, he feigned a seizure, rolled his eyes into his head and spastically shook with such authenticity and conviction she took pity on him. She went to the bath adjacent the bedroom and retrieved a wet cloth and placed it on his brow.

Then, as he said, his passion inflamed by the touch of her hand, the soft and sensual touch of her woman's hand, he immediately regained his lost senses, and pulled her into the bed beside him, filled with appreciation and devotion, intent upon returning the favor by doing just service (which she did not refuse) for one who could be so kind.

The legend did not reside in the preposterousness of the seduction, but in the story's decoration of the husband finding them at frolic in the bed and calling the police and Murphy taking flight down the stairs, exiting by the front door, to avoid arrest and prosecution, exiting in such haste he abandoned his clothing and left girded only in the brilliant wrap of a single white sheet, the mass of his milk-pale flesh a shine in the bright afternoon sun.

The legend rested in that with his exit Murphy escaped not only arrest but, for obvious reasons, prosecution and conviction as well, so in campus lingo and slang, "Pulling a Murphy" became a referent for perpetrating an outrageous stunt and avoiding the consequences of stunt; doing the unthinkable and getting away not only to tell about it, but to relate it as an unblemished comedy.

"You know," he said to Carter, "I bet he got killed over a woman. More'n likely a woman said she didn't want to make it with him anymore and he did himself in. Like the country song 'I Don't Know Whether to Go Bowling or Kill Myself." Murphy laughed.

"That's nonsense," Carter said. "Some things in life have nothing to do with sex."

"Well," Murphy said, "I wouldn't know about that, would you, Doc?"

He laughed as if he had caught Carter in a lie.

Carter took his beer to a table near the wall. He had a smart-ass answer for everything. What did he mean by that? Vivien?

Murphy pushed behind the bar and punched open the cash register and took a folded piece of paper from the money drawer.

"For you, Doc," he said, sliding the paper across the bar.

Carter circled back and took the note and unfolded it.

"How well you know her?" Murphy said.

Carter looked up, and then to the note.

"When did she call?"

"Oh, hell, I don't know. About eleven or so."

Carter crumpled the paper and dropped it into his coat pocket, and checked the clock behind the bar.

"How well do you know her?" Murphy said again.

"You've asked that question," Carter said.

"Well, when you come across a zip like that, it's worth asking twice."

"Look, Murph," Carter said, "if you got something to say, say it."

Murphy laid his huge fat hands out palms down on the bar.

"You teachers are all a little soft."

"I know," Carter said. "We have flat-feet."

"You don't understand people. You teach and you don't understand how people work."

"And bartenders do."

"We got to. Otherwise we go broke. Doc, you fuck with fire, you gonna get burned."

"Maybe we don't care about the fine-print—or moral judgments by amateur psychologists?"

"Okay. Have it your way." Murphy grinned. "But if I was messing around with a female with a rap on her that one has, hell, Doc, I'd want to know."

"Some other time," Carter said. "Maybe when I'm not already worn out with gossip."

Ten minutes later Carter made it to Ruth's apartment, and using the handrail for support, pulled himself, on the peg of his game leg, up the stairs to the second-floor. Before knocking, he waited, breathing deeply.

After a sleepless night, the pace of the walk and the arctic air, he regretted having consented to the rendezvous. He paused at the top of the steps.

His conversation with Timo, knowing she was leaving Lancaster, hung on him like a frozen, wet coat. He had not spent much time with her, and didn't know why her going should bother him, but it did. There are certain people you just don't want to lose track of, he told himself.

In reality she was done at Barker and he would not see her again. If she had gone off quietly her going would have been softened. One day someone in passing would have said, "By the way, Timo Clark has gone to Nigeria." And so it would be.

But having come to see him, to tell him, was more consideration than he expected, more than he could have anticipated. Certainly she was making the rounds. But even so he would not have imagined her taking the time to say good bye to John Carter.

When we're fond of someone, he knew, we find instances of ourselves in them. And when they go way we lose those pieces.

I should go home and go to bed, he counseled, then changed his mind. In an hour or so he would feel differently, maybe even a little better, reminded once more he was probably being overly concerned by events beyond his control.

"Things are just the way they are supposed to be," he said.

And now, Carter thought, diversion, a little diversion.

He tapped on the door, committed to the liaison, and tried to remember when he had last seen Vivien. Two days. Maybe three.

He steadied himself, and when she opened the door, resigned as he was, reminded himself again, to make the most of it, to keep the next few hours as pleasant as possible.

"Good," she said, "you got my note."

"So, what happened?'

"Oh, nothing. Why?"

"We were going to meet at Murphy's"

"I don't know. I don't like that place."

"It's pretty much like any other place."

"Murphy's a sleaze. And most of the people who work there are just like him. I don't like to go there."

"And when did you come to this?"

"I don't know."

She shrugged.

"Let's see. It's one-thirty. I know, John Carter would use a beer."

She retreated a step, then stopped and put her hand on his chest.

"Oh," she said, "John, Jesus, I'm sorry about your friend. That man? The one they found at the hospital. He was a friend of yours, wasn't he?"

"My officemate."

"The one with glasses?"

"Yes."

She didn't answer, but put her hand over her mouth.

"My god, I had no idea. Really, I didn't know he was your friend."

Carter pulled off his coat.

"Well, it's over and there isn't much anyone can do. Anyway, I'd rather not talk about it."

"But you did know him."

"Mason Oldam was the closest thing to a son I'll ever have."

Carter dropped his coat on the couch and sat at the other end.

"Do you know what happened to him?" she said.

"I'd rather not talk about it," Carter said.

The girl laid the coat over the back of the couch and sat down with her legs crossed, facing Carter.

"You know, John, You take things to heart." She paused. "I've never been around a man who cared about people or read poetry and talked about things other than sex and football."

"I talk about sex and football."

"But that's not all you talk about."

"The university is full of young men who excel at science and literature—hell, music and art."

"And sex and football," she said. "It's really a 'let's fuck babe' mentality. They aren't interested in anyone but themselves."

"And I am?"

"Yeah. You are. When I'm around you I feel like you're interested in me. John, you care about people. And because of that people care about you."

"I do," Carter said. "But I didn't know it was that unusual."

"John, it really is."

"It still seems strange."

"Maybe it is. But it's true. And you'll just have to live with it," she said and stood and stepped over the back of the couch and went into the kitchen.

The kitchen and living-room were a good bit cleaner than he remembered. The holidays. With the excitement of the holidays, people shake off lethargy and dust, tidy up a bit, and get to doing things they would otherwise neglect.

Some people, but not Carter. Carter was amused. For him holidays were less preparation and more a season of neglect. Neglect and procrastination. While people scurried about readying for the festivities, Carter languished and tarried, at times willfully so, and in this Christmas season, as usual, giving exercise to a personalized brand of nonfeasance, he had already waited nearly until the final hour to shop for presents. But then, why not?

Here was the Christmas spirit, the fantasy of snow-covered streets decorated with wreaths and bright lights, of late afternoon and early evening cocktail parties, of good will—good spirits and gifts.

And presents? For Katherine Marie. Who else? He had intended to pick up something for Vivien, a small trinket, a gee-bob, maybe a novelty, and wondered why he thought of her that way.

Then, too, the spirit of Christmas giving did not ring in high on the chart of Carter's activities. Calendar-customs. Human feelings, human kindness, regulated by the intimacy and good-heart of dollar-and-cent generosity, struck him as artificial and pretentious.

He had a sister in Miami and a brother, a doctor in Kansas City. The sister, Delores, he had not seen in twelve years, and the brother he hoped he'd never see again, stung by pangs of missing others, deceased parents, the failures of filial piety.

A good day for self-flagellation, he thought.

Actually the sister was a nice enough person, a nondescript sort of woman, who had distinguished herself in the ordeal of four marriages and a tenacity and optimism with which Carter could ill-find fault. Her resiliency, her unflagging devotion in pursuit of the elusive élan of marital bliss, he found impressive. She had two teenage sons, by a marriage other than the one she currently conducted; both sired by a husband whose face Carter could not immediately or easily envision.

The sons were strange, gaunt creatures, and from the information Carter had, as foreign in their habits and thinking as distance and dislocation from his environment might suggest. They were what he would have expected of his sister's children, bland, unimpressive, with an insatiable appetite for rock-videos, drag-racing and dope.

The sister and Carter did not often correspond, and that, too, added to the years and geography of the distance between them.

The brother was another matter.

A fifty-nine-year-old heart specialist in Kansas City, Carter had last seen him several years before, but did not now expect to see him again, at least not in the near future. The occasion of their meeting in Kansas City at a Chinese restaurant had ended in a squabble, which came within a breath of a full-scale brawl.

The quarrel sealed what had over the years become a fraternal disaffection. The brother he had never appreciated, the brother who had refused him even the courtesy of polite acceptance, seemed to drift farther into the distance with each year. Carter would have preferred it otherwise, but could not imagine how to approach the situation without adding animosity to the already bubbling caldron of reproach and insult. For that he was truly sorry.

"You've been smoking," Carter said.

"Want some?"

"There's enough on the air."

"You should," Vivien said. "It feels good."

"Maybe later," Carter said. "Is Ruth gone for the day?"

"Yep. All gone. She's at work."

"Where does she work?"

"I don't know for sure. She's somebody's secretary, some place."

When she put her arm around his neck, beneath the sweet smell of the smoke, he detected the fragrance of bath soap. Her skin was damp and soft, and the bruises around her eyes were mere shadows now. Her eyes were clear and wide.

"Carter," she said, "I've got something to ask you. The last time you were here, do you remember what you did with the TV in the bedroom? I mean, you didn't even touch it and the thing came on. I mean, well, I was thinking. Could you show me how to do that?"

"Maybe someday," Carter said. "Maybe someday."

Again Carter found himself set down in a foreign scape, a separate and distant land. He had been comforted, no, entertained, occupied by the flood of sensations, the wash of light, the firm softness of her flesh, her scent. When they slipped into the bedroom and the newly clothed and freshly made bed, he believed, at least for a short time, his decision to stay had been a good one.

"By the way," Carter said, "how's you séance with Carl Johnson and ethics coming?"

"Oh, it's okay," the girl said. "He's hardly ever there. We've only had two classes in the last two weeks."

"He's had a lot of medical problems lately," Carter said.

"He says we may not even have a final."

"Well," Carter said, "welcome to the land of the living."

Chapter XV

The following morning Carter called Ardyth again to offer whatever assistance he could, and to check on young Mason. Her voice lacked its usual confidence, but in the few minutes of the exchange Carter could not detect anything untoward in what she said or in how she said it.

"Mason did not want a funeral," Ardyth said. "Only barbarians will stand around a hole in the ground and pretend there is someone to talk to who will understand what we lost. The body will be cremated and we will have a memorial service in a month or so. That is Mason's wish. If people have words for Mason there will be a time. It is better this way."

"How did Mason take the news?" Carter said, feeling anew a flash of the boy's pain.

Ardyth paused significantly with the question, and self-conscious for having asked it, unsure of what it might have triggered, Carter broke into the pause.

"If he's there and you'd rather not talk about it, I'll understand."

"No, no, John Carter," she said. "It is true he is sitting here, but he will not mind if I tell you. His heart is broken. He is hurt because his father is dead. But he is young and strong, and we will talk about it, and he will try to understand."

She spoke precisely, carefully articulating each syllable, as if concerned she might not get the words right.

Carter agreed. No. He disagreed. He agreed and disagreed. The boy would survive the shock, the trauma.

"Again, if I can help in any way, let me know," Carter said.

He had thought about the boy often in the last day, about what he might say to him about his father, what he might say to assuage his anguish, what he could say that would be true and correct and real, as clear as a photograph, as full of life as Mason's voice.

In the living-room Katherine Marie sat cross-legged in front of the fire, sipping tea from a small china cup. She had the paper scattered about her on the floor, and Carter located the sports section and carried it off with his coffee to the couch.

"There's an article here about Mason," she said. "The police say it was suicide."

"When you finish, could I see it," Carter said.

She handed him the paper.

"John, have you ever known anyone else who committed suicide?"

The question annoyed Carter. The definition concluded Mason had done what Carter did not believe he had done. But why not? The police seemed satisfied. What did they know? What didn't they know? They didn't know Mason, although Carter didn't know if he had.

Carter thought about it.

"When I was a kid. A couple of German farmers. The oldest hanged himself in the barn," he told Katherine Marie. "Another shot himself."

A glitch in the peasant German character, at least in the German character of the rural America of Carter's experience, encouraged self-destruction.

"When I was in the eighth grade, a kid I knew a couple years younger. His father killed him, then killed himself."

"Good Lord, that must have been horrible."

"It was in the middle of summer and everyone assumed they had gone off on vacation, and they didn't find the bodies for two weeks. The whole mess was exacerbated by the condition and stench of the bodies lying undiscovered for two weeks in ninety plus heat."

Carter did not elaborate. Katherine Marie did not pursue the story, or make further inquiry.

"By the way," she said, "how is young Mason?

"How is any thirteen-year-old going to take losing a parent?"

"When is the funeral?"

"There isn't going to be a funeral," Carter said.

"No?"

"Think of it this way. If you've loved someone well, what more is there? Why bother with gatherings? Why haul your pain out into the public."

"You mean they'll have a private funeral?"

"No funeral at all. I imagine Ardyth will have the body cremated."

Katherine Marie looked away, into the fire, and sat silently as if considering the idea. Even though she did not say so, Carter knew the memory, the vivid memory of the cancer scare a couple years before had just then reappeared and settled on her.

In her silence he could see her running along a dead-end street, and knew when finally she ran out of road at the end of the enclosure, the cul-de-sac of failed inquiry, she would trot out the euphemisms and rationalizations she always used to explain the unexplainable. And, if for no other reason than that he had heard the tale a thousand times before, and had failed, at least as many times to convince her of the nonsense in the perceptions, he did not now feel up to trying again.

He checked his watch. It had stopped at six-thirty, and without saying more, he went off to the kitchen. The clock over the refrigerator showed nine-fifty. He refilled his coffee cup and found his way back to the livingroom.

He stirred up the fire with the poker and dropped on a couple medium-size logs and wondered for a moment where Vivien was.

The day before he had left her late, without plans to see her again, and thought there was an outside chance she might call.

Then he thought possibly she would not. Despite his good intentions their latest tryst had not gone well. The land of the living often provided tedious and embarrassing quirks, nature's practical jokes, just when he could least easily accommodate them.

They had gone to bed, in the teasing tangle, the delightful titillation of taunt and tease, Carter finding fascination in the usual places, the small of her back, the soft muscles of the thigh just above the knee. When she raised her arms above her head, her breasts pulled up into the beautiful contours of the smooth hollows of her underarms—the narcotics of visual and tactile beauty that warmed his blood.

Men's bodies do not provide for women the same pleasures men take from women's bodies, Carter decided. A female body is a pleasure for males, a far greater pleasure, he was sure, than a male body could be for females. But, then, he wasn't sure about this. It was probably a bad guess, at best.

Still the idea satisfied him. It explained a great many things, although it was not a suspicion he intended to share with his women friends. He could hear the howls. They would be pissed.

"What are you saying? That women are inferior creatures who cannot enjoy the same things men enjoy? Women are incapable of feeling what men feel and cannot find pleasure in a man's body?"

Well, not from this old man's torso, anyway, Carter thought. No, women have more, if not in mind, then biologically. It's genetic. What? Kids. Yeah. Selective breeding strategies to pass on genes. Everything else is subterfuge. Fecundity. Not a matter of fighting or running. Genetic success comes from selecting virile mates, slipping between the sheets, undercover, so to speak, then producing and protecting resultant progeny.

But then virile males are not always easy to find. The stock of the French people had been reduced by two inches by the Napoleonic wars. Following major wars large numbers of females of the next generation of the ravaged countries do not marry or bear children. Carter chuckled. So much for fighting. Leaving the 4 F's at home to breed. Viva la Fécundité.

And again the wails.

"What are we? Breeding machines?"

And the answer, again.

"Well, as a matter of fact in the first place. . ."

Why not? The ramifications were extensive.

At any rate, he had overcome his earlier mild despair. At least in the playpen of the carnal garden Vivien Caroline provided, he could, for a few moments, escape the outside world.

And then he could not.

The virulent parasites of depression to which the damage, the attrition of the years of wear had given host, and which pleasure and occasional good times could coax into remission, were again activated.

And what had begun with promise, the vital, sensual intoxication with which he had been overwhelmed moments before, waned, slipped, and just that quickly, faded and died. The solace and comfort he sought were not there.

The practiced eye he had so carefully cultivated for the unadorned delicacy of sensual beauty, held steady the grace and flow of the body of the lovely young woman with him. Beyond that, nothing. He was without impulse or thrust, without feeling, and, for a moment amused, bemused with himself and his failings. If this was truly a failing.

He ran his finger softly along the smooth skin of her inner thigh, up to the hairline, and could feel the tickling sensation at the tip of his finger on her skin. But nothing more.

She was lying with her head back on the pillow, chin up, mouth open.

"God, Carter, you feel so good."

She did not immediately recognize what had happened, but when she did sat up in the middle of the bed with her arms wrapped around a pillow.

"John," she said, "what's wrong? What happened?"

"Nothing I can account for," Carter said in jest.

"Did I do something wrong? I did it, didn't I?"

The white light of afternoon leaking between the closed curtains gave her arms and shoulders, the outline of her face, an alabaster radiance.

"No," he said, it doesn't have anything to do with you."

"But what happened? I mean, you were okay just a minute ago. Then you just quit."

"Wrong word, my dear."

"Well, what is it?"

"Overcome," Carter said. "Physiology is what we live by—good or bad. And physiology, my dear, is often at best weird."

She looked at him as if his words were incomprehensible and shook her head.

"No, no, no, no. John, this is really evil."

"Yes, yes, yes," Carter said, amused with her insistence. "Now you see man lives truly by a nature divided."

"Carter, what did I do?'

He took her hand and held it in his.

"My dear, darling young woman, do not suppose every failing of man or nature—in this case man and nature—is related to you and what you do."

He considered it for a moment.

"Look, you are very young and very lovely, but believe it or not, you do not make the world go."

He raised his hand.

"I know, I know. You help it along. But once in a while things beyond us have a good bit more to do with our survival than we do."

"Carter, I don't need a lecture."

She put her hands on his shoulders and pulled herself to him.

"God, it's scary. I did something wrong, didn't I?"

She held tightly to him.

"Does this happen often? I mean, you don't even seem to be bothered by it."

"Really," Carter said, "there's nothing wrong. I'm tired. Beat up and tired. Don't you ever get tired?"

"I don't think so. Not that way."

"Well, men do. Tomorrow, the next day, a little sleep and I'll be okay."

"You mean you can sleep for a while and you'll be okay? Maybe a couple hours, if we want to wait."

"Not exactly," he said rather hastily, enjoying for a moment the prospect of sleep. "But maybe. I didn't get a lot of sleep last night. And this thing with Mason has really gotten to me. In a lot of ways I didn't expect."

He took a fresh pack of cigarettes from the bedside table and striped it open, then propped himself up against the headboard.

"If we wait, maybe you'll feel rested."

"Maybe, maybe not."

"Carter, I'm sorry. I feel terrible."

"Remember what you said about apologies?"

"I know, but what else can I say?"

"Look. You're making too much of it. This isn't the end of the world. I'm not the first old fart to come down with a limp dick. This isn't the first time."

"Oh, shit, John. I just knew it. It's over between us."

She shook her head as if trying to dislodge the intruder.

"I knew it. This has happened before and I reminded you of a bad experience, something really bad. It's all my fault."

"Of course."

"When?"

"When what?"

"When was the first time?"

"Ah, ha. When I was nineteen."

She looked at him carefully.

"That was a long time ago," she said softly.

"That's right. I was about your age. A little younger."

"God, you make it sound like an everyday matter."

"Oh, look at it this way. We have a little problem here that will right itself in a short time."

"You're sure it's only temporary?"

"You haven't come across this before?"

"No. Honest to god. I didn't know this could happen."

And now, Carter thought. So she's discovered what she would not have guessed at, and should have known.

Vivien was circumspect.

"But you just lost interest."

"No, I haven't lost interest. It's still there," Carter said.

But he would not have wanted to clarify the promise. In a way she was right. He had lost a good bit of interest—in time, over the years, and now, he understood, for these liaisons.

She rested her head on his chest and for a very long time did not say anything. Finally, she drew back and lay with her hands behind her head.

"Carter," she said, "what's going to happen to us?"

"You mean individually, or to us?"

"I don't know. This is really crazy."

"Oh, you'll probably end up as a lead singer for a rock band. Make millions. Have famous men for lovers. At thirty-five you'll marry a Russian count and live a long, exotic life in Paris and Rome."

"Where did you get that?"

"I had a dream. I know these things. I'm clairvoyant. A seer."

"And what about you?"

"How about skid-row, abandoned, forgotten, but not forgiven, a proper end to complement my derelict ways. Remember, only the good die young, and I didn't make it."

"My grandmother used to say the damned can see the future?"

"Yes. They can," Carter said. "A rather painful complication, wouldn't you say? But it's the only thing they can see."

Now he wondered what she was up to, when she might appear.

He snapped on the TV, then flipped through the TV Guide. New England played the Steelers at noon. On a bitter winter afternoon, in the pleasant warmth of the living-room, it would be an easy enough way to spend a few hours.

After running across Factor in the Moon Crater, Carter had wished he had taken the time to go to a Patriots' games. The brutality of football had always intrigued him, as did the ritual and blood of bullfights, the need for blood-rites in the human mix.

When the picture came on, Three Rivers Stadium was shrouded in the white haze of the storm that had four days earlier showered ice and snow on Lancaster. The announcers were killing time, and Carter was not surprised most of the commentary was about Minus Factor. He was being compared to other great linebackers. "The Scourge of the NFL," "The Infamy of New England," he was called.

"There's the story," one of the announcers said, "about Factor going camping in Glacier National Park last summer. He was setting up his tent in a campground when four park rangers showed up with tranquilizer guns and a cage and tried to move him to higher ground."

The other laughed.

"He's too big to be a man and not big enough to be a bear."

They both laughed.

"He's as big as a grizzly and twice as mean. Did he go peacefully?"

"Well, I don't have the whole story, but they said he agreed to go. He didn't have a tent. He uses a specially made inflatable portable cave and agreed to go to a wilderness area for bears and mountain lions.

Carter had asked Factor about his name.

"Where'd you get the name Minus?"

"When I'm a kid," Factor said, "nine years old or so. There was this guy would always hang around the playground, say he was fifteen or sixteen and I was big as he was. We played basketball and in the park and he ask how old I was. Then says, 'You just two inches minus being the Incredible Hulk. Then everybody says that's Minus Two, until a couple years and I'm the biggest kid on the playground and they change it to Minus One. Now it's Minus, cause it's minus yardage."

Following a commercial the broadcast again talked about Factor.

"Last night we were with some of the Steelers and asked them about playing against Factor, and thought our audience might enjoy seeing how they were preparing for this game, and what they have to say about him."

The scene flipped to a shot from the playing field. Slowly the camera panned up and along the foothills and slopes and into the mountainous stands of a stadium as if searching the vast areas for a sign of life. It probed slowly into the distances and settled, finally, just below the press-box, focused on four huge, hulking uniformed players huddled around a fire barrel. The camera zoomed in and, as if he had been surprised while feeding and was about to be attacked, one pulled off his helmet and threw it at the camera. The helmet clattered away out of sight and he held up a large fist and index finger which he shook menacingly at the camera. Blowing and puffing on the frosty air, he bellowed and shouted.

"We the meanest, badest, best, the men who can meet the test. We gonna beat New England and their bear. We gonna make a rug from his hair."

The name Shyron Miller came on the screen beneath the face, and the other three joined in the recitation.

"We the men of steel that hunt and kill, we the undisputed king of the hill."

The camera closed on the faces as their names appeared on the screen. Folus Fowler, Henry "Mad Dog" Williams, Huey "Chopper" Atkins.

In the far background, halfway around the stadium, the camera picked up Minus Factor sprawled over three rows of seats, in street clothes, smiling contemptuously.

In the foreground, Miller raised his bare arms above his head in a power salute, shaking the wrath of heaven on Factor, and Fowler took a small branding iron from the fire barrel and burned the Pittsburgh Steelmark logo into the skin of the grinning Miller's enormous upper left biceps.

The camera crept in on the smoking brand until the clear, definite image of the logo on Miller's skin filled the screen. For a brief moment Carter smelled burning flesh.

"Well," the announcer said, "I wouldn't want to be in Factor's shoes today. Not with them after me. About as savage and skilled a bunch of hunters and assassins as ever came out of the mountains of Thessaly.

"You know, offensive linemen aren't usually known for their aggression. They're more defensive by nature. But these three are different. They've taken offense to a new dimension."

"We thought you'd enjoy that little episode."

"What I want to know," the other announcer said, "is who did the special effects for the branding scene. It looked real to me."

"I think it was real," his partner said. "I don't think it was done with special effects. They actually branded Miller."

Pumped up was the understatement of the year.

Had Miller's arm been shot up with Novocain? What else had they been shot up with?

Carter had just settled in when Katherine Marie came into the livingroom to remind him of their plans for Thursday evening.

"We have to be at Ron and Joan's at seven, so be sure to keep it open. They have a new house. Well, not new, but new for them."

Carter did not answer. Her habit of announcing without warning that "we are expected," at the Smith's, the Cavanaugh's or wherever, even after several decades of marriage, of living with females, still rankled him. Carter had not yet grown comfortable with the personal plural "we."

If the habit hadn't been so ludicrous, it would have been amusing. More than once Carter had responded unkindly with, "Since they are your friends, my dear, people I neither appreciate nor respect, whatever of converse you hold, or society you make with them, you shall hold and make without the presence of John Carter."

Ron and Joan Olsen were not two of his favorite people. Ron Olsen sold real estate, sometimes, and Joan worked with Katherine Marie. As friends of his wife, sometimes Carter endured them, sometimes. But clearly they were not people he held in esteem. Aware of Carter's disposition Katherine Marie added, "Really, John, we do owe them the compliment of decency. They have been kind to us."

"Where's the house?'

"The Bedlor place in the historic district."

"The Bedlor mansion?"

"Yes. They're having a house warming and Christmas party. Everyone will be there."

"All seven and a half billion?"

She frowned.

"Seven and a half billion?"

"That would be everybody."

"You know what I mean."

"Unfortunately. If seven and a half billion make up the roles of mankind, and seven and a half billion will not be there, you should have said 'no one will be there.' That I could believe."

The game began at six minutes after the hour. New England took the kickoff and three plays later pushed the ball down to the Pittsburgh thirty, then missed a field goal.

The New England defense came onto the field showered by boos and shouts of derision. Coming on Factor waved to the crowd as if he appreciated their greeting, a gesture that further inflamed the partisans. To complicate the conspiracy of the afternoon, on the opening play from scrimmage, Pittsburgh ran the ball straight at Factor with Miller leading the way. The meeting was aborted, however, when another linebacker slipped the gap and took out Miller and the ball carrier before they got to Factor. Carter watched Factor float along the line, easily and quickly, with the effortless grace of a large, strong animal.

The second call was identical to the first, and this time Factor met Miller head on at the line and drove him into the ball carrier in the backfield, taking both down for a three yard loss.

"The assassins will have to sharpen their spears if they want to stop Factor this afternoon," the announcer said.

"Boy, he is such a good athlete, and so determined. If they don't stop him, it's going to be a long afternoon for the Steelers."

On the next play Pittsburgh missed on a short pass and Factor came off the field with one tackle. Pittsburgh lost four yards on the series.

The camera followed Factor to the sidelines where he received a helmet slaps from teammates. He leaned toward the camera and held up a large wrapped hand and a number-one finger.

From there the hostilities escalated and the game ground down to a crawl. The snow-cover made the footing difficult, and by the middle of the second quarter neither team had advanced the ball more than twenty yards beyond mid-field.

Near the end of the quarter on a particularly brutal play, Folus Fowler suffered a badly damaged right knee and had to be taken off on a stretcher. On the same play Factor lost his helmet. The blow opened a gash beneath his right eye. Even with multiple camera angles it was impossible to see who had injured Factor, although the replays showed clearly Factor had knocked Fowler down and then stepped on his right knee. There was speculation in the press-box about whether or not Factor had intentionally gone after Fowler.

"He's been known to do things like that before," the announcer said. "When he gets the idea that someone is after him, he gets dangerous."

The following play gave credence to the speculation. On a draw intended to suck Factor into the vortex of line and backfield and pin him with three blockers, Factor's speed enabled him to beat two of the blockers, and ignoring the ball carrier, who had stopped and retreated six or seven yards on the play, Factor circled out of his way to get the third blocker, Shyron Miller. He powered into Miller, lifting and driving him five yards from the point of contact.

"Miller was extremely slow getting up after that hit by Factor," the announcer said. "Factor is really punishing the Steelers. That time he went out of his way to get Miller."

"It was as if he had the ball carrier so far behind the line that he could say, 'Okay, I can always get you, but you'll just have to wait until I get through with Miller.'"

"By the way. Listen to this crowd. They really want Factor's blood."

"Well, he's been beating up on their team."

Again Pittsburgh punted and again Factor went to the sidelines trailed by the eyes of the cameras. Now he no longer took off his helmet or wrapped himself in a cape. The sideline camera came in close on him and his massive head filled the entire screen. Carter could see the cut on his face patched with tape and blood on the bottom bar of the mask. Factor swayed rhythmically with the roar of the crowd.

When New England fumbled the ball away on the first play, Factor took the field swiftly, methodically, the first man out into position. Expecting hostilities would continue unabated, Carter went to the kitchen for a beer.

When Carter returned there was a commercial timeout, but beyond the battle between Factor and the Steelers' offensive line, there wasn't a whole lot to the game. New England led three-zip, and probably would at the half. One field-goal in two quarters. Pretty unimpressive. Three plays later the clock ran down on the half.

The snow had let up, but still the field was slick, and, at least on the TV, the gridlines were not visible. When the camera pulled back, the dark figures of the players floated like electronic specters across the dimensionless ghost-white field behind the screen.

New England kicked-off to open the third quarter. On the second play from scrimmage Pittsburgh wide receiver J. T. Roberts slipped coverage and got behind the secondary down to the five.

The announcers again focused on the contest between Factor and Miller.

"Because of the condition of the field," one said, "I'd expect Pittsburgh to run a slant left or right."

"You would think they'd want to stay away from anything around the end."

"But the inside of the defense is Factor territory, and everybody knows what that means."

"They sure do. Right now Minus Factor is not taking prisoners."

"And getting the ball through him and into the end-zone is going to fall on the shoulders of Shyron Miller."

Taking his cue from his announcers, the director punched in a close up of Factor prowling the line, huge and hulking, breathing heavily and blowing, trying to see into the Steelers' backfield.

As if he too were listening to a description of the action and expected the ball to come up behind Miller on the left, the first snap, a quick buck to the right side, caught Factor several steps out of position. In two steps, he corrected for the error and sprang into the line, now, only a step late, with a huge hand hooked onto the Steelers' center's face mask and dragged him out of the way. With the palm of his open right hand, in an arching, looping swing, he popped right tackle Huey Atkins on the ear-hole of his helmet, spun him out of the play, and as the announcer said, "Almost succeed in separating Huey's head and body."

"That play netted Pittsburgh a grand total of one yard, six inches, a badly twisted neck and a ringing eardrum."

"They've spotted the ball just inside the four-yard line, and at this rate Pittsburgh won't have enough people on the roster to get the ball down to the one."

"Vinny, let me ask you something. If you were the Pittsburgh front four, what would you do to get around, or over, or just to get away from Factor?"

"Well, he is awesome. I've seen bears have more trouble with sheep than he's having with the Steelers' offensive line. If he wants to play in an area, there is no individual to stop him. It'll take a concerted effort from everybody in the Pittsburgh offensive line, and even then they'll be lucky if they do."

"Did you see what he did to the Steelers' center, Bob Milbon?"

"He hooked his face mask. Milbon'll be doing good to turn his head tomorrow. Factor was fortunate no one saw that."

The replay showed Factor had fouled on the play.

In spite of the hype about the viciousness of the linemen in the trenches, Carter had not seen anyone play with this kind of savagery. The violence seemed excessive even for the NFL.

But then wasn't that what it was about? What were the percentages? How many had shown up? How many had not been asked to play, or would not endured the hardships and pain? How many had been driven from the field to get down to these few, among which a handful excelled.

Was this what poets praised in heroes, what Homer saw in Achilles?

Were these the splendid talents, the magnificent strategies of sinew and thews to catch the poet's eye? In the age of massive, impersonal nuclear destruction, was this what remained of the plains of Troy?

A chill rippled Carter's skin, along his spine.

Carter recalled the afternoon in the Moon Crater, Factor's indefatigable and unflappable good humor, his charisma, childlike as he was, when he laughed about Irish grandmothers and African grandfathers. It was the same zest and flavor with which he gave himself to the carnage of this brutal and mindless game.

What in the hell was going on?

Carter wasn't sure.

It had to do with Factor. And not Factor the football player. Not Factor the homespun philosopher of sorts. But something far more elusive and fleeting.

After a TV-timeout play resumed with Pittsburgh on the New England four-yard-line. This time the Steelers showed draw, and Factor, with his quickness, eager for a kill, shot the gap into the backfield, even before the quarterback tossed the ball out to his running back. Dog Williams and Atkins pulled from the right side to meet Factor, Williams going low and Atkins driving into Factor's upper body with his head and shoulders, as if Factor was a blocking sled. At the same time, Miller, who had allowed Factor to beat him through, came in from behind and drove his helmet into the middle of Factor's back. The timing was perfect and a shotgun mike caught the crack of the contact in sync with the camera's image.

Carter had been drifting, thinking about the phenomenon of sitting out in the middle of a Midwestern cornfield watching an event half a continent away, gazing at the picture, then became aware in the half-formed fuzzy images something serious and strange had occurred.

At the moment of contact, and from the source of the sound echoing in Carter's ears, from the point of contact forward, Factor was without movement.

He did not fall as a human being falls when knocked down, but dropped, as a curtain might, or as a fine piece of crystal shattered by sound will drop, not retaining its original shape, but losing its form as it goes down.

Carter stared at the set, at the image of the fallen Factor, his helmet still in place, lying on the field in the snow, knowing already what it seemed no one in the stadium yet knew.

Factor was not going to get up.

It took the officials several seconds to call time out, and a couple of the Patriot players leaned over Factor. In the background, Miller, Atkins and Williams had gone into an impromptu victory dance, with high fives and head butts.

"Minus Factor may have been hurt on the play," the announcer said, "so while they're attending him, we'll take a commercial break."

Commercial break.

Sanitize the whole thing, Carter thought. Jesus. Show the accoutrements of violence, then deny the results.

"You just killed the man," Carter shouted. "You idiots, they've killed him."

Katherine Marie called in from the dining room.

"John are you all right?"

"No," Carter shouted, "No, I'm not all right. They've just killed him and these morons are babbling about it as if it's nothing."

He next noticed her in the doorway, arms folded, leaning on the jamb, watching the TV with him.

Carter was up pacing in front of the set.

"Do you know what just now happened? He's dead. They killed him, and these crazies decide to plug in a commercial."

"Killed him? Who?"

"Factor. Minus Factor. The New England linebacker."

"Well, John, it doesn't do any good to shout at the TV. They can't hear you."

"Do you know what that means?"

"I don't even know who Minus Factor is."

Incomprehensible, Carter thought. Here we go again.

"What difference would it make who he is? A human being has been killed."

"Did they say he was dead?"

"No, they didn't say he was dead. But they don't have to say it."

She tilted her head.

"John, you're so dramatic," she said, as if he had manufactured the whole thing. "Wait until they know for sure. He's probably okay. Whatever his name."

"Dramatic?"

"Well, you don't have to act like it's a conspiracy. They're just doing their jobs."

"Wonderful. These crazies make millions staging these things and then when people get hurt they look away, pretend it hasn't happened. Their job? Covering up their culpability?"

"John, you were watching the game. If it wasn't for people like you there wouldn't be professional football."

"Seeing does not mean advocating. I don't drink Lite beer.

She left abruptly and Carter stood staring at the set, waiting, sure there was more than the announcers were prepared to admit. When the broadcast resumed he found his fears justified.

The announcers drifted into a rerun of first-half statistics, the screen filled with lists of first-downs, passing and rushing attempts and yardage.

In the far distance of the lower left corner of the screen, a huddle of people worked over Factor.

Factor had fallen face down, with his right arm bent out at an unusual angle, its large palm twisted up. His left arm was beneath his chest, but more to the point and Carter's fear, Factor had not moved, and none of the people attending him had made any attempt to move him or to remove his helmet.

The medics and stretcher crew were already on the field, preparing to carry him off. They were slipping wide straps beneath him to lift him onto the stretcher. Although Carter had seen this done only once before, he knew its purposes too well.

Factor had been seriously injured, or worse, and not merely unconscious, although it seemed to Carter extremely unlikely he would be conscious.

Finally they got him on the stretcher, and the four bearers and their unmoved, stilled burden, loaded onto a cart, made their way in somber procession to the end of the field, into the far corner of the stadium's exit crossing to the stadium underground.

"They have just taken Minus Factor to the dressing room for X rays and diagnosis," the announcers said. "As soon as we get any information on his condition, we'll be sure to pass it along to our viewers."

Carter sat fixed, eyes locked on the set, numbed by the drone of the voices drifting in and out of his hearing.

The speculation about Factor's condition remained optimistic and conservative. "I've seen players injured like that before. Most often there's a little trauma to the system, but in a day or two they are okay.

There's probably nothing wrong with him. You don't hurt players like Factor."

Even while Factor lay on the field, the replays began. Before Factor's fallen form, the form of the stretcher with Factor and its bearers, molded and cast in a single image, disappeared from the screen, the six stadium cameras wound into slow motion explorations of the parallax of the four approaching apparitions, clothed in shadow and shade, at times blurred, but always, faceless and, except for number, as they strode weightlessly to un-denied collision, as anonymous as the space men in the Moon Crater lounge.

And Carter, with millions of other viewers, came alive, appalled and fascinated and lifted, wanting, now, vindication, now explanation, to see what had happened, to inspect the details, and watched the fluid motion, the ghostly ballet of furies stirred into a choreography of bodies, of graceful animation, as they were not in real time, slowed and slowed again frame by frame, advancing in their now predetermined and unalterable paths to a point of irrevocable, having done.

During the following days, and periodically in ritual and remembrance thereafter, on anniversaries and for ceremony, the bare electronic image of Maurice Minus Factor's ordeal, his late, great and tragic fate would be replayed and replayed on TV sports spots throughout the country.

At the two minute mark of the fourth quarter, the Factor report was given.

"We've just been handed this," the announcer said. "It's from Pittsburgh General Hospital, where Minus Factor was taken for treatment after his injury in the third quarter.

"The attending physician, Dr. Arthur Carson, says, and here's the report, 'At two-thirty-one today, Minus Factor of the New England Patriot football team, died at Pittsburgh General Hospital. The cause of death was not immediately known, but an autopsy will be performed."

Carter punched down the sound and stood for a moment in silence. He could feel the shadow, the creeping black silence in the room and could hear it thinking.

Soundless images of a football game being played at a great distance flickered across the TV screen.

Carter took one step, softly, and then another, to the corner and leaned the stuffed chair forward, to better see beneath it.

"Sniveling cowardice," Carter said, replacing the chair.

"John," Katherine Marie called from the other room, "who are you talking too?"

After a pause, lacking any response, she appeared in the doorway, surveyed the room, empty except for Carter standing in front of the TV.

"John," she said, "you've been drinking too much, again. You're hallucinating."

Carter bent as if a specter had slipped up behind him, as if he expected it to touch him, then dropped to the couch.

Set down at the dead-end of a shabby back-alley, he gathered himself, prepared for a second time in a week to reconcile having lost again, breathless, exhausted, as shaken and shocked, as saddened as ever Priam was.

Chapter XVI

Carter advanced on the bathroom and the morning, and took up his daily station before the mirror. It was Tuesday of final week. Mason was dead, Minus Factor dead, and still four days to go in the week.

The tile floor shocked his bare feet. He slipped the white oval rug over from near the tub and settled his feet into the deep nap. The glare of the cabinet bulbs above the mirror hurt his eyes. He squinted down over the blur of his extended white paunch, his bag, as the Irish call it, to the childlike, boney pin-legs beneath him. No wonder, he thought. My support. A couple of thin, wobbly spindled props hinged on knobby, defective joints.

Mornings were difficult. Especially in the early winter, probing the hazy, booze-filled memories of the final few comforts of the previous evening, shaking clear of the obliterating pleasure of sleep.

Good sleep, he decided, is truly precious and gazed at the fuzzy contours of eyes, mouth, grey hair and large ears in the mirror.

He slipped on his glasses to sharpen the focus even if it wouldn't improve the image. The truth of the bright light left little of pretense to cover the sagging canvas of his face. He examined the image hanging bodiless in the glass, amusedly, then more seriously.

Johnny Cash. Cash never looked that bad. Burton with graying hair. Maybe.

No. No Welshman. A Corsican with Mediterranean hair, more French than Welch or Irish.

What else? Well, a prominent ridged brow, furrowed, gone soft around the eyes, puffy and bagged. Hazel-brown eyes, deep-set eyes.

Lips thinner now, just the slightest sag to the jowls. Deep creases along the nose, over the cheeks. Creases, hell, ruts. The paths and trails, the trials of rutting.

Fifty-five, he thought, fifty-five, and counting up to down. From where? To where?

He closed the door and settled on the stool. This was the easy part of the morning, the pleasurable part. Animal functions made pleasant to keep the system going lest we forget. One of evolution's small bonuses.

His freshman year at the University in a psych class, discussing the human nervous system the professor, a middle-aged little potato-man with graying hair and a large mole on his forehead, stated, in his opinion, at least for males taking a dump was as pleasurable as sexual intercourse.

A hush passed over the class—then a snicker, a titter and finally a voice from the back of the room announced, "Either you have never had a good piece of ass or I never took a good shit."

After the hoots and howls there was little more to say, and nothing more was said. That ended the class.

How in the hell could you know or judge a thing like that?"

What did they do, count the nerve endings? Seven thousand two hundred nerve endings in the human foot. Each nerve accommodates a factor of pleasure measure out to . . .

What about . . . ?

Gingerly Carter rose awkwardly and examined the bowl, standing for a moment regarding the enterprise of the brilliant red, the flashing red of fresh blood. Without surprise or alarm he was mildly perturbed with the inconvenience. What he had come to expect these days. Simply another malady, another indignity. He sat down again, then, with the unmistakable soft regular dripping beneath him. Several bright spots on the white bath mat caught his attention.

So this was it. The bleeding end of things. A new meaning for the British vulgarity "My bleeding arse."

Stress—attrition—wear and tear—red tears leaking and dripping away the years.

If it continued? How long? Two days, three?

He'd have to see a doctor—give the profession another chance to attempt to postpone the inevitable. The bane of modern medicine in its arrogance and magnificence, limited to affecting a mere extension of time. But nobody to solve the dilemma.

Why not, Carter thought, why not ignore it and take the chance? What were the possibilities? How far up the track had things gone wrong? Bleeding ulcers? Pain free. Another of nature's oddities. Your gut rotting away and nothing to tell you about it.

Seated still, the dripping continued, the bright blazoned drops plinking into the water dispersing into a mix about the color of cherry Kool

Aid, and just as discomforting. Life leaking into a sanitized container. Flushed away. Carter watched the drippings disappear in the swirl.

Mason going down in the chill of night, unseen. Carter had tried to puzzle out a reconstruction of the last moments, partially to fill the void of not knowing. In so doing he knew probably he had cultivated a number of crucial fallacies—one of which was that Mason would not kill himself.

On the other hand, after the initial shock, the ebb and swell of Factor's death washed over him. The enormity of the event, for ill or good, of a combatant gone down on the floor of a gigantic stadium before a throng of the rabid and maniacal was to Carter's mind both primeval and cathartic.

An assiduous commercialization of misfortune.

In a way he too had been taken in.

A barbarian, he judged, seeking immediately to quell the implications of the indictment. He would again make a pilgrimage, this time a grimmage to the True Light Baptist Church on Chicago's rat infested Southside to pay his respects, to see Maurice Factor buried, to participate in the ritual, the lowering of the remains.

Would the funeral be held there? The paper would say. The sports page. Yes, he would go. He'd make time. He'd do it out of respect, and grief.

"No luck" he told himself, "you can't get off that easily," and then wondered why he would deny the truth.

For a second day he took the morning paper with him and picked up a copy of *The Bulldog Bark* from behind the student union.

Beneath the pressing realities of exam week the campus was lifeless. The black bunting of Factor's memorial hung over the Christmas decorations on the streetlamps. Black ribbons were knotted to the poles and signs along the streets reminiscent of the square in Cork in the days of Long Kesh and Bobby Sands.

Carter had an ethics exam at ten. After writing the questions on the board (answer two of the three following) and reading them aloud to the class, he counted heads by twos. Twenty-seven. He pulled a chair to the door and opened the papers.

The Bulldog dedicated the entire edition to Factor. A photo showed him standing astride a pile of sand at a street construction sight across from the Pi Phi house. A huge crowd had gathered to watch an impromptu water-fight staged by two fraternities as part of the unofficial activities of Greek Week. Factor had climbed the sand-pile for a better view of the contest, a giant chieftain astride his mountain, surveying the valley domain of his miniature kingdom.

Between the pictures were articles. Testimonials. Eulogies.

Several alluded by innuendo, insinuation, that the rewards of running in the fast-lane had added a sprinkling of a hidden, poison ingredient to the stew of Factor's life.

The back page featured lamentations, commentary on the grizzly, graphic display of violence on Saturday afternoon.

Carter glanced over the sports page, again—the bland unaffected listing of big plays and missed opportunities, innocuous observations from coaches, the gossip and speculation, of athlete observers overloading their impoverished descriptive abilities trying to explain what they had done.

The second section featured another bash of articles. The lead article extravagant, and therefore more interesting, elevated Factor to King of the Saturnalia. A chosen, gifted athlete provided with a life of wealth and fame, who in the end must be sacrificed.

Factor would not be buried in Chicago. He had chosen a plot in a Boston cemetery. Carter tried to imagine why. Well, hell, why return to a place you'd been trying most of your life to escape?

Would the gravestone be a large marble football? Maybe a trophy instead of a monument. What's the difference between a trophy and a monument? Size?

By twelve the examinees had dwindled to seven, and fifteen minutes later Carter collected the last paper. A flier had been tacked to the corkboard on his office door, a printed announcement meant to look like a newspaper with ads for social events. Headlines and text detailed a birthday party for an English instructor name Madline Whisant who had bought a condo in the lesbian section of Lancaster.

Carter checked his calendar for the afternoon schedule, exams, appointments, just to be sure, and found the notation in red ink, "Crowly—2:00."

The Crowly meeting had slipped his mind. When he had been unable to make contact with Crowly the previous week, Carter decided Monday morning he would go to Crowly's office and get an agenda for the meeting. Then within the turmoil of the weekend he had forgotten about the agenda and the meeting.

He checked the wall clock. Twelve-thirty-one. He hadn't eaten since yesterday at three and decided to kill time he'd go downstairs for lunch.

Only a scattering of people populated the cafeteria. Carter carried his tray to a table in the sun beneath a skylight on the far side.

Later in the afternoon, with the Crowly thing out of the way he'd go to

Murphy's. He had the idea, or maybe just a hope, Vivien might be there.

At five-to-two he rode the elevator back to the fourth-floor. The scars of the vandalism in the hall had been wiped away. The broken fixtures replaced, the spattering of red paint cleaned and covered.

Goat's blood. Carter was still amused with Carl's claims for the bizarre, the exotic.

Arabic symbols?

The black letters on the glass of the office wall and doors had been replaced with even larger, bolder inscriptions for the Academic Corporate Vice Chancellor for Instruction, Marvin Crowly, B.S., M.S., PhD, Ed. and Administrative Dean of Humanities, Lamar Landeau, B.R.E., M.A., Ed., M.B.A., PhD.

Pretense and hype, Carter thought. They collect education degrees like kids collect baseball cards. Then given authority and power they set straight away to provide themselves with title and pay.

In the office Carter stopped at the secretary's desk.

"I'm here for my two o'clock appointment with Crowly," he said.

"Doctor Crowly will be available in a few minutes," she said, emphasizing the "Doctor."

She's been trained to do that, Carter knew. Doctor.

"If you will, Mr. Carter, you can have a seat."

"Professor Doctor Carter," Carter said. "Doctor of Philosophy, not to be confused with Doctor of Philosophy of Education. And since I have been summoned here for a two o'clock séance, would you to notify Crowly that it is now two o'clock and I am here prepared to proceed with whatever he has in mind? And I expect, as a matter of professional courtesy, he will want to begin on time."

The woman, Janice Watkins, looked at Carter without smiling, then picked up the phone and punched two buttons.

"Mr. Carter is here," she said.

A straight-backed, redhead in her late twenties with a blur of freckles, rumor had it she succeeded to the secretarial throne, to the first-chair of the secretaries in the vice chancellor's office by sharing her favors with both Landeau and Crowly.

She replaced the phone. A moment later the door to Crowly's office opened by an anonymous hand and Carter could see Landeau and Daly seated to the left of Crowly's desk.

Several large plants hung along the wall and window looking out over the quad to the chancellor's residence at the far end. The wall behind Landeau and Daly sported rows of framed certificates and diplomas exhibiting Crowly's certification. At the far end of the room a battery of large overstuffed chairs and an expensive couch were arranged around a large executive desk.

Carter had never been in this office before, and was a little surprised with the decor. Wall-to-wall carpeting and indirect-lighting. No doubt the largess of interior decorators and tax dollars.

Carter stopped in the doorway, nodded to Daly who offered a weak smile, then waited while Landeau finished a story he was telling. Crowly lounged behind the desk, sucking on the end of a cigar still in the cellophane wrapper, his eyes locked on Landeau. The story had to do with a guy who couldn't tell the difference between a nigger whore and a catfish.

"It's easy," Landeau said, "one has whiskers and smells and the other's a fish."

Crowly roared and Daly smiled.

Hell of a price to pay, Carter thought, watching Daly. In bed with crazies, you not only have to lie for them, you have to laugh at their sick jokes.

When Carter came into the room, Crowly looked at him, apprehensively. He pulled open the big drawer of his desk and took out something with his fingertips, a white powder, and sprinkled it on the edge of the desk top between him and Carter.

Probably baking soda to hide the smell, Carter thought.

"You'll have to tell Remcheck that one," he told Landeau, then opened a folder on his desk and paged through it as if checking to be sure everything was there.

"I'm glad to see you made it on time," he said to Carter. "This shouldn't take too long. I asked Dr. Landeau and Dr. Daly to be here so there are no misunderstandings. Dr. Norman is in another meeting, but will be informed of our proceedings."

"About what?" Carter said.

"Well, we want this to be on the up and up. We want to do this right."

Carter realized just then they were in a conversation without a subject.

"What are you doing?" Carter said.

Crowly held up his hand.

"There's no reason to be hostile."

"Believe it or not," Carter said, "questions are not a form of attack. Maybe you could start by telling me what we're doing."

Carter knew Landeau and Daly had not been invited as innocent observers. As a matter of practice, with Crowly, Remcheck and Landeau meetings were always an arrangement of three or four on one. Of habit they had a decided aversion for putting anything in writing.

"You're too distrustful," Crowly said, smiling at Carter, turning his chair and looking at the wall clock.

"It's not my attitude we're talking about," Carter said. "At least that topic hasn't been formally introduced."

"Well, in a way it has," Crowly said.

Daly dropped his eyes and settled his gaze on the floor. He showed no indication he might intervene or involve himself in the conversation.

"What are you talking about?" Carter said.

"Student complaints," Crowly said. "I want to handle this informally—I'd like to talk about it. There's no need for an onside kick. I'm sure you can explain it."

Before he sat down Carter had closed the door and wondered if it was now bolted from the outside.

"Student complaints," Carter said. "Who are the students?"

"Well, it's not that simple. Anyway, that's not important. We don't believe there's anything to it, and I'm sure you will be able to clear it up for us."

Crowly unwrapped the cigar, dropped the cellophane into the wastebasket and began licking the end of the cigar as if it was a candy stick.

"It may not be important," Carter said, "but it might be the ethical thing to do. Maybe you should tell me who made the complaint. If I'm being accused, and I don't see how you can possible have a complaint without an accuser, I have the right to face my accuser. And just to keep things in order, I'd like someone to take notes."

"That won't be necessary," Crowly said. "There is nothing formal about this meeting, and this is not a court-of-law so it's not a matter of your rights. This isn't a formal inquiry."

"Then I'll be going," Carter said. "If you have something to say, say it for the record. Otherwise, I'm not interested in your opinions or your observations."

Crowly addressed Daly.

"Dr. Daly, will you take notes?"

"Then this is a formal inquiry?" Carter said.

"Oh, let's not get excited. We'll say it's a fact-finding discussion."

Daly produced a yellow legal pad, a bit too quickly in Carter's estimation, and began scribbling.

"Did you get that, Daly?" Carter said. "This is a discussion."

"The first item on the agenda," Crowly said, "is a complaint from a student that you are not holding class."

"Wait a minute," Carter said.

He very nearly shouted.

"What agenda. I haven't seen an agenda."

"You haven't seen an agenda?" Crowly said, slowly, mocking Carter. "I'm sure you were sent a copy."

Crowly picked up the phone.

"Janice, would you check and see if Professor Carter was sent an agenda for this meeting?"

"Discussion. This is not a meeting, not an inquiry, but discussion," Carter said. "And what do you mean by first? How many items are there?"

Crowly replaced the phone.

"She says she sent you one. You must have overlooked it, or misplaced it. Dr. Daly, note that Professor Carter was sent an agenda."

"And note further," Carter said, "that I stated I did not receive an agenda for this discussion."

Landeau lit a cigarette and set it in the ashtray on Crowly's desk. For a moment it seemed he might say something, but he did not.

"We have a complaint that on at least two occasions this semester you did not hold class for the required fifty minute period."

"I still don't have an agenda," Carter said.

Crowly was licking on the other end of the cigar.

"There are three items we need to consider here," he said. "Class length, improper access and student faculty relationships."

Carter ran through the items several times, trying to decipher the coding. What did he mean by improper access?

"What class?" Carter said.

"That is not important. It is not an impossible matter. But we will need proof that during this semester you have met all of your classes for the required amount of time each period."

Crowly pushed a typed form across the desk toward Carter.

"If you'll sign this, we can move on," he said.

His lips curled back in a grin with the cigar sticking straight out, clenched in a mouth full of enormous teeth.

Carter read the form, then dropped it on the desk.

"No. I won't sign."

Crowly looked at Landeau.

"I told you. He's not going to cooperate."

"Look, Professor," Landeau said. "It would be better for everyone if you'd help us out. Why won't you sign a statement that simply says you have held all of your classes this semester for the required time? It seems easy enough. Unless you haven't. In which case the complaint may have merit, and we'll have no other choice but to proceed accordingly."

"Proceed as you wish," Carter said. "That says a good bit more than just that. It also says I have treated my students judiciously and without prejudice, whatever that might mean."

"Don't you believe you have?"

"Have what?"

"Treated them fairly."

"Certainly," Carter said, "but that is not what you want me to sign."

"Then you won't sign?"

Carter shook his head.

"No, I won't."

"Be sure to note Professor John Carter has refused to verify in writing that he has held all of his classes for the required time during the fall semester," Landeau told Daly.

"I have not been asked to verify anything in writing," Carter said to Daly. "I have been asked to affix my signature to a document prepared by the administration. Note that."

Crowly tapped his long manicured fingernails on the desk top. He had large hands, not as large as Factor's hands. Not large with long thin drawn fingers and fine veins. But large, obese hands, round and without definition, pale-skinned hands covered with long black hair.

"December thirteenth," Crowly said. "Tell us about December thirteenth."

"Tell you what?" Carter said.

"What you did?" Landeau said. "What kind of a day was it?"

His voice was pleasant and almost playful.

"Pretty much the same as any other day," Carter said, "and you know what it was like. That was last Wednesday."

"Yes," Landeau said with affirmation, as if it were a profound revelation. "The day of the ice storm and the university was closed. Yes. And what did you do, Professor? Where were you?"

Landeau's toupee was slightly off center and the light from the overhead lamp gave his head a Fred Flintstone cast. Also, the piece was a shade darker than his hair.

Maybe the glue's slipping, Carter thought.

"Did you make an unauthorized entry into the university library for the sole purpose of removing books—again, without authorization?"

So that's it, Carter thought.

It had not occurred to him someone might have known about the library, and surprised him even more anyone would care. The episode had slipped his mind, but came back now impressed with a sudden, and not altogether pleasant relevance.

So that's what they mean by improper access. They're pissed about me using the library. Their library, as if they owned the library.

Then he wasn't sure. Maybe it wasn't the library after all. But what?

"Faculty have been going in and out of the backdoor for twenty years," Carter said. "If it's such a horrendous crime, why wasn't the lock repaired or people told not to use it when the library was closed?'

"That's not our concern here," Landeau said. "What the faculty may or may not have done in the past does not concern us here. We're talking about what you did on the thirteenth."

"It is a common and past practice for faculty to have access to the library even when the university is closed," Carter said.

"If there had been a policy to that effect, we would have issued keys," Landeau said. "It was breaking and entering."

"The door was open," Carter said. "I just walked in."

"The door was locked."

"The door is always open," Carter said.

"The library was closed. The university was closed," Landeau said. "Any access under the circumstances was illegal."

"So?"

"Professor," Landeau said, "what is your relationship with Vivien Connors? What do you know about her?"

"She's not a student of mine," Carter said. "If that's what you're thinking, you've missed it. You should have checked with the registrar's office."

"We did," Crowly said. "She was a student of yours last year. And under university rules governing student faculty relations, you have violated the very first rule. The 'Faculty may not engage in personal relationships with students.' At present she is a student in this university and could be in a class of yours again."

"Learning is a personal relationship," Carter said. "Regardless of what you people make up. Classroom activity is always personal, or it's no good."

"Do you know how old she is?" Landeau asked.

"She's twenty-two," Carter said.

"She's twenty."

"She's married and has two children."

"She's single. She lives with her father at 1729 on Randolph Street."

"We don't want this to get into the newspaper?" Crowly said.

"You're going to hand it out as a news release?"

Carter stared at Crowly, who did not look at him. Sick. Carter thought.

Sick and gutless. He can't even look at me.

"Why would it get in the paper? Unless you wanted it in print," Carter said.

Landeau stuffed out his cigarette and immediately lit another. Carter watched the smoke fan out then drift ceiling-ward in a thin haze.

"You've been having sexual relations with this girl," Landeau said.

"My personal relationships are none of your business," Carter said.

"You been buying this girl alcoholic beverages. Namely beer and wine, and you've been having sex with her."

"It's none of your business. Anyway, she won't testify to that."

As soon as the words were out, Carter regretted saying it.

"You're sure?" Landeau said.

"It's still my business."

"Mr. Carter, it is also our business. What you have done with the girl is a felony. It is statutory rape. It is the business of this university, and, I might add, the business of the States Attorney as well."

Carter's mouth was dry, his pulse running rapidly. He had underestimated their viciousness and determination. Now the full weight of it settled on him. He felt as if he had just run a long way pressed by a fierce presence. A homicidal presence meant to mutilate and maim. This was no simple matter of verbal-sparing. They intended to carry it to the end, the bitter end.

Crowly stood and motioned for Landeau to follow him.

"We need a timeout," Crowly said."

They left the room and closed the door and Carter sat staring at the wall, wondering why they had stepped out. Daly did not look at Carter or speak.

When they reconvened Crowly withdrew another paper from the folder and handed it to Carter.

"Professor, we just spoke with the university's attorney, and we're prepared to press this matter. That is unless we can work something out."

"Unless I make restitution."

"You might say that," Crowly said.

"How?"

"Resign," Landeau said.

"The game plan is simple," Crowly said.

"Resign?"

"Yes."

"From the university?"

"Yes. Your position and your benefits."

"No," Carter said.

"Professor Carter," Landeau said, "this doesn't get any easier. You could save the university and yourself and your family a lot of embarrassment and hardship by resigning now."

"Goal-line stands can be costly," Crowly said.

"My family has nothing to do with it," Carter said. "Anyway, there isn't anyone who would convict a philosophy professor for sneaking into the library on an off day."

"And what about the girl?" Landeau said.

"Professor Carter, there's no reason to go on with this. We will expect your resignation by six this evening, or we will convene a committee for dismissal at one o'clock tomorrow afternoon in the vice chancellor's conference room. If you decide not to resign or not to resolve this amicably, we cannot be held responsible for what the States Attorney might do. He definitely has an interest in this case. Otherwise, we may be able to work out a deal. He does not want to see the good name of this university dragged through the mud. He's a sensible man."

Carter watched the obeisant scribbling Daly, well onto his third page of notes.

"Think it over, Professor," Landeau said. "Save your name and you may be able to find another position. Make a case of it, legal or otherwise, and you'll never get into a classroom again. We have several hundred thousand dollars budgeted to handle litigation of this kind. The good name of this university must be protected."

"That's ridiculous," Carter said. "You don't care about this university—or the people in it."

He stood slowly, weakly, to leave.

"By the way, I'll need a copy of the notes."

Crowly walked around the desk and opened the door.

"Janice, make a copy of this for the professor."

He handed her the notes Daly had hurriedly torn off the pad.

"Well, what do you think?" Carter said to Daly. "What will the AAUP do about this?"

Daly lowered his head.

"I don't see what they can do," he said.

"Have you asked?" Carter said. "Or did you decide that on your own?"

Daly didn't answer, and when they were ready Carter took his copy of the notes.

Where had Crowly gotten his information? Had Remcheck's internal spy network actually materialized? It made sense to think it had. There were any number of people who would have volunteered to report on

Carter.

Mason had vanished, had been driven out and to death, and now this.

And what about the girl? What if she was only twenty? Or was it nineteen? Where did Crowly get the information? Did he make it up hoping to get a quick resignation? Did he lie? Would he? Would he lie? Would he. But had he?

Or maybe Crowly put a sleuth on me, Carter thought.

The sensation crawled along Carter's spine. It was one thing to have the singular moment, an individual act recorded and committed to print, say, the way Factor's death had been detailed. The blow of the helmet hitting the spine, the sharp pop of the contact frozen in image and words, held in print and memory.

Factor was paid to be seen and his activities recorded. But following a mark around, meandering through a day, not trying especially to create or destroy, and stopping the journey without referent or scale, was another matter. And what would such a journey tell? How might the drift of direction on a night street, a contemplative pause in the yellow circle of a streetlamp symbolize the intelligence or intent that rested there?

Would the reporter, the writer be generous? And creative. What would he say? What story would he tell? Aggrandizement? Embellishment? The truth? And how to characterize the constant, incessant return to pleasure, a walk in the sun, the habits of drink and sex—need newly arisen?

Standing outside the details of the very recent past, Carter tried to look in with a stranger's eyes. It was a perspective from an unusual angle. Would the attendant assumptions of the view cast the events differently?

The possibilities intrigued Carter and he tried to remember if he had seen anyone suspicious, anyone hanging about too often. Suspicious? Everyone you pass on the street is suspect.

Then he recalled the day in the library. The sound he had heard but had not been able to identify. He assumed it was Vivien. But it wasn't just a sound. What had he seen?. Someone? Who? Crowly? Someone who reports to Crowly? That would account for the library. And for what they knew about Vivien. What had they talked about in the library? What had they said? Could someone have overheard the conversation?

By four o'clock the chilled fog of shock had dissipated and left Carter naked and shivering.

The plan was completed, or at least the pattern of the attack made obvious enough to see what they were after. The events of the last week, the letters of dismissal, then this. He wondered how the others were taking it.

Mason's death, precipitated, if not arranged, by Crowly and the now dubious state of his own future and fate were linked in his mind, irrevocably.

Factor's corpse hung, symbolically on the periphery, a rancid piece of spoiled, poisoned meat.

Everything, he told himself, everything, every task, every pursuit, in this society has been reduced to dollars and cents. Factor had sold his life straight away, because there was little else he could do, but despite Crowly and Landeau, Carter had not yet consented to the market-place of the classroom.

Others took degrees as union cards and joined the assembly line in the diploma-mills, watering down courses and requirements which increased the flow of dollars in and the flow of something less than scholars out. The graduating stream running from Barker State was a polluted, tepid, milky morass.

Carter wondered why he had protested.

What's needed, he decided, was a new dedication and muscle to support education. Maybe the kids in the sixties were right. Maybe we should take to the streets, Carter thought, envisioning students in the smoke-filled and rubble-strewn streets of Budapest slinging rocks at Russian tanks, at the oppression and intolerance of the invading, barbarian armor. Maybe education needs the support of an active revolt.

In the lexicon of Carter's morality, violence had been relegated to the margins. But in truth he knew there was nothing dignified about patiently suffering oppression, and striking down an oppressor had more than once served as a proper and intelligent, viable avenue to peace and security.

If you have a problem with someone and you kill him, you no longer have a problem with that person. You may have trouble with those who object to what you've done—but not with the dead man.

The question was not whether violence, physical force, was permissible. History had answered that rather conclusively. The question was only, when did it become necessary and/or feasible.

Maybe it was time for revolt, Carter thought. Maybe Kunen and the other sprouts at Columbia had it right.

And who had invited the cretins in to remodel the university? Well, Carter knew. The elected representatives of the people protected by the religious awe of elected positions. So they're the peoples' representatives. But in Carter's estimation they had seriously overstepped their representative endorsement.

Still, they had wormed their way in.

Shindel the pig farmer, who drove around in a white Cadillac with the license plate HOG 1, and whose face appeared regularly in the local news of university functions. Shindel had been elected to the Barker Board of Trustees eight years before, then in succeeding elections, by laundering university funds through bogus student and community functions, subsidized the campaigns and the elections of three of his business associates.

The duplicity, as well as the complicity of university officials was well known. But the voices of protest were for the most part individual and unorganized, and the Office of the State's Attorney of Lancaster County looked the other way. On numerous occasions, when asked about it the States Attorney Clemens said he would not intervene unless someone demanded an investigation. When a citizen stepped forward with the demand, Clemens launched what the papers called a "full scale inquiry," which lasted three days and included five witnesses, all university administrators who reported directly to Remcheck.

The frustration of the last several years pooled in Carter's chest. For the first time in his life he was seriously thinking about killing someone. Shooting Crowly would cost him what? Fifteen years? Crowly had already undone the last thirty, why not give him the rest and get a few in return? Quid pro quo. Fifteen or more? What if he lived longer? In prison. They couldn't give him any more for adding Landeau and Remcheck to the list, and whatever he served would be of little consolation or comfort to dead men.

Then he slipped into the fantasy of how he might do it. How he might do it efficiently, lacking anything of a scheme or plot, without being associated with the act. What I need, Carter told himself, is a Rambo. How about a mercenary? Murder for hire. What would it cost? Three thousand for each. Hell there are people who would do it for a lot less.

There I go, Carter mused, looking for a superman, a savior. And he knew if it was to be done, he'd have to do it. It was already too late for him to avoid association with killing Crowly. Hell, even if I didn't have anything to do with it they'd come looking for me. If Crowly died of natural causes, they'd probably determine my bacteria killed him.

"Did you breathe on him?"

There'd always be those who would know I did it. And why not?

It was wishful thinking, at best. A way to burn off the anger of the afternoon and as Carter knew, little else.

When he arrived home, coming up the walk, he noticed the Christmas tree in the living-room, the red and green lights blinking behind the lace curtains, and for just a moment did not remember the tree being there. He had the feeling he was approaching the wrong house. Inside, a newly made fire burned in the fireplace.

Without checking for Katherine Marie, without removing his coat, Carter went upstairs to the bedroom and closed the door. He found attorney Paul Absyth's number in the directory, dialed it, then sat on the bed to wait.

Absyth had represented Anselm Nolan three years before, the only bright spot in that dismal day. Then at a cocktail party several months later, offered Carter his services.

"If you or anyone else ever gets into that kind of a bind, give me a ring," Absyth had said. "I'll donate my time to the cause."

The cause, Carter reflected. Keeping university professors out of the slam. Jesus, we are an evil lot.

"Paul Absyth," Carter said, "Could I speak to Paul Absyth? This is John Carter."

Then Carter was talking into the silence on the other end, not sure for just a moment if Absyth was there.

"Several years ago, after the Nolan case, you said I should call you if I needed help. Well, I think I need it now, and I'm calling."

"I was wondering if I'd hear from any of you," Absyth said. "How many are they trying to get rid of? Who got letters?"

"I don't know for sure," Carter said.

"I saw it in the paper. Sounds like dirty business."

"This is something else," Carter said. "This isn't about the letters."

He relayed the facts to Absyth as best he could.

"Well," Absyth said, when Carter finished, "they haven't done anything yet. All they've done is threaten. Until they actually do something, there's nothing we can do. Go through the hearing on Thursday, let them do what they will, then, if it's necessary, we'll get together.

"Maybe they won't do anything. Maybe they're hoping to intimidate you."

"If so," Carter said, "they're doing a good job."

"Don't quit now," Absyth counseled, without knowing how far Carter had gone. "If they want war, we'll give them war."

"Okay," Carter said, holding his breath. "Thank you, Paul, and if need be, I will get in touch with you. Right after the meeting tomorrow."

Carter replaced the phone and sat staring at the wall above the nightstand. He was tired, exhausted, and was tempted to lie down. Instead, he pushed himself up and crossed the room to the table near the back wall.

The table was a French Provincial antique with a well-seasoned glossy top. An inlaid band of pink and white marble ran around the edge.

From there he could see into the backyard and alley. It was a pedestrian, quiet view he enjoyed. He often used the table as a desk for writing, and the top was cluttered with the usual secretarial and office paraphernalia, two small stacks of books, and a couple of Ming Dog bookends.

He slipped open the table drawer and took out the .32 Smith and Wesson he kept there, laid back the folds of white cloth of the towel he had wrapped it in, and balanced it in his hand, testing the weight and size, the comfort of steel on flesh.

The weapon had come to him thirty years before from an acquaintance who was going into the Air Force and wanted to liquidate his personal property to finance a week-long bender before going.

He weighed the hard steel in his hand, then snapped open the cylinder and dropped in six rounds, carefully, deliberately, one at a time. When it was loaded, he slipped it into his coat pocket and went downstairs and out into the disappearing afternoon to walk and think.

Chapter XVII

Walking in the night assuaged Carter and often served as a tonic for his psychic ills. Amedeo beneath Anna's window, he remembered. Restless, but with a deliberate patience, he circled the outer edge of the campus following the one-way ring-road from north to west to south.

The wind on his skin and the limited universe of vision in the dark night insulated him, drove him back onto and into himself, where he resided best. There he could account, recount and evaluate the depths and occasions of his plight.

He walked because he believed man still to be by nature a creature who perambulated, prowled, physically by whatever energy he could muster without the pretense of harnessed or guided forces.

On occasion his walks carried him into nearly uninhabited and isolated areas of the city, uncharted areas for Carter, and several times he had made it to the outskirts of town. Block on block he passed beneath the streetlamps, into the light then out again into frigid, bleak darkness.

Kant in his gray coat, Spanish cane in hand in Königsberg. Immanuel stalking the paths, punctilious on the small Avenue of the Lindens, at three-thirty, precisely, his mind wound tighter than a watch spring—along the banks of the Baltic, never more than forty miles from home. He could have gone to St. Petersburg, or Helsinki. But why?

An acquaintance once told Carter that Helsinki was about half the size of the cemetery in Chicago and twice as dead. Maybe it was as true in Kant's day. In the world of the mind, why bother?

Within the hour, slowly, methodically, he circumnavigated fraternity-row, the tennis courts and soccer fields around the stadium, the acres of experimental agricultural and student-rooming houses, giant three- and four-storied residences lined row on row with shared driveways and postage-stamp yards. On this December night the portals were huge, soft, warm yellow beacons in a dark universe. Most of the buildings were decorated with Christmas wreaths and banners, colored lights strung from the eaves. For a brief moment Carter dipped into the nostalgia, the fantasy of Christmas gaiety and warmth sheltered from the sharp winds and chilled damp air of the night.

Again he replayed the afternoon's inquisition.

"If you sign this, we can move on."

"No, I won't"

"You have treated your students judiciously and without prejudice."

Crowly wanted to set up a conflict. He's already got a stooge—he's recruited an informant to claim I have not. And why "judiciously and without prejudice?" There's a lawyer on the end of that.

"So, Professor Carter refuses to verify that he has held his classes for the required time."

What is required time? Grade school again. Are we to assign busy work? Fifty minutes on Monday, Wednesday and Friday. Seventy-five on Tuesday and Thursday.

Then this library thing. Technically, they're probably right. But I did not intend to . . . And the other thing. Vivien. What did they know that he could not deny?

"Confess!"

"No!"

"Confess!"

"No!"

Beyond the residential areas he passed the neons of McDonalds and Hardees. The early evening traffic thinned out, and along the tree block stretch of Calgary Cemetery's half-stonewall and ornate, black-iron-spear fence, the last of the cars disappeared entirely. The fence ran the full length of the cemetery, broken by an arch and pedestrian gate at the center. A hundred or so feet to either side a two way drive circled into the cemetery and then back out. The drive entrances did not have gates.

Then the "Professor Carter" crap. The formal address to attempt to legitimize their scheme. Attempting to cover their stench with formality.

Carter paused briefly at the stone steps of the entrance. The wind pushed leaves along the sidewalk and against the iron rods of the fence. In the darkness of random patterns among the stones, trees, among the cinder paths, lay bits of the scattered pieces of his history at Barker. Within the fence were interred a dozen or so people he had known.

He tried to name them, as he tried on occasion lying in bed in the morning with his eyes closed to remember the names of lovers from years past. It was a listing and naming of passions—pieces of his life. A small part of which was kept here, now. Colleagues, acquaintances, a student. No. Two. One, Carol Burgess, whose face after ten years he could still recall.

A tall, full-bodied girl, she had made a profession, a lifestyle out of adolescence. She had perfected the costume, adopted the behavior, developed the habits of adolescent acuity with an inordinate enthusiasm. She became acculturated to adolescence as quickly and deftly as another might adapt to a city or a profession.

Once she hounded Carter into dismissing class early so she could get to the Union in time for a U-2 concert. She said she listened to Heavy Metal because she needed it for her personal history.

A bright-eyed, excited, enthusiastic child, she had for a time occupied a seat in the front row. No. Not occupied. He would say graced a seat in the front row, graced a seat with the pure pleasure of living.

Her infectious enthusiasm had flattered Carter's vanity. He wanted to think the efficacy of his teaching sparked her interest, had touched her spirit, but in the end, he knew it had more to do with her than with him.

Then an ending Friday, a last weekend on a highway a few miles south of town she had gone finally, taken from the tangle of a Volkswagen mutilated by a semi, led away by an irrevocable black hand.

In ways she reminded him of Vivien. It pleased Carter, now, that he had seen fit to oblige her request. Even though he did not much value U-2.

Vivien and Crowly's accusations. What did they know about the day in the library? How had they found out about it? Who was there? Had someone seen them? Who?

He recounted what he could of the day and recalled, vaguely at first, then again in more detail, the sound, the noise he had attributed to Vivien.

And, beneath a flash of doubt, doubting himself, he believed Crowly. Everything Crowly said was true. He couldn't tell the truth unless he had dirt to use in the accusation. Crowly had talked to Vivien. She confessed. Confessed? To what? How do you confess when you haven't done anything? She had told Crowly—but how did he find her? From Murphy's.

Seamus Murphy?

Carter dropped the inquiry. Speculation meant nothing. His mind filtered through the parts and drifted back to the cemetery and its occupants.

And who among them might he choose?

After Carol Burgess. Yes. Terry Monroe. Another student. He knew her only by name—a plain featured and quiet young woman who preferred to be left to herself. She, too, died suddenly near mid-semester from leukemia, he was told, which had tracked her to Barker from some possibly distant locus.

Carter had not understood why her parents had wanted her buried in Calgary. His memory said she was not a native of Lancaster. Why then buried here? To end where you end? In view of the university? Were they following her wishes?

The empty seats were stamped in memory, wounds opened in memory. The vacant faculty offices and the empty seats filled by the tide of the living emptied into the void, another instructor, another student on another day, another taking up space—the flux of time and activity flowing into and over the wound.

For the moment he resisted a temptation to go into the cemetery, to tramp again, as he sometimes did, among the monuments.

If Mason had been buried here, he would have gone in. He would have found the newly torn and piled earth, the scar of that wound, freshly made and swollen and bare and raw. He would have talked to him, as he had the many mornings over coffee and bad weather, carried on as if nothing had transpired. He would have asked him if he knew what he was doing.

What kind of a question is that, Carter? Did Mason remember who he was? Memory. Karshokov's syndrome. Brain cells short-circuited by alcohol. Mason didn't drink. That's my number, Carter confessed. I'm the amnesiac. Mnemosyne, the bitch, complaining and trivial, without anything of scruples. Never there when you need her, but hanging about, waiting, willing to remind you of what you would rather forget.

Carter's leg ached and he pulled away from the gate, hands deep in the pockets of his overcoat, aware again of his fingers wrapped around the cool steel of the revolver.

Why did Ardyth have Mason cremated? It was inconsiderate. Just then he needed a symbol, a grave to stand over. A site for confession, a reason.

An absence of belief did not trouble him, but more what he had surmised, had assumed, what he had imagined and did not want to believe, a facile piece of reality he would have rather avoided. Just once, he told himself, just once Carter, it would be nice to be wrong, to be surprised.

The names hung in his head. Henry Caldwell, Alicia Turner. And not just names. Those gossamer faces of memory, it seemed always to appear when he looked over his shoulder.

He found the gate and pushed against the rusted hinges, surprised it gave way as easily as it did and swung open beneath the weight noiselessly.

"An embarrassment," Carter said, with droll seriousness. "What kind of a cemetery gate are you? You've failed your calling. Your chance," he told the gate. "There's no horror in silence. I mean, where's your sense of drama? What will the ghouls and spooks say?"

No horror in silence? The words came back. Silence. The greatest horror.

Traveling with only a sliver of a waning crescent moon shining through the large bare trees he had difficulty seeing the path and navigated in among the stones mostly from memory and dead-reckoning.

"Reckoning for the dead," Carter said, "deduced reckoning," and steered into a newer section of stones and markers. He stopped near an old toolshed, to calculate his position.

Who had he come to visit? From whom could he take heart? Regain a shred of self-assurance? Caldwell, of course. Henry Caldwell.

"Henry, where are you?" Carter called. "If I've come out in the night and wind, the least you can do is be agreeable."

There were several new graves and Carter wondered who and how. Where will they bury Remcheck? How about Shindel? In the hog pen, of course, where else?

Moments later he found the grave. The markings on the stone read

HENRY CALDWELL
1921 1989

and Carter sat on it as if it were a bench. The wind had subsided but there were no owls or nighthawks that he could see or hear.

"Well, Henry, how do you like it here?" Carter said, addressing the grave as if he might have been inquiring after a child in a new neighborhood. "Have you looked around? If you haven't, you know, it's pretty much like any other graveyard. Lots of stones and trees and animals—a fence. The kind of thing you'd expect. Anyway, it's a respectable place. Just thought you should know."

Carter bent to the wind, and waited as if he expected a reply.

"Henry, can you hear me? Of course you can. The dead always listen to the living. It's their fate, their punishment. They have to listen to our babbling—and why not? They haven't anything else to do."

The Henry's voice stirred on the wind and Carter listened.

It was Henry who had been conned and beaten by Joshua Laertes in the legendary golf game Laertes had played walking backwards through all eighteen holes. The caper cost Henry fifteen hundred dollars and a loss of prestige for which Henry had never forgiven Laertes. If they were not friends before, that day they became adversaries, at least in Henry's view, separated then for the next years by a rancor he carried with him to the grave.

"I should have brought your golf clubs," Carter said. "You could practice among the stones. Rattle a few woods off the marbles."

Carter supposed Henry's animosity had to do with more than the golf game. They had been members of the same department, and therein, no doubt, was the source of the game, the reason for the game. Henry losing fifteen hundred on the bet only added to the enmity.

"Henry," Carter said, "the reason academic squabbles are so bitter is the stakes are so ridiculous.

"But don't worry. You'll get a chance for revenge. There'll be a celestial fairway where you can catch Laertes and go whacking divots among the clouds."

Carter chuckled.

"Well, Henry what do you think?"

Notwithstanding his follies, his occasional misjudgments and gullibility's, Henry Caldwell had been the youngest full-professor in State's history. A Joyce Scholar, he was, in Carter's estimation, a brilliant, witty and self-possessed man, as eloquent and articulate as anyone at Barker. For ten years, until his death, Caldwell occupied the Neibold Professor of Literature Chair at Barker.

His wife, Claire, was French, a Parisian, a novelist. A small, thin woman with deep-set, intense eyes, she spent most of her time trying to convince Henry, and everyone else, that he was the more brilliant of the two. And although Carter had substantial regard for Henry's abilities, he had not been convinced.

Caldwell and Carter became friends early on, and if Caldwell had a failing professionally, to Carter's mind, it was in the classroom. He had an unbending intolerance for students, especially poorer students, students who demonstrated what he described as "the gelded mist of literary fantasy."

"They're nearly as bad as those religious spooks," Caldwell told Carter. "These people don't think, they hallucinate. Délire."

When Caldwell became ill Carter was there. He stood by those final six months and watched Henry die a slow and possibly chosen death. At fifty-eight with advanced emphysema, Henry refused to reconsider or alter his habits. He smoked three packs a day, and in nearly total belligerence and defiance, began drinking heavily.

"Cigarettes," Carter said, "cigarettes. And booze. You should have a billboard instead of a headstone. Here lies a tribute to Liggett and Myers, fondly remembered by R.J. Reynolds and Pierre Smirnoff. If the proof is in the pudding, it might as well be 90 proof. Missed by all."

Late in his illness, when Carter was certain Henry knew the end was not only impending but imminent, Caldwell made a confession Carter had not expected.

They had gone with Mason to lunch in the cafeteria at Temperly. Because of his condition Caldwell could not walk even the short distance from the elevator to the cafeteria without pausing. He was a small man, totally bald with hazel eyes and a pale complexion. He walked with great effort, shuffled, unbalanced. This day his skin was ghost-white.

"This would scare me," Caldwell said, in a weak whisper, "if I didn't have faith in God. I have always believed God will take care of me."

Carter resisted the temptation to respond. Their reflections in the glass doors of the cafeteria, his potbelly and bowed-legs and Henry's thin image, were strangely deformed, a brace of wasted twins, idling their days together. Unlike the apocryphal Descartes, with Henry it was not a matter of keeping or losing faith, but of keeping or losing his mind.

The innocent and childlike admission startled Carter, as did the cadaver-image of pale-skin and hazel eyes, and the realization a man with a mind as good as Caldwell's would drum up a religious scam to shroud his flagrant self-indulgence.

The rote recitation stayed with Carter. The lack of oxygen had delivered Henry to a younger and more innocent age. Then, too, the confession explained a bit about why Clara had always humored Henry as if he were a small boy—and also why Carter regarded him as harmless and entertaining, a friend, while realizing had he become an enemy, as he had with Laertes, he'd have been a vicious and annoying one.

Carter took out a cigarette and lit it, then dropped several more onto Caldwell's grave.

"It's too late," Carter said. "Maybe they'll soak down to you."

Carter stood and walked around the headstone. It was comfortable here, in the inclement night. He felt good. He revisited Caldwell.

"What now, Henry? God did nothing for you at all. A gelded fantasy?"

He waited for Henry's answer, to hear the rasping voice on the soft winds of memory, Henry's face contorted, ready with a well-contrived response.

"Well, now, John," saying slowly, as he always did, beneath the deadweight of consideration, saying, "John you never have wanted to give imagination its due. You need more imagination. Think of what it has done for the world."

Carter nodded as he had done so often with Henry's words.

"Brought to the world. You can't really believe that. Don't you mean, brought the world to its knees?'

Carter had read that the three most influential men in human history were Mohammed, Christ and Buddha. And that, he believed, was the sum of it, the true commentary on human imagination.

Religious fantasies spread like a mental paralysis. Marx hit on it. The world would have been a better place if religion had been the opiate of the people. Unfortunately, it did not tranquilize sufficiently, encouraging . . . ? What? Well, history is history. Carnage. Blood-witted zealots raping the countryside—physically, emotionally, mentally.

Carter walked off a few paces and stopped. Henry's voice had sobered him. Stay in a place long enough and imperceptibly, step by step, year after year the graves creep in. They surround you like the shells of rotting, half-burned wagons circled for protection.

Our annuities, Carter postulated. Instead of watching Wall Street we should keep a Dow Jones on cemetery activity. Activity on the big-board is brisk, down 6 by 3 by 6.

However, what Carter judged to be late in Henry's decline proved to be only relatively late. Several months after he was diagnosed Henry showed up in his old office. Carter saw him sitting in silence, one leg hung over the other, emaciated and gaunt, his face ashen, hands lying in his lap.

Later in the day Carter came out of the men's room and nearly walked into Henry, hunched over his cane, mouth agape, holding his ground for a moment.

"How the hell are you, Henry?" Carter said.

Henry lifted his eyes slowly, cognizant of nothing, did not speak, but tottered off toward his office.

Two hours later he had fallen in a slump, head lying on the desk, facing the wall, stone still.

Carter's impulse was to check on him. Perhaps he had already expired. Then a secretary roused him and led him away, to where Carter did not know, although it didn't seem, under the circumstances, to matter much.

Carter did not attended Henry's funeral. That afternoon, he sat alone in the living-room of the big house on College Street looking down an empty street. He sat alone with a bottle of bourbon and a candle he had lit and set on the sill.

He had never put much stock in eulogies. Panegyrics were for the simple minded. What connections there were in living need not be talked about in death. Nothing to be said or surmised by anyone would have touched what Carter felt for Henry.

The last syllables of his voice dropping onto the barren earth, Carter abandoned Henry.

To the left fifty feet or so he found the marker for Alicia Turner's grave. There had been a visitor recently. Several small bunches of plastic flowers were scattered at the center of the grave.

Not too recently, Carter inferred. An old lover, no doubt. Come to remember the good times. And there were good times. How about a night on the river bank, a spring night?

Into her seventies Alicia had the reputation and the practice of attracting younger men—numerous younger men. A bawdy old broad, an art instructor, her final and most lasting contribution may have been her penchant for decorating herself with paint and beads, anything the environment offered—including a stand of handsome, vacuous, youthful studs.

God knows, the old tart had something that attracted young males. Somewhere in the flourish of shriveled, animated animal vitality they found the musk or scent, the spoors of an irresistible sensuality. And once settled downwind in the odorous precincts of whatever she emitted, intoxicated by the fog, the ambience, their pursuit was nothing if not dogged. They followed her in a cluster, a menagerie of threes and fours, always, fops and punks in baby-blue body-suits and silk shirts, the uniform-of-the-day, trailing more than following, behind more than with her. When she swung onto the stage, her layers of brocade-lace veils covered their eyes.

A good bit of her charm, Carter believed, had to do with the illusions she created—both about her person and her life. She would sweep into a room, onto a stage, a scene, a wilting fairy-queen, mystical, gossamer in a haze of veils and gauze, always just slightly out of focus, a traveling circus of fading female fantasy and flesh come to play Barker State, to give a last, and in a sense, lasting show, not of plan, but simply because the contour, the rise and fall of the road brought her there.

One of Alicia's suitors stood out in Carter's memory. He was a tall, gaunt youth, six-three or more, thin and sallow, with a Roman nose and two teeth missing from the right side of an infrequent but decadent, invidious smile.

To add to the spectacle, he was possessed of the tiniest hands and feet Carter had ever seen on a creature that size. As a boy Carter often heard older men describe adolescent males as "all nose, pecker and feet." In this case it was at probably two out of three. Not bad, Carter mused.

More than anything, the smile intrigued Carter. The smile was not a smile in any usual sense, but a hybrid grin, a shy, withdrawn and exposed self-conscious grin, and a grimace.

His eyes were dark and sunken, circled with deep blood-blue bruised patches. He was both outlandish and fascinating, or, fascinating because he was so unusual.

Alicia's troop had about it a strange and coded rank Carter never did fully decipher. The pecking order had to do with Alicia's preference of the moment, and the menagerie seemed always to intuit and discern immediately what this might be.

She had never to ask for a drink, never to state openly she did not want to speak to someone, or tell anyone when it was time to go. They took cues from a gesture, an intonation, the cast-of-eye with which she beckoned or gave them dispatch.

Of course, there had to be a promise at the center of the connection. But a promise of what? Sexual favor? Scholastic favor? What sort of bequeath was this?

Several of the followers were not students. And none were theater or art students. So what was the glue? The companionship of the group? Carter didn't know. Maybe fashion, the lore of dress and manners—they were each mannered and polite. Maybe they were fag-hag groupies—a gaggle of girlish geese.

No one knew Alicia's origins for certain. In her late forties, speculation at Barker said she was Hungarian and had gone out during the uprising in '54.

Ten years later she passed for Spanish, a passing she encouraged and embellished with stories of a childhood in Madrid, Barcelona and Malaga.

Later, she dismissed the stories as "episodes in a place in my chronicle," or laughed saying "Yes, darling, my father was Spanish, a Diego, a superlative man of grace and wit from the Lower East Side."

Others, taking clues from other conversations, placed her origins in Moscow, Chicago and/or Paris or Rome.

Depending upon the season, the whim, the occasion, she fueled speculation with a particular and renewed zest and flourish. Her university file revealed nothing more unusual than graduate work with an MFA from Columbia and references to several Paris galleries. Carter assumed, had anyone looked they would have found she had painted her artist vita as carefully, as lavishly and flamboyantly, as she had the dozens of canvases spread about her studio-loft apartment.

Beyond his fascination with the fop-troupe, Carter had a deep regard for the old woman. Because she might have actually lived through the ordeals of one or more of the stories she encouraged, she appeared beyond the stigma of convention. Her places of convention had been usurped by idiosyncrasy. She emanated from another country, another planet, another world, with a pure and well-developed regard for what she perceived, as well as a good sense of how others perceived the world. But to his mind what she did was pleasing.

The facade of her posture, of powder and paint and veils, with an almost blatant disregard for the character she created, concealed a well-grounded practical self. She seemed at once a child in mother's clothing, on stage, playing to the audience, and yet a veritable, mature woman who had seen a great deal of a not altogether pleasant life. With part of it she indulged her troupe, the other she put on canvas.

Carter heard by the grapevine she had died of complications of an unmentionable disease, a recurring case she picked up during the depression in Italy. However, it had been a particularly nasty ending. Her hair fell out, she lost her teeth.

But for love of decoration, Carter thought, why not? Put on bells, a bone in your nose. Maybe she foresaw her end. A shameless old reprobate. And delightful, Carter would have added.

Carter squatted down, trying to read the inscription. The small afterglow of the moon did not offer much help. His eyes were not accustomed to the darkness and he could make out only the dates, 1918-1991. Was that right? The last date 1991? Probably. Was it 91? What else happened in 91?

A gust of wind scowled in the high branches of the big trees. He ran his hand over the face of the marker, trying to discern the hieroglyphic engravings. The stone-marker resembled a Victorian mirror, an oblong oval with a dancer, head back, an arm extended in the air, the other akimbo.

If memory served him, Alicia's stone had an artist's palette, brush and easel carved on it. A thin wisp of a cloud slid off the face of the moon and just then he saw a shadow between the stones to his left. Carter's heart jumped and a surge of terror flashed through his arms and legs. He froze, and oddly enough focused on the sensation of his hands pressed to the nearly frozen dead grass on the grave.

He did not respond, but tried to adjust his eyes in the dark to the spot where he had seen the shadow. He watched and saw nothing, listening for a sound, any sound above or below the sound of the rush of the trees.

Then he heard it, broken off below the wind, a low rumble carried down between the stones, around behind him.

Carter had been spooked before in a cemetery. For several summers when he was eleven and twelve, to make a few dollars, he had worked mowing cemetery plots.

The summer days were long and lazy often without scheduled or planned activities. It was just after World War II, an age when the time of children did not much matter to adults. Most adults simply ignored children and refused to be inconvenienced by them. Especially in small-town Midwest America.

Those days Carter worked two cemeteries with several hundred plots each. The grave sites were in a deep, dense wood with a single road leading in three miles from town, and two miles from the nearest house.

Twice a month the man Carter worked for, Joe Neven, dropped him off in the morning with a bottle of drinking water, two mowers and enough gasoline to last the day. Sometime after eight in the evening he would return for Carter. Usually Carter finished early and had to wait on Neven. Hungry and tired and anxious, idling in the cemetery Carter was easily spooked by the dread of being abandoned, forgotten, left out, exposed.

Waiting for Neven, in the exhaustion of his boy's mind, he would secure himself within a small Stonehenge circle of monuments, his back to a large flat stone, watching the openings between the others for any kind of movement. In the ensuing dusk the lights from the cars passing on the road played strange angles and shapes and shadows and figures among the folds of his imagination.

One evening Neven had gotten drunk and did not show up until after ten o'clock. Several of the older boys from town who knew Carter was in the cemetery alone, parked on a service road in the woods and crept in among the trees. They found him asleep in the confines of his stone-circle, and quietly and carefully slipped wash-line nooses around his hands and slowly pulled his arms back around the stone, where, without speaking or showing themselves, they bound him and left.

Exhausted by the afternoon of working in the sun, without food, Carter was not easily wakened. When he did revive, not only did he not immediately recognize or remember where he was or how he had gotten there, but imagined, when he saw the tombstones and felt the ropes, that he was being pulled into a grave.

It was a stupid thing to think, he knew, even for a twelve-year-old, and only years later did he learn the names of those who had lashed him to the rock-mast.

The drunken Neven found him an hour or so later, bound as he was, weeping, steeled to his ordeal, and Carter had never shaken the feeling, and the terror was now suddenly on him again.

For a moment, squatting on Alicia's grave, the low rumble between the stones struck him with the renewed terror of his twelve-year-old heart.

What happened next, he was not sure. The shade, the form, flew at him, almost over him, and Carter scrambled away, then, up in a sprint for the safety of the roof of the tool shed fifteen or twenty feet away. He made it to the shed and stepping onto a single wooden saw horse sitting against the wall leaped onto the low edge of the roof and heard the animal growl again and felt a weight pulling at his overcoat.

His momentum going onto the roof carried him half way up and he caught hold of the top edge. He thought the dog had lost its grip but found later the weathered cloth of the coat had given up the hold. A large triangular hole had been ripped out about a third of the way up under the right arm.

Carefully, Carter backed up the slope, up the wet and slick of the corrugated roof as far as he could while the dog made repeated attempts to mount the lower end. Each time the dog jumped it would get about halfway up, then slip, its nails scrapping down the galvanized metal. Again it would leap at the building, snarling, fangs bared, and once nearly made it, paused, hung on the lower edge, its back legs kicking furiously.

Cater watched the animal's attempts, then looped an arm over a branch hung out over the building, unzipped his pants and urinated in the dog's face.

Hung there, mesmerized, for a moment, the animal ceased growling and instinctively opened its mouth to catch the spout until it had a full recognition of the nature of the offering. Then it dropped over the edge, below and out of sight, and Carter could hear it coughing and snorting.

Broke the chain of thought, Carter commended himself, pleased with so simple and successful a defense.

The dog stayed at the base of the shed for a short time, looked up at Carter once or twice more and growled, then sulked off among the tombstones. Carter saw there were two. Then he saw a third. The animal paused several times to shake his head and drag the sides of his mouth on the ground.

"Used alcohol and uric acid," Carter said. "It gets them every time."

Relieved at having outwitted the attackers, Carter tried to zip his pants. His hands were shaking so badly he couldn't pull the zipper.

Jesus, Carter thought, what if I'd slipped or he had gotten up here? "The Cubs" again. Professor emasculated in the cemetery. A B-grade country song. Caught between the stones.

His legs were weak from the sudden push up onto the shed and from standing on the angled roof. Holding to the branch he slipped down to a sitting position and stayed seated near the top on the cold metal of the roof for another ten minutes until he was sure the dogs had gone.

Then he worked his way down slowly to the lower end and onto the sawhorse. Coming off the roof his coat swung freely and the .32 in the pocket banged against the tin shed. He did not immediately identify the sound, reflected on it for a second, then dropped to the ground.

"Jesus H. Christ," he said softly, "some presence of mind. Some warrior. Armed to the teeth and you go around pissing on mad dogs."

Carter was nothing, if not premeditated.

He took the weapon from his pocket, watching the darkness, expecting the animals to return, then walked backwards a hundred feet or so along the drive toward the street before he turned his back on the cemetery.

Just then, Carter's blood was running again. I should kill him, Carter thought, again with Crowly in mind. But then what? How about all three of them? The Holy Family. How about a little extremism in support of learning?

And then what?

At best, they'd sit your ass down in the slam for twenty years. Your last twenty. At best.

Carter then imagined he might kill Remcheck. No, it was Shindel who needed killing. Cut the head off the Inca. Then the empire would collapse.

Shindel, imposing himself upon the university community. A pig-farmer demagogue—a sniveling sophist.

How would I do it?

Quietly, of course, Carter advised.

How about a high-powered air-rifle or pellet-gun—from a distance, at night. Pop! Poof! No flash. No smoke—almost no sound. A single shot. No ballistics.

And then?

What if I only wounded the sonofabitch? What if I didn't kill him? Politicians get mean when they are wounded. What if I miss and get caught? Even though . . . Then he's a hero. If he's dead, it's another matter. Deranged professor shoots university trustee.

During the encounter with the dogs he did not notice the pain in his leg. Adrenaline, he knew. But the leg hurt now and he had to rest every half-block or so. The pain had gone into his back, and when he tried to walk erect to relieve the ache, the leg hurt even more.

"Remcheck's pets," he said. "His canine corps, guarding the dead," thinking again of the dogs—his near misfortune. "Brutes and beasts loosed among the occasionally civilized."

From the edge of the cemetery he could see Lincoln Field House and the last of the crowd making it quickly from the parking lots to the entrance. The Barker Basketball Bulldogs were playing Indiana State in their final home game before Christmas.

He could hear the roar of approval, the beast-roar muffled by the domed-roof, and guided toward it almost without intending to.

Only rarely did Carter brave crowds for basketball or football games, and this was not the time. He walked on slowly, silently, alone and dwarfed by the mushroomed expanse of the field house, through the open field on the far side and down toward the river and the Garden of the Greeks.

The problem? After this afternoon, I'm too obvious. I'd be the first they'd look for. How many other people want Shindel dead? With his reputation throughout the state and county? There were probably plenty of people who would be pleased to see him dead. A few who would probably pay for it, or at least look the other way.

What about alibis? Where were you John Carter on the night of December nineteenth at seven-thirty Who were you with? Who saw you? Again the questions.

How would he account for his presence or, as the case may be, his non presence?

The Garden of the Greeks was a rectangle of hedges and walks along the river, populated with a dozen or so limestone statues of Greek myth. There was Ares, Zeus, Aphrodite, Hermes, Perseus.

The sullen river, the black winter river running in the night stirred anew his bitterness at Mason's death, the resentment at the betrayal. The residue of anger that had propelled him through the night, surfaced again.

"I have not yet learned that lesson," Carter told himself—the astringent lessons of forgiveness and acceptance—obeisance and servility. "And I'm not likely to learn it in the near future."

The moon was barely visible again, and he circled through the Garden passing Mercury on his left. The Garden had fallen into typical winter disrepair. Vandals had spray-painted graffiti on the base over the five attendants. The statue of Hermes closest to the river had toppled face down.

The statues were a gift, a bequest of sculptor Costos Constantine, who had worked and taught at Barker during the first decades of the century. All but Hermes.

The Hermes statue was seven feet tall (a foot taller than the others) set on a three-foot pedestal. Campus lore reported a Barker State trustee, not Shindel, had visited the University of Göttingen and had been so impressed by the statue of the Goose Girl, he insisted the Barker State administration erect a similar one in the Greek Garden.

The students could, the argument went, as students in Göttingen do, kiss the Goose Girl upon graduation.

After a good bit of debate and cajolery, a compromise was struck and it was decided, why nobody seemed to know, to commission a statue consistent with the Greek theme of the garden. Thus Hermes.

Hoping to avoid the embarrassment of openly displaying a university expenditure gratuitously honoring a randomly selected deity, then Chancellor Harold Roland had the statue set in the woods near the Faculty Center, where it remained for ten years or so.

Why a statue of Hermes? What was Hermes connection to the Goose Girl? Carter didn't know. Why not Apollo? Why not, Carter asked? Hell, why not Mike Fink? How would you like to kiss that hairy, mud-coated ass?

As president of the trustees, Shindel sponsored a program into place to have the woods cleared along the river by the farm house for low-rent student housing to replace the low-rent student housing that had been displaced by his high-rent student housing project adjacent to the campus. Thus, Hermes took up a new residence in the Greek Garden, near the river.

The early winter freezing and thawing had undermined the footing of the pedestal. The body and base of the statue were still intact, but the head and left arm with its caduceus had broken off. The arm lay in a single line of pieces, pieces glistening in the lights from the field-house, as if it had been pulled apart in segments.

Carter did not see the head and speculated for a moment that the statue had not fallen. Maybe the spray-painters had pushed it over and collected the head. It had happened before. The offending fig-leaf and genitaila of Epstein's Sphinx guarding Oscar's tomb in Paris was one night chiseled away. Then Cater saw the head at the edge of the river, lying face up partly submerged, staring blank-eyed out of the water at the winter sky.

"The pathfinder," Carter said, "the god of the stars. You can't even see the stars."

Carter pointed to the heavens.

"That way. Up. Polaris right there. Just off the tip of your nose."

Slowly, Carter circled to the left.

"You're a mess. Pathfinder."

The lights from the windows of the field house hung on the hill above the Garden, a miniature Milky Way of artificial suns. The roar from the game tumbled down the slope and for a second, just a second, Carter was reminded of the Acropolis, of the Parthenon.

"Hermes," Carter said, "you worthless orphan. How will you lead us? To what? Justice? To justice—into the flood waters of justice. What do you see with your stone eyes? What have you seen? Not only eyeless, but headless."

With his foot, Carter scraped together the pieces of the arm and stacked them at the neck of the statue. He stepped into the water and retrieved the head, turning it over in his hands. It wasn't as heavy as it should have been. A piece of his petasus was missing. A wing had been broken away.

Hamlet fingering Yorick's cranium.

Whose head now? Carter wondered.

A month after his execution, Thomas More's daughter Margaret took More's head off the paling of Traitor's Gate and kept it with her for the rest of her life. How would it feel to hold Crowly's head in my hands? Whose head? I'll tell you whose head. Mine. My head. They want mine.

"Imperial Caesar, dead and fashioned in clay."

African tribesmen keeping and sleeping with the skulls of their fathers.

The loathing of his dilemma, his cowardice, his failure of commitment to the task, had already curdled into the gall of contempt. It was a special form of self-flagellation Carter had come to several times in his life. Outrage. Faulkner called it "impotent outrage."

Carter knew, now, the seething and hatred he held for Remcheck and Shindel, the poison seeping into his heart, their venom, was poisoning him. And because of it he would, for a long time, hate himself, as he hated them. He would loath his cowardice in failing as he hated their stupidity and arrogance.

Carter set the head down facing the river on the small pedestal of pieces he had piled up. He paused, regarding the head.

"Why did Apollo forgive you? And what about Argos? A hundred eyes and still he sleeps."

And what about the ethics of violence? Without absolute morality—which prohibits violence and then breeds it. What are the perimeters of violence? What is justified and what is not?

Years ago, in Texas, if a man caught his wife in bed with another man, he could kill them and claim justifiable homicide.

During the sixties, expecting the black hordes to come swarming out of the city ghettos hell-bent on trashing and looting, the Nebraska legislature enacted laws to justify "killing in defense of property."

Within the year seven defendants (all white) cited the law as defense for killing business partners they claimed "were about to miss-invest the company's funds."

In Williamson County, Illinois, in 1924, twenty-five mine strikebreakers were executed in a graveyard, and no one, not one person did any prison time for the killings. Clearly, killing scabs in a graveyard at night was not even a misdemeanor in the coal county of Williamson in 1924.

Where did Immanuel's call to duty originate? And what would Jeremy have said? Is it honorable and morally permissible to kill a few so a civilization can survive? What is the utility in killing human beings? And will Homo sapiens survive, anyway?

The night, the events of the day, had brought a deep disgust to Carter's heart. This was not the Garden of Olives. Not Gethsemane. And I'm no messiah, he thought.

And still what he had not done tormented him—what he had hoped he could do and had not done.

He had walked the university world around and this was the best of it. Junk food parlors, mad dogs, the roar of crowds in arenas and stone remnants of a vanished civilizations lying ruined by the river.

Chapter XVIII

Carter crossed the campus at Cato's Walk in the bright sun of the beckoning solstice. The sun's fire in the trees burned down from the end of a phosphorescent rod, white and blazing. Fire falling from the sky washed the bare trees and walk with a luminous brilliance. In the southeast, the far space of southeast, the sun hung motionless.

Who will call it back?

Carter wondered.

Coming onto the quadrangle he heard shouting and waited as Betty Sutter overtook him.

She came up in a rush, carrying a thick briefcase and a stack of books under her arm.

"God, glad I caught you," she said. "Do you mind if I walk with you? I'll be late for lab, but that's okay. It won't cost me anything but an ass-chewing."

"No, not at all," Carter said.

"I saw you go past the Union, but thought maybe you preferred to be alone."

"It's all right," Carter said.

He suspected he knew what she had in mind, or could at least guess along with her.

"No," Carter said again.

"I heard what they are doing to you," Betty said, "and I want you to know we think it is a shame."

"We?"

"You have friends on this campus. They will support you."

"Well, I'm glad," Carter said.

In truth he took little encouragement from the promise. The power of academics resided always latently in their ideas and opinions. Otherwise they were impotent.

In the long run they could affect an enormous influence, catastrophic or beneficial on a society. But their short-term powers were anemic.

"Well, I'm glad to hear that," Carter said. "But what makes you think I need support?"

"You're being sacrificed."

Her voice was soft and kind, as if she was talking to a small child.

"Am I?"

"They intend to make an object-lesson of you. John, it's not difficult. If Remcheck and Crowly can get rid of you, this faculty will be so frightened, it will do whatever it's told."

"I hadn't thought of it that way," Carter said.

"You have embarrassed them. They think you are radicalizing the faculty."

"They? Who?"

"Remcheck and Crowly. In their eyes, you are an evil spirit."

"My spirit may be a bit malignant from time to time," Carter said, "but it's not evil."

"These aren't sane men. Remcheck is crazier than Zeus. Crowly thinks you are a Vietnamese spirit out to get him."

"He thinks I'm an evil spirit."

Carter watched her intently. A tiny woman, with a large square head, he had thought of her as a gargoyle. The description still seemed appropriate. Her skin was snow-white in the pure light and her features grotesque and beautiful, thick, yet fragile, with the delicacy of fine porcelain.

"You mean, he actually thinks I'm a sappy spirit chasing after his ass?"

"Yes. An evil spirit seeking revenge for what he did during the war in Vietnam."

"Revenge? Those people don't need an avenger. History will do that for them."

"All the same, he claims a Buddhist monk in Saigon put a curse on him and said Thanh hoáng would avenge the Vietnamese people. Crowly thinks you're a monk. He believes you have been incarnated with the spirit of Thanh hoáng."

Shortly after Shindel's election to the Barker State Board of Trustees he had led a crusade to replace University President Harold Roland and to appoint Remcheck president. After a search, that was, despite its claims, neither national nor sincere, the board stepped over six applicants, all far better qualified than Remcheck. When asked about the board's choice, Shindel told the press "God told me to pick Remcheck." Carter had wondered about God's choice of prophets and about his dialect. Pig Latin, no doubt.

Professor Cornford's observation that religion is geographical. There are no Muslims in the Arctic circle. Few Hindus in Rome. A psycho starts it. Infects the countryside. Then they all come riding down the mountain or across the plain with flaming swords and laws.

"Crowly actually believes I'm a made-over spirit of a Buddhist monk?"

"Yes. I'd say so."

"That's idiotic. Rational people don't believe stuff like that. No. It's a pretext, a red-herring."

"I don't think so," Betty said. "Look at it this way. Crowly can't use that as cause to dismiss you."

"Why not? Shindel used it as a reason for appointing Remcheck."

"Well, it's not the same. Shindel can get away with it. I doubt if Crowly could. Anyway, I've heard him talk about it a couple of times. He really believes it, John. He thinks you will get his soul."

"I may at that," Carter said, "if I could be sure he had a soul. I mean, it's one thing to kid around about spirits. But to actually believe it. Anyway, who told you this?"

"That they are crazy?"

"No. About my sacrificial state."

"They have asked Charles to sit on the Hearing Committee."

"Charles?"

"Lessiack."

"Why?"

"I don't know. He says he doesn't know either."

"Who else?"

"They didn't say, but rumor has it Harry Gotsch was asked."

"The entire faculty. Why Gotsch?"

"He's a very powerful man, John. He writes speeches for both the governor and for Senator MacMillian."

Just then Carter was on the outside looking in. What had Lyndon Johnson said about putting Hubert Humphrey on the ticket?

"Better to have him inside the tent pissing out than outside pissing in."

They had a thousand connections.

Here he had been flubbing about in Einstein's universe, amused with the links of consciousness and cosmos, paddling the muddied waters of illusion and paradox, and they were peddling influence, padding their nests and coffers, prepared to orchestrate a neat little sideshow at his expense. Talk about a shell-game.

Why Lessiack and Gotsch? To legitimize the hearing. The only positive note was Lessiack. Carter's fondness for him tempered his rancor. But that's what they want. They want it to look good. Bad wine in a new bottle. But it still smelled.

Now Lessiack and Gotsch were part of the plan. They fit into Remcheck's political scheme.

"Be careful, John," Betty warned. "They've already killed one person."

She paused a moment, a moment too long, as if she wanted to say something she shouldn't say.

"One person?"

"John, nobody but the police believe Mason Oldam killed himself. I've worked at the hospital on the psyche ward—on the fifth-floor. The rooms have security screens on them, which are better than bars. People don't jump through security screens."

"Goldenstein said Mason had gotten to the roof."

"Goldenstein is not going to tell the truth about anything. He's a psychiatrists—when it comes to facts he's more than a little inventive. Psycho facts."

"Then what happened?"

Sutter shrugged.

"Maybe we'll never know. Unless a volunteer comes forward with information. Even if a patient saw something, who would believe it?"

"Well, speculation isn't proof," Carter said.

"Just because we can't prove our suspicions, doesn't mean they're incorrect. We're always dealing with the out-of-sight, but it doesn't mean nothing's there."

"Or that it is there," Carter said.

"If I had my way," she said, "they wouldn't do this to you, you wouldn't be banished. You are among the best here, John. Among the very best."

"I thank you," Carter said. "But don't worry. The old man of Crete can take care of himself."

He watched her walk away, just then determined to ride the beast, to wait out Paul Absyth's counsel.

"Until they actually do something, there's nothing we can do."

Nothing grows here, Carter counseled. The soil repels the roots. And it's been that way since Shindel and Remcheck took over.

Carter rode the elevator to the fourth-floor alone thinking about what Sutter had said.

"They have already killed one person."

What did she know? He had the feeling she was not telling everything.

One person? Mason? Poor Mason. It all seemed so long ago. A hundred years ago.

In his office he reviewed the questions for an Intro exam he had at ten. After the exam he returned to his office. He found his mind returning repeatedly to the other end of the hall and the Vice Chancellor's Conference Room.

Why Lessiack and Gotsch? What else? Would they give silent consent to Crowly and Landeau? Following the Intro exam he found a small vase with a sprig of mistletoe on his desk. A note scrawled on a card with a smiling face was stuck to the vase. It read, "Travel with Aeneas. May you find safe passage in the Golden Bough. Good luck John."

Carter put the mistletoe in his pocket, took a small pad he used to scratch out lecture notes, and shortly before two o'clock pushed up the hall to the administrative offices. Janice Watkins hovered over her keyboard watched by the glazed white eye of her PC monitor. Three other women, secretaries at various tasks of typing, filing and eating, stirred among the desks and file cabinets.

The office was overly bright, and the pollution of perfumes and powders clouded the air. Staking out territory, Carter thought.

These were not among Carter's favorite people. They were vacuous, officious and petty, if not vicious. In addition to their menial tasks they perpetually indulged in a brand of gossip that often bordered on slander, with opinions of pure fiction, as vindictive as anything he had encountered. The Furies, encouraged by Clytemnestra with Orestes brand wagging in her chest. And, for the most, they were immune to censure, reproach or common decency.

Watkins had seen Carter coming and did not bother to look up.

"The meeting will be held in the Bolgia Room," she said.

Following her words, Carter veered off to the long hallway on the left. These rooms were usually reserved for board gatherings and Carter wondered at the significance of having the meeting here instead of in the

Vice Chancellor's Conference Room.

He navigated the corner and followed the corridor, reading the names on the brass plates on the doors. Jules Bolgia Room. Named for a former Barker State trustee and benefactor.

Outside the room Carter paused for a moment. The annex of the dead.

When Carter entered the room, Crowly and Landeau and Daly were already seated in a knot at the far end of the long conference table. They had file-folders and legal-pads and a telephone on the table before them. They did not look up or otherwise acknowledge his presence, and he took a seat at the opposite end, facing Crowly.

He eased into the chair and his side and back hurt where the dog had bitten him.

The night of the canine attack, following his orbiting odyssey, his journey in darkness, he had and examined himself in the bathroom mirror. The spot on his back was an ugly black-blue hematoma with a white center.

The animal's teeth had not broken the skin, so Carter assumed there was no chance of rabies or tetanus, but all the same he watched the discoloring with interest as it grew hourly into a disc the size of a saucer.

Carter had not been in the Bolgia Room before.

Two full-sized classrooms had been gutted, the wall between them removed, and the ensuing room made over. Behind Crowly on the far end to the left a miniature waterfall rippled over the rapids of plastic rocks and ceramic logs. To the right of the falls a huge felt-tapestry with a Barker State seal hung behind a high, antique oak entertainment center with a coffee urn and a small Christmas tree.

Dean of Students, Robert Lovell, and a woman Carter had not met but had heard a good bit about, Margaret Martin, were at the coffee urn. They joined Crowly and Daly and Landeau at the table and for a moment Carter suspected they may have been replacements for Lessiack and Gotsch.

Lovell, a retired Marine Corps tech sergeant, had come to Barker with the Remcheck company. The Martin appeared to be in her early or mid-thirties, had russet hair, large eyes and a quick smile.

Along the left wall, recessed individual glass cases held pictures of the current seven members of the Barker State Board of Trustees. The pictures were wrapped in a blue-velvet manta and the interior lighting gave them a strange and cadaver-like appearance. A brass name-plate and a plastic flower had been set in front of each picture.

The seven deadly sins, Carter judged, and tried to match the faces with the practices. How about Shindel? Gluttony? Pride? Greed? Avarice?

There wasn't enough to go around.

The deities of the university. Self-selected and appointed, mindless elected hacks who by a public vote of the unaware and illiterate insinuate themselves into the corridors of learning bringing the plague with them. People willing to put up thousands of dollars for an elected position that pays nothing. Ego, Carter was convinced. And power. Power over people. And graft.

On his note pad, Carter scribbled a line he remembered from Tacitus.

"Lust of power is the most flagrant of all the passions."

He had to keep that in mind. Another from Camus.

"The mind that must be right is a very vulgar mind."

Prestige and privilege and pretending.

At graduation trustees wore doctoral robes, and only two, to Carter's knowledge had even a B.A.

So, Carter reflected, my assignation place, my invitation to the dance, the slave market in Gaza, eyeless I sit in contravention, the counter-point of discord, to be immolated. Across the room from the pictures, the walls were hung with wreathes. Below the pictures were three small tables with group photos of administrators and trustees.

In one, Remcheck and Crowly posed in military dress—Remcheck in lion-tans and Crowly in the leopard-spots of camouflage. Crowly held the leash of a dog Carter judged to be a husky. The dog had a white eye. The inscription at the bottom was partially hidden by the frame, and from his position at the end of the table Carter couldn't have read it anyway. He assumed it had been taken in Vietnam.

Lovell and the Martin had just been seated when Lessiack and Gotsch came in. They nodded to Carter as they passed.

"Do we have assigned seats?" Gotsch asked. "Or can we select something at random."

"Fifty-yard line or end-zone," Crowly said.

For a moment, Gotsch stood watching the waterfall.

"Is the chancellor going to be here?"

"I don't know," Landeau said. "He said he'd try to make it."

"The chancellor may stop in later," Crowly said to Landeau. "He has a couple of small matters to clear up first."

"Well," Gotsch said, "we're supposed to play racquetball tomorrow and I'm not sure I can make it. I've got this bad back. Second time I hurt it in two weeks."

Crowly glanced at his watch, then picked up the phone and punched in three numbers and Carter could hear it ringing down the hall. Moments later Watkins came into the room carrying a stenographer's pad.

"Janice, close the door, if you will," Crowly said.

She had been standing in the doorway with her hand on the knob, but before she could pull the door closed Carl Johnson leaped in from the hall only narrowly missing Watkins.

He was dressed in a red blazer, green tie and yellow shirt and slipped into the seat next to Carter. He was breathing heavily as if he had run a long way.

"Ah," he said, trying to catch his breath, "I see I'm in time for the rite de passage."

"Carl, what's going on?" Carter said. "What are you doing here?"

"My dear man, if they are seeking your blood, the least I can do is bear witness to the letting."

Johnson's face was florid. The skin below his cheeks showed large bruise-like blotches. He had been off for several days for medical evaluation, the second time in three months, and Carter assumed his appearance was symptomatic.

"They think it's cancer," he told Carter. "Leukemia."

"Parkinson's Disease," he said on another day.

"Possibly hepatitis," on yet another.

He had lost weight. His eyes were sunken and hollow. His neck poked out of his now overly large collar like a shriveled stalk and he had lost a good bit of hair.

Age, Carter speculated. They call the fifties "cardiac corridor."

"Dr. Johnson," Landeau said, "we are not seeking anyone's blood. This is a hearing committee, and you are not a member of this committee."

"If you're not on the roster, you're not allowed on the field," Crowly said.

"I'm Professor Carter's counsel."

"That's correct," Carter said. "I asked Dr. Johnson to serve as my counsel."

"This is irregular," Landeau said. "Unprecedented."

"That people have counsel?" Carter said. "Unprecedented? In what country?"

Crowly leaned toward Landeau, head down, hand over his mouth, and for the moment nothing more was said.

"That scattered the vultures," Johnson said softly.

"Thanks a lot," Carter said.

"Jesus," Johnson said, "it took me fifteen minutes to find where they had taken you. This place reminds me of the catacombs."

"How about the labyrinth?"

"Ah. And the Minotaurus conducting the inquiry."

"They threw criminals to the Minotaur."

Without saying anything more Crowly opened the file-folder on the table in front of him.

"At Chancellor Remcheck's request, as Vice Chancellor of Instruction, I have convened this committee, and officially open this hearing.

"We are here to review the case of Professor John Carter, specify the complaints against him and to offer a recommendation to the chancellor concerning the adjudication of this case.

"First of all," he said, "I want to thank all of you for taking the time to serve on this committee. Special team assignments are always difficult."

He looked around slowly.

"Since it's difficult to know the players without a scorecard, I'll introduce everyone.

"Going clockwise, to my left is Dr. Landeau, Administrative Dean of Humanities, Professor Andrew Daly, Department of Education and AAUP President, Professor Charles Lessiack, Physics, and Professor Harry Gotsch from English.

"At the far end of the table are Professors John Carter and Carl Johnson, Department of Philosophy, and on this side of the table, Dr. Robert Lovell, Special Assistant to the Chancellor and Dean of Students. Next to him, Margaret Martin. Margaret has recently been transferred from Student Activities to the Office of Public Relations. My secretary, Janice Watkins will take notes."

Throughout the introductions Carter watched Martin. Although they had never met, the grapevine had it that she too made the rounds of top administrators and board members.

Her latest assignment, or at least her most recent assignment, had been the Chairman of the North Central Evaluation Committee, Wesley Evans, a vice president of a small college in southern Minnesota. During their visit Evans and the NC committee had been housed at a Ramada Inn just off campus, and rumors suggested that Martin as director of committee liaison and accommodations, not only spent her days at the Ramada but gave freely of her nights as well.

Another from their stable of corporate whores, Carter thought.

Crowly read from a typed copy and Carter speculated about the origins of the document. Probably a whip from the law firm the board employed had prepared it. One hundred seventy dollars an hour to write speeches for semi-literate ex-jocks and military misfits who want to pretend they are educators. Management counseling, they called it. Risk management, crisis counseling, Carter called it. Catastrophe capitalism.

Whatever it was called, it was a lot easier than practicing law. Over the last several years, with typical adversarial arrogance and aggression, the firm had counseled Barker State into several millions of dollars in law suits—which it, of course, litigated.

"This is not a court of law, so we do not speak of charges, Crowly said. “We do not have to establish guilt, since no one will be convicted. We are only interested in desirability. We are operating on behalf of the university as any committee might for any business, to review and recommend a winning strategy.

"The chancellor has asked me to inform you, that it is the university's position that tenure shall not be a question here. The Board of Trustees recognizes the seriousness of removing a faculty member from his position. However, tenure at Barker State is a matter of board policy. The board grants tenure, and the board has the right to deny or withdraw tenure."

Crowly's eyes crept across the page, line by line, pausing as his voice paused when he had trouble articulating or stumbled on a word.

"Now, Professor Carter, as you know, we have had numerous complaints from students and their parents over the last year that habitually, as a matter of policy, you do not hold class the fully allotted time specified by contract."

"I always knew your students didn't have any class," Johnson said.

"Your student evaluation ratings are extremely low. You are one of the two poorest rated members of the Philosophy Department."

The classroom evaluation system at Barker was especially odious to Carter. Early in his reign, Shindel had decided the Barker faculty needed to be evaluated. Evaluated as prime pork might be evaluated. "Held accountable," he said. And for the purpose of devising a system, a fair system, Crowly and Landeau were directed to prepare a student questionnaire to be used as an evaluation tool. This they did in a matter of ten minutes or so.

The drift of the questionnaire, Carter found, had little to do with teaching or classroom procedure. Professors receiving grants or otherwise providing the university with income were exempt from evaluation.

The questionnaire was not only poorly conceived, but in many cases students did not comprehend the questions. When asked if the instructor had provided a good atmosphere for learning, one answered, "No. The goddam room was always too hot or too cold."

As a matter of self-defense and for information, Carter devised his own questionnaire, and for years gave it to his classes on the last day of the semester.

"May I respond?" Carter said.

Crowly did not answer.

"You'll get a chance. As soon as Dr. Crowly is done," Landeau said.

"It won't matter," Carter said. "What is said will not stand up separately or severally. And nothing I can say will have any bearing on this sideshow, anyway.

"On any number of occasions, I have asked for the names of those who accuse me. Each time I have been denied the information. The practice of allowing and encouraging anonymous accusations is both educationally unsound and unethical. If a student has a complaint about classroom procedure or methods, let him bring it to me. If it cannot be settled there, then have it brought before an impartial body for discussion.

"The problem here is not the complaints, but that you have encouraged students to file complaints so you can use them on the faculty as you are doing here."

"Doctor Carter," Landeau said, "this hearing is being conducted by a legally constituted university committee, and it would help if you could refrain from invective and personal attacks on its personnel. No one is using anything on you."

"Invective? You're trying to throw me out. You're after my head and you accuse me of invective? Maybe you need a course in linguistics and logic."

Landeau was a small man with thinning hair and gray skin from too many hours indoors. Carter pictured him as a boy, an adolescent, small but not weak, timid but already with a penchant for deceit, rat-like with a pointed nose and small eyes—a rat with a sickly pallor always scrambling to get off the bottom of the pile.

Carter sat back in his chair and did not say more. He crossed his legs and noticed the edge of the inside sole of his right shoe was dotted with small specks of red paint he had picked up in the hall. Red paint and mud. Red paint. Goat's blood. Mud and blood.

"Furthermore," Crowly read, "your unconventional and eccentric opinions and views have alienated and estranged students, which in turn has caused them to drop classes and to withdraw from their studies. The drop rate in your classes is nearly twice the mean. This has cost the university thousands of dollars in unclaimed revenues, reimbursed fees and lost book sales.

"Within the course of this semester," Crowly said, "the office of the Dean of Humanities Division has received no fewer than six complaints from various churches and religious establishments that you are using the classroom as a forum to attack religious organizations and their programs.

"The Illinois Human Rights Act section dealing with higher education prohibits creating an 'intimidating, hostile or offensive educational environment.' On at least two occasions you have offended students by teaching someone called Thomas Aquinas in your ethics class. Another student has filed a complaint that you are not teaching material relevant to what the students are to be learning. You told a class you had your neighbor chained up in your backyard. This was not only a lie, but frightened one student into dropping your class."

"An example I gave the class," Carter said. "It was a problem I gave the class about people harming themselves"

"Well, I'll tell you how you have harmed yourself," Landeau said. "You're going to be dismissed because of stories like that."

Crowly raised his hand, ending Landeau's interjection.

"Professor Carter," Crowly continued, "you had a class read a story about cooking a man in an oven. That, Professor Carter is encouraging violence, and cannot be tolerated."

"It's a well-known essay," Carter said. "'The Case of the Obliging Stranger.'"

"How about 'Hansel and Gretel'?" Carl said.

"The policy," Crowly said, "of the Board of Trustees of this university, as amended June 22nd of this year, states that the university's mission requires that instruction which is actually provided is that which is intended to be provided. It gives charge to university personnel to aid students in reaching their goals, a policy you have clearly and knowingly violated."

So, Carter thought, this is it. My Nielsen's are down a couple of shares and I'm being canceled. Well, I'm not surprised. Philosophic inquiry has never been popular.

On several occasions students had complain that Carter did not ask the proper questions on tests. When he inquired as to what would be a proper question, he was advised that the questions should be "handed out in class, as other professors do." This he understood, referred to faculty providing detailed outlines and examination questions to assure everyone in the class with a grain of memory would get a perfect score. They were called "study guides."

Carter had often heard instructors refer to themselves as performers. Teaching as acting. But he never expected to have the concept used on him.

Carl Johnson's voice rode over Crowly's to snap Carter's attention back to the table.

"What you should do," Carl was saying, "is dismiss those students from the university as uneducable, persons without the sense or sensibility to be educated, rather than using them as a standard for instruction."

Crowly continued reading and Carter spread his handkerchief on the table. He took the mistletoe from his pocket and placed it just left of center on the handkerchief. Crowly looked up in mid-sentence, then stopped reading to stare at Carter's end of the table, and the mistletoe.

Now Crowly looked directly at Carter, who sat hands folded, head down and eyes closed. Crowly's mouth fell open, slack and twitched at the corner.

Carter lifted his head slowly to canvass the faces at the table. Nothing. Absolutely nothing. They were bland, without expression or apprehension. They were empty-eyed, tilted and angled. Easter Island heads. Landeau had his hands in front of him. He was bent with his nose very nearly poked into his hands, his eyes focused on the ashtray at the center of the table.

Gotsch settled into his chair, a bloated deity, corpulent and puff-faced. Daly clicked his pen. They reminded Carter of exhausted peasants, dropped and stuck to a canvas. A strange brigade, Carter imagined, my defense, or maybe not, the jury, the executioners? In any case, their presence and appearance offered little of inspiration or hope. Philistines. Florentines.

The voice continued, "Furthermore, Professor Carter, on December thirteenth, by your own admission, you entered the university library without authority, on a day the library was closed and appropriated books without notifying the librarian. This is theft, pure and simple. And the university legal staff is prepared to press charges to recover the lost property and to prosecute you for this theft."

After an initial survey of the books, after reading several chapters on schizophrenia Carter gave up and the books had gone no farther than the front hall table. The morning after his initial meeting with Crowly and Landeau, he had dropped them in the book-drop outside the library.

"In addition, on the day your broke into the library, you had a university student, name Vivien Connors, with you. This is the same student with whom you have been conducting a sexual liaison. Again, this is a violation of university policy. It has been a standing policy of this board and this administration that students and faculty members of Barker State University not consort sexually, and socialize only with the consent of the proper university authorities.

"Moreover, you have violated the law by purchasing alcohol for this student. This has been brought to the attention of the District Attorney's office, and they are prepared at this time to bring charges against you."

Carter often reminded classes that, "The moral thinking of those who judge man as an important creature differs considerably from those who at the other extreme see him as a worthless and depraved, self-seeking animal bent only on pleasure."

How would Crowly and Landeau attempt to define human nature? Carter wondered. What would they say? Would they agree with Hobbes? And their assumptions? Carter did not think it would make a pretty picture.

Sensibilities fired by temperament. Another chapter for his book.

"A Sashay on Under Human Standing."

"You have been given a full accounting of the university's reasons for your dismissal. Speaking for the Barker State Board of Trustees, I have no recourse but to ask for your resignation. If you fail to resign your position as professor of philosophy by noon tomorrow, Friday, December twenty-second, a special meeting of the board will be called to terminate your employment."

Gotsch raised his large head, his dewlap swinging as he rotated to watch Crowly.

Landeau closed the folder and looked up.

"If you have anything to say, Professor Carter, the committee is prepared to listen."

"Committee," Carter said. "Inquisition."

"Professor Carter," Landeau said, "this is university committee, duly organized and authorized by order of the Board of Trustees."

"Merry Christmas," Carter said. "Welcome to kangaroo-court. All the authority in the world will not sanitize or sanctify what you are doing—or dignify you in having done it. This smells. You people smell."

"Professor, we are not interested in your opinions," Landeau said. "I suggest you confine yourself to the issues at hand. This is not a personal matter. You're just the first duck across the pond. If you have nothing more to say, we need not go any farther."

Carter was tired. A wave of sadness washed over him. He had never at his cynical best imagined anything like this. He had a sore throat, and his stomach burned.

"There is," Carter said, "a place in the collective human soul, a vast and sloping ground, a lost place of stone as black as the cliffs that seal it. And in this we have come to such a place.

"You claim, a stretch of an untested logic, that I have driven off students and/or seriously injured others. I would like to remind you that education is a difficult and often painful business, an enterprise not for everyone. The very reason, I might add, so many people end up with degrees in education and business.

"In my years here at Barker I have encouraged students, good students, at every turn, to expand their intellectual universe and have done nothing, in or out of the classroom that teachers have not done for centuries. What you have accused me of, in only one instance has to do with my teaching. Your other accusations are an invasion of privacy. What I do on my own time is my business and of no interest to the university."

"Professor Carter," Landeau said, "the reputation of this university is at issue here. You have exhibited a flagrant and wanton disregard for students, your colleagues, the university and the community."

After his initial presentation, Crowly did not speak. He watched Landeau, waiting, Carter sensed, waiting for a cue.

"You say I am injuring students," Carter said. "How so? What do you mean by injury? I haven't harassed anyone physically. I mean, I haven't pushed anyone out of a helicopter. Or off a building, or anything like that.

"Charles, what do you think?" Carter said.

Lessiack smiled.

"I suppose there could be merit to the charges. None of us perform in the classroom as well as we might."

The sun falling into the room painted Lessiack's face with a somber, shadowed mask. Carter could see the outline of his skull beneath the skin, the tight skin stretched drum-like over the bone.

"Professor Lessiack," Carter said, "will every student in the physics department graduate?"

"The physics department is not at question here," Landeau said. "The sciences have their own requirements."

"Sciences?" Carter said. "How about the humanities?"

"The rules are different," Landeau said.

"The rules are whatever you want them to be at the moment. Anyway, these are not charges. There is nothing at all legal about this."

"This is a legal meeting. We have legal status."

"In other words, you have already decided what you're going to do, and this gathering, this coven, has been called to provide a paper-trail."

"At this moment, no decision has been made," Landeau said. "Your fate is up to you."

"Fate?" Carter said. "Destiny maybe. But fate? Fate follows us around like a bad-dream, but we certainly do not control it."

"If you resign, nothing will be said or done."

"If not?"

"Then we'll have to decide."

"What do you think, Charles?" Carter said.

Lessiack was still smiling.

"I think Dean Landeau has stated his position clearly."

Crowly raised his hand.

"It's half-time," he said. "We need a chalk-talk. Let's take a break, give everyone a chance to stretch."

In a few minutes Carter and Carl Johnson were alone in the room.

The prospect of leaving Barker, bereft, with empty pockets, did not greatly distress Carter. He had not put much stock in money, or prestige, although his removal would probably necessitate a major restructuring of his life.

The house had been paid for and Katherine Marie was gainfully employed. He would not end up in the pauper ward or debtor's prison. The prospect of reading and writing without the burden of the classroom appealed to him. What troubled him most was having to leave Remcheck and Crowly to their schemes. If their kind could control and intimidate the universities, no one was safe, the entire society was at risk. Certain cultural entities, Carter believed, had to be subsidized. The arts, education, the glue holding life together.

The closest thing to an absolute in human terms was culture—art, music, philosophy and custom, laws—a fabric woven from the disparate threads of human lives. And it could go wrong. Rather than moving toward a more livable and meaningful provision, it might make a wrong turn. Clearly, to Carter's mind, Barker State had taken a wrong turn.

And though Carter's contributions had been minuscule, had they been greater, Remcheck and Crowly would not have behaved differently. They had flagellated him with senseless technicalities. Arresting Lautrec for having short legs. When asked why he did not jail Sartre for his criticism of the French government, de Gaulle is reported to have said, "You do not put Voltaire in jail."

Well, so much for de Gaulle. What about Voltaire?

"Il avait de diable au corps," and ". . . into whose hands hell had given all its powers."

For his services Voltaire spent a good bit of time in the Bastille.

Carter knew his position was without merit.

There were a few who value education, but not many. Most understand it as a troublesome undertaking—to be tolerated if it can produce cash, eventually. And those who provide the grit-and-grist of scholarship, and teaching, are not to be trusted, but maligned, and never protected.

And what was the academy, anyway? A collection, at best, of people who investigate and expand thinking about the world and about thinking. A loose collection of individuals brought together, assembled in a few rooms. Certainly not the grounds, the buildings, or the administrative hierarchy. And what if they did not assemble? The diaspora of the academy would still be an academy. A villa in a garden-grove of the mind, Epicurean, where a society of arts and sciences might flourish.

But just then he stood alone, outside the garden, outside anything he could define as a human community. Convention, custom, habit, prejudice and bigotry and stupidity had bunched humanity into a seething, stinking huddle. Hobbes hadn't missed it by much.

Teaching he took as a moral obligation, an imperative, a categorical imperative. He occupied the chair at the end of the table in this room, not because it was the right thing to do but precisely because it was the only thing to do. He had chosen the position, Galileo called to Rome. He had taken the stance that led to the inquisition as surely as if he had selected the seat. He had called himself to Rome to be tormented.

Carter, too, had a vision of how life should be lived and what civilization could be. And he would not assent to theirs. To do so would have been a form of moral suicide.

So, Carter thought, open season on the academy. Professor duck. One hell of a position to be in, staring down the barrel of the gun with a maniac's finger on the trigger, a maniac with glazed eyes, a drool, hell-bent on adding foul to the fowl in the pond.

But the taste was bitter, the sponge of gall did not satisfy his thirst or ameliorate his pain.

"Suppose I am right," Carter said to Carl Johnson, "what use is my defense? The people I must sue for relief and remedy are my persecutors."

Chapter XIX

When the room emptied, Carter spoke softly to Carl.

"Are the others having hearings?"

"From what I've heard," Johnson said. "That's the MO. These are dissemblers and crafty men, John."

"I'm going to have coffee," Carter said, "you want a cup?"

"Black," Johnson said, "black for black Thursday. By the way, if you're up to it, when this is over, I have a flagon of hemlock in my office."

The clock above the plaques showed two-forty-seven. The time had not gone quickly. Carter crossed the room on shaking legs. The burning in his stomach had subsided, but he still felt weak. Verbal combat of this type was new to him. The uselessness of the conflict and its absurdity was old-hat.

"This is not a personal matter," he told Johnson. "They're telling the truth, except as it serves their personal whims."

Carter handed Johnson the Styrofoam cup.

"I'm a very small pawn. They intend to reconstruct the entire university—turn it to profit. The university as their private property. Barker State as General Motors. In a way it's the Nixon argument—elected office as personal property. An instrument of ownership rather than a cloak of trust. But it won't work unless you have an excess of resources. Even then it's inefficient and unworkable. But to do it they have to get rid of people like me."

"How about Buchenwald," Johnson said.

"Dammit, Carl, I'm serious."

Johnson smiled. "So am I. Will no one rid me of this turbulent priest?"

"I'm not a priest."

"You might as well be. Teaching has always included the vow of poverty. What's left? Obedience, chastity? My dear man, you have broken all your vows and they are intent on excommunicating you."

"The other night I was looking at *The Chronicle*, and it seems to me the curators of the better schools, say the Ivy League schools, and the better schools here in the Midwest, are really working to support scholarship. These clowns are doing just the opposite.

"Instead of protecting us from law suits, they threaten us with them. Instead of standing behind the faculty faced with students who want a grade for nothing, they encourage attacks on the professorate by the students—and all the while violating the civil-rights of both faculty and students."

Carl was right. Just then Carter saw himself as a man without a profession. Set adrift on an open sea, refused entry to a country of origin or choice, would a man also lose his nationality? Well, maybe not. But what difference would it make?

"You're dangerous," Carl said. "You're undermining their beliefs. The faculty must be kept under control."

"Certainly. I oppose their beliefs."

"Ah, but there's more. War and business are good for the soul. They believe that. Oh, they wouldn't say it in those terms, but then maybe they would. Anyway, it's true. The bureaucrats had to get rid of Socrates."

"I'm not Socrates."

"Oh, not a priest, not Socrates. Then why are they after you? Who are you?

"And it's not just Socrates. How about Hume and Galileo? John, you've got the Pope pissed at you. You're disturbing his universe. You're just uncontrollable. An ingrate, a malcontent."

Carter had heard it all before and didn't put any more stock in it now than he had before.

"Lord, lord," Carl said, "Anyone who disagrees with Shindel and Remcheck is anathema. Think of it, John. The activities of our genitals submitted to moral analysis. Socratic scrotum-scrutiny. My dear man, your privates are no longer private. Well, at least not private for which they were intended. The purpose of life according to Crowly is professors shall not have erections. You naughty man."

"Well," Carter said, "maybe it's better this way. I don't suppose there's much choice. If we abdicate, they'll succeed by default."

"Entropy," Johnson said. "The massive black cloud of entropy. Once we were good men picking our way among the ruins. Today we are the ruins."

"Do you believe in dreams?" Carter said.

"Heavens yes. Half of my life is guided by dreams. The other half is a dream.

"Ah, to dream is to create. The nurturing enterprise of all science and art. Those figments and fancies that reveal the world. The closest to nature and living beings are the truest. They tell us about the reality we are. Symbolism."

"Well, that wasn't what I had in mind." Carter shook his head. "Not exactly. Dreams as sketches of what we feel about what we live."

"Maybe dreams are recorded experiences to make us remember and feel."

"Neurons firing at random."

"John," Johnson said, "nothing is random."

"For several months, now, I've had this recurring dream. I'm on a runway or highway or parking lot or something. A large asphalt surface—a black surface at night and there are lights everywhere, small lights, spotlights, flashing lights, and a large crowd milling about. Some of the people are happy and laughing, others are crying, others just watching. Each time, I'm in the back of the crowd, trying to see over the heads to what must be a startling or curious event to have brought so many out at night. Once or twice I felt I could almost recognize the faces.

"I've been teaching 'The Men in the Cave,' too long. It's like being chained in place with a fixed point-of-view and shadows coursing along the wall in front of you.

"When I wake up, I feel things have gone wrong, or something's lost—maybe someone. As if an airplane crashed. One moment the pilot and the people are alive and well and then—Boom!! I want to run time backwards and correct the error before the irretrievable becomes irrevocable."

"Maybe you saw a plane crash when you were a child and don't remember it," Johnson said. "My dear man, it's all a bad-dream. A bad-dream with a seventy-year run."

He reached over and placed his hand on Carter's arm then straightened the edges of the handkerchief.

"I've been admiring your altar-cloth and mistletoe. We should have a mass for the dead."

"The golden bough," Carter said. "For safe passage."

"You should have brought the entire plant."

While they were talking, Lessiack came into the room. Then the others followed. Landeau and Crowly were in the hall at the door and Carter could hear their voices, but could not make out the words. Then they, too, came in and closed the door. On his way to his chair Crowly circled wide, staying well away from Carter.

"You called a recess so you could consult with your attorney," Carter said when they were again seated.

Crowly looked at Landeau, but neither answered.

"Have you been directed by legal counsel about proceeding with this hearing?"

"We consult consul on matters of this kind," Landeau said.

"We keep in touch with our people in the press-box," Crowly said.

"That's what I thought," Carter said.

He leaned toward Johnson.

"This is a trial, Carl. In spite of what they say, they're conducting a trial."

"We have one more matter to discuss," Crowly said, "concerning Professor Carter's case."

"Now it's a case?" Carter said.

"At any rate I haven't finished. I haven't finished answering your earlier accusations."

"Right now you're fourth-and-twenty-five," Crowly said. "You should be thinking about punting. You're playing without an offensive line."

"I'm not interested in your silly sports metaphors," Carter said. I am not assuming I have lost anything. Nevertheless, the record should be corrected.

"Item one. Hawthorn Library. In custom and practice, for as long as I've been at this university, teaching and research personnel have had free access to Hawthorn. Access has never been at issue in memoranda or in any other form of communication with this faculty. Your accusations to the contrary are not only frivolous but also slanderous. You have implied I have stolen books and damage university property. The accusation is an attack on my character. I do not take it lightly.

"Likewise, your insistence that I have wronged my students by not conducting classes every period for a full fifty minutes is ridiculous. The classroom task is to educate students, not to hold them captive until their sentence runs out. If in my judgment their time can be better spent in other educational activities, then it is my duty to adjourn classroom sessions in favor of the other.

"There are no time-clocks at the classroom doors, and before I can even entertain this as a serious complaint I will need from you a list of other faculty, a list signed by those faculty who have not held class the full-time on even one occasion this semester. And I will expect each and every one of them will be brought before this committee, or another, for the same purpose as I have been brought here.

"It's bad enough you have taken the time and energy to bring these accusations against me. It is sadder that in this institution, this society, you have found the permission and support to do it. There is something fundamentally diseased in a society when people in public office put their personal politics and greed above the public welfare."

Carter paused to empty his coffee cup and glanced at Johnson who was nodding defiantly, his chin in the air.

Throughout Carter had watched Lovell and Martin. Martin had not spoken to anyone but hung at the edge of the proceedings like a poorly painted trinket. How quickly these people fall in line with their mundane office routines, setting up football pools, collecting for birthdays. They were in the halls constantly coming and going, spinning the web of a shuffling, babbling enterprises.

For Remcheck's birthday Martin had taken up a collection from the hundred and fifty support personnel and provided a large cake in Crowly's office for a party. The white sheet-cake with red-rose-frosted trim was lettered with Happy Birthday Chancellor Remcheck, Our King. A small golden crown had been set at the center of the cake.

That had been Martin's idea.

Lovell supplied a video tape he had made of a party at Remcheck's of the entire administrative higher-echelon indulged in a drunken frenzy that ended with the revelers stripped down and splashing about in Remcheck's huge swimming pool.

The merriment and fun of children's sex-party games. Friendship and camaraderie and companionship among the insipid and ridiculous, the entertainment of watching the frivolity of another party. Watching the watched watching each other.

Did they ever have anything to say beyond a grunt, beyond sexual innuendo or football scores? Maybe Vivien was right.

"What goes on in my classroom," Carter said, "that is relevant to the understanding, the teaching and discussion of philosophical thinking is none of your business—and I wouldn't expect you to understand it anyway.

"The bad opinions I am accused of holding, come from traditional and highly respected academic sources. What I think—no, not what I think, but what I want my students to think about, comes from Schopenhauer, from Kant, from Hume and Marx and Dewey and Ayers, and yes, from Einstein, Bohr, Heisenberg, Paule. My bad opinions, as you call them, reflect the greatest thinking of many of the western world's greatest geniuses.

"Voltaire said, 'My trade is to say what I think.'"

"And you are a long way from Voltaire," Crowly said.

"Your claim that I have injured students and the university by drumming out those who do not and/or will not work, who will not learn, and that my actions are undemocratic and un-American, as well as inconvenient for you, is ludicrous.

"I have been associated with this institution for twenty years, have seen it grow from a college to a university, and have never asked of my students anything but their best.

"I resent the insinuation that I have been remiss and morally deficient because I will not allow simpletons and the intellectually incompetent to remain on the educational dole. When I go before a class, it is incumbent upon me to instruct and examine and judge and by judging to certify those who are there.

"This society is shot through with people from Wall Street to the slums who want something for nothing. People who want to do something without actually doing it. People with bogus degrees and preposterous titles. But they will not come out of my classroom—not if I can help it."

"You people have created your own myths," Landeau said. "And we are going to expose them."

"I might add," Carter said, "one of my duties here at Barker is teaching a senior ethics seminar. And from whatever point-of-view, even Machiavellian, if you want to go that route, there is a strange and disgusting irony that an institution, in which ethics courses are taught, should be operated without regard for ethics. It is insufficient in any but the most primitive and rudimentary and deceitful mentality to apply principles after the fact to excuse what has been done, rather than using them before hand as a guide for what will be done.

"Otherwise, my private life is my business, not yours."

The years of lecturing, of leaning into the uncompromising winds of indifference and reticence had tempered Carter's oratory. Once he would have carried on, emotionally, vigorously. But now, in face of the arrogance, the unflinching arrogance and intolerance before him, he again lost heart.

Why spill reason and good sense upon acidic soil? A professor he had studied with at the University of Chicago had referred to the university as, "A steaming, fetid pit of yelping jackals watching wolves in sheepskins casting imitation pearls to the swine." The description stuck in Carter's mind, and if it insulted everyone, too often it seemed appropriate.

He glanced around the table, to Gotsch, then to Lessiack and Daly. During the recess Gotsch had stopped to talk to Carter.

"This is a distasteful business," he said.

His words caught Carter off guard and he answered abruptly, "It certainly is."

Carter thought possibly the proceedings had annoyed Gotsch and made him sympathetic.

"How did we get to this?" Carter said.

"We are all men of worth," Gotsch said, "not great men, but men of letters and worth."

The emphasis should be on worth, Carter would tell Gotsch later. The idea of quality in the university was too often neglected and seldom rewarded.

From the tone of the exchange and Crowly's failure to repeat his last statement, Carter sensed the hearing was winding down.

They are nearly done with me, he thought. They've had their fun, used up their allotted time, killed off a sufficient part of the afternoon.

"There is another matter," Crowly said again.

He nodded to Watkins and held up an index finger and Carter went back to his notes.

There were several items Carter had wanted to clarify, but decided now he had said enough.

Watkins disappeared into the hall, and for the moment of the lull everyone in the room shifted and stirred and Carter relaxed.

"One more matter?" Johnson said to Carter. "What is that?"

Johnson looked past Carter to the door. Before Carter could answer, he nodded. "No doubt she's part of it," he said.

Carter had been studying Johnson's face and followed his gaze to the door. Watkins came into the room followed by Vivien. Watkins ushered the girl into a chair near Martin.

Vivien wore a white blouse and beige knee-length corduroy skirt and white, low-heels. For a moment, she seemed out of place, as she had at his kitchen door the morning of the ice-storm. She appeared older and more distant, but he couldn't tell immediately if her coloring came from the makeup, from eye-shadow and lipstick or from the winter out-of-doors.

Although he had seen her without clothing, he had never seen her dressed in anything but Levis and sweatshirts, and never with makeup.

He would not, until then, have described her as overly attractive, and was reminded again, and poignantly, how the accouterments of paint and decoration could master the human eye. How beguiling to sight and mind a little paint and cut-of-cloth could be in the lives of creatures starved for beauty.

Her appearance reminded him of the day the previous summer, home alone at mid-morning in an usual disheveled condition of consciousness and ill-repair, he had been called to the front door by the bell, where he found two young women who announced with wonderful smiles and winsome voices that they were "working for the Lord," and wondered if they could read to him a passage for the day from the Bible.

Carter shook his head, but his failure to verbally give them dispatch held them, and him, as they read from the Twenty Third Psalm.

He judged the older to be seventeen, the other maybe fifteen. Both were impeccably dressed and finely groomed. The older girl, the prettier of the two, had such soft black hair, white skin and blue eyes, Carter could not tell what had been made up and what of nature was showing through.

The proportions of her face and neck and shoulders, her superbly rounded breasts and hips beneath her sheath dress, blended so perfectly with her smile and voice that even hours after she had gone, deep into the shadows of late afternoon, her image stuck in Carter's mind.

She had touched him with more than sound and sight, or the idea that "The Lord is my shepherd." Indeed, for a time, he was captured in the experience of a young woman he did not know even by name.

Vivien smiled, a weak pale smile, when she saw him, and just then, in the mystery and impending implications of her appearance, he could say only, "Hello."

She did not acknowledge Carl, and Carter assumed that even at this late date of the semester they may not have yet reconciled their differences.

Crowly greeted Vivien, and by the casual enthusiasm of the introduction, Carter guessed this was not a chance appearance. More than that her presence, having her in this room with these people, filled Carter with foreboding. For this he blamed Crowly and his disdain and contempt became loathing.

"You sleazy sonofabitch," Carter said to Crowly in a barely audible voice.

"I'd like to introduce Ms. Vivien Connors," Crowly said.

He shuffled through the folders and pulled out several type-written pages and handed them to Landeau.

"Ms. Connors has information relevant to this hearing," Crowly said.

"Disgusting," Carter said again, this time loud enough for Johnson to hear.

Landeau shifted his gaze to Carter.

"Professor Carter, you could save yourself and everyone else a lot of trouble and humiliation. It would be the sensible thing to do."

"You can resign," Crowly said. "It would be easier. When asked about the German invasion of Austria, Mussolini said, 'When an event is inevitable, it is better it should take place with your consent rather than in spite of you, or still worse, against your will.'"

"What I don't understand," Carter said, "is why you would quote a criminal who was machine-gunned and hanged by his heels so his subjects could pay their respects by spitting on him."

"By the way, I'm sure Il Duce will be glad to know you are eternally grateful to him," Johnson said.

Crowly ignored the remark and spoke to Vivien.

"Ms. Connors," he said, "have you met Professor Carter?"

Vivien looked at Carter and smiled.

"Yes," she said. "Yes, I have."

She spoke softly, in a frail voice, an anxious nervous voice, as if she was unsure of what to say. Coming into the room she hesitated when she saw Johnson, before moving cautiously to her chair.

"Would you tell us about your relationship with Professor Carter? About how you met."

Again she glanced at Carter, as if seeking approval, and for a second, a fleeting second, he thought she did not understand the nature of the gathering, or what was going on, and might think she could help him by telling them what they wanted to know.

How in the hell had Crowly found her? Had they been trailed? What kind of information did he have? And how did he get her to come here?

Were they in this together? Had Crowly sent her to his office?

What had Crowly told her? And then, what would she tell? What would he ask her to tell? Carter braced himself against the distaste and horror of having his private life exposed, held up and examined and ridiculed. Again he had underestimated their viciousness and was filled with a new rage.

"What do you mean?"

"Where did you meet Professor Carter? Was it in his office, in class?"

"I was in a class of his last year."

"Which class?"

"I don't know for sure. I think it had something to do with philosophy?"

"An Introduction to Philosophy. Philosophy 150-07," Crowly said.

Vivien nodded.

"So you've known Professor Carter for a long time."

"No. I wouldn't say that."

She looked down at her purse on her lap and began picking at the strap.

"He was very nice," she said. "He is a very good teacher."

"How long have you known Professor Carter?"

"Oh," she said. "You mean like, well, I only really met him a couple of weeks ago."

"And how was that?"

Carter didn't know what he expected her to say, but her answered was matter-of-fact, he thought, and without rancor.

Jesus. So far so good. Maybe he had it wrong. Maybe she told them something else. But what? They brought her here for a reason and Crowly already knew the story. He wouldn't have mentioned it unless he had verification.

"I stopped in his office and asked him to help me with a class."

"Then what happened?"

"Not much. He wasn't very nice—but we became friends anyway,"

Landeau was still reading from the list of questions.

"Where did you go when you left his office?"

"I waited for him on the quad."

"Then what?"

"Well, when he came out, I talked to him."

"Ms. Connors," Landeau said, "would you tell this committee your age?"

Vivien lowered her head and hesitated.

"Nineteen," she said finally, reluctantly.

"Then what did you do?" Crowly said.
"What did I do?"
"You and Professor Carter."
She looked at Carter and blushed, then smiled as if she had been asked to reveal a secret she alone held.
"I don't know. Nothing."
"Nothing?"
Carter pushed his chair back and leaned forward with his elbows on his knees and his head in his hands. Jesus Christ, he thought, how do I pick them? Of all the females on this campus, in the world, I get one who never got past show and tell.
"We went out for a beer."
"Then what did you do?"
"I don't know. It was snowing."
"A couple days later you met Professor Carter at Murphy's Bar," Landeau said.
Vivien starred at her purse, nervously turning the ring on her left index finger.
"Yes," she said, "we met there."
She spoke softly in a monotone, in an exhausted and distant voice.
"Would you tell us what you did at Murphy's?"
She did not answer immediately, but looked at Landeau as if she did not understand the question.
"We sat down," she said, raising a whisper of amusement around the table.
"Well," Landeau said, "did you do anything else? What did you do after you sat down?"
"I don't know," she said. "I guess we talked. We had a cigarette."
"Did you have anything to drink?"
"Of course we had a beer," Carter said. "For Christ sake, what do you do in bars if you don't drink beer?"
She nodded.
"We had a beer."
"A beer? How many?"
"Two or three," she said. "I don't know."
"Ms. Connors, the time you met Professor Carter at Murphy's. What did you do when you left Murphy's?"
"I've already told you."
"Yes. You have. But would you to repeat it for the committee?"
She looked at Carter for verification.
"We stopped at the Cap and Cork for a bottle of wine."

"He bought a bottle of wine."

"Yes. I didn't have any money."

So, Carter thought, we are done with the facts. Now they want to punish me, to expose and embarrass me. Sack-cloth and ashes. Flagellation. My sins are far too mortal and grievous to merit mere condemnation. I must be flogged and racked. Carter listened as she spoke, as Landeau read the questions and as she spoke and detailed the chronology of their liaisons, the facts of their contacts the last several weeks.

"When you left the Cap and Cork, where did you go?"

"We went to a friend's apartment."

"And you had sexual relations with Professor Carter."

"Yes," she said, not smiling now, but with a calm, detached voice he no longer recognized. She could have been any woman.

"How many times have you had sex with Professor Carter?"

"Three times. Well, two times."

"Could you give us the dates?"

"I don't remember exactly."

"I can give you the days," Landeau said. "December third, December eleventh and December fifteenth.

"Now where did this take place?"

"At my friend's apartment."

"What is the address of the apartment?"

Before she could answer Landeau took a stack of papers from his folder and passed them around the table.

"This should be of interest to the committee," he said.

When the stack came to him Carter took a copy and passed on the rest. The packet had been professionally printed with a cover sheet identifying the document as "Conversation—December 11." It appeared to be printed like a movie script. Then Carter saw his name at the top of the page.

Carter
Are you awake? It's after seven. I have to go.

Connors
You don't have to go. You don't have any place to go. Anyway, if you go, you'll just have to come back. So why go?

Carter
I have to visit a friend.

Connors
You're already visiting a friend. Don't be greedy.

Carter
Do you think there's hot water? There certainly doesn't seem to be any heat.

Connors
Visit your friend tomorrow. Stay with me.

Carter
I'd rather stay. Much rather.

Connors
Good. Then it's settled. We'll stay here for the rest of the night.

Carter
By the way, when do you expect Ruth?

Connors
I don't know. But it's not a problem. She doesn't mind sleeping on the couch.

Carter read the words slowly, not only with a disgust for the details, but also with a shocked revulsion for the satisfaction Crowly and Landeau had taken in preparing the document.

"Just a few questions about this conversation," Landeau said. "First, what day was this?"

"The cover page says December 11," Carter said.

"Do you recognize the conversation?"

"What I recognize is an invasion of privacy," Carter said. "This is a violation of my constitutional rights."

"Our lawyers don't think so," Landeau said. "Where were you when this conversation took place?"

Carter did not answer. Substantial pieces of his life were unraveling. And if not everything, still a great deal of what he had lived in faith would come undone.

Landeau directed his questions to Vivien, and Carter sat back, the murmur of her voice fading in the distance behind him.

As an undergraduate Carter had fallen under the spell of a Jesuit philosopher, Wade Williams, a displaced Texan who as much as anyone had molded Carter's professional attitudes and opinions. In what Carter considered a profound insight, Williams pointed out that in his opinion man could not live without something to believe in. "Man needs to believe. If not in God, then in whatever he holds greater than any other."

The observation did not register with Carter as an enduring truth—not then. But of late he had reconsidered. While prying himself free of religion, without intent or design he had become a true-believer, as dogmatic and unyielding in his assumptions as even the most ossified, lunatic bishop. Buffeted about as they were and fading in and out like radio signals in a storm, the ramifications of his self-erected doctrines and credos edged into focus only a bit at a time,

When he left the Greek Garden that night, Carter had decided to bypass Murphy's and return home, but in the passage at a corner found himself abreast the remains of Newton Hall. The sight of the old building, the basilica, its rubble stacked beneath the high neck of the Pettybuilt crane had truly saddened him. The east wall had been totally demolished and the filament of the crane's long cable hung loosely and oscillated in the wind above the headache ball lying on the bricks.

The cell of a second-floor classroom had been halved, the blackboard still intact against the inner wall. The door at the end of the room hung open on a twisted hinge, exposing the black rectangular artery leading to the labs and offices, the honey-combed inner-sanctum where over the years scientists had percolated their concepts and formulas, meticulously separating the facts of legitimate inquiry from the foibles of assumptions and guesses. Here lives had been spent chopping into the forest of creation, and in small part the known micro-particle connections of the material world were analyzed and arranged into a kaleidoscope of the infinite verities energy, space and time allow.

As an Instructor in his early placement, Carter was assigned a room in Newton for an Intro class. Three mornings a week for four months he eased into the shabby, regal cloister of the old building, a novice, a voyeur in a hall lined with opaque half-glass doors, the air permeated with the ambiguous whirr of small motors, bubbling electrical pods and the smell of hot glass and seared metal. When by chance or choice a door stood open, his gaze lost itself in the tangle of metal and glass and blinking tubes shrouding the banks of the lab counters. Men and women in white coats, at peace and ease, waited, it seemed forever waiting, at the counters, braced on the heels of their hands, over manuals or other documents.

Then Carter would pause to follow by eye the tubes and wires, the stems of the clamps and frame-works, to sort through the structures, the connections the mechanicals made with one another. Invariably, however, he stumbled and lost his visual way. But when the door closed or time and sense required, when he abandoned the vision, he took with him a child's view and awe, the scrambled awareness of the complex and mysterious.

In their search for the beginnings of matter and the universe the white-coats had unfolded the cloth enshrouding the basic elements of human life, as well as the possibilities of its ends. Herein, Carter believed, might lay the link between the natural world and man's soul.

Inspired by the power of the vision he approached his classroom those days not so much as a stage, but as an acolyte might approach a sanctuary, the keep wherein resides the golden idol washed in the brilliance of the fountain of white-light.

Those days he lectured as if he approached the unknown, as if words might be found, finally, to describe the fleeting link of the creative surge that pulsed along the chain from thought to word to energy into matter. If in the beginning there is a logos, then the word was no longer those days with God, but in Carter.

The vision of the old building pained Carter and further pushed him off into the darkness of the night. As if the building's destruction were Crowly's doing, a link in logic Carter had easily made, he found himself in the church parking-lot across from Crowly's house. A car was in the driveway. Carter could see into the well-lit but what appeared to be an empty living-room.

He had not had even curiosity enough about Crowly to want to know where he lived, and was surprised the building looked pretty much as any other modern suburban house, well-kept and unaffected by the rot and rancor, the black prejudice Carter felt the structure might show having consented to shelter a man like Crowly.

Instinctively, needing something to hold to, he wrapped his hand around the handle of the .32 in his pocket—impulsively he would say later, then crossed the street and stood for a time at the edge of the driveway.

What caught Carter then, was not so much a desire for revenge, although he could taste the sweetness of the fantasy, but an overwhelming fear. He looked over his shoulder, quickly, having not yet shaken the shock of the hassle with the dogs in the cemetery. He had no fear whatsoever of what he might do, might of impulse or imprudently or impetuously do. Carter believed he would face whatever that brought. His fear, the concern that hung on him like a weighted black cloak, was a fear of failure, for himself and for those around him. The kind of sinking sick sensation that comes with an awareness of being saddled and harnessed into failure by the limited sensibilities of those around you, of knowing now the cause, the war, the battle to which you are committed is irrevocably lost.

When Crowly sold the house, would the realtor feel obligated to tell prospective buyers about the building's character, as they sometimes did when selling a property that had harbored a murder or other gruesome aberration?

Carter had a prepared speech.

"This dwelling served as a bastion for a deranged man, a man who gave appearances of normality, but harbored vicious, unnatural antisocial destructive tendencies.

"He insinuated himself into the ranks of those given the responsibility of protecting life, and like a parasite that destroys the host upon which it depends, by a meanness of heart and malevolence of spirit, further dimmed the lamp of enlightenment."

Who would buy such a building? Carter wondered.

I should kill him, he thought, although he did not know even if Crowly was home. He stepped into the driveway, with a full view of the living-room, though not prepared for what his new visual vantage-point would provide.

Sitting in the center of the room watching the television in the corner was Crowly's wife, Glenda, and their seven-year-old son, Marvin, Jr., a child with multiple-sclerosis who Carter had heard of, but had never seen, and thus did not remember.

The child's mother was dressing him for bed, and Carter was struck by the boy's small, frail features, the design of misaligned genes, struck by the irreversibility of nature's accidents.

Carter stood for a few moments, no longer thinking of Crowly, Marvin senior, but filled with the awful awareness that the boy could just as easily have been his, as Mason and Factor could have been.

A son, he thought, suddenly aware that when he imagined those connected closely to him, he always felt they would be the best, the strongest, the most intelligent.

Then he withdrew slowly, his rancor and rage diminished, reduced, made foolish and petty, wondering what other burdens of the heart and mind with which the child's father, his nemesis, Crowly senior might be afflicted.

Now listening to the drone of Landeau's voice he traced the location of the .32 to where he had left it, in the pocket of his overcoat in the hall closet at home, relieved not to have the weapon at hand.

When Vivien finished, Carter confronted Landeau.

"The room was bugged," he said. "You had the place bugged."

"Not quite," Landeau said, "but it worked."

He turned the page.

"At the time of the conversation you were in bed with Ms. Vivien Connors. You had just had sex with her. Isn't that correct?"

When Carter did not answer, Landeau continued.

"Then on December thirteenth you were again with Ms. Connors. That day you went to the library. Ms. Connors, would you tell us about going to the library with Professor Carter?"

"The picture," she said.

"The picture?"

She did not answer the query, but sat motionless, stock-still, frozen to the chair.

"What about the library?" Landeau said. "How did you get into the library?"

"The phantom. He had blood on his hands."

Then only the murmur of the water trickling over the ceramic rocks and logs disturbed the strained silence of the room. The bluff and play, the mocking irreverence Carter had come to associate with her was gone.

"The phantom? Who?"

Crowly had watched the girl. He pushed himself away from the table, clearly agitated with her answer.

"You were in the library," he said.

"Yes."

"With Dr. Carter on December thirteenth."

Crowly's voice rose. He almost shouted the last words, as if he had suddenly absorbed her lost energy.

"Was there a third person with you?" Landeau said. "Who's the phantom?"

"There's no phantom," Crowly said, impatient with Landeau. "There's no phantom."

"Sure there is," Carter said.

"Everyone knows the phantom," Johnson said. "He guards the books and makes certain only reasonable people handle them."

"Blood," the girl said. "He can't see. His eyes."

Landeau looked at Carter as if Carter might further decipher the girl's words.

"Blood?" Landeau said. "Goat's blood?"

"That's enough," Crowly said, pointing to Watkins. His face was red and puffed with a white border along the hair line. The veins in his neck bulged above his white collar and Carter knew he was seriously angry.

"You can go," he said, barely controlling his voice, and she stood automatically, puppet-like.

"Thank you Ms. Connors," Landeau said.

Watkins sensed the urgency and took Vivien's arm and attempted to escort her to the door.

"But that's not all," Johnson said. "At least we should be given the courtesy of interviewing the witness, if we have questions."

"Do you have any questions?" Landeau said.

"As a matter of fact we do," Johnson said.

"We don't need to go on with this," Crowly said. "We've already heard enough. What more do we need to know?"

"For me," Gotsch said, "I'd like to hear Dr. Johnson's questions. That shouldn't do any harm."

When Vivien was again seated Landeau leaned around Lessiack to face Johnson.

"You have five minutes. Please limit yourself to five minutes."

"Would you repeat the witness's name?" Johnson said.

"She is not a witness," Crowly said. "Her name is Vivien Connors."

"Among others," Johnson said. "How about Phillips. Have you ever heard of Michelle Phillips?"

Crowly shook his head.

"Her name is Connors."

"How about Jinx?" Johnson said. "Who's Jinx?"

"That's her sister," Carter said.

"You have a sister?" Johnson said. "Why don't you tell us about your sister?"

Vivien pressed her lips together tightly. Carter recalled what she had said, how she felt about Johnson, the animosity. She shook her head.

"I don't know," she said. "Do I have to answer these questions?"

"Not unless you want to," Crowly said.

"That's not a good question," Carter said. "Or a fair one."

"Oh, all right. If you don't want to answer, don't," Johnson said. "But why should anyone introduced here as Vivien Connors answer to the name of Michelle Phillips in my classroom. No doubt you have a twin?"

"Is Michelle Phillips your sister?" Carter asked. "What about Mary Ann?"

He could not recall the last name.

It was an affectionate question. Wishful thinking he would call it later. But just then he did not feel her betrayal, if that's what it was. He could not reconcile what she had told him about herself and with what Crowly had said about her.

With her he knew a little less than he might have—a little more than he should have bothered with. From the beginning he was aware of her frailties—and found a warming charm in her naiveté, even for a young woman, especially for a young woman. She was innocent and vulnerable.

She put her hand over her mouth and stared pass Lessiack. Her eyes filled with tears.

"What's the penalty for taking another student's place in a university classroom?" Johnson said. "For doing someone else's work? Frankly, I don't believe anything you say Ms. whatever your name is."

"That's not part of this inquiry," Crowly said.

"It most certainly is," Johnson said, "unless you're telling me. . .

"Anyway, your witness is not reliable," Johnson said. "But then, I suppose you've had a good bit of experience with unreliable stories."

He looked from Crowly to Landeau to Daly.

Carter raised his hand.

"Carl," Carter said, "that's enough. That's plenty. "I'd like a short recess," Carter said.

"Is that necessary?" Landeau asked.

"As much as anything else," Carter said.

He stood and Johnson followed him to the door. In the hall Carter made his way to the far end, slowly, wondering how much he wanted to tell Johnson, how far he wanted to push the inquiry.

Michelle Phillips. Carter remembered the name. Then he remembered the face. He would not have put the two together. He did not until then. But he could recall vividly Michelle Phillips, and what he had known or assumed about her and could feel and see, now, his perception of Vivien and the image and sense of her he had come to know over the last few weeks as it fit or did not fit the image and sense he carried in memory of Michelle Phillips. Were they sisters? He didn't know.

"Look, Carl," he said finally, "I really appreciate what you've done, but I'm not sure there's any merit in going on with this."

"Well, maybe not for you. But I'm in this too. What about me? Who is that horrible child? What is this? The *Return of the Body Snatchers* or *Aliens?* Who is in that body anyway?"

"Carl, they're going to do what they want regardless. There are implications in this you don't understand. Her sister has cancer. She's dying of cancer. Maybe she was sitting in for her sister—taking notes."

"Taking notes for a dying sister? Why? Notes for the dead? Of the generosities one might have for a dying relative, that is the strangest. I agree.

I don't understand."

"I don't know," Carter said, "hell, maybe her sister's hoping to get back on her feet. Maybe she plans to return to school. People have hoped for sillier things."

"Then they can do it on their own time."

"Carl, let's just drop the whole thing."

Johnson stalked away, indignant, back straight, hands in his pockets.

"This is a sham. The school, these people. And if that's not bad enough, now I find out I have Mata Hari or the great imposter, or God knows who, in the front row. Next she'll tell me she's a clone. How many are there? Five? Ten? What is she? An unlimited-limited edition?"

He paused and regarded Carter.

"You want to protect her," he said, his voice quizzical and accusative. "Why do you want to protect her?"

"No," Carter said. "Not protect. It's not a matter of protection. How about decency?"

"John, there's not a decent person in that room—much less a human one."

"But whatever we say about her will not affect this—this what?—this joke. Nothing will come of it."

"Maybe not, but at least I'll get the satisfaction of knowing I've exposed an imposter. You don't just allow duplicity of this kind to go on."

"Carl," Carter said.

He was shaking his head.

"I don't want to go on with this. Not this way. This is not the place or time for it."

"Well, she certainly is not going to get a grade from me until I know who she is."

"That's okay. But let's do this my way," Carter said.

Carter re-entered the room thinking now of retreat. He had seen it through as Absyth advised. He had seen it through, given them their say, without seeking or pressing for vindication. Now he wanted out. No job—no position was worth this kind of trouble. Capitulation, he admitted, I'll capitulate, abdicate, bail out. Just then the solemnity of solitude and silence beckoned him.

"I have a final statement to make," Carter said. "And I say this in good faith and with sincerity.

"When people contrive to fabricate malice, they not only do their society a disservice, as well as damage their friends and neighbors, but they poison themselves and their lives. They corrode their souls in a way not easy to rectify.

"By participating in this travesty, each has marked himself, if not for the first time, then again as one unwilling to reason and judge as a decent human, and as willing to sell himself for whatever profit might be at hand. In either case, I am sorry for you. Sorry your contact with an institution that could exemplify the very best in the human mind and character has had so little influence on your lives and your actions."

"Well, nobody's perfect," Landeau said. "But we are deeply touched by your concern for our souls."

Carter had been standing at the end of the table with Johnson behind him. He retrieved his notebook and handkerchief and the mistletoe, then passed his hand over the empty Styrofoam coffee cup. A red Carnation appeared beneath his hand in the cup.

A small gurgle came up from Martin's throat, along with several smirks of surprise from the others. While Carter spoke. Landeau grinned and shook his head. Now he did not smile.

Carter leaned forward and placed the cup and the flower near the center of the table. In a single motion, as if it might explode, Crowly jumped to his feet, knocking his chair backward as he stood.

Crowly's face had always reminded Carter of a crudely fashioned flesh plaster-cast. The brow seemed at once flat and prominent and yet inadequate for the eye-ridges pushing out beneath two lines of heavy black hair, which nearly touched before dropping into a thick, wide nose. Despite the size of his head, his mouth and teeth were over-large and out of proportion.

But just then the vision, and Carter's opinion of Crowly, took on a new and subtle hue. What had been in the gaze of passing observation, of simple loathing, now beneath the insight of closer inspection shifted to pity and fear.

Clearly, this was not a man to be ridiculed and dismissed as an idiot, although his mental capabilities were at times meager. Just then, Carter caught a whiff of the corpse, just the slightest scent of decay at the center, and of the ominous.

Crowly's fury had subsided, and his face was now pale and washed out. Carter had heard boxers and soldiers talk about opponents and enemies who were not merely determined and capable, but also marginally deranged, willingly mad, and who, in madness, contained the cunning and intelligence to find excuse or reason for their pathology. What Carter had known about Crowly for some time, he now understood.

Conceptualization, psychologists call it. From the Conceptualists. Carter classified the process quickly. To apprehend in reality what you have, for a time, carried in your head.

Carter observed this, at other times, in Crowly's body chemistry, as if he sensed the paths he walked had been rigged with traps. In whatever he did, his was an uneven pulse, a tremor at the core, the spring wound too tightly. He reminded Carter of a large animal, plucked from a jungle habitat and dropped in the middle of traffic at a busy intersection, facing threats from all sides, wary, prowling slowly, and not knowing which way to retreat or attack.

Crowly backed away toward the waterfall, his eyes locked on Carter, his hands held out as if to ward off an attack.

"No," he said, "no," as Carter slipped to the side of the table. "You can't. Get away."

Carter had intended to leave, and glanced back at Johnson who was watching Crowly with an amazed and amused fascination, his face expressionless, as if he was viewing a truly pleasurable, phenomenal event.

"Go on," Johnson said to Carter, quietly. "Go on. Walk toward him. See if he'll jump into the water. "

Crowly retrieved the chair and held it with the legs pointed toward Carter.

"Get him out of here," he shouted. "Get him out."

"Go on" Johnson said. "Put a spell on him. The Devil wants his soul."

Johnson stretched his right arm toward Crowly, his hand cupped with the fingers extended claw-like, as if he was about to turn the dial on the combination lock of a giant safe.

"You have sinned," Johnson said, "and the spirits of the underworld will rise and take your soul."

Crowly's eyes were glazed. He shook the chair at Carter and Johnson.

"C'mon fuckers. C'mon. Nobody's gonna get me."

He crouched and walked back and forth with the chair as if they were large cats and he was holding them at bay.

"See what you can do," he shouted. "I'm tougher than all of you. You hear? I'm ready."

He was shouting, red-faced, again, eyes watering. He was seriously overweight and had trouble breathing when he exerted himself of became agitated.

Carter watched Johnson for a moment, then drew away. The drift of the smell was stronger now.

When Crowly picked up the chair Lovell scrambled to his feet and stepped behind Martin's chair. Landeau slapped his hand on the table and stood abruptly.

"Meeting adjourned," he said. "I want to thank you."

"C'mon," Carter said. "Let's go, Carl"

Johnson stood with his hand still pointed at Crowly, stopped in mid-sentence, mid-incantation, smiling at Carter.

"Jesus," he said, "this is fun. Maybe I should put a hex on him. Put him in the circle of evil and call down the fiends of Osiris."

He looked at Crowly who had stopped behind the chair, breathing heavily, wheezing and hissing, struggling to get his breath.

"You," Johnson shouted at him, "you will kiss the Devil's arse and nothing, nothing will be left but your blackened, scorched skin with a hole in it the size of a pin-prick where your sad little soul fell through."

"C'mon, Carl," Carter said. "This is absolutely insane."

Johnson dropped his arm and followed Carter to the door.

"You're right," he said. "We might as well go. La farce a fini."

Chapter XX

Carter stopped in the living-room and poured out half a tumbler of bourbon and fell onto the couch. The silence of the room, the dimmed silence of the room with its browns and shadows calmed him. The Seth Thomas in the hall struck the half-hour.

The afternoon had sapped his energy. The rancor and poison of the hearing had settled in his muscles. He would have to call Absyth, to tell him what had happened, but just then he did not have the strength or confidence to call anyone.

He was still slouched down on the couch, the drink cradled in both hands on his stomach when Katherine Marie came in to remind him they were expected at the Olsens' at eight.

"They have a new house," she said. "An old house, but new for them."

"The spoils of largess," Carter said, wearily.

"Inheritance."

"A euphemism for the dole."

"John, there's nothing wrong with inheriting money. We give gifts to people all the time."

"Largess," Carter repeated.

The engagement had not slipped Carter's mind. He had allowed it to slip away, so when the time came he'd be irritated by the intrusion.

In a more conventional frame of mind, he'd have objected to attending a Christmas party at the Olsens', even though in the end he would have gone along with the plan. Now he didn't care.

So the Olsens were not his favorite people. So what? What difference would another uncomfortable evening make? Very little, he thought. In fact it might be good for comic relief.

Whenever he saw Ron Olsen, Carter saw a sign stuck to Olsen's chest announcing, "Local Boy Makes Good As Real Estate Agent." With a new and obviously larger house, and certainly the place would be larger than the last, the night would no doubt be more of the same.

Two years before with Ron Olsen's father's death, his mother had died a few years earlier, as an only son he inherited several millions in property as well as the father's business, Olsen Chevrolet, the largest auto dealership in Lancaster. What that translated in dollars, Carter could only guess. But then, in matters such as these his imagination usually fell short.

No matter what, Carter could not shake the madness of the afternoon. It bled into his thinking, and the more he thought about it, the more bizarre it seemed. Crowly the insane, crouched behind a chair. Carl putting a hex on him. My god! And this was a university.

Carter stopped in the hall still wrapped in his coat and dialed Absyth's office.

"Paul, this is John Carter," he said. "I think we have something to talk about, now."

Absyth listened as Carter delivered a narrative of the afternoon, then suggested Carter come to his office the following day.

"How about three-thirty? We can take as much time as we need."

Katherine Marie insisted she drive to the Olsen's and at seven-fifty Carter dutifully slipped into the passenger's seat of the red Nissan.

"I know the way. And even on the best nights it's unlikely you'll be sober by eleven," she told Carter.

Carter acquiesced. If he was going along for the ride, it might as well be literal, and minutes later strapped in and clinging to the dashboard handle he was being wheeled and careened along a narrow street, through sloping curves, past stands of large barren trees.

"Jesus," Carter said, "I didn't realize nobility had made it to Lancaster."

"It's the oldest part of the city."

"And you know where you're going?"

"Yes," she said. "Yes I do. And wait until you see this house. You'll love it. It's wonderful."

They spun through a pillared entry of a stonewall into a neighborhood of mansions secluded in what in the night looked to be a well-tended woods. In the darkness Carter could only get an approximation of the size of the buildings and grounds, but those he could see were enormous.

Katherine Marie slowed the car at a sharp left curve, accelerated down a long asphalt drive dropping into a dense patch of trees, then rising abruptly along a steep slope. Still, Carter could not see the house, and was about to ask, when they entered another gate onto a large circle-drive leading to what was more of a chateau than a house.

"My god," Carter said. "Is this the place?"

"Yes," Katherine Marie said proudly, as if it were hers.

"Don't you just love it?"

"Love it? That's not a house. It's a hotel."

"Would you believe forty-two rooms?"

"With or without baths?"

"No. There are seventeen bathrooms."

"Just in case one is busy."

"And three kitchens."

"A hotel," Carter said. "The Olsentatious Hilton. Where's the slave quarters?"

"This is Chateau du Monde."

"Chateau du Monde?" Carter repeated. "How about Robber Baron Manor? My god, there are people who live ten to a room."

"Not here," Katherine Marie said. "Some people need a lot of space."

Two couples waited outside the massive wooden doors beneath the cut-glass chandelier of the columned-portico. A well-lit Christmas tree was visible through the sidelights and the fanlight over the door. The men hunched against the wind. The women were wrapped in furs.

"Too bad there aren't any hunters in the area," Carter said. "Or trappers. They could reclaim the furs and get a second commission."

"These aren't tree-huggers, John. Just average Americans, like you and me."

"Who's gonna be here?" Carter asked, wondering now why he had consented to come here.

"Oh, just a few friends. Nobody you know. Other than Ron and Joan."

Katherine Marie pulled the car around to the lower point of the crescent at the end of a long line of cars and squeezed the Nissan into the escape space between a Cadillac and Porsche.

"We're right on time," she said.

"On time? The whole city is here."

"Or they will be. It's quite an honor to be invited, John. Everybody who is anybody will be here."

"Yeah, I know," Carter said. "A few friends. Nobody I would know. You already told me."

The walk around the circle-drive approached the entry on a crest. After riding in the Nissan with his legs cramped Carter had trouble unbending his sore knee.

"Why don't we call a cab," Carter said. "We need a ride in from the parking lot."

Along the left wing Carter could see over the hedges into the first-floor rooms. The walls were covered with bookcases and large paintings. An occasional light shown in the windows of the upper two stories and beyond the portico the right wing disappeared into a dense thicket of large shrubs and trees. No telling, Carter thought, how far it goes. Do they have fox hunts in the halls? Carter had read that the royals once held fox hunts in the Palace of Versailles.

Carter tapped the knocker. Overhead the glass tear-drops of the chandelier clinked softly.

Within seconds they were joined by another couple, and even before they could exchange greetings, Carter decided to keep his observations and opinions to himself. In the rot of opulence he would not easily find a sympathetic ear. He decided to keep his mouth shut.

Despite the resolution, or possibly because of it, he was already ill at ease.

Ill-will, Carter called it. Good will can be directed and guided and cultivated, but ill-will is intractable and shrinking. Carter turned from the door.

"I'm surprised to see you here," the man said.

When the voice came in from the darkness, it took a moment for Carter to place the face.

"No telling where I'll show up," Carter said.

"I know," the man said smugly. "That's what I've heard."

The man was Ralston Burk, a Lancaster lawyer Carter had not seen in over five years. He was a short, fat man, who was even fatter now. He had red hair in small thin patches over his ears, puffed eyes and a bulbous nose. Burk's name came up often in the politics of the Lancaster lunatic right-wing. By reputation he was loud, short tempered and often abusive when he drank.

Burk had represented the people who sold Carter the residence on College Street. Near its end the transaction soured and had very nearly fallen through when Carter discovered Burk had added a thousand dollar finder's-fee to the previously agreed-to sales price.

It was a matter of placing a one in front of the seven on the seven hundred dollars in taxes Carter was to pay. Only accidentally did Carter catch the overcharge and thwart the scam.

When he confronted Burk with the fraud, unwilling to give up on a good thing, or possibly hoping to preserve the appearances of legitimacy, Burk insisted the number was correct. Then he claimed he had found the house for Carter, since he had initiated the contact, and was therefore entitled to the same fee from Carter he had received from the seller.

Carter refused to pay, and Burk threatened to sue. Carter ignored the threat, paid what was due the bank and heard no more about it.

But it had come within a hair of squelching the deal, and Carter could only speculate on how many times the scam had worked.

"Too bad they don't still burn people with red hair," Carter said.

He looked at Katherine Marie.

"You said everybody would be here. Not anybody."

When the door opened, Katherine Marie took Carter's arm and leaned toward him.

"John," she said, "this is a party. Don't start with me. Let's get through the evening without an incident. Don't embarrass me."

But at the moment, Carter did not think about what he might say or do. He stepped inside and stood regarding what he could only describe as the extravagance of an enormous central entrance foyer. Was it an atrium? In a house? In a castle?

The floors were matched red granite, as were the walls. To the right a wide staircase with a polished mahogany banister curved along the wall to the open balconies of the second- and third-floors.

A giant fully decorated blue-spruce occupied the gentle curve of the stairs. The top of the tree reached upward eight or ten feet past the second-floor balcony toward the third-floor and the ornate carved-wooden panels of the ceiling.

Opposite the entrance, a line of small columns and arches, reminiscent of Roman baths, separated the hall from the various doors leading to the rooms at the back.

Not reluctantly, but slowly, Carter surrendered his scarf and coat to a young man-attendant and followed Katherine Marie through the arched passage into the sunken living-room.

What appeared from the outside to be several rooms was in fact a huge rectangular room with hatched-windows and stone walls. For the most part the walls were taken up with floor-to-ceiling bookcases filled with knick-knacks. Large Persian rugs of beige and brown and russet covered parts of the parquet floor dividing the room into small, separate islands.

Chandeliers hung from the beamed ceiling, three on either side. At the far end a fire burned brightly in a large fireplace, and along the left wall, near the center of the room, another fire burned in another fireplace. The interstices of the stone walls, between bookcases and paintings were set with marble busts and hung with large green Christmas wreathes.

A bar had been set up near the larger fireplace and young men in white waiter's jackets and white gloves circulated through the crowd of twenty-five or thirty people standing in small groups or seated in the black leathers sofas and chairs set about the fire places.

When they came into the long room, Joan Olsen met them at the steps. She was sixty or so, an engaging and vivacious woman, who looked in Carter's estimation, a good bit younger.

"John Carter," she said with a dramatic flourish, as if they had long been close friends. "I'm so glad you could make it."

Joan Olsen's attitude about him had always struck Carter as indicative of just how impervious the Olsens were to the world around them. In the four years of their acquaintance, in the infrequent contacts Carter had with them, he had carefully avoided anything that might speak of intimacy or true friendship. He tolerated them, he suffered them, nothing more. But to his knowledge they never caught on.

Maybe everyone treats them that way, Carter thought. Maybe she knows the truth but is holding out hoping I'll buy a house or a car.

Ron Olsen trailed a few steps behind his wife. When Carter and Katherine Marie entered the room, he broke off a conversation with a man standing at the smaller fire place, and came toward Carter, with his hand extended. He grinned from ear to ear, as if Carter's presence were a capitulation or surrender and tribute and shook Carter's hand as if having him there was a triumph.

What did Paul Nelson say?

"You can always tell when the dog has been rolling in shit by the way he comes trotting across the yard grinning at you like a fundamentalist."

Maybe it was Carter's disdain for money and the tall-corn of prestige that fascinated Olsen.

"We are certainly glad you and Kate could make it," he said.

He stood beside Carter as if they had suddenly become comrades.

"Well, what do you think of the new place?"

"It's fit for a baron," Carter said. "Do you really have fox hunts in the halls?"

Olsen cocked his head and looked at Carter momentarily, then shook his head slowly.

"No," he said, not sure about the joke. "No, I don't think so. I mean, who said that? Who would say a thing like that?"

"Just a rumor," Carter said.

Joan stepped around Katherine Marie in front of Carter.

She said, "Ron, would you get us a drink?" then to Carter, "I've got someone I want you to meet."

Carter picked up a faint choral of piped-in Christmas songs. "Hark the

Herald Angels," or maybe "The First Noel."

A drink, he decided was precisely what he needed.

"Bourbon," he called after Ron. "A double."

The room was stuffy and close. Joan Olsen smelled of a cosmetic counter. No subtleties here, Carter thought. Nothing here of mystery or intrigue, of the taunting to tantalize. What you miss in quality, you get in density.

Carter followed along to the far end of the room where a small crowd had gathered around a large black sofa in front of the fireplace.

A man Carter did not know had the floor expounding on the success of the Barker State football team. Joan edged into the group, pushing her way into the center of attention.

"All right," she said, "break it up. This is a Christmas party and I refuse to allow shop talk. Do that on your own time.

"Here, I have someone I want you to meet. This is Professor John Carter from the Philosophy Department."

While she spoke she looked directly at a man seated at the end of the couch, as if the introduction was meant specifically for him.

"John, I want you to meet our newest member of the Barker State Board of Trustees. This is Patrick O'Rourke. Pat, John Carter."

O'Rourke rose from his seat to shake Carter's hand.

"It's not often I meet board members," Carter said.

"Nor I, professors," O'Rourke said.

With Carter's introduction the group fell silent. He had seen it before. The mention of philosophy dampened the fun and legitimacy of football scores and real estate deals. These people were intimidated by words such as philosophy.

It had taken several years in the classroom for Carter to realize most students equated philosophy with the occult. Astronomy as astrology, chemistry as alchemy.

Then there were the questions of god, paradox and the contradictions, the failure of proof on proof. He may as well have been reciting fairytales. And tall-tales, for all the good it did. Is the universe a clock by design? Is good, good because God says it's good or because it is good in itself?

And what about philosophers? Shaman. Witchdoctors. Sorcerers. The mystical mix of mist and charm.

We are the dirty ones, the untouchables. The kiss of death, Carter thought.

Without excusing themselves the celebrants drifted away, moving off to the bar, leaving Carter alone with O'Rourke.

"Sit down, Professor," O'Rourke said.

A waiter, a plump youth with a cherubic fleshy face handed Carter a drink. Carter thanked him, then sat down at the far end of the couch.

"You're new on the board," Carter said.

"Yes, two months."

"Baptism by fire."

"Well, not in the strict sense. Actually everyone has been very helpful. Dr. Remcheck is very capable. He makes sure we understand everything beforehand. Before we have to make a decision. The board is lucky to have him? Don't you think?"

"I suppose there are people who think so," Carter said. "And there are those who might disagree."

O'Rourke smiled.

"A true philosopher. Everyone has an opinion. That's what makes the world go round."

"I would have classified it as a matter of fact, not opinion," Carter said. "And some opinions have more veracity than others. Our task is to decide who is legitimate—or honest and informed."

"Well, these positions are difficult. You can't please everyone."

"Does he please anyone?"

O'Rourke stared at the floor for a moment, then looked at Carter. "Yes. The board. He satisfies the board."

"With what?"

Again O'Rourke did not answer immediately, but waited as if he needed to consider the significance of Carter's question.

"By doing his job well," he said, finally.

"Which is to please the board."

O'Rourke smiled.

"Now you understand, Professor."

"Then who's keeping the store?"

"What do you mean?"

"Well, if Remcheck's job is keeping the board happy, who runs the school? And who monitors those running the school?"

"You make it sound ominous," O'Rourke said. "You sound like a man who's got his underwear in a knot."

"Perhaps," Carter said, and smiled in spite of himself. The conversation bordered on talking in a vacuum. Not even an echo of insight or reason, Carter told himself, and raised his glass to O'Rourke.

"Salute," he said. "Here's to a long and satisfying career on the Barker State Board. And Merry Christmas, too, Mr. O'Rourke."

Carter pushed up from the couch, abruptly, emptied his glass and approached the bar for a refill. With a new supply of bourbon in hand he took up a spot at side of the fireplace. The logs on the andirons flared and he set his glass on the mantle.

Already the party's population had grown by thirty or so. Near the center of the room he could see Katherine Marie talking to Ralston Burk and another man. Joan Olsen came around the fringe leading a woman toward Carter.

Clytemnestra, Carter suspected, supplying me with what I desire least and need even less.

"John, this is Martha Rothwell. Martha, Professor John Carter, one of our most distinguished faculty members."

The woman, Carter gauged to be in her early forties, had short, almost totally white hair and horn-rimmed glasses, her soft face caked with enough paint and powder to cover a damaged cadaver.

"Martha is the new curator of the Barker State Art Museum."

Carter nodded to the woman.

"How do you do," he said.

"I'm doing very well," she said, in a surprisingly husky voice.

Other than her face, she did not appear overly plump. She was big bosomed, dressed in a white blouse and brown full-skirt. A flat gold chain decorated her thin, freckled neck, curving over the ridges of prominent collar bones. The bracelets on her right arm clacked and jingled as she extended a multi-ring-fingered hand to Carter.

"I'm pleased to meet you, Professor," she said. "I've heard nothing but good things about you."

"I can imagine," Carter said. "You've considered the possibility your sources are unreliable?"

Martha smiled.

"Of course."

"Curator?" Carter said. "That's a new position. What happened to Solomon Boggs?"

"Resigned," Joan Olsen said. "Didn't you hear?"

"As a matter of fact I didn't. What was there to hear?"

"A real scandal. I mean, it wasn't that big. He was selling university property, or something. Everybody knows about it."

"Selling property? University property?"

"That's what they said."

"They?"

"Dr. Remcheck. He said Mr. Boggs did not have authorization to sell university property."

"So they fired him."

"Well. He did break the rules."

"Whose?"

"Oh, I don't know. There was more to it. But it's over. Martha is the new curator. It's done."

Joan stepped away and gave Martha a fond, appraising look.

"And I just know she'll do well."

"I'm sure she will," Carter said.

"Professor Carter, to which department are you assigned?"

"Assigned?" Carter said, amused by the prospect.

Assigned as a child assigned to an orphanage, a prisoner to a cellblock?

"My assignation place?" Carter said. "Philosophy."

"You are assigned to philosophy?"

"Sometimes."

"And what is your philosophy, Professor?"

Her teasing lifted Carter's spirits a bit.

"To eat, drink and be merry. Life, liberty and the pursuit of. I'm a teacher not a guru."

"Well stated. A well-schooled professor?"

"As you are well sculpted and painted," Carter said. Her face softened, moderating slightly Carter's reticence and suspicion. Still, he wondered how she had ended up on the Barker State payroll. Whose bed, or what beds had she taken to?

"Indeed," the woman said, "Dr. Remcheck has spoken highly of you?"

But not I of him, Carter thought.

"Has he?"

"He said you're a member of the old guard. He speaks quite respectfully."

"Of age and foolishness," Carter said, "everyone is respectful."

She excused herself and Carter held his ground, both annoyed by the misdirection of the conversation and rankled by Remcheck's flattery and praise. The sonofabitch was truly Machiavellian. Cocktail party chatter. Say one thing do another, then cover it up with the fog of rhetoric and babble.

Carter had downed the drinks too quickly, and he hadn't eaten since noon. He felt uncomfortably warm. The fire had burned lower, thankfully, and he located a cool spot of fresh air buffeting in around the large hatched-window behind him. He needed to get off his feet and gather his strength, to catch his breath, but the chairs and couches were occupied.

He placed his empty glass on the mantle, then steadied himself on the smooth oak beam. Despite the open fire and the air leaking in, the room had a heavy, musty smell of mold and perfume.

The soft strands of "Tannenbaum" drifted down over Carter's hunched and sweated form. Voices rose and fell about him, penetrating, knife-edged voices.

"Did you see the Steelers' game?"

"That was something."

"Man, did you see that?"

"Yeah. Especially when Sambo got it."

"That was the best part of the game."

"Football's still a white man's game. Put the shines on the field and let em kill each other while the real people sit and watch."

"Give niggers enough money and they'll do anything—even kill each other."

"New England lost their minus factor, and lost the game."

Carter breathed deeply, waiting for his head to clear. His fascination with their foppery and comic pretense at sophistication and gentility, this house, this room, this grotesque and opulent display of dwarfed and failed sensibilities had lodged in his chest.

No matter how often he gave them the benefit of the doubt, these were not good people. They were parasites. There was nothing here of service, of giving. Nothing of compassion and generosity, unless it be fashioned for a handful of cash. These were leeches, blood-suckers, moving from host to host, from the dead to the dying.

For several semesters he had assigned his ethics students a list of social problem/situations and asked which of the problems in their opinion needed to be acted upon. The list was short, a teenage druggie, a cheating husband, a businessman lying to the IRS, contractors discriminating against blacks.

What he did not know, did not even believe for the first few semesters after he received the results, was ninety-five percent of his students did not consider racism a moral or social problem. They not only accepted it, but believed it was a good idea.

And now this crap.

Coming here had been a mistake. He longed to be alone.

The day had taken its toll. The afternoon had dealt him serious damage. He had not recovered from the shock and now considered retreat, escape. Maybe he could get lost in the maze of upstairs rooms.

Behind him the drone of revelry rode over the party. Then the pernicious cacophony broke, for a moment, stilled, before mounting again, accompanied by the muffled popping and slapping of hands.

At first glance Carter could not locate the purpose of the applause, although most of the people faced the far end and the doorway leading to the entrance hall, suggesting someone or several someone's everyone knew had arrived.

He scanned the crowd again. Still nothing.

A third survey found Joan Olsen's blond head in a group of seven or eight men, most of whom he could not identify, but one he recognized immediately, recognized with a visceral presentiment.

Remcheck's shaven head, the round head, round as a bowling ball is round, bobbed at the center of the crowd. He was smaller than Carter remembered. Even among the salesmen, the hucksters and market gnomes, who were none of them big men, he was small. Small and grinning a white-toothed grin, and shaking hands.

Christ, Carter thought, the lion's den and there's the motherfucking lion.

He had not expected this.

But it made a sort of primitive sense. Political sense, as politics is social. The university of money and favor.

Attracted by the applause, O'Rourke was already on his feet headed toward Remcheck.

A dog looking for a tail to wag it, Carter thought. Bearing tribute to Caesar.

Remcheck, the slick, glad-handing s-o-b. But that's what the board wanted. The board had created him, given him the position, as it was, without adequate counsel or recommendation. Now they acted as if he were a deity. They create god, then stumble over each other in worship. That was Shindel's doing.

And as act follows thought, Shindel emerged from the crowd, at Remcheck's side. Whenever he had seen them, they were always traveling in tandem. When they could, board members and half the university employees avoided Shindel. Capitulations to cowardice. And for good reason. Strange things happened to people who displeased him.

For years there had been rumors about Shindel's vindictiveness, but for the most they seemed only to be rumors. Then with Shindel's open and obvious control of board elections, a citizen watchdog group, an ad hoc committee, calling itself Citizens for Truth in Education, formed.

Among its other attempts to influence the politics of the Board of Trustees the founders of the committee, Wilma and Horace Chetler, filed a formal complaint with the State's Attorney on Shindel's apparent conflict of interest in voting on the University Road Residence Project.

Following the complaint, in a rather unbelievable but substantial run of supposedly coincidental bad luck, under a storm of accusations and threats over a loan made to a friend, Wilma lost her job as a loan officer at Lancaster First National Bank and Trust.

A week later the Lancaster department store where he had worked for fifteen years, dropped Horace from its managerial ranks, and in direct contravention to state law, their insurance, home and auto, was canceled.

After protests and threats of lawsuits the insurance was reissued, with high-risk premiums. Two months later their street was zoned commercial and the area in front of their residence, where they normally parked, set off as a no parking zone.

The police regularly patrolled the street, made occasional stops at the Chetlers' to ring the doorbell, often at two or three in the morning, to ask if they had seen anyone who looked suspicious.

The Chetlers' complaints against the police were answered with more harassment. And finally, they too capitulated, sold the house and left Lancaster.

Carter knew the dangers as he knew the enemy.

Now it's my turn, he thought.

But it was more than that. He had not attacked Shindel, although given the opportunity and half a reason, he would not have hesitated. But then, he surmised, maybe I have. With people as power hungry and paranoid as these, imagined wrongs could suffice as antagonisms.

Shindel had inherited most of his money. The youngest of four brothers, he shared in the fortune the elder Shindel had collected in construction and manufacturing.

When Papa, Big Bill Shindel, a man of something less than exemplary character, died, the older brothers took up the business as a committee of three and distinguished themselves during the next couple decades by making more money, a not altogether startling accomplishment having begun as they had with baskets of millions.

The younger Shindel, to become Carter's nemesis Shindel, had been given positions as a functionary, a warehouse manager, then an office clerk, for a salary, and required to live off the profits his brothers made for him, a situation of which they continually reminded him.

Sometime after his fiftieth year, Shindel got into real estate and through the boom of the seventies made more money. He bought up several pig farms and made even more money. By then his wife had died a mysterious alcoholic death, and his oldest son a Lancaster lawyer had killed himself.

Another son, a Shindel Corp executive, abandoned his family and disappeared, word had it to a California commune with a teenage prostitute, and had not been heard from in over ten years. And what Shindel had lost in authority over his disintegrating family, he now exercised at Barker State.

Boosted by the family name Shindel ran for the Barker State Board of Trustees and won handily. The rest was, as Carter fondly noted, unfortunate, corrupt history.

Shindel took careful note and made frequent references to employees in his charge he had fired. New university administrative employees were often encouraged, unofficially, to purchase houses from his agency, usually at a price in excess of the property's true value.

After thinking about it, Carter knew he had done something worse than attacking Shindel. Shindel expected attacks, enjoyed the nastier aspects of political combat.

Carter had not attacked Shindel, but had made him uncomfortable, had made him nervous. In his complaints and protests about the failing academic standards at Barker State, Carter had pressed Shindel and Remcheck at the source of their deception.

These were money-mongers who knew nothing and cared less about education. Their interest from the beginning had been money, the money the university provided for their manipulation and divestment, those three hundred and ninety million dollars a year in the coffers of the university's yearly budget.

The tremors of Carter's complaints, which passed unnoticed for a time, finally suggested a larger and far more serious threat. The appearance of legitimacy of their schemes resided in the facade, an intricately carved facade of public relations and business connections, a facade that covered their activities with the assumptions of monies well spent, authority properly exercised. And because Carter's discontent came from the inside, it had shaken the Shindel scheme's stability. If others took up the protest, or found merits in his complaints, the entire plot could be threatened.

Shindel and Remcheck were well-aware of what people like Carter could do.

Again Carter revisited the intrigue. And what about Mason? What had he done? Why had they gone after him? Or had they? And the others? The selection may have been arbitrary or mistaken. But then again, maybe not.

A shudder ran along Carter's spine. Regardless of what he felt or said, these were not men of whom he merely disapproved. These were dangerous men, men who in their greed and mindlessness threatened to twist and mutilate the most precarious bonds of the human community.

The afternoon had seriously wounded Carter. He hurt without broken bones or torn muscles. He felt unsure of making it to the other side of the room—and equally unsure of what he might do if he got there.

Pushing off he abandoned the solitude and refuge of his fireside station and ventured off on less than reliable legs, set himself adrift around the couch, advancing along the archipelago of Persian rugs.

Chapter XXI

"Harassment," Paul Absyth said. "Certainly Harassment. But a real threat. Normally this would go without prosecution. States' attorneys have more pressing matters to deal with. But they do have the option to bring charges. And when politics gets in it, well there's no telling. You'll have to decide what you want to do."

Carter sat silently before Absyth. Just then he wasn't sure. Faced with the inevitable, why bother?

"What about the States Attorney? Clemens? Would he listen to reason, if we ask? I mean the girl is over eighteen."

"But not old enough to drink."

"She misrepresented herself."

"She'll testify otherwise. Look, John, if she says she was in bed with you after you purchased alcohol for her, the law takes care of the rest. Whether you knew her age or not is of no importance. You should have known.

"Have you talked to her?"

Carter shook his head.

"Can you talk to her? That's the question?"

"Reason with her?"

"It seems to me their case rests on her testimony. If she won't testify, they have no case."

"I don't know."

"It would be worth a try. What she said at the hearing is not admissible evidence."

"It's not?"

"If she were to recant under oath, I don't think there'd be much of a case. She may refuse to testify. It probably wouldn't stop the people at Barker. They could still do what they wanted. But at least the criminal charges would be out of the way and you'd have a better chance."

"She has to lie. To say she lied."

"Have you ever heard a young female take pleasure in that?" Absyth said. "Parading around at the center of attention? Look, we're dispensable. The law takes care of the rest. Whether you knew her age or not is of no importance. You should have known.

"To say there was nothing unusual in your relationship with her, however she wanted to say it, could destroy their case."

"Otherwise?"

"It is a criminal offense to buy an underage female alcohol and then take her to bed."

Criminal offense.

The words had a strange, almost comic ring. Criminal for doing what he'd been doing the last forty years. For doing what men had been doing since the beginning. Man's two favorite pastimes—screwing and drinking. Drinking and screwing.

And now it was criminal and he was a calendar-crook. Crime by the numbers. How long before she'd be twenty-one? Her birthday? She had mention her horoscope. What did she say? But when? Six months? Three days? An hour, maybe two? Were there mitigating circumstances? He couldn't think of any—at least not any that mattered.

"I don't know," Carter said. "I'd like to think I knew what she would do, but I don't."

"Why not talk to her? What would it hurt?"

The suggestion annoyed Carter.

"I'd rather not."

"You have a better idea?"

"No, but I don't think it'll work."

Absyth propped his chin on his hand, elbow on the desk.

In profile his nose curved cleanly away from a straight Nordic forehead. His carefully styled and groomed soft brown hair gave him a fastidious, antiseptic cast. The smooth tan skin of his boyish face seemed strangely angelic and out of place in the conversation.

A choir boy and . . . what?

Carter glanced around Absyth's office another time.

Where was this? What was it? A psychedelic wonder-world housing law books. The kind of place that proliferated the sixties when bars and shops sprung up in old buildings—grain elevators and warehouses, abandoned railroad stations, cubed-off with sheets of plywood, painted magenta and orange, then lit with strobes and colored floods.

No Picasso's here. No Rembrandt's. No paintings or pictures at all. The monotonous row on row of state statutes, row on row of identical proper spines, the backbone of civility, marked and labeled, filled a wall of bookcases. And that seemed simple and usual enough. To Carter's mind this was what you had to expect. The tedium and pedantry of law, the bland thinking of precedent and feasible argument. Hadrian's Wall, the status quo, within which change comes slowly, grudgingly.

The other walls, however, were not what Carter had learned of law offices. Away from the books the world passed, shifted rudely in time and space, to a different referent.

The plaster-board had been painted black, black as the night sky emblazoned with a bright red scimitar, a crescent moon and a star. A large lead-framed stained-glass Star of David hung from a gold chain over an otherwise bare window.

The Pentacle? Where? On the floor just inside the door. Where else? A purple pointed astral pentagonal set in and outlined by the white ceramic floor-tile.

"You don't pay rent for this?" Carter said.

Absyth looked at him blankly.

"No," he said, "I own it."

"And you can't afford an interior designer,"

"What you see, already cost me over seven thousand dollars."

"Seven thousand for black paint and scrambled symbols."

"What difference does it make? It pleases me."

A choir boy, still, Carter judged. And for a moment doubted the wisdom of giving his confidence to a novice.

"How old are you?" Carter asked.

Absyth redirected his gaze to Carter.

"I'm fifty-five," Carter said.

"And you're worried that I'm too young."

"Twenty-nine," Carter said.

"Six. Twenty-six. Next month."

"When you were born, I was three years older than you are now."

"And what were you doing that year? Where were you?"

"At twenty-six? In a coal mine. Trying to collect enough money to go back to graduate school."

"Married?"

"Had been. Fumbling at it. The shock of marital failure."

"I scc. Why did you ask my age?"

"Maybe I should get an older lawyer."

"Like a younger wife? Well, hell. Maybe you should. Older attorneys many times have agreements, arrangements, can sometimes make arrangements. You know, old debts being paid. Favors. It may be a way to go."

"Then again, maybe not," Carter said. "All you can do is save my job. And actually that's not worth much."

Absyth rotated away.

"You think so?" Absyth said. "Well, at least I'm glad to know we're involved in a common but worthless enterprise."

Carter nodded.

"Even if I could get back into the classroom, I'm not sure I'd want to."

"What about the criminal charges?" Absyth said.

"You think they'll go through with it?"

Absyth stared at Carter and Carter took out a cigarette.

"Then you'd better get to work," Carter said.

"You intend to resign?"

"No," Carter said.

"Talk to the girl."

Carter waited for the realization to settle in.

"Okay," he said. "For whatever it's worth."

"By the way," Absyth said, speaking slowly and calmly. "I agree with you about the significance of getting your job back. Even if we keep a positive attitude, it may not be the best thing for you."

The statement surprised Carter.

Absyth could suggest that Carter might not want to return to the classroom, but judging his competence was another thing. Was that the nub of the insinuation? Had his teaching slipped so far? Had he fallen from the grace of professional competence? What did the profession require? What profession? Maybe competence had to do with enjoyment. He didn't know.

Lectured by a child. Lectured and counseled by a fledgling. In face of the accusation, however, the warm voice gave him a renewed confidence. It was only kindness he had found recently.

"Who is on the hearing committee? Is there anyone there you can talk to? Anyone to argue your case?"

"Daly. He's AAUP president."

"Will he listen?"

"I don't know. I doubt it."

"Anyone else? If you could get two people it might help," Absyth said.

"Charles Lessiack. Harry Gotsch."

Absyth raised his eyebrows and whistled.

"Harry Gotsch?"

"You know him?" Carter said.

"I know he's connected to the governor."

"A speech writer or something."

"Or something."

Absyth held up an index finger.

"Numero uno. He's the governor's right hand man on education in this state. Very little goes down that doesn't go by Harry Gotsch. Even the education budget."

"Which means what?"

"Talk to him. Tell him they are attacking the professorate. Sacking the university. Maybe he'll talk to the governor about it. You're not going to tell him anything he doesn't already know. Lean on him. Tell him you'll go to the Governor."

"Gotsch isn't going to believe me. I don't have any power."

"Power is getting those who have it to use it. If there's anything politicians love, it's the status quo. They do not like waves, not even ripples. Certainly not scandals. Even odds, Gotsch has more dirt on Shindel and Remcheck and Crowly than you can imagine. What's it hurt to ask?"

"I suppose I'm thinking professors shouldn't have to stoop to things like this."

"Stoop? Stoop to stand up? Maybe this is part of the profession. Why not? What keeps the university professorate from politics?"

"What we do in the classroom."

"But not what you do outside the classroom."

"Look, the courtroom is political. You're always trying to get the judge and jury to vote for you. To do that you have to convince them of your case," Carter said. "Politics is natural for lawyers."

"What are you doing with your students? Aren't you trying to persuade them to think? To reason? Hell, that's politics. You can't separate one from the other."

"Why do you think it would be better if I quit teaching?"

Absyth stood and walked around the desk. He laid his hand on Carter's shoulder. He was taller than Carter remembered.

"I know a good bit about the law," he said. "And right now I'm learning more. I know nothing about teaching. Or what makes a good teacher. So I'll take your word for it. I'm not going to tell a man his business."

"And I shouldn't tell you yours."

Absyth smiled.

"Something like that."

Carter gathered up his coat from the chair near the door, then shook Absyth's hand.

"Think about it," Absyth said. "Talk to Gotsch. Meanwhile, I'll get busy. If you have anything, give me a call. By the way, Merry Christmas."

On the way out Carter passed Absyth's secretary, a red-faced middle aged woman with short, brown hair. Carter nodded and stepped through the glass doors to the street.

Now he set a steady pace, a true course for Murphy's and a booth in the backroom to drink and think, to shake himself down to a self, to a residue John Carter could recognize. He had to prepare himself for the tedium and boredom, then for the stench and holler of a barroom brawl.

"They want blood," he told himself, "then blood it will be."

The prospect of a fight pleased him. Now he had a plan, if not of action, at least he was pointed in a new direction. Absorbing the shock of the attack had weakened his resolve. He had been revived, felt alive, rejuvenated.

He thought about Vivien.

At the moment he did not want to talk to her. Not just now, and decided that later, much later would he return home to face Katherine Marie, to be reminded of the tattered ends of memory, the reminiscence of the Olsen's party that swirled about him.

The near end of the night remained still just beyond recall. Coming home, he remembered climbing the porch steps—but could not even imagine how he got there. He couldn't have walked. That explained what? But who?

Katherine Marie had spent the night on the couch wrapped in an afghan, a pillow over her head. Guessing she had had a restless night and needed sleep, he stayed in the kitchen most of the morning. By midmorning she disappeared from the couch. He heard her overhead in the bedroom, but didn't see her until noon as she passed the living-room door on the way to the kitchen, without speaking or otherwise acknowledging him.

More in curiosity and mischievous little-boy trepidation, than with compassion, unaware of the source of her distress, Carter followed her to the kitchen. More than her displeasure probably had to do with too much wine, and him.

She had not dressed or put on makeup. The kitchen painted her face with an electric, ghostly glow. She looked very old. Her eyes were red. She had been crying.

"Are you all right?" he said.

She shook her head and looked at the floor and began crying, again.

"Carter," she said, "how could you?"

"Oh, I don't know," Carter said blithely, "it wasn't exceptional."

She looked at him, for the first time—then looked away.

"You're a bastard. Do you know that? God, I'm so ashamed to be married to you."

"Ah, shame, my dear, is good for the soul. It's akin to the other absurdities we endure. It'll make you a better person—if you don't mind learning to hate people."

"You're disgusting."

"What'd I do that's so shameful? Marry you?"

"How can you joke about this?"

She had not brushed her hair and it stood out in a bush. A new style, Carter thought. The heavy wrinkles of her face she so skillfully shaded and shadowed with makeup seemed now more like scars. She dabbed her eyes with a handkerchief.

"Oh, hell," he said. "For Christ sake, I'm sorry—for whatever it is."

Just then he did not have much of an appetite for intrigue and soul searching. The whiskey of the previous evening had not yet worn off. His legs were shaky, his stomach uneven.

"You're always sorry," she said.

"Look. I'm just a sorry-assed ill-content. Now do you feel better?"

"Whatever you say, it doesn't mean anything."

"Well, I don't know. I'm sure it means something. It'd probably have even more definition if I knew what I'm apologizing for. When you decide to tell me why you're crying, or what I've done, I'd like to hear about it."

Carter went to the living-room. Nothing out of the ordinary came to mind, immediately or readily. Then it did. She had gotten wind of Vivien. Vivien? Who spilled it. Who? At the Olsens'. And what. How much did she know?

Well, shit. Here we go again. My business is my business. Another invasion of privacy. The marriage syndrome.

The thought annoyed him. The insignificance of a few random trysts molded into a major moral issue.

It always comes to this? To what? What had he done?

In the kitchen he resumed the inquiry.

"What did I do?"

Katherine Marie leaned back against the stove, arms folded. Her eyes were set on the distances beyond him.

"What did you do?"

She eyed him suspiciously.

"You're serious, aren't you?"

"What are you pissed about?"

She looked at him blankly.

"What did you say to Remcheck?"

"What did I say? About what?"

"John, I was standing right there. I heard the whole thing. You don't have to pretend."

"I'm not pretending. But I will tell you what I am doing. I'm getting sick-and-tired of this simple-minded, whimpering. If you have a complaint, then let's hear it. If it's serious, maybe we can work it out."

She threw her head back and turned away.

"What does everything have to be negative?"

"Because it is negative," Carter said. "It's vulgar. It's obscene. And there's no other way to describe it."

"You're an educated man, John. You don't have to talk that way."

"And you're a not-too-bright female who has no place prescribing behavior for anyone. I suppose that's what education means to you. Sound good or pleasant or some other such nonsense. Well maybe it's time education is redefined not in terms of PR hype and pleasant images but in terms of the real world and what it puts into people's lives.

"I haven't the slightest idea what education means in your lexicon, but I'll tell you what it doesn't mean for me. It doesn't mean trying to look good at the expense of everything else. The point and power of symbol is not reality, no matter how much you think it is. The shadows on the wall are just that—shadows. All the education school and business degrees will not make educated, and therefore, better people of those misanthropes at Barker you seem to admire so much."

"How convenient for John Carter. You make an ass of yourself—and of me—then don't remember."

"You?" Carter said. "You? If what I did had to do with the great-and-grand you, maybe I should hear about it. What is this a military court?"

She was whispering now. A pissed whisper, Carter thought. When did she practice this kind of thing? Where had she learned it?

"Last night you called Remcheck a worthless sonofabitch."

Carter starred at the floor for a moment. A soft sense of relief came over him, then gratification.

"I did? Is that all?"

"No. That is not all, as you put it. You insulted Mr. Shindel."

"What did I do? Maybe it wasn't an insult. Maybe whatever I said was true."

"You insulted him. The President of the Barker State Board of Trustees. You called him a pig-fucker."

"Not a fucking pig?"

"How smug. Your arrogance is impossible."

Carter smiled.

"Arrogant? Well, you're right. I don't have any proof he fucks pigs—although I wouldn't put it past him. I knew his brother when we were kids. The brother always said the only thing in life he wanted was a cow that was stump-broke. Which goes a long way toward explaining why he married his wife."

"You called Remcheck a killer. And there were at least a dozen people who heard you."

"Citizens to bear witness," Carter said. "I'll bet that was good for a few uncomfortable moments."

"I left. I've never been so embarrassed in my life."

"How'd I get home?"

"I don't know, and I don't care."

She started to cry again and struck the top of the stove with a delicate, but clenched fist.

Oh shit, Carter thought. Here we go. A full blown tantrum. She took a small pan from the top of the stove and whirled and hurled it at him.

"You're sick," she screamed. "You're sick and demented."

The pan missed Carter and clattered across the floor.

"Because I call a fucking pig a pig-fucker?"

"You said—right in chancellor Remcheck's face—you said, 'Remcheck you're a sadistic killer, a real sonofabitch.'"

Carter played back the words briefly, tried to envision the scene, but nothing came to mind.

"Well," he said finally, "I'm impressed. I should have said that a long time ago."

"You said you knew he had killed Mason."

"Yeah," Carter said. "Yeah, he did."

"Do you expect people to believe that? John, that's preposterous."

"Why?"

"Why haven't the police arrested him?"

"How should I know? They don't arrest people for emotional murder."

Carter watched her face.

"Or is that too abstract for you? Remcheck killed Mason. Remcheck and the little," he almost said pig-fucker, "the little squint-eyed prick, Shindel. It's not hard to understand when we destroy an environment, we kill whatever lives in the environment."

"That's ridiculous. University trustees and chancellors don't go around killing people."

"I know. You told me."

"But it's ridiculous."

"Is it?"

"Nobody believes that. Even Morgana Carmichal thought your behavior was uncalled for.

"Morgana. She wasn't even there."

"Yes she was. You were just too drunk to remember."

"Why are you quoting Morgana? I thought she wasn't your kind of woman. Now suddenly you're bosom buddies?"

"She said you always take things personally."

"Well, she's right about that. Though it seems hardly a criticism. Everything those clowns do is an affront to persons of integrity and goodwill. And intelligence, I might add. We have an obligation to object. I've talked to Morgana about this a hundred times, and our views don't differ that much. So I'd suggest you leave her out of it.

"Look. Remcheck's policies have reduced the university to a stack of bricks inhabited by a bunch of babbling self-serving idiots. This isn't a university. It's a K-Mart for cheap degrees. Junk bond education. If there were any educational regulations—even as anemic as the SEC—the board, the administration of this esteemed brickyard, and half the faculty, would be under indictment for fraud.

"You may not see it, my dear, but the tenets you feed on are the entrails of a wounded, dying beast. Why don't you tell me about the mall and classroom crap you've been running around here babbling about for the last several months?"

The conversation with Absyth had improved Carter's disposition, if not his prospects. The Olsen farce was decidedly ex post facto, and since he did not expect Shindel and Remcheck would call off the hounds, the episode hadn't done any damage. They were probably pissed, and would be more determined, but now it seemed inconsequential to Carter.

The girl posed the bigger problem. He had to ask her to recant. But how? What did they have on her? And who in the hell was she, anyway?

After the hearing Johnson had walked back to the office with him.

"Where'd you get the bit about Michelle Phillips," he asked Johnson.

"From the registrar," Johnson said. "She's been using a couple of different names. She's enrolled in classes under at least two names—maybe more. I don't have it all. It doesn't make sense, but she was listed in my class as Michelle Phillips."

"Your ethics class."

"No. That was last year."

"She's not in your ethics class."

"Not this semester."

"You're sure?"

"Absolutely."

"She told me she was in your ethics class."

"No," Johnson said.

"Then who is she?"

Johnson shook his head.

He had labored through the conversation and now took a deep breath and leaned back, looking at the ceiling. A moment later he leaned forward, bending over with his arms wrapped around his stomach.

"Are you all right?" Carter asked.

"I will be," Johnson said.

The conversation had ended there. For a long time Johnson had not looked well. His complexion varied from florid to pallid, his eyes bloodshot as if he had been smoking dope, or drinking, both of which Carter doubted.

Johnson sat for a few moments then rose, nodded to Carter, and left the office.

Crazy, Carter thought. The world's gone bananas.

Carter went straight to Murphy's from Absyth's office.

He didn't have a number for the girl. Maybe, he thought, she'd be at Murphy's. Or he could leave a note. Always she had found him or left instructions about where he could find her, and when.

The tables in Murphy's backroom were stacked in a corner and Sam Perrin, in the booth beneath the single window, the blinds raised, leaned over a newspaper he had spread on the table. A spot of sunlight illuminated the table in a clean circle.

Sam the innocent, Carter thought, the clean, washed clean and made holy.

Carter found a stool at the bar. The heavy damp smell of tobacco and sweeping compound scented the air. Through the door to the office to the left of the bar, he could see the back of Murphy's bulk hunched over the desk. A twelve-inch black and white TV on the desk flickered over the five o'clock news.

A bartender Carter did not know brought him a beer, and he tried to concentrate on the large TV above the bar.

Every few minutes his mind reverted to the puzzle. What did Lessiack and Gotsch think of the inquisition? What had Gotsch said?

"We are all honorable men, here."

What did he mean?

Carter poked through the change on the bar. When he looked up Murphy was leaning in the doorway behind the bar.

"That woman find you?"

"What woman?"

"You know. The one looks like she belongs to the Adams Family. The one comes in here with those two chinks that work at the observatory."

"Sutter," Carter said.

"She's been in twice in the last hour. Hell, you ought'a set up an office here."

"And I get a percentage, right?"

"Well, she'll probably be back."

"What'd she want?"

"Who knows? What do any of em want?"

Murphy's cavalier attitudes about women annoyed Carter, although at the moment they seemed a bit better seated in fact, a bit less unrealistic.

"By the way, what do they want?"

"Money. Or its equivalent. And that means men who will give money for sex. It's easier than working for it."

"Nothing more?"

"Nope. Not if you want to be truthful. Doc, in case you haven't looked, there are two sexes. That divides the world in two. And one always wants what the other's got."

Sutter? He had thought about Sutter. He had thought he might call her. Maybe she could tell him about Lessiack, his impressions of the hearing, his intentions. Maybe he could encourage her to do a little lobbying on his behalf. How much influence did she have with Lessiack? They spent a good bit of time together. What else? Was there more to their affiliation? How close were Gotsch and Lessiack? He simply didn't know, but Sutter had chased him down that morning on the quad. Why?

"By the way," Carter said, "I do want to thank you for trying to warn me."

"About what?"

"About crazy females."

"Hell, Doc, you ain't needed warning, you were just short some information. I mean, you ain't known only about half of it. See, I know the whole family. Her old lady used to come in here loaded and get pissed and get into a temper-tantrum, and every once in a while throw a beer glass at somebody. Got so I had to blackball her. Keep her out unless she was sober—which wasn't often those days."

Murphy wiped his hands on a bar towel as if he was finishing up a particularly messy task.

"Anyway, it's a helluva poor reason to lose a perfectly good job. For a cheap piece-of-ass."

"Where'd you hear that?"

"What?"

"About my job."

"Oh, hell, news gets around. People talk"

"Well, she doesn't have anything to do with my job. They want me off the faculty, and if not for this, then it'll be something else. And it's not losing a job. It's losing a paycheck, which I don't need anyway.

"Look at it this way," Carter said. "You run a bar because you make money at it. That's why most people do what they do. To make money. But what I've been doing for the last twenty years for money, I would have done even if there hadn't been any money in it. Of course I would have to feed myself. But that's another story.

"So I'm having a bit of bad luck."

Carter looked toward the backroom.

"Sam's lost himself. Fortunately I haven't had that kind of luck. At least not yet."

Murphy leaned back, and looked at the ceiling.

"Doc," he said. "You don't expect me to believe that, do you?"

"Well, to tell the truth, Murph, I don't care what you believe. It's true."

"Yeah, I know. And people can live on love, too."

"What about Vivien?" Carter said.

"What about her?"

"You know her sister."

"Which one."

"How many are there?"

"There," Murphy pointed to the front door. "I told you she'd be back. Right on time. An she's got the slope with her."

Betty Sutter hesitated inside the door, and then exaggerated a wave as if she was polishing a window, as if they were still a great distance apart and she was afraid he might not see her. She wore a heavy wool red, white and blue sweater and washed-out Levi's and sneakers.

"Dr. Carter, I need to talk to you."

Carter did not recognize the woman with Sutter but assumed a connection with the physics lab.

"Sounds important," Carter said.

"I think it will help you," Sutter said.

"Well, hell," Carter said. "You know me. I need all the help I can get."

"Can we talk?"

Carter looked into the backroom. Sam was still in the booth with the newspaper.

"Yeah" he said. "Murph, I'm gonna set up a table in the back."

Murphy grinned his little-boy-best and nodded.

"Suit yourself. It'll save Sam the trouble."

"Can Sam have a cigarette?"

"Un huh. If you watch him smoke it. Make sure there's nothing left."

Sam was sitting with his hands folded in front of him, examining his thumbnails. When Carter came in Sam looked up and watched him as a child might watch a stranger. Carter lit a cigarette and handed it to Sam, who puffed it into a grey cloud.

Carter set his beer on the pool table, then lifted down a table and carried it to the far side of the room.

Sutter and her companion followed docilely, watching as he collected chairs from the stack in the corner.

"What about him?" Sutter said, referring to Sam.

"Nothing," Carter said. "Whatever he hears, he leaves it here when he leaves here. He can't remember his name or the day."

Carter sat with his back to the wall facing the door, watching Sam.

"The biggest concern is he'll forget a lit cigarette and incinerate the place."

Murphy set two empty beer glasses and a pitcher of beer on the table. On his way back to the bar he leaned over the pool table and snapped on the plastic Tiffany.

"I'm glad I found you," Sutter said.

She put her hand on Carter's arm. "Dr. Carter, this is Lui Chan. She's a research assistant in Crompol Lab."

The girl smiled and bowed, without standing, in the way many Asian woman have of exaggerated acknowledgment of males they assume have power or position.

Several years before two Japanese women had appeared in Carter's intro class. And as if their difficulties with English and the concepts of Hume and Kant were not enough, at every turn they bowed and nodded, with ingratiating obeisance, acquiescing with whatever he said, regardless. They assigned a grand significance to every word he uttered, making communication all but impossible.

He had wondered at the time how a man could live with that, unless he had already dismissed women as mindless creatures. Then it made a sort of inverted sense.

Perceiving they were at the mercy of men, the women submitted, only in trumps, while securing with their ohhing and ahhing and bowing and smiling a substantial privacy and freedom from anything else the men might have been inclined to demand from them.

He had come to view the behavior almost as a comedy routine, a stage act, but reading their papers and scoring their exams, he discovered they were both quick-witted and intelligent—the brightest students in the class, which further added to his perception they were toying with him, and maybe with all men.

Lui Chan he judged as twenty-three or four. Her profile was nearly flat, although straight on, her face was quite pleasant. The tawny brown of her skin, he thought, more Thai than Chinese, although he hadn't any reason beyond Murphy's slurs to think she was Chinese.

While Carter filled the beer glasses, Sutter extracted a manila folder from her brief case.

"Look at this," she said, pushing it across the table.

He took the sheaf, and opened the cover. The cover-page appeared to represent an application, he thought, maybe a grant proposal.

"Where'd you get this?"

"The physics department," Sutter said.

"Why show it to me?"

Sutter smiled, what Carter thought without knowing her well enough to judge, a conspiratorial smile.

"It's a prospectus for a government project Crompol Lab will be working on for the next three years."

"So?"

"Well, look at it."

Carter flipped through several more pages.

"Now what?"

"John, it's all wrong."

"What's that mean?"

"It means," Lui Chan said, in a voice totally devoid of accent "somebody's been trimming and cooking. That's what it means."

"John, the government has given Barker State six million dollars for this project, and there isn't a grain of truth in the proposal."

"Who did it?"

"You want to guess?"

"Somebody in physics. Lessiack?"

Sutter exaggerated a nod.

"Lessiack, Crowly and Landeau."

"You're sure?"

"We couldn't make a mistake on this," Lui Chan said.

"But why wouldn't anyone else catch it?"

"Who? Nobody else has seen it. Who's going to turn down six million dollars, or have to answer to appropriation committees for squelching a grant this size? John, this is big bucks. The kind of grants universities live on."

Carter pushed back from the table. He had heard rumors, but hadn't imagined it would be this obvious, this blatant.

"How long has this been going on?"

"We're not sure," Lui Chan said. "We've found some of the altered worksheets. There are more."

"Why bring it to me?"

"It was Chan's idea," Sutter said. "We thought you could use the information. When the board hears about this they'll have to do something."

And there it was again.

The dumb belief in the integrity of power, when everything suggested just the opposite.

"Did you ever think maybe, just maybe the board knows about this and maybe the board even instructed or encouraged this?"

Sutter had ignored the beer Carter had poured for her. Now she gathered in the glass with both hands and sat starring at it. She shook her head slowly.

"A bit of the old Daly regime in Chicago," Lui Chan said. "Corruption was the only system they knew. Honesty was corrupt and went against the way things were supposed to be done."

"It's even worse," Carter said. "You're from Chicago?"

"Yes. The University of Chicago."

"Can I take this with me?"

Sutter nodded.

"Yes," she said. "That's a copy."

She took a sip of beer.

"But I still think the Board of Trustees would do something if they knew about it."

"What?"

"I don't know, Professor Carter. But surely something."

Chapter XXII

A block from Murphy's, Carter dropped the folder in a trash barrel. He walked another block before retracing his steps and retrieving the papers. Worthless as they were he could not overlook even a remote possibility—at least not yet.

He did not share Sutter's faith in the great "someone." He did not know who she was referring to, and suspected she did not know, either. Who cared about this kind of thing?

"The board would act if they knew about it," Sutter had said.

They'd kill the messenger.

Sutter's great "someone" was the epitome of academic fantasy. Gotham was under siege and Batman was nowhere in sight.

Maybe, in the end, maturity came down to being shed of illusion. Maybe the truly wise were those who, stripped of pretense, could anticipate the corruption, the cunning double-dealings of human enterprise, as well as the arrival and passing of love. Maybe that was education. The inadvertent purpose of our lives. To be apprised of human propensities—hatred, folly, deceit, vengeance. And love.

Carter came onto the porch and paused at the mailbox. A handful of bills and magazines, *Foreign Affairs, TLS.* American Express and Visa. A utility bill.

In the hall he dropped the mail on the table and went to the kitchen for a beer. The silence was broken by the faint murmur of distant voices just beyond the kitchen, and he leaned over the table to see into the yard. Probably Mrs. Elmore, that worn caricature from Rabelais. But he could not see anyone. Sound carried through the heat ducts. Maybe he had forgotten to turn off the radio he kept in the upstairs bathroom. The Seth Thomas in the hall showed ten-thirty-three. He listened for a moment. It wasn't ticking. He had forgotten to wind it. He checked the stove clock in the kitchen. Katherine Marie wouldn't be home for another hour or so.

At the desk in the far corner of the living-room he opened the packet and laid out the papers as best he could.

Twice more Carter's attention was taken from the papers by a low grumbling, he thought of voices, crawling along the floor behind him. He gazed out into the yard for a time, watching for blowing leaves, the bare branches of the maple near the drive shaken by the wind. At just the right compass angle and velocity the wind rising and pushing into the eaves of the old house could resemble a soft, deep throated, distant thunder.

The papers were in two packets. Each carried a cover-letter addressed to the National Science Congress. The letters bore Lessiack's and Crowly's signatures, but amounted to little more than the usual political, public relations, grant rhetoric. The forms and lab reports were, however, extensively detailed mathematical formulas and diagrams and graphs with occasional supplemental prose explanations.

The proposal had been divided into two parts, with different time frames and areas of funding. The first entailed a two year development research phase for one million two hundred thousand dollars. The second extended over three years and involved an additional two million.

A cursory reading confirmed Carter's suspicions. As with the sheaf of science articles he kept in his desk drawer in Temperly, he could, at the beginning, decipher a small portion of the calculations. From page twenty on, however, the prose appeared less frequently, then vanished altogether. What remained reminded him of intricately designed wallpaper.

As far as he could tell the second packet matched the first except for the notes, and what he guessed were corrections in the margins. And while the differences in the numbers and computations were small enough, he knew in the lab they could delineate clearly the margins of success and failure, of legitimate scientific investigation and fraud.

Without the original data, which it appeared Sutter and Lui Chan had, there would be no way for anyone to detect the scam. Cooking and trimming they called it. In his ethics class Carter used a video tape called "*Do Scientists Cheat?*" But he had not guessed it might be going on in the labs at Barker.

Still, in the precious ore of discovery there had to be dross. There had to be people who did not want to shoulder the yeomen's work science required, who found it easier to manipulate the situation.

He stood starring at the documents, undecided about what to do, then, as if inspired by the deception, propelled into the depth of the deceit, he spun abruptly and walked across the living-room into the hall to the sewing-room door and paused before opening it.

The mumble of voices that had hummed in the hall and living-room were now silent. Katherine Marie was seated at the far end nearest the windows. Vivien had been on the couch, but when she saw Carter she stood, and stepped around to the end, putting it between them. Katherine Marie remained seated, back straight, hands folded in her lap, watching Carter.

A Madonna pretense, her Holy Mother pose, Carter thought.

"What are you doing here?" Carter said, looking directly at Vivien, suggesting he already knew.

"We're talking," Katherine Marie said. "I invited her here so we could talk."

"I know," Carter said, "you're discussing the variables in the national economy."

Again he said to the girl, "What are you doing here?"

"There are some things we need to clear up," Katherine Marie said.

"I'm talking to her. She's a big girl. She can answer for herself."

He didn't know how Katherine Marie found Vivien. Someone at Barker had called. Maybe her name came up at the Olsen's. That he doubted. If Katherine Marie had known she would have used it before now. And he knew if he asked, the answer would be replete with acrimony and insinuation.

Vivien sat down on the couch, leaning forward, arms together on her knees, looking at her hands.

"You don't have to be rude," Katherine Marie said. "You aren't exactly guiltless in this matter."

"A significant non-sequitur," Carter said. "Guilt to vulgarity? And what matter might that be?"

"You know what I'm talking about," Katherine Marie said. "Taking advantage of your students."

"She's not my student," Carter said. "This is not a case of student as nigger. Nobody took advantage of her. Nobody in this room, at any rate, unless you've got something in mind."

"John, I have the whole story," Katherine Marie said. "There's no point denying what you did."

"You have never had the whole story. You haven't even an idea for a story," Carter said. "What you have is a bit of scattered data and a stack of silly assumptions."

"We don't need to go through the details. We need to decide how we're going to handle this."

How "we" are going to handle this?

Well, here we go, Carter thought, the all-inclusive mythic "we."

The marriage postulation of oneness, a merging of identities, blurring the distinctions of self. The biblical nonsense wherein male and female had been wheeling and dealing over the eons, whipping the pretense into a froth, mapping out turf for dominance and exploitations in a system that enslaved both mistress and master. A system to indulge misfit and masturbator alike.

Early on Carter discovered that while Katherine Marie clung fervently to the trappings of the marriage cadaver, her conjugal loyalty was at best spurious. It hinged on the advantage of the moment, so the bits and pieces of his not-so-admirable past he had given away at simpering moments or brought up as conversation, she hoarded with miserly efficiency and often served back to him at her best advantage to make a point or remind him of his failings. Mishaps she read as premeditated acts, ascribing evil motives to accidents, as she did the time Carter stabbed the dog.

On a late summer's eve he had set up the grill on the back porch to avoid a soft rain that had been falling for two days. He pushed the grill nearest the far rail, away from the kitchen door, hoping the smoke would drift out from beneath the porch canopy. However, repulsed by the curtain of precipitation, after a short time it curled back and hung between the posts and the back wall in a weighted, thickened haze.

The thought came to him, then, a fan might disperse the smoke and send it on its way into the saturated atmosphere. He went to the kitchen for the ten-inch oscillating fan he kept in the pantry. Having retrieved the appliance, to avoid making another trip, he picked up a spatula and a seven-inch, thin butcher-knife he had ground down, specifically to use over the outside grill.

He had already done significant damage to a fifth of Jack Daniels and paused unsteadily at the screen-door, attempting to juggle the fan, knife and spatula into an arrangement to free-up one hand.

The dog, a five-year-old medium-sized brindle Katherine Marie had taken in as a pup, ran into the kitchen and as was her habit, without warning leaped toward Carter.

The practice of jumping at men, only at men, even in fun, Carter attributed to Katherine Marie's encouragement and rewards, although he was not sure how she had trained the dog. He had never seen any conditioning or training sessions, and imagined it had been done by some twisted, psychic aberration. Maybe she had done it with ESP or some other such alliance of canine association.

At any rate, Carter struggled with the door, juggling the fan and the utensils and did not see the animal coming. The dog, for her part, launched through the air and impaled herself on the knife, running the better half of the blade into her right eye. Pushed, and then pulled from Carter's grip, the knife slashed into the palm of his left hand.

The force of the animal going onto the blade knocked Carter against the wall and dislodged the fan from his grip. Anesthetized as he was, Carter did not immediately perceive he had been cut, and was surprised at the splattering of blood on his arm and hand. For a moment he thought the dog had bitten him.

As he remembered it, the animal dropped to the floor, almost in slow-motion, whimpered, then sagged to her haunches, and toppled, stiff as a ten-pin, and just as dead.

It took eighteen stitches to close the wound on Carter's hand and the following day, an hour to scrub up the blood.

Not only did Katherine Marie refuse to clean up the mess, and so the blood dried on the floor and wall, but she would not accept, by virtue of a careless, albeit, playful habit, the dog had initiated the incident.

Of course she grieved the dog, excessively by Carter's estimation. She placed small pictures of the dog at optimum places and kept its food dish and a ragdoll it often played with in full sight between the stove and refrigerator—no doubt to better legitimize future references to the incident. When she needed a particularly nasty retort, she'd bring up the dog's death.

Carter dismissed accusative references to the dog's demise as a loathsome weakness of mind—a cheap-shot, betraying confidence. Another burr in the blanket of matrimonial comfort.

But this day had more to it.

As much as anything, Katherine Marie enjoyed the "we women" and "you" game. The arrangement rested on a primal remnant similar to the lion-pride of females choosing a male and then legislating which other females would be allowed in.

When he found them, his first-impulse had been to have nothing to do with either of them, especially within the already established closed confines of female filiations.

Vivien had gone along with Crowly, for whatever reason. Katherine Marie had gone out to find her, and Vivien had come here at Katherine Marie's invitation. At any juncture the chain could have been broken. But it had not, they had not broken it. They wanted this as surely as he had wanted to avoid their emotional, verbal clutter.

And still he did not walk away.

The nonsense of the pretense intrigued him. If they insisted on exercising a short stroll into the absurd, he'd accommodate them.

Of previous dalliances, on occasion, he had been accused, blamed. But he had not been confronted face to face by two females, one wife—the other a quasi-mistress—questioning, or at least discussing the ramifications of his sexual proclivities, and he guessed, his improbity, in which both had been involved. Warily, Carter entered uncharted territory.

Katherine Marie was still angry about the Olsen charade. And not just pissed at him, but with "them." The male "them" as oppressor, as he had come to believe, rooted in the substratum of the female psyche, the genetic knee-jerk of the procreative equation carried over from the ancient past when child-birth enslaved females, and men were obviously to blame for the bondage. So even in modern times, with the kid-game little more of enslavement or bondage than an option, the choice clearly a woman's, whether and with whom to breed, when men could no longer be rationally held as the source of the discomforts and dangers of child-bearing, the party-line still held men as the enemy.

"You are not involved in this," Carter said. "You haven't been involved in this in any way."

"I'm married to you. I'm your wife. So I'm involved."

"Married?" Carter said. "Is that what it's called?"

The marriage constitution needed to be reworked, reinterpreted. What did the contract imply? Certainly not a lifetime of affection. The best anyone could hope for these days was toleration. Putting up with another's peculiarities without going off the deep end and maiming or killing.

"Marriage?" Carter said. "If you think I've violated some sacred nuptial trust, it's nothing compared to what you've done. What do you want?

The security of marriage—whatever the hell that is? Maybe a place to come to at the end of day. Maybe footsteps in the hall or a handy-man to build a fire in the fireplace or a bozo to escort you in public.

"But I don't need a roommate and I surely don't need a mother or any other moral-matriarch telling me what is and is not proper and acceptable.

"To be perfectly honest, I've never been able to depend on you the way most people can depend on partners. I've supported you at every turn. And you've seen me as the enemy. As your jailor or keeper or something I never was."

He stopped in front of the girl who did not raise her head to look at him.

"I make mistakes," he said. "Sometimes I make serious mistakes, but then it seems human enough."

"But I do care about you, John," Katherine Marie said.

"No," Carter said. "Money. What you care about in this marriage is a few thousand dollars-worth of property. Nothing more."

"There's my name. I have a name to protect. People I work with. It's only sensible. I don't want this to get out."

"You don't want what to get out? You could change your name."

"I think it's rather obvious. I could be ruined. All the years I've put in building a reputation could be destroyed by this."

"Ridiculous," Carter said. "If your name and reputation are destroyed by the action of another, I'd have to wonder seriously about the nature of your business.

"What you're really talking about is greed. Greed and fear."

He stopped beside Katherine Marie.

"You're so involved with hustling the buck, and placating the money-changers, you can't see anything else. You've reduced your self-image to a couple of dollar signs painted with mascara. You're being used, and the sad part is you haven't the slightest awareness that you're being used.

"Now you've set me up as the villain. My god. For twenty years I've encouraged you, backed you, helped you. What more could I have done?"

Carter squatted down in front of Vivien.

"And look at you. A lovely human being. A fine young woman. A woman I've tried to befriend and truly care about. And you set me up. Why? Fear? Because you're afraid? And while I can understand your fear, it doesn't change the results, or what it does to the soul to give in to that kind of evil.

"You want to talk about love and honor. I've loved both of you. And it's not just a matter of sex and the stupidity of marriage. And what do you do? Is there not even a semblance of friendship? You allow these clowns to use you, both of you. Why?

"These are bad people. Not men, not even animals. They're mean-spirited, hateful minds in human form."

He stood and walked to the end of the couch.

"If this gets out, no one will ever look at me in the same way," Katherine Marie said.

"And how might that be?" Carter said. "Maybe you should go wipe the mascara off the dollar signs. Maybe you should look like a sixty-year-old human. What would be wrong with that? Maybe you need a new image. Then you wouldn't be bothered by what people think, or how they look at you."

"I wouldn't be able to face anyone. They'd think of me as that poor woman married to that horrible man."

"So you're not keeping honorable company. Well, let me tell you a bit about honorable company. You know why that creature is sitting there? You know why Crowly and those other misanthropes are after me? Because I've demanded a little bit of integrity, a little but more than educational business as usual. I'll tell you a little about honor and decency."

Carter shifted back to Vivien who sat starring at the floor.

Vivien wore an old sweat shirt, Levis and dirty white tennis shoes. Opposite Katherine Marie, she appeared in yet another pose, portraiture, the shade-line and color tempered and rearranged in Carter's mind. Her hair was tied in a pony-tail and doubled up.

"John, there's no reason for hostility."

"Oh yes there is. Injustice should always be met with hostility. When people fail to act reasonably, as compassionate humans, there is a definite need for hostility."

"This young woman came here at my request."

"I know. You said that."

Carter stepped toward Vivien and stood looking down at her.

"Who sent you?"

When she did not look up, he reached down, took her by the hair and lifted her head.

"Look at me," Carter said.

"Carter," Katherine Marie shouted. "You take your hands off that child. You leave her alone."

"Is this how females go around getting beaten up?" Carter said.

Even before he finished, he knew the question had been miss-stated. He stepped away, and put his hands together in front of him.

"No," he said, "that's not right. The question, would be, is this what females do in order to keep from getting knocked around?"

Vivien dropped her head again and began to cry.

"Who sent you?"

"It's time we get to the bottom of this," Katherine Marie said. "Obviously you've been lying to those who trusted you. Maybe you could explain your position to us."

"'To us?' The great ubiquitous 'us.'

"My position? I'm presently standing in a small room in a house on College Street in Lancaster, Illinois, in the northern hemisphere of the planet earth, in a solar system, galaxy and universe that is at the center of nothing. Is that precise enough?"

The girl's appearance at the hearing had surprised Carter, and he thought possibly she had not known what the gathering was about. He had been further surprised by her candor. In his experience, most women were reluctant to divulge the details of a liaison they had initiated. Unless, unless. Unless there was more to it than he knew.

He had called off Carl's inquiry about the girl's name and background, certain Crowly was using her and he (Carter) could more easily endure the indignities than have her embarrassed or damaged by the fallout. In a sense he blamed himself for having involved her.

"This is not," Carter said to Katherine Marie, "no matter how you see it, one of your ad-agency get-togethers. I am not a client. This is my house, and I resent you sticking your nose in my business. Your position in life, in my life, does not afford you the right or the privilege to play mother-counselor, private-eye or whatever it is you're into."

He asked Vivien again, "Who sent you?"

Not only did the idea have merit, but Carter perceived just then, the first thin threads of a connection.

"Your old man. You told me your old man beat you up. But it wasn't your old man. Who was it? You aren't even married. And the crap about kids. Yeah. A nice touch. "

He paused for a moment.

"Who would beat up women? He probably works for Crowly."

The name crawled out slowly, a patina of slim on his tongue. A vile taste.

"Crowly," he said again, letting the ideas germinate, before bringing them together.

"I asked her to come here," Katherine Marie said.

"I'm having a bad time with people answering for other people," Carter said. "Right now," he pointed to Katherine Marie, "I'd suggest you not talk unless someone asks you a direct question."

"Carter," the girl said, "there's nothing wrong with what we did. I don't know why you're so angry."

"Why I'm angry? It's not what 'we' did. You're right. We didn't harm anyone. But it's what you did. What'd you tell them at the hearing? Am I losing my mind or did you dump out the details of the last couple of weeks for those vultures to feed on?"

"But there wasn't anything wrong with what we did."

"How about what you did? What about the transcript? You knew the place was bugged, didn't you?"

"I didn't think it made any difference."

"Why was Ruth's apartment bugged? Who did that? Ruth? Is that how she gets her kicks? Playing back tapes of her conquests. Or yours?"

"We didn't do anything wrong."

"But they think it is wrong. No. They don't think it's wrong. But they will play it up as a violation of some eternal absolute ethical code they're entrusted to uphold. As if I've trespassed on the sacred tenets of civilization, the same civilization they are destroying."

"But you said you didn't care what other people think."

"Usually I don't. But there's no reason to give them a whip and chair. Nobody in his right mind would want his private conversations published."

"You said if you try to cover up something, you're as bad as they are?""

Carter shook his head.

"Why don't you run around the streets without clothes? Well, maybe you do. But people keeping their personal lives personal is not covering up anything. What people do on their own time is their business.

"So you think I'm as bad as they are, and you intend to show them I'm not by getting me fired?"

"John," the girl said, "you don't realize how much I admire you—the kind of person you are. I don't want to spoil it by making it into a cheap lie."

On the wall to either side of the window facing the backyard were large pictures of a white dear standing in a green glade, head up, ears forward, alert. Carter leaned with his hands above his head, palms pressed to the glass.

It didn't make sense.

"No," he said, "that's too easy. There's more to this than protecting your warped image of me."

Katherine Marie seated herself on the couch beside Vivien and put her arm around the girl's shoulders.

"John, may I say something?"

Carter watched her, but did not speak. A gleam reflected off her black hair.

"We wouldn't do a thing like that intentionally," she said. "I think this young lady was confused. As a professor you have a tremendous influence over students. I think she's telling the truth."

"You're as crazy as she is," Carter said.

"Why do you have to insult everyone," Katherine Marie said. "You're so insensitive."

"That wasn't an insult," Carter said. "And don't give me the insensitivity bit. Anyone who objects or questions your failure to comprehend even the slightest facts about reality, is insensitive. If I whisper the word 'no,' you think I'm shouting. If you want to talk about insensitivity, let's talk about this little fiasco you've drummed-up here. Self-indulgence. That's what it amounts to. And you don't give a good damn who gets hurt by it, or whose life is inconvenienced."

"What you did is your doing, John. What you need to do now, is explain it to Dr. Crowly. He's a good man, and I'm sure he'll understand."

"What I need to do, I'll do," Carter said. "Without instructions from you."

"Well, you haven't done very well so far, John."

"My politics are sufficient for the situation—my track record's a lot better than yours," Carter said. "And I guess that's what disturbs me most about this. I've worked at education as a means of encouraging students to better understand their world. I've done it without asking for the accolades of prestige and/or money. And what do I get? Not only have I not received anything of respect or appreciation, but I've been belittled and mocked and condemned by a pack of equivocating, self-serving parasites who have not provided a thing of value for this society or anyone in it, but for themselves."

He gestured to Vivien.

"And now you come in here telling me you want to protect my image. You literally aid in the destruction of whatever chance I might have had to help people in the future, and you talk about saving my image. You are twenty-two, or twenty, or however old you are, and you haven't even the rudiments of understanding that your actions affect the lives of others.

"And in the end, I don't believe you. I don't believe the tripe about admiring me. There's more to it. Crowly put you up to this. Or better yet, you're protecting yourself—from what I don't know, but whatever you're into is as destructive as it is worthless."

"It's difficult to respect someone who takes advantage of children," Katherine Marie said.

"A moment ago she was a young lady, before that a student, and now she's a child. Which is it?" Carter said. "If you want to get to the bottom of a matter, and you already told me you do, then maybe we should begin by calling things—and people—by their correct names. Let's start with Mrs. Caroline Vivien Connors or Michelle Phillips or whoever she is.

The girl began crying again.

"John, that's contemptible."

"Contemptible is an accurate word," Carter said. "It's not sex or money that make people bad. It's how people use sex and money. And that is contemptible. In fact it's obscene. If the city had obscenity ordinances both of you would be in jail."

"We don't have to put up with this," Katherine Marie said.

"Again, we agree," Carter said. "You can leave any time. Nobody's going to stop you. In fact, if you want I'll help you pack."

He stepped to the door and pushed it open.

"Here, I'll hold the door for you. Is that genteel enough for you?"

Katherine Marie stood. Her eyes were moist, now, the tip of her nose red.

Well, here we go. When in retreat weep and whine, Carter thought. Bluster and irrationality to get your way, and when it fails, go into a weeping fit.

He suspected, just then he wanted out more than either of them.

"Okay," he said, "I'm finished. I've said too much already. I'm truly sorry for the rant. But this has to end."

A moment later he regretted saying it, then knew in spite of himself, it was true. There was nothing left. He had known this for some time, although his childlike hopes had kept him from admitting it.

He went to the kitchen for a beer and to gather himself, to assess the shock and turmoil and heard the front door close. Ten minutes or so later he tentatively, meekly, edged into the hall, then into the living-room, listening for sounds. But there were none. The door had closed once. Had they gone out together? Christ knows where.

"Fini," Carter said aloud. "Just like that," and fell into his favorite corner of the couch to revisit the events of the last few hours.

When will it end? Just when I think it's over—Christ. Maybe this is the last of it.

But is it?

This is what you got old buddy, he told himself. A screwed-up situation with people trying to end your career and your old lady, for whatever it's worth, pulling-up stakes and making a run for the door. Well, it's not what you planned, but it'll have to do. You'll just have to make the best of it. He emptied the beer. Some philosopher.

Maybe they had it planned. Maybe it had worked out for the best. Hobbesian old woman hell-bent on self-interest. Indeed, the animal ministrations of a nasty, brutish and short life.

And then for a long time he sat and stared out at the gray day, the bare trees bending and waving in the wind, the awareness of his newest status gathering around him.

He could not see himself as an oppressor. His ancestors, Irish and French had come to the land of the Illinois as visitors. Voyagers and farmers, they traveled males without females, married native women, adopted the habits and customs of the women, so much so to incur the disdain of later arrivals for having become indistinguishable from the "savages."

He approved of that. The word "savage," replete with wisdom and savvy, an acute and mystic sense of nature.

In his liaisons, even in philandering, he had been amendable, adaptive. He too had adopted the habits and customs of his connections, as much as possible. And if the truth were known, he had been used a good bit more often than he had used anyone. At least he had not indulged in the pretenses and madness of sexual possession.

Vows. And what vows had been broken? To love, honor and obey. Nobody, but nobody has ever given a reasonable definition of love. Whitehead thought it ridiculous to speak of "love" among savages. The ancient Greeks didn't give much play to heterosexual love.

So what about it? What about this hormonal, visceral, animal reaction? Affection? Bonding?

And what about honor? Money. Without food, shelter and adequate means there is no honor. Only the deranged could insist on the fantasy of poor but honorable. Fortunes, or as it may be the misfortune of scarce resources, not only diminished honor, but impaired both the ability and inclination to honor.

This, Carter suspected, lay at the base of the vast majority of marriages. Females honored money. American females honor money. Lorca. "American women's wombs are filled with gold."

How far would Katherine Marie go? She had a vindictive streak, but she wasn't a fool. What she lacked in intelligence she made up in cunning. What was she plotting?

He got up and plugged in the Christmas tree, decorating the late afternoon with the small red, green, blue and white blinking bulbs. As the day darkened the lights reflected on the window behind the tree, deepening and extending the room into the darkness outside.

Carter liked Christmas trees. The festive solemnity of the symbolic. He had not spent Christmas alone in several decades and was amused by the novelty of having the house to himself.

What would he do? Sit by the fire and listen to music, to the wind and watch the choreography of flames in the fireplace.

After retrieving a tray of ice from the kitchen he took a favorite tumbler from the liquor cabinet and poured a drink. When the fire caught among the dry, sweet smelling oak logs, he loaded the CD player with "Christmas Eve at King's College, Cambridge," "Carols from Winchester Cathedral," Britten's "A Ceremony of Carols."

The music and drink, the pleasant, soft light, filled him for a time. Back to Epicurus. Was this the garden? The sense and pleasure of sound and light, those masters of information, stimulation to please or horrify.

The harmony, the ecumenical synchronization of voices resonated and lifted into the webbed and ribbed vaulting of Carter's imagination. Here the beautiful mingled with the possible. Here gifted voices, trained and schooled, a chorus of scholars, reached for the nearly impossible, creating a world of magnificence and beauty.

A short time later he again edged into the sordidness of his dilemma. It persisted in the rancor to which he had been brought, and for what? So someone, anyone could feel she had her say.

He imagined the confrontation had to do with Katherine Marie's Catholicism, her moralizing fantasies. For the most part he ignored her religious proclivities, unless they became active and malignant.

"Believe what you will," he told her often enough, "just keep it to yourself. It doesn't seem sane for adults to go around talking about their connections with Santa Claus."

Here was mystery, lying at the edge of the known and the obvious. He detested conflict, and yet seemed often to be wandering into the fray. He preferred peace but found his immediate, short-termed history had been decidedly out of sorts with this. Maybe it was in him. Maybe he did encourage discord and difficulty. But could he have avoided it? Well, hell. By staying in bed all day.

But what would he do if they returned? What if they reconsidered? What if they returned saying they had made too much of it?

Well, he had lived with two women before, but not under the same roof at the same time. It would no doubt test everyone's equilibrium, their diplomacy. The prospect amused him.

The phone ringing in the hall snapped his reverie. It jangled a third time before he picked it up. He said "hello," and without more the line clicked and went dead.

Chapter XXIII

Even on frosted nights Carter slept with the sash nearest the bed opened a few inches. Sunday morning, Christmas Eve, the bells from the Presbyterian Church woke him. The clock showed nine-forty-five, and he appreciated the good sense of the presbyters. No doubt the Catholics had been afoot with bells tolling since dawn. The Calvinist had probably not gone to bed at all.

In the kitchen he waited for the coffeemaker, poured out a cup, and paged through the morning paper. The results of the Factor autopsy report were splashed across the front page. "Drugs, Not Football Killed Factor."

A minor problem with cause and effect, Carter knew. Drugs and the fast-track. Football killed Lyle Alzado. It maimed him, disfigured him, then killed him. A vicious business. Mental and physical brutality, encouraged and supported by chemicals, then disability and early death for a recompense of shekels and the howling approval of a few thousand fifty-yard-line-no-names.

Carter took a second cup to the living-room.

Saturday morning while he was out Katherine Marie had removed her personal effects. The inevitable had come to pass and she departed. The dust-marks and clutter of her leaving were scattered about, a vacant spot on the wall from a picture she had taken, a stack of clothes in the hall for which she would return. A brilliant sheen flooded the room providing a well-painted setting for the silence and his solitude. He promised to think about Katherine Marie's going and if it might be possible for her to come back. If he wanted her back or not. Would she want to come back? Probably not. That made sense. He would have to examine how he felt about living alone. There would be time later to act, if he decided he should.

He drifted into thinking about Sutter and Lui Chan and their ardor for sleuthing, their find.

For the moment it pleased him to think things might change. A spark of hope? Of course, in the end it came to nothing. Still, he would show the document to Absyth.

Anyway, it didn't much matter. He snapped on the TV and sat on the edge of the recliner holding the warm cup in both hands. At night he lowered the thermostat. In the morning before showering and shaving he reset it. In sub-freezing-weather the furnace labored for hours to catch up.

He flipped through the channels, to the weather, then back to the news.

He would not return to Barker. The decision, not unlike Katherine Marie's going, had been there, he realized, and had come finally, surprisingly easily and settled into his mind. For a moment it felt good, and made sense.

He switched channels.

Commercials for the last minute shopper. Mattel. Ken and Barbie. The cash registers ringing.

Channel 4 carried a brief news update. He lingered for a moment.

"I'm standing in the parking lot of the Hy Vee market on West Park Street. Last night a man was seriously injured here," the reporter said, "when he was struck by a car."

Hit and run, no doubt. Another incident in the city of our lives. How to avoid the last minute Christmas rush. Check out, permanently, pay the last check.

"According to witnesses, the incident took place right here."

The reporter was wrapped in a heavy coat and long black scarf, his hair lifted by gusts of wind. Random snowflakes blew across the screen.

"At approximately ten-thirty last night," the reporter pointed to the store, "the victim came out of the door. He was accompanied by a woman who was not injured.

"Witnesses report the car, a blue Volkswagen Rabbit, was parked over there."

With a gloved hand, he directed the camera-eye across the lot.

"It had been there for some time with its motor running, possibly waiting for the victim to leave the store.

"It came around a row of cars parked here."

He indicated where he was standing, then faced the camera.

"And headed toward the front before striking the victim.

"The injured man was taken to Barker Medical center where he remains in a coma and is listed in critical condition.

"Police identified the injured man as Marvin Crowly of 2329 Covington Place, Lancaster, the Vice Chancellor of Instruction at Barker State.

"The driver of the car was later arrested at her home and has been identified as Ardyth Oldam of 1732 Palvar Street. At air-time she is being held at the County Correctional Facility. Charges are pending."

The news switched to the weather. Temperature thirty-two, winds out of the northeast at five.

Carter sat for a moment trying to get a handle on the announcement. Crowly. Somebody had run over Crowly. Ardyth. She had run the sucker down. The Marvin Crowly?

He had difficulty bringing the two together. Apparently more trouble than she had. It didn't seem possible. People like Crowly do not customarily get nailed. They're invulnerable.

How many Marvin Crowlys were there? How many could there be? In Lancaster? At Barker State? Jesus. It was Crowly. The sucker got popped.

And Ardyth Oldam.

They said she had been arrested.

Ardyth had gone after Crowly and had been arrested. Leaving the scene? She ran over Crowly in the parking lot at the Hy Vee. High drama in the parking lanes. Just like that. She took him out.

Then he was sure she meant to do it. The coincidence was just too improbable. She meant to do it. She knew he was in the store and waited for him. She had stalked him. Followed him. Or maybe she saw him at the meat counter and decided to do it then.

How long had she been planning this? At ten-thirty he had been at Murphy's indulging in his newly realized freedom. He didn't remember hearing a siren. But then he wouldn't have.

Carter sat back holding the coffee cup close to his chest. How long had she been stalking Crowly? How long had she planned this?

He was still thinking about Crowly when the phone rang. It was Ardyth. She was calling from the Correctional Center. She had been told she had the right to one phone call. Would he come to visit. To talk to her about getting a lawyer?

He said he would. The conversation ended.

Just then he could appreciate the company of her anguish. Anger had driven her, and the car. But she had taken the next step. The step he had been unable to take.

For another moment Carter sat in silence. He pictured Crowly lying in the hospital. The arrogant, mindless Crowly, the witless, pathetic Crowly, pale and helpless in a white gown, connected to a life support system, the motionless and now harmless Crowly, quite possibly the life seeping out of him.

Carter emptied his cup into the sink. He pulled the plug on the coffeemaker and taking his coat from the hall-tree went out into the frozen morning.

The three-storied yellow brick soot stained and crumbling Correctional Center, was set back alone in an open treeless field several hundred feet from the street. Its grim continence stood as a monument to the comic corruption that had put it there ten years before.

During a humid summer twelve years before, while most of the citizens were busy with other things, without even a pretense of public consent, the County Board and the city's Aldermanic Council in a rare joint venture devised the scheme for the project and raided the public coffers to finance it.

Following only the shallowest tributaries of protocol and necessity, they selected an architect—in this case the Mayor's brother, Shindel's son in law—summarily and quickly let supply and labor contracts and proceeded with the construction before opposition groups could organize or respond.

Within days silver shovels were passed around, ground broken and pictures taken of the dignitaries, the Mayor and the County Board Chairman. But because of the size of the kickback pie, and opportunities for front page pictures and quotes, what began harmoniously, quickly fell into disarray. In a tower of rabble-babble scenario, the project crawled into cost overruns, work stoppages, union and management squabbles and political haggling.

Before the doors opened for business, parts of the roof sagged and leaked and cracks the thickness of a man's hand appeared in the cinderblock walls. The second- and third-story slate window-sills which were set at nearly forty-five degree angles came unglued and slipped out, and on several occasions crashed to the sidewalk below.

In a letter to *The Lancaster Sentinel*, after an afternoon in the center on business, a wag wondered if the climate-control system had been modeled on a hybrid of the green-house affect and a polar-winter. In July workers wore sweaters and mufflers to their desks. In January and February they worked with the windows opened, the ceiling fans running. The pollution-control system failed frequently, and at least twice the central electrical-control board blew up.

Half way up to the building the narrow sidewalk circled out to either side around a red granite stone-based statue of Benote Lancaster, the land baron whose name the county and city had taken, along with his political and economic habits. A green Christmas wreath decorated the base of the stone.

Three rows of rectangular, barred casements along the front face of the building were interrupted on the first-floor by a set of large glass doors. Above the doors, in case someone might not know where he was, a bronze-cast name-plate announced Lancaster Correctional Center.

Carter came through the glass doors into the lobby and stopped at the information desk. Red and green bunting covered a good part of the handrails on the stairs, and a large Christmas tree in a wooden pot filled the area between the stairs and the backdoor.

The lower floor included the county jail, the sheriff's office and the city police headquarters. The glass doors had been hung with a green plastic wreath.

"I'd like to visit Ardyth Oldam," he told the woman.

She stared at him blankly, and when he said, "I'm Professor John Carter from the university department of philosophy," she printed his name at the top of a form attached to a clipboard, and handed it to him to sign.

"You can wait over there."

She pointed to a bench set against the wall behind a six-foot dracaena.

"It'll be a few minutes."

Carter sat down behind the plant.

Another elderly painted woman at her station seemed to have little to do. She filed her nails, waited near the phone. Pork-barrel. Mothers, wives, aunts, and friends, supporters, providing the lug to finance the power-brokers upstairs. Keep it in the family, or at least in the clan.

Sunday and Christmas Eve, and the place had an oppressive air.

In spite of the high, open spaces, the grey beyond the three stories of windowed-walls, he could find nothing of warmth or comfort. The attempts to make the halls as agreeable as possible had not succeeded.

A deep disturbance had leaked into the hold of Carter's consciousness. For although he had relegated violence to the last page of the human lexicon, there were those even among the civilized who had not, and who with provocation, or with little provocation, often responded violently.

And then he was consumed with a profound regret, an abiding disgust—a disappointment that people would actually attempt to carve out careers by mistreating other people and take a chance that nobody would elevate the stakes or expand the rubric of engagement.

Violence in the ivory tower.

What about Iowa?

A gun bearing physicist injecting a bit of laboratory reality into the political squabbles of theoretic physics. A definitive statement, marking out clearly the results misconnections can bring. Or the tragedy the lack of misconnections can bring. Old moth balls Schlick bathed in the "Consistent Empiricism"—of gunshots.

Remonstrance. Regret, remorse and then revenge.

Vengeance. My god.

What had finally brought Ardyth to the parking lot? How had she focused on Crowly?

It was easy. She knew him. The women on campus knew him. How he operated. The women's groups would be pleased to see him dead.

But she had done it.

The incredible and terrible anguish. Carter didn't know.

What would the miners have said about Crowly? Carter had heard it often enough.

"If ever a sonofabitch needed killing, that was one."

But was there no other way to expunge people who endangered the society, who relentlessly and mercilessly measured the value of their lives, their personal success, in the harm they could do to others. Was there no way beyond physically and violently tearing them from the social fabric for a society to rid itself of these predators?

Surely, Carter knew well, you could not ignore them. Turning the other cheek meant only both cheeks, and then your nose and mouth would be blooded as well. As Ghandi discovered. But in India, not America. And Martin King. Yeah, that was America.

After a few minutes a young uniformed officer appeared at the information desk and retrieved the clipboard and approached Carter.

"Carter," he said, "John Carter?"

Carter stood.

"Follow me."

Carter fell in behind the man and trailed along a narrow hallway with offices and workers on either side, then through a small courtyard. A guided tour, Carter thought.

The complex was a good bit larger than it appeared from outside. No wonder the fighting lasted as long as it did. There was a lot of graft to organize. Enormous sums to funnel into kickbacks and payoffs.

On the far side of the courtyard they passed through a swinging barred-door into an alcove, through another steel door to a hallway, into the visiting area, then through still another set of doors. Here a second officer patted Carter for contraband and weapons.

He was a small man with an easy smile. "Are you prepared to be assaulted by a licensed sex-offender?" he said, running his hand along the inside of Carter's leg.

"It's alright," Carter said. "The best offer I've had today."

"You must really be in bad shape."

"Yeah," Carter said. "It's been a long, hard day."

They laughed.

The visitation chamber was a long low rectangular box with a row of carrels at the center divided by Plexiglas. The partitions were substantial enough to prevent passing contraband, as well as physical contact, hostile or affectionate. Each carrel had a telephone. Through the meshed panes along the top of the walls Carter could see the curled rows of razor wire above the enclosed exercise yard behind the complex.

Carter picked out a carrel and waited another five minutes before Ardyth appeared at one of the two doors along the opposite wall behind which he assumed the inmates were housed.

She was dressed in a drab-green prison dress and white tennis shoes and was followed by a rotund matron in a police-blue shirt, tie and skirt. The matron had a yellow patch on her right shoulder and carried a large ring of keys. She stopped just inside the door. The round white clock above her showed eleven-forty-nine.

Ardyth came in slowly, as if she wasn't sure where she was being taken or why. And it came to Carter he was the first to visit her—no one else had visited her, not just yet. She paused briefly, then seeing Carter, smiled a faint, pale smile. She walked toward him, her hands held together in front of her, although he did not see cuffs or shackles. Still, she did not seem to know where she was.

She had pulled her hair back and tied it with a small pink ribbon and looked as she might have on any day, any morning about to clean the house or simply relax in front of the fire with a book.

Seeing her here, with the matron, in the confinement of the glass partition, the full awareness of what she had done came over Carter. Imprisoned by the forces of the disapproving world, she was also incarcerated by the passions she embraced and her decision to submit to the indignity of an inevitable captivity for doing what she intended. Certainly this woman was not a criminal. In fact, what she had done might not be criminal either.

Carter was aware he had misjudged her alliance with Mason, the true tenor of their connections. Of course he could not have done otherwise. There was precious little on the surface to suggest the depths. Once or twice, she gave intimations of it; say the night at the Koto Gardens. But that's the way it is with some people. Until Mason died, possibly even she didn't know the extent and intensity of their alliance.

She sat across from Carter, and he lifted the phone and spoke, watching her face.

"Are you all right?" he said, hoping she might confirm what he supposed was not the case.

Again the faint smile.

"As well as I may be under the circumstances," she said.

Carter nodded.

"They are treating you well?"

"Yes, John Carter. They have been friendly."

The conversation had an ethereal echo. He could see her clearly, but in the hollow of telephonic transmission she seemed at a great distance.

Her cheeks were flushed as if she had been out on a fresh morning or the cell they had given her was quite cool. She sat erect and proper, looking straight at him, holding the phone a small distance from her ear. Her eyes were clear, and did not show anything of sadness or distress. She tried to smile.

"It is a terrible thing," she said. "But I knew you would come when you heard. That is why I called"

"The news," Carter said. "I heard about it on the morning news."

"Yes. I would think they will have a great deal to say."

"Terrible people," Carter said, "cause good people to do terrible things. But maybe we shouldn't talk about this."

Carter looked past her to the matron standing at the door at parade rest, her fat arms, from the elbows down, hidden behind her.

Were the phones bugged? Probably so.

"I do not think about it much," she said. "Last night I did not know how it had happened. The police came to the door today just after six o'clock."

When she spoke Carter caught a quick elusive shift in her eyes, ever so slight, off-center, as if her sense of her life and who she might be had been severely savaged.

She spoke with the same lilting, staccato cadence with which she had always spoken. But now, as best he could tell, listening to her through the device, her speech carried an echo, as if she spoke hearing a voice she had never heard before, a voice she had not yet identified or accepted as her own.

"But I am happy to see you John Carter. Coming here, you make me feel good."

"Do you have a lawyer?"

"No. I have not thought about a lawyer."

"If you want, I'll call for you. Do you have a name?"

"You would know more than I would," she said. "Yes. I will be pleased for you to hire a lawyer for me."

"Have they charged you?"

"They have taken my fingerprints. And my picture. Maybe I will be famous in the post office."

She paused.

"But I have not been told what they intend to do."

"Well, they'll have to have an arraignment. As soon as I leave here, I'll call Paul Absyth—a lawyer I know—and have him contact you. Then we'll see about setting bond and getting you out of here."

"Yes," she said, "but Mason is at home alone. He is alone. He has not been the same since his father died. I worry about him. He should not be alone."

Now the matron stood behind Ardyth and touched her shoulder.

"Time's up," she said.

Carter checked the clock.

"Paul Absyth will get in touch with you. Keep your chin up. I'll take Mason home with me. He can stay with me until we get this straightened out. Everything will be all right."

But he wasn't sure.

Following around at another's command, waiting to have doors unlocked, then locked behind him, had depleted his bravado. He had heard cons talk about prison life. "It's not the walls," they were fond of pointing out. "All buildings have walls. It's the doors that get to you finally. Not being able to unlock and open doors. That's the real anguish of prison life."

What he wanted, would have preferred, was to return to Ardyth and stay with her. No telling what they might do to her. She should have someone with her. Then he knew better.

"I hoped you would come," she had said.

For the moment she would be safe. More than that, her confidence and toughness had encouraged him. Her sanity, her well-conditioned rationality gave him hope. He felt a sense of companionship, as if another was in this thing with him. He wanted to be with her.

For his benefit, he wanted to be with her, and outside once again, swerving around the statue of Benote Lancaster, he made his way down Palvar Street toward the Oldam house.

He expected young Mason would be home, although he didn't know who or what else to expect. Had the relatives convened? Who were the relatives? Ardyth had a sister, he remembered, but had concluded from the snippets of years passed that the sister was older and lived in India—southern India—with a cithara player, maybe. Who else? What had happened to Masons family? Carter knew Mason's father and mother were dead. But who else?

Well, Ardyth's request had been straightforward.

The muffled chime of the bell was answered by a young woman who opened the door several inches but did not speak. Carter could see only a slice of her face, her brown hair. Probably a neighbor come to comfort young Mason, come bearing tureens of soup and salads, to infest the household with the illusion of safety and well-being the smells of food cooking can provide. No telling what they had shown up with.

"Ardyth asked me to stop in," Carter said, "I'm a family friend."

Behind the woman voices filled the hollow hall.

"We have everything under control," the woman said, and closed the door.

For a moment Carter waited, then rang the bell again. The door opened, a narrow slit, and a voice from someone he could not see said, "Go away. We don't need help."

Carter set his right foot, heel down against the door and pushed, and was surprised when it gave in as easily as it did, that it opened with the woman behind it holding to the knob.

"I came to see Mason," Carter said. "His mother asked me if I would."

The woman did not speak. She kept the door between them, looking out, starring at Carter.

"Is he here?" Carter said.

The voices had subsided and Carter thought Mason might be in the living-room. From where he stood he could see part of the Christmas tree and its dead bulbs.

"No," the woman said.

She was smaller than Carter, several inches smaller, with brown eyes and a thin, angular face with cream-smooth skin and short brown hair. She held a cigarette in her left hand.

"Where is he?" Carter said.

"I don't know. He's not here."

"And who are you?"

She did not speak or move, but watched Carter.

"He's not here," she said again.

"I know," Carter said. "You said that. But I happen to think he is here. Now, here?"

The woman stepped past him into the living-room and took a stance with her back to the Christmas tree.

"You've got no business here," she said.

"Look," Carter said. "I'm not going to get in a debate over territory. I just came from the correctional center. I spoke with Mrs. Oldam and she asked me to stop in and talk to Mason. This is the Oldam house, and that's what I'm doing."

"Well, now you can go," the woman said in an unaffected monotone. "Anyway, there is no Mrs. Oldam. There never was. Her name is Ardyth Spencer-Whitehall-Oldam."

"You're related to the family, right?"

He waited, but for what he wasn't sure. The woman did not answer.

"And if not, then who are you?"

Another woman appeared from the kitchen. She was a good bit heavier than the first, but just as short, with jet-black, cropped hair. She wore glasses and a powder-blue Barker Bulldog sweatshirt and black stretch-pants. She had a large black mole on her forehead just above her right brow that looked like an askance third-eye.

"We're seeing after the house," the second woman said.

"You're Ardyth's sisters? Mason's aunts? I know," Carter said, "you're long lost relatives, who have in this moment of crisis just appeared in the nick of time to save the Oldam household from certain disaster."

"Yes. We are taking care of a sister in a time of trouble."

When she talked only her lips moved.

"A sister? You cleared this with Ardyth?"

The woman with the cigarette took the coffee saucer she had been using for an ashtray and held it in her left hand. Keeping her eyes on Carter, she tapped the cigarette on the rim of the saucer.

"Yes," the woman with the cigarette said. "When a woman is in trouble our duty is always clear."

Carter was about to say something about people making silly assumptions, but did not. He watched the women, held tenaciously to their positions, with nothing more than what they believed was required of them. The macabre. Surreal.

"Where's Mason?" Carter said.

"I said he's not here. He's being counseled."

"And I don't believe you. He's upstairs."

"We'll take care of him."

Take care of him. The words chilled Carter.

"I'll bet you will," he said. "But I'll tell you what. I don't know who you are—or you," he gestured toward the woman in the doorway. "I don't know how you got in here, or what you intend to do. But I'm going to go upstairs. If I don't find Mason, even if I do, when I get back down here, you two had better have a better story than you've given me at this point, or be gone. Otherwise I'm going to call the police and have you arrested for breaking and entering."

When he looked up the stairs, Carter was wondering what exactly had happen to Mason, if anything, and didn't hear the woman behind him. Then he was propelled forward and felt the hot end of the cigarette against the back of his neck.

It was a simple, nearly silent, swift act. Not only did she burn him with the cigarette, but pushed him forward into the wall.

By the time he regained his balance she had already retreated and was then in front of the Christmas tree, feet apart, crouched, head forward, holding the saucer in both hands in front of her as if she were carrying a football, prepared to feint and dodge him.

He suspected she might be entertaining the high theatrics of the improbable, and intended to throw the saucer like a Frisbee. Too many James Bond movies, Carter guessed.

The viciousness of the attack stunned Carter. Words he expected, but nothing as pathetic and petty as an assault with a hot cigarette. By then the burn on his neck came to life. His eyes teared.

"What are you doing?" Carter said, rubbing the wound with his fingertips, then examining the fingers.

"Get out," the woman said in a surly tone.

"You're evil. The devil sent you. Get out."

By then her face flushed. Her cheeks were inflamed, her lips pale. Carter watched her. He covered the burn with the palm of his hand and stepped back to the stairs.

"Mason?" he said, "are you there?"

A latch clicked on a door opening and Mason appeared at the top of the stairs. The last time they met the boy's confidence and self-possession had given him an air, a magnitude larger than his size. Alone at the top of the stairs, he appeared smaller than Carter remembered.

The boy nodded.

"Yes," he said. "Yes. I'm here."

"Do you know these people? These women?" Carter said, trying to see the boy and watch the women at the same time.

The woman in the stretch pants came in behind the cigarette lancer and took a karate stance as if she was about to smack a brick or chop a two-by-four.

Mason shook his head, but did not speak.

And for a time they stood fixed, momentarily transfixed, in their postures. A thirteen-year-old boy at the top of the stairs, waiting obediently, observantly. The strange and pathetic women, Carter thought, nearly comatose, as if set in stone, surrounded by the bark of a radio and a drab Christmas tree, prepared to defend by attack, if need be, the territory they had usurped or at least commandeered as theirs of right by the malefaction of a logic so twisted and skewed as not to resemble logic at all.

And, of course, John Carter. John Carter the intruder, the interloper at the bottom of the stairs, watching himself while watching the boy and the women, out of a sense of duty to a friend, hoping to help only to find he was not wanted, having already suffered in the pitiable scramble a symbolic if not serious wound.

"Mason, get your coat," Carter said. "You're going with me."

The woman in the karate stance edged forward, closer behind her accomplice and Carter lifted an umbrella from the hall tree behind the door. He held it with the crook outward.

"I'm taking Mason with me," he said, "and if either of you get in the way, so help me God, I'll drill you."

"That's kidnapping," the cigarette woman said.

"Good. Then call the police."

The boy came down the stairs with his coat and passed behind Carter. When he was outside, Carter backed out and closed the door.

"Are you okay?" Carter said, after they had reached the street.

"Yes. But it was very strange. I suppose I should thank you."

"Who are those women? Do you know them?"

"No. But they are from a woman's group. When my father died, Ardyth went to one of their meetings."

Ardyth. A support group? He was aware that fringe groups often attached themselves to the hull of the academic ship like so many barnacles. Universities were full of them. Parasites clinging to the scholarship.

He had not thought enough about Ardyth's anguish—how he could have helped and reprimanded himself for his failure. But then how do you know? He had been kind and offering. What else could he have done? Should he have been more insistent? Would it have been an invasion of privacy. He could not patronize her.

They were still several blocks from Carter's house, and he wondered how much the boy knew about his mother's situation.

"Do you know why they came to your house?"

"I'd guess to see Ardyth."

"But Ardyth isn't home."

"Yes. She said very early this morning that she would be gone for most of the day, but I shouldn't worry."

"Have you eaten?"

"I had breakfast. Before the women came."

"Are you hungry?"

"Yes."

"There's a McDonald's just across from Murphy's. How about a Big Mac?"

"I have only a dollar," Mason said.

"And I've got a ten. Think we can make it on that?"

Mason screwed up his face.

"If you don't eat too much," he said and smiled and Carter smiled.

"Yeah," Carter said, "helluva way to spend a Sunday."

He touched the burn on his neck with his fingertips. The anesthetic of the December air had soothed the wound, and he wondered if the women were still in the house. He wouldn't call the police. More than likely they didn't intend to take anything—they weren't thieves, just nuts on a bizarre but well-intended mission.

"Ardyth told you to come and get me, didn't she?"

Carter nodded. "You may be staying with me for a few days. If you need clothes, we can go back later. You might want to get your presents from under the tree."

"No," Mason said. "There aren't any presents. Ardyth doesn't believe in presents. She says giving presents at Christmas misses the point. The idea of Christmas is peace and harmony."

Carter carried the umbrella he had taken from the hall tree, carried it like a small cane.

"Is this Ardyth's umbrella?"

"Yes," Mason said. "She has had it for a very long time. I was nine when she got it in New Orleans."

Carter examined the smooth plastic handle. Was it the same umbrella they had used at the Koto Garden? That he had held over Ardyth as she helped Mason make his way to the car?

If it was, well enough. Even so, Ardyth liked it and he liked that.

Mason walked a few steps more then paused.

"How is Ardyth?" he said. "She didn't tell me, but I know what happened."

Chapter XXIV

At home with Mason, Carter spent the remainder of the afternoon on the phone. Morgana called to ask if he had heard about Ardyth. He assured her he had.

"John," she said, "after everything else, I hate to tell you this, but Carl is in the hospital. He collapsed Friday night at dinner. I was talking to Councia Brown. They were at the University Club. He hasn't been looking well lately.

"And this is the worst of it. They're pretty certain it's AIDS. He's at Lancaster General for the moment, but they want to transfer him to a hospital in Chicago. I offered to go with him, but his brother is in town for Christmas and said he would stay with him. He didn't think there was any need for both of us to be there. He wants to be alone with Carl. Going down with a defunct immune system is not a pretty sight."

"How bad is he?"

"Not good. I guess they don't give him much of a chance, or much time. I'd be surprised if he ever gets home again. His brother said by last night he was resting quietly, but wasn't responding to anyone."

"Then why would they want to take him to Chicago?"

"I don't know. It's just talk.

"You're sure there's nothing I can do to help Ardyth?"

Carter told her he had young Mason with him and was just then preparing to call Absyth to see if they could get Ardyth released.

"I knew this would happen," Morgana said. "It was bound to."

She hesitated.

"I heard about your meeting with Crowly," she said.

"Meeting? The inquisition? Brought before the Inquisitor General. Flogged and wracked for my indiscretions."

"You always were indiscrete, Carter. Trying to teach and work under these conditions is a major indiscretion. You should know that.

"But I'm sorry about it anyway. I didn't think they would do something like this. I guess none of us is safe."

"We never were," Carter said. "Security is a fantasy. It's hard to remember. Anyway, it's over now."

"But isn't there something you can do? My god, John, twenty years before the mast should be worth a bit of respect. Common decency requires some consideration."

"Time spent and a-job-well-done mean nothing to these people. They don't even know what a-job-well-done means."

"Is there anyone who will listen. Anything you can do."

"I have a lawyer. If legal defense means anything. But, then, they have lawyers too. They've got a whole law firm. In fact they have two law firms. And they have more money than I have for a legal fight. They've got a key to the taxpayers strongbox. If they choose to use it.

"It'll come out in the wash."

"Well, as I said, if I can help," Morgana said.

Carter thanked her then hung up the phone and waited a moment before going into the living-room.

The news about Carl hurt. Not that it wasn't expected—but now the worst had been confirmed.

So Carl has AIDS. The solution to the medical mystery. Jesus Christ, poor Carl. What a Christmas present.

Carter wondered if the stress of the hearing had precipitated Carl's collapse. Will it never end?

As soon as they came into the house Mason asked about the television, and settled in front of the set.

"Ardyth doesn't approve of television. After Mason died she gave our set to Goodwill," Mason told Carter.

Just then the boy was luxuriating in a newly found freedom. And why not? Carter stood looking out beyond the Christmas tree reflection. The winter afternoon closed along the street.

That explained Carl's florid appearance, the absences.

Mason had died, mysteriously, or at least without Carter knowing how. Crowly's wounding had been a bit more public and so, not quite as mysterious. But they were both out of action. Ardyth was in custody, and now Carl Johnson was in the hospital—dying.

It took three calls for Carter to locate Absyth at the home of his in-laws. Two hours later Absyth called back to say he had found a judge and met with him in a parking lot behind the university gym to arrange bail. If Ardyth could come up with five thousand dollars, she could be released from the correctional center by six o'clock.

Carter had several thousand in one checking account and four in another and Absyth had given him the name of a bail bondsman.

The number had been disconnected, so he called Murphy.

"I need to get a friend out of jail," Carter said. "Know a bondsman?"

"Who's the friend? Anybody I know?"

"You probably heard about it on television."

"I figured the woman that got Crowly. Must've been one pissed female."

"Can you help?"

"How much is she in for?" Murphy asked.

"Fifty thousand," Carter said.

"Five big ones," Murphy mused. "They're serious."

"Yeah, I know. How much will the bondsman need?"

"He'll take a check," Murphy said. "If you want, come on down around five. I'll see if I can get him here."

"Who is this?"

"His name is Wilson Martin."

"One more question," Carter said. "What's in it for you?"

Murphy laughed.

"Oh, hell Doc, there's a finder's-fee. But we'll be generous. Everybody wants to be home for Christmas. Let's say two hundred dollars."

"And if not we'll have to wait until next week."

"Yeah, something like that. I'm asking a man to come out and do business on Christmas Eve, and a Sunday at that."

"You're an asshole," Carter said. "A real asshole."

"Yeah, I know," Murphy said. "But we both know it takes just a little of that to get by in life."

Carter hesitated.

"Listen, Murph, I do appreciate the help."

"I know," Murphy said. "That's why I'd do this. Anybody else, shit, Doc, they could sit it out."

Carter hung up the phone and immediately Morgana called a second time to say she would be leaving town on the twenty-sixth for a week and could be reached in Philadelphia at her mother's.

At four for Carter put a pizza in the oven for Mason.

"It'll be done in about thirty minutes," he told the boy. "Of course I expect you to help yourself to whatever is in the refrigerator. There's coke and milk. Anything but the beer. The beer's mine. If the phone rings, let it ring. Don't answer it. Don't answer the door. Keep it locked. I should be back in a couple hours.

"When the fire burns down a little, put on a couple of logs. Keep it going."

"I am king of the fireplace," Mason said. "At home the fireplace is always my job."

"Good," Carter said. "Then I'll expect the king to know what he's doing."

Carter got to Murphy's a little before four-thirty.

Sam Perrin was sitting in a booth near the front with a newspaper spread out before him. Two men were at the pool table.

"Not much business," Carter said as Murphy set a beer in front of him.

"Till about eight," Murphy said. "Won't be many students, but you'd be surprised how people cooped up with relatives and the kids all day want to get out, or maybe stop in on the way to a party."

"How about Martin?"

"He'll be here," Murphy said.

Carter sipped his beer and kept an eye on the clock and the front door. Just before five a heavy man, about Carter's height, with a wide, bloated, corpulent face and black plastic-rimmed glasses came in. His mud-colored hair was parted in the middle and hung to either side to his ears. He had a stub of a burned-out cigar clamped between his teeth.

He stood inside the door looking along the bar to the pool table, his bulk blocking most of the doorway. His brown overcoat was open, exposing a large stomach bulging beneath a rumpled white shirt. He wore a wide maroon tie knotted loosely. The collar taps of his shirt were turned up.

Murphy had been running water into the sink below the bar. When the man came in, he shut off the faucet, took a bar-towel and began drying his hands. But neither spoke.

Slowly the man walked along the bar past Carter to the far end and where he stopped with his back to the door of Murphy's office. Seamus took down a bottle of bar-whiskey, poured out a generous amount into a small beer glass, carried it down and set it in front of the man.

In one well-greased motion, with a thick, fat hand, he removed the cigar stub, took up the glass, lifted it, drank the whiskey, set the empty glass on the bar, and replaced the cigar.

"You got business," he said in a deep, gravel voice.

He talked with the cigar gripped tightly in his teeth, moving his thick lips around the cigar, and then only as necessary.

"Yeah," Murphy said, looking at Carter, then back to the man.

"This is Doc Carter. He's got a friend being held at CC and he wants to get her out."

"What'd she do?" the man said. "Who is she?"

"Her husband taught at the university," Carter said. "He died a couple weeks ago. She ran over a man with her car."

Without an introduction Carter assumed the man was Martin the bondsman.

Nothing discernible registered on Martin's face. He simply stared at Carter as if he already understood the intricacies of the statement.

"What's the charge?"

"I don't know," Carter said. "Paul Absyth said her bail was five thousand."

"Fifty thousand," Martin said. "You can spring her for five."

"Okay. Yeah. I think so," Carter said.

"What's her name?"

"Ardyth Oldam. A r d y t h," Carter said.

Martin took a folded paper from his inside coat pocket and opened it on the bar, then pulled out an vintage fountain pen, screwed off the cap and began filling in the form.

"This is a contract," Martin said. "How do you spell her last name?"

"O l d a m," Carter said.

"You got the money?"

"A check."

Martin looked at Murphy, who nodded. Martin resumed writing. He pushed the paper toward Carter.

"Sign the bottom."

Carter looked over the paper quickly before signing it.

"One check for five thousand. Another for four hundred fifty," Martin said.

"How about two checks? One for two thousand and another for three? Two accounts," Carter said.

"Suit yourself," Martin said.

"How long will it take?"

"I'm on my way. Say an hour or so to get the paperwork ready."

Carter had not dealt with the underside of the legal establishment for a number of years. Bondsmen, he calculated, were only a step down from ambulance chasers, a step up from bounty hunters. A poor but pragmatic trade-off in face of even poorer alternatives.

Martin pocketed the form with the checks.

Murphy poured another supply of bourbon into the beer glass and Martin picked it up and tapped it on the bar several times before emptying it. Then he glided away toward the backdoor, as if there might be an inherent danger in parting by way of the passage he had entered. He proceeded with small steps, floating around the tables and chairs. His head did not bounce or lift and fall. Nor did his shoulders sway. And at the door, apparition-like, he vanished.

Carter ordered another beer.

"Where'd you find him?" Carter said.

"Turn a rock over with your toe and you'll find all kinds of things," Murphy said.

"Well, I do appreciate your help."

Carter wrote out a check for two hundred fifty dollars and pushed it across the bar.

"But you're still a sonofabitch. Does that cover your trouble?"

"Trouble?" Murphy said. "No trouble, Doc. Pleasure. Pure pleasure. It's a wonder to get paid for doing good."

"Well, I hope it's the end of both the trouble and of the pleasure of this," Carter said.

"I'd say your friend's troubles are just beginning," Murphy said. "Except as the powers want to keep it quiet."

"Why would anyone want to keep it quiet?"

"Hell, they put her on trial, you don't know, the stench might reach to Springfield." Murphy laughed.

"Where'd you get that? What are you talking about?"

"Oh, you know how it is. People talk. They don't just come out and say it. But a piece here, or there. A word or two. A smart-ass remark. If you got any kind of memory, hell, a morning or two later you wake up and it hits you. So that's what they were talking about. That's what it's about.

"There are people in this town—people with lots of money who have parties—parties with, should I say, mature, but young females. The more the merrier."

"Such as?"

"That female you were hanging around with."

"Vivien."

"Let's say her rep ain't exactly snow white. Maybe she was snow white but she drifted. Cept Snow White did live with them dwarfs. All seven of em."

"She's married," Carter said.

"Yeah. She was. Lasted six days. Then the guy run off with her sister."

"You know the sister."

"Everybody knows the sister. Well, most everybody.

"I tried to tell you, Doc. I got your best interests at heart. Fucken females like that can get you a shit-load of trouble."

"Yeah, I know," Carter said. "But what else is new?"

"Hell, Doc. I know the whole family. I think I told you about this once before. How her old lady used to come in here loaded and get pissed and throw temper-tantrums. Some kind of Indian. Finally had to blackball her. Keep her out unless she was sober—which weren't all that often.

"See there was this, what you might call, business. Just a little thing. So a spender wants a party and needs to liven it up—maybe a couple females who weren't too particular about who got on em. For a couple hundred bucks or so."

"Crowly?"

"Not sure about him. But whoever it was made a decent piece of change."

"Crowly was running a service?"

"Don't know. What I said is that ding-bat you been hanging around with is in the stable."

"Stable?"

"Well, sort of. Her friend Ruth's been doing that kind of thing for a long time.

"But if they ever put her on the stand, I'd expect all kinds of heads to roll. Hell, Doc, the people at the top ain't gonna take the heat. They'll blame everybody in sight. Who do you think? The females will get nailed—anybody hanging around. That's how the game is played."

"What about the Red Dragon?"

"Yeah. That's how they passed out assignments. An address or phone number stuck up, maybe on a bulletin-board. You see them around, look at the bottom. There's a phone number, could be an address."

"Phone numbers on the wall of the pisser?"

"But these were assignments."

"What about the red dragons stamped on the walls in Temperly and Lincoln? 'We owe it to the Red Dragon.'"

"I don't know. Coulda come from the slopes. Four or five of em. They got into the business. Were told they'd be handed over to immigration and sent back if they said anything. I'd guess they got up a campaign. Went around marking up the walls."

"And Vivien?'

"Connors' old man was in the Crotch with a couple of the people running the operation."

"Connors?"

"Connors. Caroline Vivien Connors."

"With Crowly?"

"Don't know," Murphy said. You never know. Maybe not. Hard to say."

"What happened to her father?"

"He got tore up. Stepped on a mine. Blew his right leg and his nuts off. When he got back the old lady ran out on him."

"Where is he now?"

"Today? Who knows? Alaska. Mexico. Return to sender. Whereabouts unknown."

"I wasn't an assignment."

"She was probably freelancing with you. Maybe looking for another customer. Maybe just having fun. Who knows what goes through the head of females?

"Maybe Crowly got wind of her connection with you. He'd been messing around with her friend Ruth, and after a bit of a discussion, should we say, when she objected, Crowly beat the shit out of her."

"And Ruth Lessiack?"

"Same thing. She's been passed around by Crowly and Landeau and Remcheck. Her brother was in on writing them bogus grants and I'd guess they threatened to turn him in if she didn't cooperate."

"Who told you this?"

"Like I said, Doc, a lot of people come through them doors and they bring with them the bits and pieces of their lives. Then the pieces just fall in place. Sort of a jigsaw puzzle without anybody havin to fit them together. Crowly sponsored a golf tournament in the spring. That one for the sick kids. I play in that."

"You play golf?"

"Yeah," Murphy said. "Don't you? What's your handicap? I shoot in the low eighties."

"So what about the tournament?"

"Doc. You hang around these people and they tell you things. And at times it's not too subtle. They just come out and say it."

"But you didn't say anything about it."

"Look Doc. It don't mean zip to me. Do I look like a cop? Nobody gets hurt. I mean, not really. A few bucks pass hands. Even the slopes get to stay in the country. If a female wants to screw for money, it might as well be good money. No matter how them cunts were treated, they'd been worse off in China or Indonesian. This way everybody gets a cut for the trouble."

"Jesus," Carter said.

"Business as usual," Murphy said. "Shit. Money's money. Some do a helluva lot worse than that just to stay alive.

"Doc, when you come in that one night, the night of the snowstorm, when you come in with that female, hell, I figured you were in the loop. And it's none of my business to interfere with a man's pleasures. I sure'n hell ain't gonna tell you how to spend your money.

"But a couple days later, now ain't I tried to tell you about her?"

"Then Crowly could have known Vivien through her father."

"Could have."

"Who told you about Crowly in Vietnam?"

"The graft of life seldom gets interred with time," Murphy said, raising his head. "It's a small world. You know Billy Boreman?"

Carter wasn't sure.

"That short blond dude with the beard. Comes in here to play pool. You've seen him."

"I think I know who you're talking about."

"Well, believe it or not, that little fucker's got a Silver Star. An you don't see too many of them around here. One tough little son-of-a bitch. He got into Headquarters Company in Saigon just after Crowly and Remcheck were sent home. I told you it was a small world."

"And he told you this?"

Murphy grinned.

"Not all of it. But some."

"So maybe Crowly knew about this. What about Remcheck?"

"Well, who knows? I don't hear much about him."

"Boreman told you this."

"No. Boreman told me about Saigon. About the helicopters, and the shit Crowly and Remcheck got into. It don't take no genius to put the pieces together. Then I got a friend who belongs to the Elks Club. He tells me if I ever want to have an after-hours party, it can be arranged. Police protection and all. He's talking about it, and you don't have to be a genius either to get the drift of what he's talking about."

"Let me ask you this," Carter said. "A couple weeks ago somebody vandalized the fourth-floor of Temperly. Any ideas?"

"With goat's blood."

"Where did they get goat's blood? And why?"

"From goats, where else. Maybe they know a vet. There's a goat farm just out here near the edge of town."

"Who did it?"

"Just speculation. Boreman's gook stories sound about the same."

"From Nam."

"Boreman says when he read about it in the paper, it was like deju vu. I guess Remcheck and Crowly were into some pretty heavy shit. Sensational enough to even make the headlines in the killing fields.

"Then there was a problem around the secured areas in Saigon. It looked like the gooks was getting in and vandalizing the secured areas. Nobody knew who was doing it. I guess Crowly caught a couple ROKs outside the compound. They had cutters and red paint trying to make it look like Cong had got in. Probably where Crowly got the idea. Otherwise it's one helluva coincidence."

"Hell, maybe it was red paint," Carter said.

Murphy finished filling the sink and Carter watched the reflections of the warped light of the Miller sign in his beer glass. He finished the beer, thanked Murphy again, and on his way out tapped on Sam's table as he passed. Sam was still hunched over the paper, but straightened up and smiled and nodded.

"By god, somebody needs some luck," Carter said.

The night was gathering, the streetlights coming on. In the blocks of beginning darkness, again he replayed the scenario. He understood a bit of it. Another episode from *The Godfather*. Disgusting.

Only finally on the porch, key in hand, unlocking the front door did he awaken from his trance.

Could this be true?

Was it true?

The disregard for human life. A mentality so devoid of humane instinct the malefactor could not expect ever again to be treated as a human being.

Is this what gave rise to the Forfeiture Principle? For one to deny his humanity so thoroughly no one else could ever again affirm it. The Third Reich rabble came to mind.

Aristotle, Carter knew, believed humans chose evil because of a lack of education, miss-education or perversity. In the length of his experience Carter had never truly, until this moment, attributed actions, human actions to perversity. Folly, stupidity, ignorance, even pathology, but not perversity.

In the end the truth was apparent. Remchecks and Crowlys had the better of it. In an absurd universe they had been the most absurd. By comparison Carter's transgressions were dwarfed. He was a rank amateur.

"Well, Carter," he told himself aloud, "you are not the fierce, ferocious bad-ass cynic you always pretended to be. You have been assigned to the back-row of the second rank."

The hallway was warm and smelled of pizza and he could hear the voices from the television. In the living-room Mason was camped with his plate and a large empty milk glass on the coffee table. True to his word he had kept the fire aflame.

But even a seat in the last row would not change Carter's situation. He remained an accused man, accused of crimes insignificant in nature compared to those of his accusers. Victimless crimes. Crimes manufactured by his accusers. But crimes they were, nevertheless. And his rationalizations would do little to shift the reality.

Then he remembered Ardyth.

He checked his watch. He would wait another hour before going to the Correctional Center. He poured out an ample supply of bourbon and fell into the overstuffed chair near the Christmas tree. His left leg was still sore, his back pained him.

From there he could see Mason on the couch in front of the television, leaning forward, his smooth, cherubic face white with the light of the screen.

Outside Christmas voices rose from the street and crawled over the ledge of the window behind him.

"God Rest Ye Merry Gentlemen."

Carter was amused. By all means. He stood and bent to see. Ten or so young men and women in red and green wool hats and long scarves and heavy coats stood in the crescent beneath the streetlamp caroling the early evening.

They sang "The First Noel," then concluded with "Silent Night," and for a moment Carter slipped into the nostalgia of the season. Here for the sake of song and good cheer, and nothing more, a small group of people had added a softness to the evening. And here for just a moment, again Carter felt the associations people might make, when they have a mind for it.

At six-forty-five Carter arrived at the Correctional Center. The building appeared deserted, with only a single light in the main lobby. He rang the emergency bell and waited. Momentarily a security officer materialized, pushed through the glass doors, then opened an outer door to Carter.

"I came to get Ardyth Oldam," he told the officer. "Her bail was made this afternoon."

The man nodded, and ushered him into the building.

"I think they already picked her up," he said.

"Someone picked her up?"

"I don't know if they've left yet. But I'm sure that's who they were after. About thirty minutes ago."

"They?"

"A couple women. I let them in."

"Could you check for me?"

"Sure," the officer said.

He took the phone off his belt and punched in a number. The handset buzzed and cracked and a voice squeaked over the small speaker. The officer mumbled a reply, then replaced the instrument on his belt.

"They're on their way out," he said. "Give them a couple minutes. You can wait here. They have to come out this way."

The "they" startled Carter. Then he knew exactly what had happened although he did not yet understand how. The fems had come to get Ardyth.

A moment later he had an uncomfortable premonition. Not only had he assumed Ardyth would know he was coming for her, but he had also assumed earlier the combatants he had faced at the Oldam house were freelancing, maybe NOW entrepreneurs, opportunists operating on their own. Both assumptions sprung from his hopeful affection for Ardyth, but were not grounded in even a smattering of fact.

Then, too, he didn't know how much Ardyth had been told—if she knew he had paid the bail. How could she have known? The Correctional Center minions could hardly give you the time of day, much less anything personal or legal.

When the women came into the lobby, Ardyth made straight away for Carter and held out her hand.

"Thank you, John Carter," she said. "Thank you for paying for me. On Tuesday I will take money out of savings and repay you."

Carter took her hand, her very small hand and held it for a moment.

"There's no rush," Carter said. "I won't need it right away."

Ardyth looked past Carter to the front door.

"Did Buddy come with you?"

"No," Carter said.

"Thank you for not bringing him. I would not want him to see his mother in jail."

"He's watching the fireplace for me."

"He's watching the fireplace and watching the television," she said.

She smiled a small smile, as if she had caught Carter in a minor deceit.

"That, too," Carter said. "Corrupting his thirteen-year-old mind."

"I do not worry," Ardyth said playfully. "It is already corrupted. He is a man. It is a good for him to be corrupted that way."

The women with Ardyth hung behind, poker-faced, watching Carter. Both wore heavy winter coats and wool hats which concealed whatever might have concurred with Carter's visual memory and made identification difficult. Without looking directly at them he could not be certain they were the ones he had run into earlier. A moment later he decided they might be Ardyth's relatives, although it seemed a long guess, under the circumstances.

"Have you told Buddy what about this?"

Carter shook his head.

"No, but I'd imagine he's heard about it from the news. There's not much else to report on Christmas Eve."

"Yes," Ardyth said. "That is unfortunate. I hope he was not alarmed"

"He hasn't said anything," Carter said.

She nodded to the women, then without speaking, returned to Carter.

"I have been thinking since we spoke this morning, John Carter. Could Buddy stayed with you for a few days until I decide what I should do?"

"That will be fine," Carter said, the surprise barely contained in his voice. "That will be okay."

"He was to go to his grandfather's in Atlanta on Wednesday. And it would be better if he did not hear about this problem every day. He does worry too much."

His father's son, Carter mused, with a twinge of recognition. Recognition edged with regret. Like his father, with a genetic peculiarity for obsessive introspection. The tight tungsten winding of the mind burning itself out.

When Ardyth offered her hand to Carter, there was nothing of the affection or intimacy he would have hoped for. Her touch was as formal as her speech. She took his hand, shook it firmly, briefly, without conviction or enterprise, then stepped back.

"I would prefer to go with you John Carter," Ardyth said. "But it is better this way."

At the moment Carter felt like an intruder, a teenager who had inadvertently wandered into a party to which he had not been invited.

Now he wanted to be done with it.

"Well, I'm glad you're out," he said. Then added, "And you have friends to see you home. I'll look after Mason. Give me a call, or I'll call you tomorrow about getting him to Atlanta. I may be able to help."

He hoped Ardyth might say more, but she did not and he left with the officer holding the door. He said goodnight and Merry Christmas, then followed the main walk toward Murphy's.

Waiting at the corner for the light, he could see the women standing in a bunch in the Correctional Center lobby.

"Well, so much for nonsense, Carter," he told himself. "So much for your adolescent fantasies. So much for your good Samaritan impulses."

Then he was angry for wanting more than a handshake, a thank you. Why should time and friendship matter for much? But there was always an essential missing, even on Christmas Eve.

True to Murphy's prediction the bar had taken on a festive atmosphere. A dozen or so patrons filled the booths along the front wall. Another group had taken up the backroom. Middle-aged men in suits and ties and brightly colored sweaters, women in heels and dresses. Nothing this night of the ragamuffin scruff of students. These were business folk who frequented Murphy's in afternoon, when Carter was seldom around.

Carter took up residence at the far corner of the bar with his back to the wall and ordered a double. From there he could see the front door, although he did not expect the visual position would yield much of interest. Bing Crosby and *The Bells of St. Mary's* flickered unnoticed on the television over the bar.

The episode with Ardyth troubled him. His impulse, after his annoyance subsided was to excuse her—to find excuses. Maybe she needed women to talk to. She only knew him as a family friend. And even with Mason dead, she would not change quickly. He supposed then she had a good bit on her mind. Needed people to talk to. Women might be better at it, at least for her.

He ran the tips of his fingers over the burn on his neck. The spot was sore to the touch.

He tried to think through what he might have said. Had she confided in him? What would any sane human say? Beside the clichés.

Carter, he told himself, you can't even counsel yourself. How could you help her? And for a moment he was glad she was not with him and he did not have to face the obvious, the trite and true, and talk about it, to renegotiate the verbal terrain until the words themselves lost meaning.

He ordered another drink, instructing the bartender to leave the bottle. Determined then to get on top of the disappointment with Ardyth, and with himself, for being a fool. He reminded himself again that things were just the way they were supposed to be. A bit of stoicism helped.

An hour later the bar had crowded up again by half. On the stool, even in the corner leaning against the wall, Carter's back ached. With his back pressed to the wall he tried to relax. Beneath the chatter of the crowd and the TV he heard the slightest sounds of water running. Probably one of the tubs beneath the bar leaking. Then he looked down and the man next to him was standing in a pool of urine.

The man, Geno Melchioni, Carter recognized from previous episodes in Lancaster bars. He was a day-labored, dressed this night in a blue shirt, a tie pulled loose, and tan pants, standing with both hands propped against the bar, his eyes closed. Carter assumed he was too drunk to find the pissoir, too drunk to even care, and as he had on at least one other occasion had given in to relieving himself then and there.

The miners Carter had worked and drunk with had often expressed the sentiment of wanting a place to drink where "you can spit on the floor." In Carter's estimation pissing on the floor in a crowded bar on Christmas Eve, seemed a bit extreme.

Carter caught Murphy's attention and motioned to Melchioni with his thumb. Murphy nodded and came around the end of the bar, followed by one of the bartenders. Melchioni had not opened his eyes, and for a moment Carter thought he might be asleep.

Melchioni had a reputation of barroom disturbances, and on occasion had spent several months in the county jail for his indiscretions. Carter wondered if tonight would merit another lock-up.

Without speaking Murphy took Melchioni's coat from the wrack behind Carter, hung it over the man's shoulders and said, "Let's go Geno." With the attendant bartender holding one arm and Murphy the other, Melchioni did not resist. Quietly they walked him to the side door and gave him leave to the frigid night. Moments later Murphy returned with a mop and bucket. He wasn't pleased.

Carter stepped back and Murphy motioned for several patrons to avoid the urine puddle. He was about to swab the floor, but paused and looked at Carter.

"Doc," he said, "we lost Sam."

"Sam is already lost," Carter replied.

Murphy shook his head, obviously distressed.

"Doc, you never did get it about people. Sam is gone. He disappeared this afternoon."

He looked at Carter poker-faced. "And don't give me that philosophy shit. It don't help. When somebody's gone, they're still there, but you can't see em." He paused again. "It ain't they just disappear. Sam could've been my old man. People like that only come around once. An when they do you better pay attention."

"But he's gone?"

"Yeah. I don't know how. I had the door locked, like always. Hell, Houdini couldn'ta got out of there. When I went to check on him the door was open and he was gone."

Instinctively Carter turned to the backroom and the booth Sam often occupied in the afternoon reading the paper. Though surrounded by patrons standing with drinks, talking, the booth was empty. A single shaded hanging-lamp cast a yellow circle on the table, a clearing in the wilderness, evocative more of absence than light.

"Have you notified the police?"

Murphy shook his head. "What could they do? There's no record of any kind. You know Sam. I know him. But who in the hell would they look for? And how would they know if they found him? There's no identification. No fingerprints, no record of any kind. Not even a picture. Couple weeks ago some of the Saturday afternoon pool players took a picture with him. But I don't even know who they are. I mean, what could the police do? What would they look for?"

He shook his head again. "Doc, he's just gone."

Murphy stood for a moment shaking his head and Carter wasn't sure what he would do. Then he dipped the mop in the bucket and prepared to swab the floor.

"Doc why don't you move over to a booth so I can clean this up? I'm gonna have to blackball that fucking Wop sonofabitch."

Carter took the bottle and slipped off to a booth. His view of the door was obstructed, but he no longer cared. He wasn't waiting for anyone. He was tired of watching people come and go. Tired of looking over his shoulder. Of people pissing on the floor around him. He wondered how it felt to walk home or to the next bar on a winter night in wet pants. Probably the same as it felt after falling into a moat at the Koto Gardens. He was tired of people disappearing.

The bright green and red lights on the front window blinked rhythmically and with the cardboard cottage setting behind him and the cotton-snow drifting down, through the cigarette smoke that shrouded the TV, Crosby was singing "White Christmas."

Two drinks later Carter decided to give up on the night and head for home. Mason was alone and he didn't want to be gone too long. He was about to exit the booth when Kerm Soliski appeared at the booth.

"Mind if we join you?" Kerm said. "Looks like seats are going to be hard to find tonight."

The "we" caught Carter. He looked around to Kerm's right to see who was with him.

"There's just the two of us," Kerm said.

The woman with Kerm smiled at Carter and slipped into the seat across from him.

"Have you two met?"

It took a moment for Carter to recognize Vivien. She had been made over in a red wig and sunglasses and bright red lipstick.

"We've met," she said.

"I'll get the beer," Kerm said. "Carter, you need anything?"

"Nothing you can buy here," Carter said.

Kerm slipped off into the crowd and Carter sat for a moment with his elbow on the table, hand on his forehead.

"Jesus," he said finally, "what happened to you this time? Get the shit knocked out of you again? Had to redo your whole head."

He had tried to control his voice, but the inflection was still bitter and more sarcastic than he wanted.

"Well, I guess I'm persona non grata," Vivien said.

"I guess you are."

"You don't seem very friendly."

"You can be whatever you please," Carter said.

"Look, Carter, I know you're angry with me, but . . ."

"Quite the contrary. I'm not angry. In the lexicon of emotions, my dear, anger is a poor substitute for real feelings. What I felt for you in the beginning is still there. But not anger. I mean, you're like a daughter."

"A daughter you screw."

"In the least a screwed-up daughter. One I cared about. So I'm incestuous. Hey, look. Males are attracted to females. That's nature. Then civilization comes along and makes it a crime.

"What are you doing? On a new case? Have you told Kerm about you're recent adventures?

"To be truthful, I didn't expect you to protect me. But I did think you might have just a hint of decency about you. And I'll tell you this again. You have a warped sense of loyalty, if that's what it is you have. All you had to do was keep quiet. That's all. And what do you do? To preserve the sense of my rather absurd and scattered existence, as you see it, you tell them exactly what they want you to tell them."

Carter tipped an abundant supply of bourbon into his glass and waited for the girl to respond. When she did not, he continued.

"Kant postulated good will as the only unqualified good. And you do not have anything of good will. In spite of your pious smiles and protestations either you're lying or you've got a severely warped, perverse nature. I'd guess it's a little of both.

"You couldn't even give me your correct name. As if I'd care about names.

"And the nonsense about your sister. What sister? And kids. There's something seriously wrong with your head. You're going to need more than a five dollar wig to cover your problems. A vital part of your brain is missing."

The girl did not say anything and looked away. Although he could not see her eyes, Carter thought she was about to cry.

"It just didn't seem important, Carter. I thought if I had kids, you wouldn't think I expected you to be serious or loyal or any of the other crap."

"And the scam with Crowly. Do you have any idea how far off the chart you are?"

She lifted her head and looked at the ceiling.

"You don't know that man. H was crazy," she said. "I didn't know it at first. When I figured it out, it was too late. I didn't mean to get you involved.

"Remember the day we were in the library? Crowly was there. I ran into him while you were looking for a book."

"What was he doing in the library?"

"I don't know. Ruth thinks he was probably stealing stationary or something. He'd take things. Sometimes he took the small potted plants from the library for his house. He always did that kind of thing. If he made a ten-cent phone call from home he'd charge the school for it."

"And you ran into him."

"He threatened to turn me in for breaking into the library if I didn't go along with him."

"And you knew about the tape recorder at Ruth's"

"I heard it was there, but honest to god, John, I didn't know it was on."

"You turned it on. What'd you want? To preserve the moment for posterity. How'd he pay you? By the word?"

"John, it was voice-activated. I thought if I went along with what Crowly wanted, it wouldn't hurt anybody and he'd forget about it. I had no idea."

"That's the truth. You really have no idea."

"But you got to believe me."

She reached across the table and touched his hand and Carter pulled away, recoiled.

"John, I didn't mean to hurt you. I'd want to be your friend. I mean, we had a really good time. I know I should have been honest and not made up the stuff about a husband and kids. But it really doesn't change anything. What I told you, about why I came to your office, well it's true. We were good for each other. I really want to be your friend."

Kerm carried two beers back to the booth and slid in next to the girl. He was talking about the history of Christmas decor and the theory of the Protestant Reformation.

Kerm spoke in oblique, rounded stories of extremely loosely connected analogies. He constructed word mosaics of juxtaposed colors, sounds and forms, and after a time, left them hanging like exaggerated wall-paintings for the observer to make into a whole.

On numerous occasions Carter had spoken with Kerm and afterwards was not always certain what had been said. Water painting, Carter thought, projecting iridescent patterns onto a mist. Nothing held. The shapes and curves disappeared, the mist fell and drained away in snake-like rivulets.

Kerm's accounts of fishing trips did not end with a claim of having caught a fish twice the size of any he landed, but began with an insinuation of having located a special river or lake and having landed a fish of a variety so rare and treasured none other could, or would, measure up to it. It had to do with the fantastic, and in a sense the incredible and preposterous.

Kerm's stories were at the base of his declining artistic production. Rumor had it Kerm had stumbled into the dust and erosion of an artistic ravine and had not for several years now produced much in the way of art. His verbal acumen depleted his creative energy and left him on artistically fallow ground.

Carter poured another drink and Kerm focused on the bottle.

"You didn't drink all of that?"

The fifth was a little more than half empty. Carter held the bottle up and tilted it.

"Most of it," he said.

"That's incredible. That's actually incredible."

"Oh, I don't know," Carter said. "I could have done in the whole thing. We philosophers have a penchant for drink. Did you ever hear the 'Philosopher's Drinking Song?'"

Kerm shook his head and Carter sang.

Immanuel Kant was a real pissant
who was very rarely stable.
Heidegger, Heidegger was a boozy beggar
who could drink you under the table.
David Hume could out consume

Schopenhauer and Hegel,
and Wittgenstein was a beery swine
who was just as sloshed as Schlegel.

Thomas Hobbes was fond of his dram
and Rene Descartes was a drunken fart
"I drink, therefore I am."

Yes, Socrates, himself is particularly missed,
A lovely thinker, but a bugger when he's pissed.

Chapter XXV

Carter answered the door, surprised and then annoyed at finding Harry Gotsch standing shoulders hunched, the collar of his gray overcoat set against the wind.

Probably sent over to sniff out the remains, Carter thought.

"You got a few minutes?" Gotsch said.

Carter hesitated. "Yeah. Sure. C'mon in."

He closed the door and pointed to the hall-tree for Gotsch to hang his coat.

Gotsch's face and large nose were ruddy from drink, the weather or both, Carter didn't know.

"Thought I'd stop by and talk to you about the troubles."

Gotsch's voice was mildly buoyant.

The amused tone annoyed Carter even further. Maybe he enjoys this. Maybe he gets off on other people's misfortune. Then Carter remembered what Gotsch had said at the hearing.

"Troubles?" Carter said. "As in Ulster."

"Yeah. Something like that."

Carter led the way into the living-room.

"How about a drink?"

"Sounds good," Gotsch said.

"What'll you have?"

"Oh, a little ice and a double would be okay."

"Bourbon?"

"That'd be just what the doctor ordered. If I was a doctor."

Carter poured out two drinks according to Gotsch's directions. He handed Gotsch a glass.

Gotsch looked around. "This is a nice place," he said. "What'd you pay for it?"

"Ninety-two."

"Not bad. Lots of places for books. Old time fireplaces just beat hell out of them new energy savers. When I sit down in front of a fire, I want to feel it. So what if it costs a dime or two more.

"I got that sitting around a fire from hunting with my daddy. Hell, I was hardly walking and he'd have me out coon hunting. We'd be up in the woods most of the night, till I got too tired to stay awake and he'd say 'Har, you go on back to the fire and get comfortable and I'll be along in a while.'

"So I'd throw on some twigs and bark and set down close on the blanket I had there. Never did see him come back. By then I was asleep. Next thing I knew it'd be daylight and he'd have breakfast cooking on the fire.

"You hunt?"

"No," Carter said. "I grew up on a farm. The first twelve years. And to tell the truth, whether it's an open field or woods, it's all work to me."

"That's a shame," Gotsch said. "Hunting's mixed up with the primitive. I'd guess there's comfort in just doing it. A shame to get that knocked out of you."

He stood and walked around the couch, inspecting the bookcase to the left of the fireplace.

"What you been reading lately?"

"I don't know," Carter said, distracted. "Pretty much the same stuff I always read. The Greeks. Descartes. Hume. Mills. Rawls."

Gotsch took a book from an upper shelf and held it spine up.

"*Avondale*, by Harry Gotsch," he read aloud. "You know, some people call this poetry."

"Wouldn't you?"

"Yeah. Sort of."

"How many titles you have?" Carter said.

"Eight," Gotsch said, "if you count that little anthology I helped Councia with. Three novels, two books of stories. This and another book of poems."

He set his drink on the mantle and paged through the book.

"You know who Jesse Stuart was?"

Carter shook his head.

"A novelist?"

"Yeah. Six or seven. He sold a few million copies. He wrote a lot of stories and poems that show up in high school anthologies. From the mountains of east Kentucky. Anyway, every time I look through this book, it reminds me of Jesse. We were at a writer's conference one weekend in Huntington, at Marshall, and went off in the afternoon and got to drinking and started talking about how we got on to writing and he told me a nice little thing it's kind of hard to forget.

"He was about six or seven at the time. Maybe a little older, since kids up in the mountains don't usually get to school too early, if they make it at all. He said after about a week or so in school, after school he come home and went running out to the field where his daddy was working, and he says 'Daddy, I can do something you can't do.'

"I guess the old man just kind of stood there looking at him and says, 'What's that, Jesse?'

"Jesse says, 'I can write my name.'

"Man. That's just how I feel about this book. It's like writing my name for the first time."

"But you didn't come here to tell me about hunting or ask what I been reading."

"No, as a matter of fact I didn't," Gotsch said. "I guess you heard about Crowly."

"Yeah," Carter said. "I heard he's in critical condition in the hospital. In a coma. If that's what you mean?"

"Yeah, well, that was yesterday. I just got the news he didn't make it. He's a dead man now," Gotsch said.

A surge of trepidation and despondency, disbelief passed along Carter's arms to his neck.

"Crowly's dead?"

With Mason in front of the TV Carter had not watched the news.

"When?" Carter said.

"Sometime yesterday. About noon. Hell of a Christmas present," Gotsch said.

Carter placed his glass on the mantel and dropped onto the couch. His eyes burned. He covered his face with his hands. Jesus. Another casualty to the absurd.

He hadn't shaved in two days and his face felt coarse and uneven—coarse and uneven, the events of the last several weeks.

Poor Crowly. Poor sad Crowly trying to compensate for his demented fears and climb free of his warped life by messing up the lives of others. The slow-witted and frightened Crowly who life had wounded far more seriously than anything that happened to him in Vietnam.

"I didn't expect this," he said. "Crowly was a tough man. I really expected he'd pull through. I figured he'd make it."

"Hell," Gotsch said, "it's an easy way out of your problems."

Carter wondered. Who would take up the pursuit? Landeau? Norman? They didn't seem likely. And then what. Ardyth had been charged with malicious assault. Would it be murder or manslaughter now?

Gotsch laughed.

"You keep tormenting the natives and one of em's gonna get you. Messing with people can be dangerous. You just never know when one's gonna lock and load on you.

"We had this old boy back home who everybody knew was beaten up on his old lady and kids, but nobody wanted to get into it. Then the kids grew up, the boys were about thirteen and fourteen and the sheriff found him out on a back road with a couple bullets in his head. There was pretty strong feeling the kids had more to do with it than they should have, except what had been going on in the family, and the sheriff wasn't too much interested in pursuing it. He had more important things to do, playing poker and keeping his car washed.

"It passed on as a case of what happens if you mess with people too long.

"But that's not what I come to tell you. Hell, Carter, I come to deliver you season's greetings from the governor. Yule tidings from the governor's mansion in Springfield wrapped with a red and green ribbon, which is more than most get from the government."

"And what's that?"

"You have been plucked from the lion's den. The States Attorney and those yo-yos at Barker have found it in their hearts to overlook your transgressions and infidelities."

"What's overlook mean?"

"Well, they ain't forgiven you, but they have decided to forget. That way other people will forget what they done."

"Like what?"

"Oh, hell, I'd imagine they got a whole barn full of bones they'd rather not have people rattle."

"The Red Dragon."

"Or whatever it's called."

"At Barker. My resignation," Carter said.

"They've reconsidered."

"Because Crowly died."

Carter stood and retrieved his drink from the mantel.

"No, no. I just told you about that cause I know you were fond of him and would want to know about that. It doesn't have to do with this other thing."

"What thing?"

"Well, it seems the States Attorney isn't going to take anything to the Grand Jury. He doesn't think there's enough evidence. Landeau and Remcheck have decided to forget about the meeting they had on you the other day."

"All the charges or complaints are being dropped?"

"Far as you're concerned, Yeah. The States Attorney doesn't have enough evidence. Just another way of saying he's been told to drop it. The Grand Jury would indict a dead horse if the state's attorney wanted it."

"Why doesn't he want it?"

"There's one stipulation," Gotsch said.

"What's that?"

"Well, the deal Absyth worked out says you have to take a year off from the university. An unpaid sabbatical."

"Absyth worked a deal. A trade-off."

"Yeah, I figure so."

"So I'm sentenced to a year in limbo."

"Oh hell, just a matter of bargaining. Pride. Even when they get caught with shit on their hands, they want to come away with something. What they want for you is better than trying to explain it all to a judge."

"What they want is my absence. They want me out for a year. Then what?"

"You come back as an assistant professor," Gotsch said.

"Assistant professor, with a reduction in pay. Something to embarrass me."

"I suppose that's part of it. But hell, Carter, look at it this way. You don't have any kids. There's nothing to say you can't go off and work for a year. If you want to."

"A pound of flesh. They're never satisfied. Even when they're wrong they have to punish someone, to inflict pain."

"Course there's nothing to say they're wrong. Just they got caught fucking the dog.

"But for the time-being things are back to normal, if they ever were. And I'll give you odds, you come back in a year and both Shindel and Remcheck are gone. And that means Landeau and Norman, too. Hell Crowly's already gone."

Gotsch laughed what Carter labeled a good-old-southern-boy laugh, a laugh sufficiently broad to include the misfortune of another, even the fatal misfortune of another.

"What about Ardyth Oldam?" Carter said.

"That one run Crowly down?"

"Is there any way of getting the charges dropped? Any chance of getting Clemens to let her go?"

Gotsch held up both hands.

"Whoa, hold it right there, big dog. Now, I got this settled for you. That wasn't the easiest thing I ever done. I don't know about that woman or why she did what she did, or what Clemens is going to do with her. And as a matter of fact, I don't want to know. In her case, Crowly dying gives everything a different slant. Nobody's gonna want to talk about it for a while. And when they do it's probably gonna be in front of a jury."

Carter went back to what Gotsch had said. Charges and complaints dropped.

"How did this happen," Carter said.

"I'd guess you know Paul Absyth called me."

"I talked to him about the problem," Carter said. "But I didn't know he called you."

"He had it in mind that maybe there'd be an outside chance we could get this settled without dragging everybody through the mud. I told him in good part that had already been done and it'd be pretty hard to undo what's once done.

"I don't mind telling you, this is not a good business. But it ain't just this little episode. If everybody at Barker got hauled in for his peculiarities and transgressions, there wouldn't be too many of us afoot. Course there's more to it than that. The ought-to-be don't get it. You ever heard of Rodney Langston?"

"Langston? Was he a student at Barker?" Carter asked.

"Some time ago."

"Ten years, maybe fifteen. It's been a long time."

"What you know about him?"

"If it's the same one, not much. He was a bright kid. Got called in a couple of times in other classes for papers he wrote. They were too good. Nobody around here had seen a student with those kinds of writing skills.

"I tried to get him to go into the graduate program in philosophy."

"Now, goddam, Carter, why would you waste a good mind on philosophy?"

"He decided on law school instead. Maybe Harvard or Yale. Got a perfect score on the LSAT. The only student I ever had who did that."

"Well, he's in Springfield, now. Talk about pissing away a good mind. Works for the governor. The day after your little scramble with Crowly and Landeau, I had to go to the capital for a budget conference. That was last Friday. They were trying to get everything done before Christmas.

"Absyth called me Thursday and I got the idea to talk it over with Langston. See if the governor might be interested in this thing. Usually politicians want to stay out of other people's business, unless they got a point to make or, maybe in this case, want to send a message, without using Western Union.

"Anyway, there's been rumors around the capital for a couple months now about Shindel not exactly using public funds to buy up land, but let's say borrowing, or holding onto the money the university has in his bank for a few extra days without paying interest. He's been using the money as collateral to finance land deals.

"Then there's a little difficulty the governor had during the last election with Shindel giving what might be considered a substantial campaign contribution to, shall we say, to the wrong people? Course you hear things all the time. But when the rumors hang around, you get the idea that maybe they not just rumors.

"To make a long story short," Gotsch laughed, "which I don't often do, Langston didn't say much but must have figured the governor would appreciate hearing a little about the politics at Barker. By the way, Langston said to tell you hello. Said you were the best teacher he had. He still remembers what you told the class about Jeremy Bentham. Said to tell you that you were right."

Carter retraced what he might have said. What would he have said fifteen years ago about Bentham and Mill?

"What did I say?"

"Hell, who knows. He might have thought you meant just the opposite of what you said. Students do that. No telling what they remember. They get away from school for a few years and everything takes on a golden glow. Sort of the memory of the good-old-times."

"I doubt Langston would do that."

"Something about you getting him through tough times, personal problems."

Carter shook his head.

"I don't remember," he said. "I don't know what it might have been. I was just trying to remember if he was married or what it could have been."

"Oh, hell, it don't matter. He likes what he remembers about you. Thinks you did helped him, so I didn't have to talk too hard to get in to see the governor. We been working on next year's budget. He wants to improve the higher education funding, and to be honest, this could poison the legislature. Any ripples will sink the boat. Like that ol boy back home used to say, 'It'd be striking me upside the head with a pine knot.'

"Course I didn't know what to expect. Then a couple days I got wind that a message had come down that the governor was prepared to send treasury agents to Lancaster to look over the university's use of state funds."

Gotsch held out his empty glass to Carter.

"Now I don't know if he'd do that. But it's a helluva good suggestion. Goddam, I bet that sent those misfits scrambling. Then Langston called and said Remcheck agreed to drop the thing with you and after a little talking, the States Attorney's Office, agreed with Langston—that there wasn't enough evidence to take this to the Grand Jury. John Clemens managed the governor's last campaign, and there's talk he's in line for an appointment to the Illinois Supreme Court."

Carter splashed Gotsch's glass half-full with bourbon and handed it back.

"Merry Christmas," Carter said.

"Course I figure the governor was looking to send a message.

"Then Crowly gets hisself run over. Makes the governor look like a genius. I figure there's more here than anybody's telling. If they don't keep the lid on, all hell's gonna break loose. They'll burn this place down to the water-line. And that may happen anyway."

"Jesus," Carter said, and sat for a minute looking into the fire. "It's over."

"Since nothing official's been done, I'd expect there won't be a statement made," Gotsch said. "Unless something comes up big that I ain't heard about, this whole business should die of its own weight. Just kind of sink into the water, out of sight. Unless you decide to make more out of it, which I wouldn't advise."

"Will they keep their word"

"Oh, I'd guess so. Hell, once a deal is made it don't pay nobody to go back on his word. Sort of a gentleman's agreement.

"When I was a rookie reporter with the *Sun Times* in Chicago, we had a crime-writer who did articles on the mob. A couple pieces started investigations, even led to convictions. I could never figure out why the crime-writers weren't whacked. I mean, nobody even called to complain.

"Then it came to me, kind of slow, a little at a time, that what got in print was what the traffic would bear. The editors knew what they could get away with, and the mob knew that the stories could always get worse. Nobody was happy with the arrangement, but the alternatives weren't very attractive."

"Could we go back to this other thing for a moment?" Carter said.

Gotsch looked at Carter quizzically.

"What about it? You don't believe your luck."

"Well, I appreciate the hell out of what you did. But I need to get it straight in my head."

"Langston knowing you was the luck. It ain't for him we'd been pissing into the wind. No telling why people will help you, or why they won't. Then Shindel did his part. I knew about MacMillian having his nose out of joint over the campaign contributions. I just didn't know how bad it was bent or what he might do, given the chance.

"Not so much what an investigation might turn up. It's the stink of the thing in the papers. Bad PR scares these people to death. More'n anything. They can always get a smart lawyer to keep them out of the slam. But once the smell gets out to the public, it's bad business. They don't savor this kind of notice. They want to pull the strings without anybody seeing it."

The idea of a year off, even an enforced year away from Barker had a certain allure for Carter. It would mean time, time to read, to think, time to visit places he had always planned to visit but never seemed to get to.

"I don't suppose I have any reasonable choice but to accept the deal," he told Gotsch. "Hell, I planned on a lot worse than this. It could have been another kind of sabbatical. An extended sabbatical."

He thanked Gotsch again on the porch.

"This is one of the better Christmas presents I've had in the last few years. I do appreciate your trouble. I owe you. Keep that in mind. If I can ever help you, be sure to ask."

"Hell, Carter, you don't know how much of a favor you already done for me. You see, when Remcheck and Shitwell get wind that I was in on this, it'll back those clowns up a little farther into their corner. That means I won't have to mess with either one. And they won't mess with me. That's worth something. Anyway, this is fun."

Carter watched Gotsch get into his car, then retreated to the livingroom to let the idea soak in.

In the early afternoon Ardyth called to check on Mason.

"I do not think it would be good for him to be at his house," Ardyth said. "I have made arrangements for him to go to his grandparents in Atlanta."

"Are you planning for him to stay?" Carter said. "I mean, is he going just for the holidays?"

"I do not think so, John Carter. We have made arrangements for him to stay with his grandparents for a month after Christmas, but now it will be better if he does not come back until this is finished. He is the only grandchild and they will be glad to have him visit."

"Then I have a suggestions," Carter said. "He'll probably have a good bit of luggage, if he's going to be there semi-permanently, and that would make it difficult either on a train or plane. Why don't I drive him to Atlanta? I need to get away for a while anyway. And it isn't a bad drive."

Ardyth hesitated for a moment.

"It would not be trouble for you?"

"I would. And no trouble. In fact I'd rather enjoy it."

"When would you leave?"

"Well, it's up to you. I'm free now. When are your parents expecting him?"

"He could be ready by Thursday."

"If we left Thursday afternoon," Carter said, "we could be in Atlanta early Friday morning."

"That would be nice of you John Carter. I will have the money for you then and will give you money for gas."

"Gas money won't be necessary. Let's just say I was headed to Atlanta, in the general direction, anyway.

"Otherwise, how are you doing?" Carter said.

"I am doing well."

There was a significant pause on the line, a troubled pause filled with the awareness that Crowly had died.

"I have spoken with Mr. Absyth for a long time on the phone and will be going to his office this afternoon. This is a serious matter, but he thinks we can, what he calls 'beat it.' So I will need to wait and be patient."

Carter hung up the phone and opened the drawer to the hall table where he had placed a white envelope with a green tag taped to it. The day after Katherine Marie left, Carter received a notice in the mail for a certified letter. He paid little attention to the green card which required him to go to the Maltus Street Post Office branch to accept the letter. A Christmas package he assumed and dropped the card in the drawer of the desk in the living-room. Saturday morning he remembered the card and stopped at Maltus Street.

The clerk handed him a white envelope with a bright red and blue New England Patriot logo. Carter inspected it several times, then pried open the flap.

The stationary displayed the Patriot logo at top-center of a white page with a large watermark football. Carter read the clean type print.

> Dear Professor Carter,
>
> The New England Patriot American Conference football team is pleased to invite you to be our guest at Superbowl XXXI in New Orleans on January 28, 1996. Included with

two tickets for the game we have enclosed tickets for Superbowl Week festivities.

We hope you will enjoy the week long entertainment in New Orleans, and that you will continue to support the Patriots as the best NFL franchises.

The Very Best in Sports

Carter read the signature and then located the name on the mast head of Patriot dignitaries on the left side of the stationary. Winsloe Bulgari. A senior vice president for public relations.

Carter stood for a long five minutes rereading the letter and fingering the tickets, the game tickets and a packet of at least ten others.

The second page listed the events and times and locations. This had to be a package NFL teams put together for their fans, for their most, what? Prestigious fans. Important fans? But then why me, Carter wondered?

He pocketed the letter and tickets and left the post office, thinking there had been a mistake. He hadn't had that kind of interest in football or any connection with the Patriots. If Minus Factor had been alive he would have done something like this.

But that was what had happened.

At the Moon Crater Factor had said he would send Carter Superbowl tickets. Carter had not thought much of it at the time. What had Factor said? "I'll send you a ticket?"

No that wasn't right. But it didn't matter. Carter looked at the date again and counted back. The letter was dated two days after Factor died. Monday December 18. Maybe he put in the order or request before the game at Pittsburgh. But the Pats weren't going to the Superbowl. And for another several walking blocks of minutes, Carter was numbed. Somehow before he died Factor had gotten tickets for him. A gift from a dead man, a man Carter truly liked, reached out across the abyss, the gap between the living and the dead, the vast desiccated wasteland of memory and intention.

So why not? Why not take Mason to Atlanta and then go on to New Orleans for Super Bowl week? Hell it was as good a plan as any other.

After his conversation with Gotsch, Carter made a mental list of what he needed to do, and then prioritized the list. He was fairly certain Katherine Marie would not cooperate. She would object to whatever he suggested. So he needed someone to look after the house. The post office could forward his mail to the hotel in New Orleans.

There were two piles of exam papers on his desk at Temperly and final grade rosters had to be submitted to the registrar. The phone company, cable service and newspaper office. The utilities would have to stay on. What else? He would have to clean out his office.

He stood for a time watching Mason camped in front of the TV. The boy had come down while he was talking to Gotsch and gone immediately to the TV.

In the two days they had been together he had become more attached to the boy, more than he had been to anyone in a very long time.

And then he was consumed with a profound grief, a grief he would not have expected, for the dead Crowly, a grief for his children, the two boys, one with Multiple Sclerosis, one seven the other five, for their vanished father.

The mad forces of driven people punishing and penalizing the innocent. My god, he thought, what have we done?

Maybe he should call Crowly's wife Glenda and offer sympathy, condolences. Surely she would not know he and Ardyth were close friends, and so, if she did, so what? Maybe, he thought, later in the day. Later in the week.

"I have to go to the office for a few hours," Carter told Mason. "If you can hold out until I get back, I'll cook up something for us to eat."

"That is good," Mason said. "Can I get a snack?"

"Yeah," Carter said. "Just don't fill up on the garbage."

"But garbage tastes so good," Mason said.

Mindful of his last official duties for the university Carter took an empty briefcase and headed across campus toward Temperly, to read and score the last two sets of final exams.

Alone in the old building, in the silence, several times he had to override the impulse to give everyone an A. But that was exactly what Crowly and Remcheck had encouraged. The university as business. Give the client/customer what he wanted.

Several instructors Carter knew had dummied down their courses sufficiently to allow them to send their students cards at the semester's end printed with the rhyme

> For all you do,
> This grade's for you.

The King of Watered Down Beers clumping around the classroom. Carter wondered what the reaction would be if the grade was a D or F. Clearly the card was meant for A and B grades. Otherwise the sentiment would be sarcastic, viciously so.

Carter read and marked the papers with care, as an obscure artist might put the final strokes on a last canvas, knowing it will never be viewed, and would not, even if it was seen, bring a pittance of praise or notice.

He finished the last paper at one-thirty, filled out the grade sheets and dropped them in the box at the registrar's office. By two o'clock he was standing in the middle of his office trying to determine where to begin and what he wanted to save.

The Monday after Mason's death Ardyth boxed up and removed what Mason had left. Mason had already carried off his books.

Carter pulled open the long drawer to Mason's desk. A rubber band, a broken Bic and a small pile of paper-clips were all that remained. In the side drawer he found a green book, hardback, with a worn and tattered cover. A book plate Ex Libris carried Mason's signature and an address Carter recognized as the small house on Campbell street where Mason and Ardyth had lived just after they were married.

The bottom of the title page was inscribed with Ardyth's name. Carter had difficulty decoding the script, but it said something about their first anniversary. He wondered why the usually thorough Ardyth had not taken the book or at least thrown it in the wastebasket.

Fifteen years ago she had signed the book as a gift and Mason had inscribed his name inside the cover. A matter of ownership, although the marks of his hand and the object inscribed had outlived him.

Enquiry Concerning Morals.

It was the Open Court reprint of the 1777 (Edition R).

On the back Carter read, "At the beginning of his anti-religious Of Miracles, Hume remarks, 'I flatter myself, that I have discovered an argument. . . which, if just, will, with the wise and the learned, be an everlasting check to all kinds of superstitious delusions, and consequently, will be useful as long as the world endures.'"

Hume, arguably the most important philosopher ever to write in English. And maybe the most important in any language, Carter thought.

Reading Hume as an undergraduate Carter had not been overly impressed. Just another philosopher propagating his particular brand. Certainly reacting to rationalism, Carter remembered thinking, but so what. What was so iniquitous about rationalism? He didn't know, at the time, but he knew now. He knew now with a clarity and focus and intellectual contempt he did not often direct at other habits of mind.

In the following years, the long years of observing the idiocy of assumption, superstition and out-and-out illogic and mendacity of the populace generally, it had been Hume's beacon, the focus of his soothing voice that assuaged Carter's anguish. Here was the reason, the logic, the cool integrity Carter had come to rely on and cherish.

During the summer of 1984 Carter was in London, and made a pilgrimage to Edinburgh to see what remained there of Hume. He had gone among the crowds on a brisk Scot's day with the pipers and fiddlers subsidized by the city fathers, playing at corners throughout the city center, past the over wrought monument of Walter Scott, the infamous architect of costume melodramas.

Within a few hours, however, his enterprise of discovering David Hume faltered. Even the student at the information center at the University of Edinburgh had not heard of Hume and could not find anything in the general information provided by the university about him. Not only were there no monuments, there were no exhibits, no displays. Nothing set aside to commemorate his life or his work.

At the Edinburgh Public Library Carter was told there had been an exhibit in 1976 on the bicentennial of Hume's death.

Why not birth? To celebrate his death? Death as a cause for celebration? Apparently.

All was not lost, however. After a further series of inquiries and signatures Carter was directed to the south reading-room where he would be allowed to glimpse copies of first editions of the *Treatise* and *Understanding*.

What else was available, he didn't know.

By then his puzzlement had subsided and he had come to understand the disgust and disappointment Hume had felt when he noted that his *Treatise* of 1740 "fell still born from the press" with not "a murmur among the zealots."

If what was true in Hume's day, that few people in Britain were capable of understanding and even fewer of appreciating his originality and genius, was not true today, there still had not been any attempt to raise a monument or to honor Hume's genius.

Why not?

Well, people did not encourage renegades. Hume's atheism had caused a scandal. The religious fantasizing that had passed for so long as philosophy had received a broadside and was listing severely. Now agnosticism had to be taken seriously. After Hume, there could be meaning in saying "I don't know."

Because of it Hume had been denied a position at the university. But of course. And even though that was more than two hundred years ago, the aggrieved petty and childish do not forget, and they most certainly do not forgive, not even genius.

When Carter entered the reading-room none of the people at the large tables looked up. With pens and notepads at hand they bent over books and papers browned and cracked with time, moving slowly, deliberately over the pages, line by line. The dedication and intensity of consulting the sources, these first-fonts, the solemnity and seriousness of the enclave with its huge wooden tables and bookcases, high pressed-tin ceiling and large mahogany doors elevated Carter's senses.

The librarian who had met Carter at the door took his card and directed him to a chair at the end of the far table. When he was seated, on a small paper Carter listed the two volumes he wanted and handed it and the card to the woman. She took the paper to her desk and sorted through a file listing the library's holdings of first editions of Hume's work. Then Carter waited as she disappeared through the door at marked Staff Only.

Outside the noise and clutter of Edinburgh's streets filled the day. From the reading-room Carter could see the cars and pedestrians, but could not hear them. Traffic simply slipped into his view from one side and disappeared at the opposite, the images of a monotonous silent movie, run in from nowhere, going nowhere.

Because of the silence and isolation, even the smallest, most insignificant sound was amplified and each motion exaggerated, made larger and more expressive.

An elderly man with a brilliant white beard and a fringe of gray hair above his ears read from a book printed in characters Carter did not recognize. The gold of his horn-rimmed glasses glowed in the sunlight falling in behind him with a deep yellow fire.

To the man's left a young woman Carter judged to be thirty or so bent over a newspaper or broadsheet, her nose and glasses very nearly on the page. The gleaming from the large transoms gave her features a conspicuous and prominent resolution and clarity and tone. A slight whiff of bath soap, maybe a soft disinfectant, drifted Carter's way and for a moment he was appreciative of her hygienic.

Promptly the librarian reappeared with two books, one brown, one black, two very old books, and placed them on the table in front of Carter.

For a number of minutes Carter sat with his hands on the table, palms down, staring at the books. He imagined Hume had handled the texts and when he took the first book and opened it, in the contact of his hands with Hume's turning the same pages, something settled in Carter, something came full-circle.

He sat in the clear, bright shimmer, touching his fingertips to the words, to the print of the cream-colored pages, the raised ink print of the seventeenth century presses, as if in touching them he might intuit the magnitude of the ideas and the brilliance of the mind they represented.

But there was more to Hume for Carter than the depth and turn of the ideas, as brilliant as they were. There was always the man Hume who Carter could not shake out of his mind.

Hadn't Hume written early on about the moral power of benevolence? This kind, gentle man of genius, ignored and scorned in his own day and today, even by the religious bigots and partisans, even after giving them a lesson on what it means to be human.

For four hours that day and five hours for three more days that week Carter occupied a space at the table in the warm, nurturing opalescent of the south reading-room. He reread the first editions of texts he had read in part and in total at earlier times in later editions, seeing the ideas, the arguments in an altogether different and enlivened way.

Carter knew that when a man died and his books were listed and stacked on library shelves, whether he was dead six years or six hundred, the man, the living man was absent. Those days in the library had put the man, the living man David Hume into Carter's mind, deep in Carter's soul in a way he had not been there before, in a way he would always be there.

Walking out of the Edinburgh Public Library for the last time the afternoon he was scheduled to return to London he paused on the steps, trying to refocus his eyes, the impressions of the Edinburgh street rush, its people moving hurriedly along the dirty walks, his mind adrift and laboring in the discourse and arguments of the eighteenth century becoming 1984, thinking at the time he had been touched across a span of two and a half centuries as he supposed people are often touched by a mystical, spiritual presences.

Hume's treatment, the lack of recognition even in the late twentieth-century became a powerful symbol for Carter, and at times a saving consolation. But Hume had triumphed—even though the religious crazies, the inane and banal, had not permitted him access to their university or allowed a stack of stones to be raised and dedicated in his honor.

Carter leafed through the pages, of habit, absently thinking again about Mason until he found a torn page, then another. The pagination skipped from 66 to 94. This was the book Mason had torn up during the ravages of his first break. Those pages, Hume's words, had ended wadded-up and tossed around the office floor like so many dirty popcorn balls.

It wasn't so much how Ardyth had overlooked the book but why Mason had kept it. In Mason's mind had Hume gone wrong—or was he simply too correct. What was Mason thinking? What connection had he made with this torn and mutilated remnant of his slip into the abyss? And having overcome it for a time was it a souvenir he kept to remind himself of what he possibly knew waited for him?

Carter decided to keep it as a memento, a piece of damaged property that bespoke the anguish of the mind that damaged it. He flipped through the pages again, this time stopped by two small snapshots he had not seen before. The smaller picture was of Ardyth and Mason, without much definition, from a time Carter gauged to coincide with the address and the gift of the book.

Ardyth looked frail and cheerful, smiling, holding onto Mason who still had all his hair. But that was before their life had gone wrong, seriously and drastically wrong.

In the other picture Ardyth and a woman Carter did not recognize were seated on a park bench. The color of the leaves on the trees behind them spoke of early autumn.

Carter was tempted to keep the pictures.

From his own desk he collected a stack of file-folders with clippings he had gathered and read but never taken time to reread. There were articles from philosophy, physics and anthropology. A brown folder bulged with pages torn from *The Bulldog Bark*. Another was filled with faculty senate minutes he had saved for reasons he could not now locate.

He dropped the folders into the waste can. He would leave a note for the cleaning lady with the bequest of the jade plant. It would be hers to carry away, leave or destroy. A nice way to slip responsibility, he thought.

What would he save? The laminated clippings of his Chicago days. He un-pinned them from the wall, rolled them together and placed the roll in his briefcase. The calendar of philosophers and authors he would save, again as a souvenir until he no longer needed souvenirs of Barker. And the pictures of Hume and Locke.

He laid the large calendar on his desk and leaned over the faces and names and quotes looking for something appropriate for leave taking, disembarking Barker's scholarship, the woof and arf of academia.

He emptied the drawers of staplers and the three-hole punch, chalk and pens and notepads, the tools of the paper-pushers of the academy. He pulled out the top drawer to empty the bits and pieces of bent paper clips, pencil stubs and dust into the waste can. When the drawer slipped from his hands and clattered to the floor and a small, metal button device stuck to the outside edge of the back of the drawer popped loose. The device clicked to the floor and rolled away like an errant coin.

Carter retrieved the mechanism and examined it carefully. He had not seen anything exactly like it before, but felt confident of its purpose.

"I knew it," he murmured. "I knew it. I knew it. I knew it. Why didn't I look for this?"

It appeared to be a small transmitter. He pocketed the device, then took it out and examined it again. Absyth came to mind. He could take it to Absyth and ask about a violation of his constitutional rights. What? Privacy, of course.

Carter deliberated for a time. Wasn't this akin to wire-tapping? Could the university tap an office phone without notifying those using the phone that they were being monitored? Why not? Of course they could.

Even when the courts ruled school administrations demanding teachers sign off on grade changes violates the teachers' First Amendment rights, Carter knew of at least three cases at Barker where this had occurred.

The instructors were told they would be dismissed for insubordination if they refused to make the changes and sign the rosters. Not wanting to risk the inconvenience and hardship of going without a job or pay during a long court battle, the instructors caved in.

What was seldom considered or discussed was why the chest-thumping patriots of university and college administrations would disregard principles decided by the courts as law.

Newspapers regularly reported primary and secondary school administrations' attempts to circumvent Supreme Court dictates on racism as well as on the separation of church and state by including religious benedictions and prayers in school functions.

Carter had no proof that someone had planted the bug. Hell, it could have been there for years. Who had the desk before him? It came up from storage several years ago. Could he run a trace on the device? Jesus. Talk about a grain of sand on a beach. He didn't even know if the thing worked.

Maybe he should have it framed with an appropriate caption and pass it on to the university museum. They could display it with their other ludicrous relics and treasures of academia.

He packed the odds and ends into his briefcase and snapped it shut.

The first few days he had let Mason forage the refrigerator and cupboards. Then he determined to monitor the boy's meals. Today he wanted to get back before he came down with the hungers. That could be any time now.

Carter checked his watch, took the briefcase and left the fourth-floor, going down the old wide stairs to avoid whomever might be on the elevator. From the first landing he saw the woman, a young woman, in the dim winter light coming toward him and thought he recognized her. She looked up and watched him as she came onto the landing. When he paused to let her pass, she stopped.

"Dr. Carter," she said. "Do you have a minute? I was hoping I'd find you here."

"You're Ruth Lessiack," Carter said.

The woman nodded.

Ruth Lessiack had her brother's wide eyes and smile, a striking resemblance Carter had not caught that afternoon in the long ago of the month before when she appeared at his door with Vivien. During the struggling moments in memory and recall of faces and voices he found familiarity, but nothing of recognition. Now he saw it. They could have been twins. As much as any brother and sister.

"Do you have a moment?"

"A moment," Carter said.

"I came here to try to explain what happened. I want to tell you, because Vivien won't tell you."

"She doesn't seem to be in such bad shape. I saw her the other night at Murphy's with Kerm Soliski."

Ruth smiled.

"I know. I'm so glad. He's just what she needs right now."

"What she needs?"

"He's kind and understanding. Carter, she's been through a lot."

"And she made damn certain to drag everyone else through it with her."

"No. It's not like that."

"What is it like then?"

"She's embarrassed, and I think a little frightened."

"Frightened? Of what?"

"You. She's afraid of you. You have a strange power over her. Carter, she thinks a great deal of you."

"Yeah. I know," Carter said. "But hardly enough to keep her mouth shut."

"After talking to you the other night she felt just terrible. She's been depressed and wanted me to talk to you."

"Why you?"

"Well, at least part of this is my fault. I introduced her to Marvin. If I hadn't done that, the whole thing would have been different."

"So she's without volition or a mind of her own."

"You don't understand. She had to do what she did, Carter. If not . . ."

"What? If not what?"

"She was scared."

"Yeah, I know."

"She was scared. And not just of you."

"Crowly?"

"Yes."

"Why?"

"He was a dangerous man, a driven man, Carter."

"I know."

"Did she tell you about us? About my relationship with Marvin?"

"No. As a matter of fact she spared me those details."

"Well, he was crazy. Carter, you have to respect that. He was crazy. The night he found out Vivien had been at my apartment with you. He beat the shit out of both of us."

"And you didn't turn him into the police."

"No. You can't just do that."

"Why not?"

"Carter, the cops are no fucking good. Whatever you've been through, it will only be worse if you go to the police.

"Then there's the other thing."

"What other thing? Crowly had the goods on your brother."

"Yes. Charles has been suspended."

"For writing bad grants. For fraud," Carter said.

"I don't know. Yeah. Along with Landeau and Miller."

"The director of Crompol Lab."

"Charles wanted me to tell you he is sorry he didn't give you more support at the hearing last week. And since you and he have been friends, he was wondering if there was anything you could do. Maybe you could talk to Harry Gotsch for him."

"Talk to Gotsch? Why should I? Why Gotsch?"

"You know Gotsch better than most people and Charles thinks Gotsch is pushing the investigation. If you were to talk to him, well, he knows the States Attorney and most of the Barker board members."

"You're trying to build support for your brother."

The girl looked at him and nodded ever so slightly.

"You could make a difference. Everybody knows you and trusts you. You're one of the most respected people on campus. That's why Marvin was after you. He told me you were the one person the faculty trusted and because of that he was afraid of you. He said he had to get rid of you. He was afraid you would cause a lot of trouble if you really wanted to."

"Well, I appreciate the underhanded vote of confidence," Carter said.

"Although I'm not sure what it means coming from Crowly. His perception of me was as warped as his other fantasies. And I don't know Gotsch very well. Not well enough to ask him to represent your brother to the States Attorney.

"What brother Charles needs is a good lawyer. If he's been involved in falsifying government grants, it needs to be straightened out. I'd suggest he get a lawyer."

"But that's not the whole story, Carter. Scientists write balloon grants all the time."

"And they get sanctioned all the time," Carter said. "The whole story is you and your brother, and whoever else, Landeau and Miller, and that friend of yours, can't see the whole story. You can't even see across the room.

"Look," Carter said, "what's done is done. Spilt milk. Maybe it did work out for the best. The administration and its bogus policies are in retreat. That's something, at least. Your brother, who I really do like, and his colleagues have been stopped from injecting their heresy into the scientific canons.

"Maybe my position here at Barker wasn't important. Maybe losing a job of this nature is a small price to pay for getting the rabid dogs out of the academic chicken-house. I don't know.

"But what I do know, is next year, the year after that, another bunch of idiots will come along with another scheme. Another pack will scale the garden fence and the academic process will be damaged still further.

"You don't need to apologize to me for Vivien or ask me to help your brother. You're right. I like Charles, but at the moment it ends there.

"You people need to apologize to yourselves for the damage you've done to your own lives. And I don't mean screwing for money. In face of what else has happened your traditional habits look almost angelic."

Carter reconsidered.

"Look, it's an old idea," he said, "a very old idea, but the Greeks, a few of them, believed it was better to suffer an injustice than to do an injustice. And to understand what an injustice is, you need a handful of smarts. Not even wisdom. That would be requiring too much. But at least a basic intelligence beyond infantile self-interest. Which is precisely what you don't have.

"I'm not very inclined to accept anyone's apology, except in what we learned from this. If so, then maybe, just maybe there's sense left in it, and the apologies and remorse will have veracity and validity."

Carter left the woman on the stairs and made his way out into the frigid afternoon, relieved, just then, at having had a bit of his say, even to someone as insignificant, and he assumed, as deaf to his words as Ruth Lessiack.

He crossed the quad in the bright air headed for College Street, wondering, what food was left in the refrigerator to fix for Mason. Christmas Day they had celebrated by watching football and ordering pizzas from Dominos. They had ordered three large pizzas, a pepperoni, a supreme and a sausage, and had eaten pizza for the next five hours. Carter suspected ordering out again might be a good idea.

Chapter XXVI

Ardyth dropped off Mason in the near mid-afternoon. Carter watched from the second-floor bedroom as they stacked the boy's suitcases, computer, guitar and several small taped-up boxes on the porch steps. Carter set his suitcase in the entry hall and went out intending to talk to Ardyth. By the time he got to the porch she was driving away in a car he had not seen before.

The authorities probably have the killer-machine in captivity, Carter thought.

He instructed Mason to collect whatever he had of clothing from the guestroom, and went to the garage and pushed open the large overhead door. The car, a silver sixty-four Bonneville, was covered with a fine coat of dust. The left rear tire needed air. He hadn't driven it in two months, and when he opened the door, the musty scent of the too-long-neglected greeted him.

Carter was fond of the car. It had belonged to Henry Caldwell. Carter had got it almost as a gift. When Henry died Claire planned to return to France within a few weeks, and wasn't particularly interested in making money on the deal. That was 1980. The odometer showed twenty-seven thousand and the interior was impeccable.

Carter gave her four thousand for it.

Now he was sorry he hadn't driven it more. But as with most university campuses, Barker was seriously over populated with motor vehicles, and he found it easier and more convenient to walk. Then walking became a habit.

The engine churned lethargically, cranking up, slowly, and after what seemed a very long time, fired, then caught. A haze of blue smoke blew up behind the machine and drifted out into the alley.

Even in the depths of winter, and after so long, the engine ran evenly, though laboriously, and Carter fidgeted with the dashboard switches. He checked the blower, the lights, the wipers, snapped on the radio. The small clock at the center of the dash still kept time. He pulled up the collar on his coat and settled into the deep, comfortable cushion of the seat to wait for the engine to warm up.

An initial anticipation had already begun, of travel, of the different and new, of having slipped from beneath the weight of deceit and duplicity, rancor and malice. He was not yet sure how long it would take to shake off the stench, but for the first time in months, maybe in years, he felt free and alert and safe. The old Pontiac was part of it.

In another several minutes Carter backed the car into the alley and circled the block to the front of the house.

When Mason finished loading his suitcases into the back seat, he came around to the rear of the car.

"Maybe we should try to get your luggage in the trunk with the boxes," Carter said. "It's a long ride and you might want to stretch out on the back seat or sleep."

Mason nodded and retrieved the bags.

The length of College Street was quiet in the crisp morning. Without acknowledging Carter, a man in a Cossack hat and car-coat with a dog on a leash passed on the sidewalk. As they passed, Carter watched the dog, an Eskimo with a white eye. His grandfather claimed a dog with a white eye could see the wind, wherever in the hell he got that.

Just beyond the front walk the dog stopped to pee on the large ash between the sidewalk and the street. When Carter arrived at College Street, the tree had been an anemic sapling wound in a strangle of vines. And although it was on city property, the City showed little interest in its welfare. Carter cut down the vines and pulled them from the branches. Over the years he burnt off the bag worms and kept it trimmed. It had prospered and taken on substantial proportions, a decent addition to the College Street milieu.

As Carter stood watching after the man with the dog, a white sedan swung around the corner. The car slowed noticeably coming up the street toward him and Carter could see two men checking house-numbers. They pulled up abreast of him and the man in the passenger seat rolled down the window.

"Is this 1413 College Street?" the man said.

"Yes it is," Carter said.

"You wouldn't happen to be John Carter?"

Carter had left the engine running and to avoid the Pontiac's exhaust stepped closer to the car.

"I'm John Carter."

The man opened the door and stepped out. He was a good bit shorter and thicker than Carter judged he might be, slightly balding and round-faced with eyes the color of the high blue winter sky. He wore a charcoal serge suit and a white shirt and brown tie. A prominent scar ran along the right side of his neck just above the collar line.

"Looks like you're leaving," the man said.

"Or just arriving," Carter said.

The man smiled.

"Which is it?"

"Maybe a little of both."

The man took his wallet from an inside coat pocket and opened it toward Carter.

"You live here," the man said, nodding toward the house. "1413 College Street?"

"Yes," Carter said. "Who are you?"

"I'm agent Sanderson from DCI. We'd like to talk to you."

Carter had been unable to read the imprint on the badge and wondered how he might verify the man's claim.

While they talked the driver backed the car toward the curb and pulled up to where they were standing.

"Maybe we should go inside," the man said. "It would he more comfortable."

"It's fine here," Carter said.

"Suit yourself."

"DCI?"

"Department of Criminal Investigation."

"Talk?" Carter said. "I was told there wouldn't be charges."

"No charges. I don't know. We're looking for information."

Carter waited as the driver joined them, and then looked to check on Mason who was in the front of the Bonneville with his arms folded on the back of the seat, watching through the rear window.

The second man was slightly taller than his partner, with gray hair, but dressed in the same colored suit and tie. The uniform of the day, Carter guessed.

"How well do you know Ardyth Oldam?" Sanderson said.

"Very well," Carter said. "I'm a friend of the family." He motioned to the Bonneville. "That's her son there in my car."

The agents shifted to regard Mason but did not otherwise acknowledge the boy.

"Mr. Carter, we're interested in your whereabouts on December nineteenth? Say after seven o'clock?"

Carter did not answer immediately. He counted back the days. This was the 28th. Nine days. Two back and then seven. Tuesday.

"That was the second day of exams."

"Did you have a class that night?"

"No," Carter said. "I gave up night classes ten years ago."

"Were you home that evening?"

Carter nodded. "Yes."

"All evening?"

"What's this about?" Carter said.

"What time did you get home from class?"

"Hell I don't know. I'm not sure."

"Was there anyone at home with you?"

"My wife."

"Who else?'

"No one. What's this about?"

"Mr. Carter we have information that you were not at home the entire evening."

"Information?"

"We have witnesses who saw you outside Marvin Crowly's house."

"Witnesses. Who?"

"That's not important. What we want to know is what you were doing there."

"If I was there."

"You were there," the taller agent said. "We're sure of that."

"Are you?"

"Yes."

"I see," Carter said. "Is this witness personally acquainted with me?"

Carter didn't know what could have been seen. What had he done or what might have been incriminating or suspicious? He remembered standing in the darkness at the edge of the driveway. There had been lights in the windows, but he had not seen Crowly. What else? Had he taken the Smith and Wesson out of his pocket? He didn't think so. But there would have been no other reason for his presence on the street outside Crowly's house. Maybe he had come for tea. Or at least a beer. Maybe it was an accident. He had lost his way.

Someone speculated he was there to mess with Crowly, or at least that he intended to do Crowly serious harm. It wouldn't take a genius to figure that out. Everyone knew how he felt about Crowly. He had made his contempt for the man known. How could it be otherwise? Surely they had heard about his troubles with the administration. But who was everyone?

What could the witness have reported? It was dark. Jesus. Who could it be? Walking along the street at night is no crime. Now he was certain he had not taken the weapon out. Who could have known he was armed?

What had been reported? Who were they? What kind of information did they give?

Thinking about the weapon, Carter tried to remember if he had locked his briefcase. The Samsonite attaché case was behind the driver's seat on the floor, packed with its usual contents. Several pens, a notebook, a bottle of bourbon, a glass and the revolver. It was on the floor beneath Mason's computer and several boxes of computer paraphernalia. A concealed weapon. He wondered if they intended to search the car. Would they go through the boxes and suitcases of clothes and books?

"Mr. Carter," agent Sanderson said, "it would be better for everyone if you'd clear up your activities that night."

"Look," Carter said. "I think my lawyer should take part in the inquisition. Now if you aren't going to arrest me, then I'll need to get back to what I was doing."

"Mr. Carter, we have reason to think Marvin Crowly was involved in highly questionable activities. And more than questionable, possibly illegal activities. We're trying to determine if Mrs. Oldam had anything to do with it. We don't know. You know anything about that? What you were doing at Crowly's that night?"

Ardyth and Crowly. The connection hadn't crossed Carter's mind. How could he imagine a link between people who occupied opposite poles on his emotional spectrum? Ardyth he loved and respected with an extended and deeply appreciative devotion.

And Crowly?

A sense of relief passed over Carter. For the first time in weeks he was innocent of the accusation of wrongdoings imagined or real.

Then he sunk into a new regret. Rather than Ardyth, he would have preferred it was he they suspected.

For a moment he chilled with the realization that in a strange and foreign land of human possibility it could be true.

"No," Carter said softly. "No, I don't know anything about Crowly's extra-curricular activities. Crowly was the vice chancellor of instruction and we had a disagreement."

"About what?"

"About my unauthorized use of the library. I could get into the library whenever I wanted. I'd been doing it for years."

"How'd you get in?"

"Oh, hell, there was a backdoor that had a worn lock. If you lift the door handle and pull, it pops open. Philosophers don't always operate on an eight-to-five schedule. I never took anything I didn't return, but Crowly tried to use it to fire me."

"Fire you for going into the library?"

"Yeah."

Sanderson smiled. He shook his head. "That's what you meant by being charged?"

"Yes."

"Did you go to Crowly's that night?"

"Yes I did. I was going to talk to Crowly, but changed my mind."

"You didn't see Crowly."

"That's right."

The taller agent seemed satisfied. "That sounds right," he said.

He took out a small notebook and a pen and scratched out what Carter assumed was his name.

"Did you know Mrs. Oldam was going to kill Marvin Crowly?"

"No," Carter said, "and to tell the truth, I don't think she knew it either."

The taller agent focused on Carter.

"It's a little hard to believe she'd wait in the parking lot with the motor running for half-an-hour to do something she hadn't planned."

"Did she ever say anything to you about Crowly?" Sanderson said.

"No. I don't think so. I'd say it was an accident. A fortunate accident, not for Mrs. Oldam, but certainly for everyone else. Crowly was a pig."

The older agent shook his head. "Professor, thank you for your trouble. And by the way, what do you know about Michelle Phillips?"

"I know the name," Carter said. "That's all."

"And Vivien Connors."

"Are they the same person?" Carter said.

Sanderson nodded. We think they are."

"That's what I heard," Carter said.

"Did you meet her through Crowly?"

"No," Carter said. "She came to my office. If I had known she had anything to do with Crowly, I'd have thrown her out."

"But you didn't?"

"Throw her out?"

"No. You didn't know about her connection with Crowly?"

"No," Carter said. "That I didn't know."

"Okay," Sanderson said. "By the way, where are you headed for the holidays?"

"Atlanta. Then the Superbowl," Carter said.

The men smiled.

"Superbowl! Damn. Some people have all the luck. Must be nice."

"Yeah," Carter said. "Must be."

Carter retreated to the sidewalk as the agents re-entered their car. They talked in the encased silence of the vehicle for a few moments, checking their notebooks, then drove off slowly without looking at him again.

"So much for that," Carter said, and motioned for Mason to take his suitcase out of the back seat.

On their way out of Lancaster, Carter stopped at a Mobil station across from Calgary Cemetery. He checked the oil and tires. The left rear tire needed air. He filled the car with gas and picked up a map of the southeastern United States. The clock in the station showed four-forty-two.

"Well, you ready for this?" he said to Mason.

"I am not sure," he said. His voice was uncertain.

"Have you ever been away from home before?"

"Only for a few days. But then I was with Ardyth and Mason."

"But Lancaster will still be your home," Carter said.

"No. Ardyth said it will no longer be our home. She will leave when she can."

"I would think any place we stay for a number of years remains a home," Carter said. "I lived in Chicago for a while, and in a way I still think of Chicago as home."

"What about your friends?" Mason said.

"Yes, you're right," Carter said. "They are gone."

"I will see Ardyth in a few months," Mason said. "But it will probably be a very long time before I see any of my friends."

"Maybe they could come and visit you."

"I think Jimmy Rongey will. He's my best friend."

Mason's voice rose.

"You know what he did, Carter? When he found out I was going away he made this huge banner and hung it across the back of our homeroom at school. It must have been twenty feet long."

"What'd it say?"

"It said, 'General Oldam Marches on Atlanta.' We had just finished studying about Sherman's march."

"When was that?"

"Oh, a couple days before school was out."

"When'd you get out?"

"The twenty-second. We always go to the last minute."

"Well, General Oldam, I guess we should get on with your march."

The boy grinned and nodded.

"We will be good travelers together," he said.

Carter guided the Pontiac onto the highway south and forty-five minutes later merged left onto the Interstate 64 southeast for Paducah, Nashville, and Atlanta.

"You hungry?" he said to Mason.

The boy shook his head.

"Not yet Carter. Ardyth said I should eat. She gave me two hamburgers and a bowl of soup."

"Well, when you need food let me know."

Carter pushed the dial along the FM band to a St. Louis classical music station.

"There's something you didn't know," Carter said.

"What?"

"Radio stations east of the Mississippi begin with W and the stations west of the river begin with K."

"How about WIL and WEW in St. Louis?" Mason said

"I don't know,' Carter said. "I guess they're an exception."

"I heard WEW was actually on the Illinois side," Mason said. "I think I read it a couple years ago in a radio almanac."

"So that leaves us with WIL."

They rode through the dusk of southeastern Illinois, the Shawnee Forest toward the Ohio River. Just beyond Mt. Vernon they lost the St. Louis station and Carter picked up a PBS station from Carbondale.

"You always listen to classical music?" Mason said.

"Mostly," Carter told him. "Some folk, old time stuff."

"What kind of old stuff."

"Oh, you know, rhythm and blues."

"Not Presley or Pat Boone."

"No. No. Sam Cooke. Chuck Berry. Fats Domino."

"God. You scared me, Carter. I thought you had lost it."

"You mean Presley and Boone."

"Yeah. For a minute you really had me worried."

"But you're feeling better now?"

"Carter, you got to promise you won't do that to me again. I mean, this is going to be a long ride. Something like that could ruin it for both of us."

"Something like what?"

"I mean, if you liked Elvis Presley you know what I'd do? I'd ask you to stop the car and I'd get out and walk."

"No. Don't worry about that.

"But you like Fats Domino," Mason said.

"Yeah."

"Boy, the Fat Man could sing. If I was a singer, that's how I'd sound."

"You're not going to be a rock-singer?"

"No. Ardyth won't hear of it."

"What are you going to do?"

"I don't know. I want to do something that makes a difference."

"Such as?"

"Maybe work with the ACLU or the EPA. Today too many people just think about themselves. They spend all their time thinking about making money and the world is falling apart."

"That sounds like a good idea."

"Should I be a teacher?"

"Like your father."

"And you?"

"No. I wouldn't encourage anyone to be a teacher."

The boy did not answer immediately. Carter assumed he was listening to the music. Then he spoke.

"Do you know anything about the Bible?"

"A little," Carter said.

"Remember what Christ said about teaching?"

"Go ye forth and teach?"

"No. That's not right. The Old Testament said the thing about multiplying."

"But that's the idea."

"The Old Testament says 'Apply thine heart unto instruction, and thine ears to the words of knowledge.' The New Testament says of Christ 'And he began again to teach by the seaside and there was gathered unto him a great multitude.'"

"I guess you know that chapter and verse."

"Yes. I do. The first was from Proverbs, 23:12."

"And you're worried about me and Elvis. You start preaching and I'll be the one out on the road walking."

"Oh, it hasn't got anything to do with religion, Carter. Ardyth wouldn't allow it. But the Bible has a lot of nice ideas."

"You are your father's son."

"You really think so? Thank you. Have you ever heard that the boy shall be father to the man?"

"Yeah. I've heard that. My crazy first wife used to recited that. She didn't have the slightest idea what it meant."

"You do not like women very much."

"Son, if you had dealt with the women I've run across, you might not care much for them either. Of course there were good ones, just as there are good and bad men. But some of them were bad."

"But women like you. I've heard Ardyth say that."

"Some women," Carter said.

"Ardyth thinks you are a very important man. Ardyth did not run over Crowly just because of Mason. My father's problems were very difficult. She was exceedingly upset about what Crowly did to you."

"Upset enough to kill him?"

"Carter, my mother is a very strong-willed woman."

"I believe that," Carter said.

"I saw what that woman called Carol did to you with her cigarette."

"Carol?" Carter said. "Carol who?"

"She calls herself Carol Zygote."

"Zygote? That's her name?"

"Do you know what a zygote is?" Mason said.

Carter laughed. "As a matter of fact I do."

"Well, she says she has only recently been conceived and is now becoming a new person."

"And when she has become? What then?"

"I guess it depends on what she becomes."

"She's already taken a bit of a violent turn. Maybe she'll become a homicidal fetus."

Mason started laughing.

"God. Carter, then when they came to abort her she could fight back."

He held his hand up.

"I can see it now. Doctor wounded in battle with violent fetus."

"Did your mother ask those females to come to your house?"

"I don't know. I don't think so."

"I had the impression she didn't know they were there. Or why would she have asked me to stop by to see how you were?"

"Maybe she was worried they would be there."

For a long time then they rode in silence, the only sound the whistle of wind and the hum-drum of the tires on the pavement. Mason took a pillow from the back and lodged it between the doorpost and seat and settled back to watch the passing landscape.

Carter could see the cut of Ardyth's nose and chin in the boy's face, although his eyes and mannerisms were thinly veiled copies of his father's.

So the dead live among us, Carter thought, carried back to Mason sitting on the floor of their office tearing pages from a book and wadding them up.

The words of his inquiry hung in Carter's head, and he wondered now what John Carter would do? Certainly he did not have a clear vision for the immediate future, although he had a growing, if somewhat vague sense of direction.

Certainly he'd leave Barker. That much was clear. In spite of his tenor and tenure of years in the academy he had never been as tightly tied to the university as many of his colleagues. Had the opportunity appeared earlier, he would have been on the road sooner. True believer or not, it wasn't Carter's nature to cling to a dying or hopeless cause. He would take it for what it was worth. He'd leave. At the moment he did not intend to return.

Down to the last seventy or so hours of the year and the decade, the car's clock might as well have been a sundial on an overcast day. Minutes and hours no longer mattered.

Time's arrow could be unwavering as the needle of a compass hangs slightly off true north, but he could still seek out and follow other compass points. Atlanta was out there at the end of the road, sooner or maybe later he would arrive, but that was a matter of energy, and whim—what took his interest and the digressions he might make along the way. He would arrive in Atlanta in darkness or in sunlight. It mattered very little to him which.

The old car ran smoothly south along I-57 and he watched the gauges. Temp, amp and oil. The gas needle rocked just to the west of the half-mark.

Now he was toying with the idea of taking Mason with him to the Superbowl. Factor would have smiled about that. Bringing the young into the tribe. A silly, vicious tribe, but a tribe nonetheless. Then he decided against it. The boy needed to be in school and would require a week or so to get settled and registered.

Then, too, Carter had had enough of other people, be they young or kind, or both. Emotionally he had worn down a good bit more quickly than he thought he would.

He would deliver the boy to his grandparents, excuse himself gracefully but quickly, and move on.

An hour later they were in Kentucky, looping above Kentucky Lake on I-24 headed for Nashville.

Mason had given up trying to sleep in favor of watching the night lights of the highway and countryside.

"Carter," the boy said, "what's it feel like to get old?"

"You think I'm old?"

"Yes. Sort of. You look old. Your face is wrinkled."

"Why do you ask?"

"Well, you see, I was trying to think what it would feel like to be a woman. I mean, to wear a bra and have a different set of privates."

"A different set of privates?"

"Well, you know, like having one leg, or maybe three legs. Like having green hair."

"Or no hair?"

"I wasn't thinking about how people would look at you or how they might say stupid things and stare at you or not talk to you. I was wondering just how it would feel. Like getting old?"

"Something like that."

"Like having one leg?"

"Maybe four legs, two legs or three, and a different set of privates and green hair. All of that."

"All of what? What do you mean?"

"Well, it's all the strange things in the world happening to you at the same time, only you don't see them as strange anymore. You don't really care."

"You don't care about sex or how you look?"

"I wouldn't go that far. But there is a story about Sophocles as an old man of eighty. The younger men were kidding him about not being of much value to women. Sometimes age does that. Anyway, he is reported to have said, 'Thank the gods the demon is off my back. Now I can get on with serious things.'"

For a time the boy watched the passing signs, the highway markers.

"Do you think it will happen to me?"

"To all of us," Carter said. "It's a part of nature, the conditions of our bodies, and minds."

"I see," he said. Then after a while, "That's depressing, Carter."

"No," Carter said. "It's part of growing up. Of course a lot of people don't make it. They get old and never grow up. I'd guess it could be annoying. Your body changes and at sixty it's telling you something a lot different than what it's telling you at thirteen."

"But I would rather be thirteen than sixty."

"Because you'd have your whole life ahead of you. But if you were six you'd have even more of it "

"Wouldn't you want to be thirteen again? I mean, if you had the chance?"

"You want to go back to what you were at six?"

Mason shook his head.

"No. No, I don't think so."

"Then why would anyone sixty want to go back to thirteen?"

"Well, thirteen is a lot better than six," Mason said.

"Did you think that when you were six?"

"No."

"In other words you thought six was the ideal age when you were six and now you're thirteen you think thirteen is the ideal age That's called chronocentrism "

"What's that?''

"The belief one age is better than another."

"How did you pronounce that."'

"Chro-no-cen-tri-sm."

Mason nodded.

"When I was a teenager," Carter said, "my dad always told me I was living the best years of my life. Now I don't know what the old-man had in mind besides other than he wanted to stay a kid all his life, and pretty much did, but those were in no way the best years of my life. They were years I'm glad I don't ever have to go through again. Adulthood and the fleas and ticks it collects is still better. And aging is just a part of the process of not being a kid all your life."

"Do you think I'll grow up? I mean, like when I get older?"

"Yeah. I think you will. Seems to me you already got a pretty good start."

"But you think fifty-five is the ideal age, don't you?"

Carter shook his head.

"No, I'd say it's another age, probably no better or worse than any other. Think of the things people twenty-five and thirty have to do I no longer have to do."

"What things?"

"Well, they have to work for mean people. They want homes and cars and kids and good lives. Then they have to suffer, to see their ideals and goals rot away before their eyes."

"But isn't there good? I mean, you enjoy your life, don't you?"

"Oh, yeah. I met some wonderful people," Carter said. "People I've really loved. Great students. And I've seen people do magnificent things. I've enjoyed great art. Marveled at the depth and dexterity of minds producing fantastic ideas. But now, I don't have to put up with that anymore, either. With the magnificence and pain and frustration of wonder and beauty. Unless I want to. And it doesn't mean I won't choose to. Only right now I have more choices than I've had in the past."

"I see," Mason said. "It's like you don't have to worry about it. I mean, the other set of privates and the green hair."

They circled Nashville just after ten-thirty. They ate at a McDonald's near the Kentucky-Tennessee border. Then Mason fell asleep.

Driving alone in the night, with the boy asleep, invigorated Carter, for reasons he did not fully understand. Freedom, possibly freedom, buoyed up. The weight had been lifted. Freedom and the darkness, the solitude and quiet of the car rumbling along anonymously in the night. And primal urges. The pure exhilaration of travel and endurance, of not having to answer to time and place, and persons.

He had entertained the idea he should stay around for Ardyth's trial. Then he dismissed the impulse. His closest connections with her were his fantasies and she had plenty of moral support from other quarters. Why tempt the fates and give the violent fetus another chance?

He would not rule out the possibility of returning to Lancaster for the trial, if there was a trial. Who knows what kind of a deal Absyth could swing? But he would not return just for the trial. One reason for doing something was not usually enough. But five reasons could make it worthwhile. At the moment he did not have even three good reasons

And Sam was gone. Escaped. Vanished. Disappeared as Murphy said. The absence hung in Carter's head. The old man, old man, gone off alone, walking some disserted street, a lone highway, looking for a comfortable rock to rest on, to pass his last hours as family and tribesmen took to the higher altitudes with their herds migrating to seasonal pastures.

Carter wondered what he would do tonight if he saw such a man. Several times he had offered a ride. As he did one morning he found a young woman passed-out on a Lancaster street corner. He stopped for a red light and saw her lying next to a bus-stop having feinted, or worse. The several pedestrians waiting at the corner were unmoved by her condition, ignored her, and stood looking down the street for the bus. Carter parked the Pontiac around the corner, encouraged the woman to her feet and following her somewhat confused directions, found her house and delivered her to an older woman who answered the door. He did not ask her name.

There had been another time or two, out on the road, when he offered people rides. Several times hikers refused his offer. Of course they had a right to their loneliness, their solitude.

Would anyone offer Sam a ride? To where? He didn't know. Even if Sam arrived at wherever he was going, he would be unable to give the who and where from and where to and why. He could not make a reasonable or meaningful reply. The consciousness of Sam Perrin sprung loose in the world of matter, of things, had disappeared or at least could no longer account for itself.

Carter watched the road, thinking, maybe Sam had made it this far.

Maybe he was still alive and out there someplace and prepared to recover what was lost. Fantasy, he concluded, pure fantasy. A child's dream.

But what more was there? To pass the hours of white-line monotony, he dropped into reviewing the events of the last month, the anger and anguish again in his chest and throat, and resolved to give up idle speculation of his recent history and to concentrate on the future instead.

After he delivered Mason he would take a sharp left and head for the sea. From there he'd go along the coast to Washington.

D. C. would be sufficiently miserable this time of year, the air soot-filled, the homeless, the disenfranchised—the center of high political theatrics and stacks of solid-rock marble tributes to the dead past.

As a young man, even into his mid-forties, on vacation in London or Dublin, he always expected he would return. Now he knew it was improbable. At age fifty-five it was highly improbable he would get back to London or Edinburgh. A return, he knew, would be purely accidental. There were just too many cities and simply not enough time.

And since he did not expect to come this way again, he would visit the Library of Congress and the Smithsonian.

Within the next few days he'd call Norman and officially accept the sabbatical for the spring semester.

The prospect pleased him.

For the last two days the newspaper had carried feature stories on Lessiack and Landeau. The Sutter-Chan papers had gotten into the power-structure and the axe had fallen, albeit probably with a blunt blade. Lessiack, Landeau and Miller, along with two others Carter did not know had been suspended without pay.

Without Crowly to run interference, or to take advantage of Crowly's demise and blame a dead man, the grant scam had sailed onto the rocks. From what Carter could make of the news any number of people were washing their hands of the fallout and waste. Hell, the corruption was so hot the pipes in the physics department probably glowed in the dark.

Even the national press had picked up the story.

The university promised a full internal review, but States Attorney Clemens wasn't sounding very accommodating. He was talking in terms of a federal grand jury investigation to determine if any laws had been broken, and promised to co-operate fully with the federal attorneys.

The vibrations emanating from Springfield were unusually vitriolic. Carter wondered what and how much Gotsch knew about the situation when he visited. Why did he refused to talk about Ardyth's incarceration? Maybe the politicals want a trial not so much to get Ardyth for sticking Crowly, but to raise a forum to investigate and explore the Crowly-Landeau-Remcheck schemes. And Shindel.

Later he would write a letter accepting the deal Absyth and Gotsch had worked out. One year. He didn't know where he might be in a year, but he could consider that when the time came.

The best way. And what would Daly and Norman think? It would please the bastards to no end. They'd piss-and-moan about his evil nature—his turpitude. The festering of the bureaucrat's malady. For all things there is a complaint, someone to blame, even when the results are peasant.

Eventually he'd return to Lancaster to settle his affairs, sell the house and whatever else there was. Katherine Marie would no doubt get a lawyer. She had left the Olsens and moved into an apartment with a coworker and was already making noises about wanting her share of the furniture, and what he owed her.

The formula.

Whatever equity the building held, would be eventually pissed away in legal fees. Still, he couldn't bring himself to care about it, to find rancor or disappointment in it. He did not know what he owed Katherine Marie. What might she owe him? And how could it be calculated? She didn't owe him anything, obviously. Her lawyer would play on her sense of deprivation, the emotional economics of having been cheated, and weave it into a package of dollars and cents. That's what they do for humanity. Giving everyone his due. And what is due? Vengeance? Revenge? Retribution?

Selling the house would probably be easy enough. When he called the woman who answered the phone at the Magnuson Realty Agency took his name, phone number and address and within the hour a bespectacled female with a briefcase appeared at the door. He did not think it was the person he had spoken to on the phone, although he wasn't sure.

Forty minutes later they had a management contract signed.

"Just look after it for a month or so. I'll keep in touch."

The slipping away of dollars he had never intended to collect was not a matter of much concern for Carter. If need be, and he assumed it would be soon, he would live on whatever meager means required. A place to keep his books, another six feet long to lie down, a couple pounds of food and a few ounces of bourbon a day would service him well enough.

Now driving in the night he tried to list the books he would take with him—an exercise fitted for Epicurus' garden. Then he gave up on the futility and idiocy of the activity. The list grew as his library had grown over the years, so each additional title found another book to influence or redirect it.

Carter pushed the old car through the northern Georgia sunrise, along I-75 past the Chattahoowee Forest at Dalton and on to Calhoun and Carterville toward Atlanta. By four-thirty the eastern sky was aglow and traveling in the lower latitudes even after the winter solstice the sun appeared closer to the center of the horizon.

At five-fifteen clean shafts of sunlight spiked through the trees. The highway rose in the foothills and dipped along the rivers and lakes in the mountains of northern Georgia.

Mason slept peacefully his head propped against the door on his pillow. He had slept through Tennessee and the night, through two gas stops and a piss-call, stirring only occasionally.

Carter needed to make a pit-stop for gas before Atlanta. He did not want to disturb Mason and decided to go another forty miles or so. Then he'd wake the boy. They could have breakfast and Mason could see Atlanta as they came in.

He took the slip of paper with the address from his shirt pocket. The morning was still not sufficient for reading, and he replaced the paper and tried to reconstruct what he could of the directions from memory.

They came in on the expressway toward downtown Atlanta, running in a welter of morning rush-hour traffic.

"Well, General, there's the city of your fame," Carter said. "Now that's a right decent skyline. Don't you think?"

Mason sat up straight looking from left to right and then back.

"But they didn't burn it this time."

He paused.

"You know Carter, I'm glad for that."

"Well, history doesn't always repeat itself."

They rode through the center of the city on into the Burrnburry Park on the southeast side. Near the middle of the 700 block of Jefferson Davis Avenue Carter slowed the car, trying to determine the house-numbers.

Burrnburry appeared to be an older and more secluded section of town. The antebellum mansions were back a hundred feet or so from the street, shrouded by large trees and enormous bushes.

"You ever been here before? Do you know your grandparents' house?" he said to Mason.

"A long time ago," the boy said. "When I was six."

"You remember the house?"

Mason leaned closer to the windshield, examining the houses as they passed.

"Carter, they all look like the one I remember."

At the end of the block Carter decided to turn around and get out and walk.

"We're going to have to get closer. I'm not even certain these houses have numbers."

"There," Mason said. "That's it right there."

"You're sure? I mean, you're one hundred ten percent sure, without a doubt."

"No," Mason said. "But at least it's better than not knowing where we are."

Carter looked at the boy.

"I drove you all the way to Georgia for you to tell me how fortunate we are to be lost in Atlanta."

The Spencer-Whitehall residence was a two-story affair of imitation classic Greek architecture, the mythic theme echoed throughout the South.

On the right side a long narrow drive passed between two large live oak trees to a portico of fluted columns. Beyond the portico Carter could see an asphalt parking lot and a three car garage with a large weather vane.

"What's your grandfather do?"

"He's a doctor," Mason said.

Carter checked his watch. Eight-thirty. The trip had taken nearly fifteen hours. No doubt Ardyth had phoned to say they were on their way with an approximation of when they would arrive.

"Yes, this is it," Mason said, pointing up the driveway. "Everyone comes in this way. They will be glad to see us."

Carter waited in the car while Mason rang the doorbell. Moments later an elderly woman, Carter guessed to be in her seventies, answered the door. She had white hair, glasses and was dressed in a brocade housecoat and slippers. She opened the door, smiling and quickly embraced the boy.

Together they came over to the car and as Carter disembarked, Mason introduced the woman.

"See, Carter, I told you this was it.

"Grandmother this is John Carter, our friend. Carter this is my grandmother, Mary Spencer-Whitehall."

The woman spoke with a soft southern accent, and apologized for her husband's absence.

"He had rounds at the hospital at seven. He would have been pleased to meet you.

"Please come in."

After the long hours of sitting behind the wheel sagged down in the soft seat of the old Pontiac, Carter's leg ached and when he stood he had difficulty straightening it. The discomfort of the wound from the dog bite had diminished considerably in the last days, and when he stretched he could only barely feel it. He was thankful.

The woman graciously offered him breakfast but he declined.

"We ate about an hour ago. But thank you."

"Surely you'll have coffee."

Carter agreed, and followed her through a large hallway to what he assumed was a sitting-room. The bay had a high ceiling and tall thin windows hung with thick magenta drapes. The morning sunlight fell onto the parquet floor and thick Turkish rugs with the delicacy and shimmer of a silken web.

Carter was seated at an antique French Provincial table near a window with Mrs. Spencer-Whitehall across from him. There a young black maid served them coffee and Danish pastry from a fine porcelain service.

The woman was eloquently articulate, warm and possessed of an uncanny gift for knowing very nearly what he would say next. She asked about his position at the university, which he abbreviated and shifted the conversation so she might hear what he could tell her about Ardyth's situation.

For over an hour they talked about Mason senior's death, about Mason junior and Ardyth's circumstances. She listened attentively to Carter's explanations.

An hour later they unloaded Mason's gear, and Carter declined an offer to meet her husband and stay on for the holidays. Carter thanked the woman for her invitation.

He said to Mason, "Well, old friend, this is good-bye for a while."

"We could have gone all the way to South America without any trouble," Mason said.

"You think so? How far do you think we'd have gone before we would have had to turn back?"

"Maybe all the way to the South Pole. Remember, we're both named Carter."

"You know," Carter said, "I didn't remember that."

"From now on I'm going to use my real name. My name is Carter Oldam."

"Well, Carter, you know this thing with your mother will turn out all right. It might take time, but it will be okay. Meanwhile you have to carry on the Carter Oldam tradition."

The boy's eyes were moist and Carter wasn't sure, but supposed he was thinking about his mother, the situation in Lancaster.

"I know," the boy said. "We'll meet again. Then we'll be old friends."

"Here's something," Carter said. "There's no reason you can't come visit me when you get a vacation. Hey, we could sit around and listen to the Fat Man sing and talk about the revenge of the violent fetuses. Hell, we might even start a violent-fetus fan-club and hall-of-fame."

Carter Mason was looking at the ground.

"Where will you be?"

"The Chinese say you should live facing the sea with the mountains at your back," Carter said.

"California?"

"Oh, I don't know. But it'll be nice. Until then you take care of Sherman's Atlanta, General. We'll keep in touch."

The boy tried to smile, but stood as if he were rooted in the driveway.

"By the way, I almost forgot," Carter said. He took the book he had found in Mason's desk from the glove compartment and handed it to Carter Mason.

"I found this in your father's desk in our office. Your mother gave the book to your father just after they were married. There's a picture of Ardyth and Mason in the book. I'd say it was an early picture, maybe about the same time she gave your father the book."

The boy took the book, his eyes moist.

Carter shook the boy's hand, the boy's soft pliable hand, thinking more he was holding the hand than shaking it, and nodded to Mary Spencer-Whitehall, then got into the car.

At the moment words weren't working very well. Having lost his father, his mother and his home in a matter of a few weeks, Carter thought the boy was holding up extremely well.

There would be a time, Carter could believe, when Carter Mason would break down and cry, when it would be safe enough to cry and to admit to himself the sadness of the changes in his life for which he had no culpability whatsoever.

Anyway, there wasn't a whole lot more to say.

Carter would have preferred to take the boy with him and serve, minimally, as a surrogate, a minor replacement for the boy's lost father. But that was a fantasy, and a counter-productive one. As with so much of the beauty he had discovered, he had no legitimate claim to the boy or to the connections they made in these final few days. And that, in Carter's estimation, was a shame.

He edged the Pontiac into the street, waved good-bye a last time and headed east, southeast for Highway 20 to Augusta, on to Columbia. He'd need to stop for gas and for a couple quarts of motor oil to keep the old engine lubricated.

He hadn't slept for nearly twenty-four hours and needed to get off the highway into a comfortable bed. He intended to stop in Augusta and hole up there for a day or so, to collect his senses, before moving on. He had a bottle of bourbon, for starters, and a copy of Hume's *An Enquiry Concerning Human Understanding* to rethink, to bring into line with his suspicions about the philosophy of the mind. And what better place, he decided, to spend a holiday than in the recesses of an icon of the weather-beaten and shoddy American culture, the cardboard-cutout ubiquitous Holiday Inn, cradled in the genius and fertile mind of that fine and pleasant Scot, David Hume?

The notion came to him that after D.C. he might go on to New York. He had not been to The City in thirty years. But there was nothing or anyone there he cared enough for to make the trip. And the city itself was neither enticing nor inviting. While there were museums and theaters, the streets were for the most a swamp of dope and dog shit.

Is there life in New York City? Not unless you can afford a thirty-second-floor apartment. Certainly there was nothing there for Carter. And time was running down.

No. When he had his fill of driving around observing the manifestations of D.C.'s poverty and power, which would not take too long, he'd head for New Orleans.

Here he was struck by the irony of having two tickets to the Super Bowl in his pocket, a couple slips if thin card-stock for which countless Americans would enthusiastically sacrifice a good part of their material fortune, and for which he had no regard whatsoever. No regard for the tickets and the opportunity to view the game, but no regard for the game either. A fool's paradise, Carter thought.

If after the Superbowl binge, the anguish, the solid rock-bottom, gnawing obstinate ache of insult, and of his dsappointment, had subsided, he would head back to Lancaster to liquidate his holdings and set his affairs straight. If not? He didn't know.

Either way he'd take out for Missoula. He had some time left, ten, maybe fifteen years of months to rethink the years that floated out behind him in a bizarre dream, to see if he could salvage anything of esteem, to see if he could find reason in what he had been doing the last twenty years.

He had heard a lot about Missoula. About people living in the mountains only forty minutes from town. He had heard life in the western Montana winter during the first months of the year could be spectacular and vicious. He wanted to see just how bad it could be, to see what was in it, suspecting deep down inside he would be only trading one wilderness for another.

WAYNE LANTER

Wayne Lanter, English Professor Emeritus, Southwestern Illinois College, is a Writing Fellow from the University of Iowa's Graduate Program in Creative Writing and the former Aspen School of Contemporary Art Writer's Workshop. He has served as Contributing Editor of the *St. Louis Literary Supplement* and of *St. Louis Magazine.* He founded and for ten years edited *River King Poetry Supplement.*

His books of poetry include *The Waiting Room, Threshing Time, At Float on the Ohta-gawa, Canonical Hours, A Season of Long Taters,* and *In This House of Men.* He has edited *New Century North American Poets,* an anthology of contemporary American and Canadian poets, and has published non-fiction works, *Defending the Citadel: A Personal Narrative* and *If the Sun Should Ask: Witch Doctors and Parables.* His work has been anthologized in the United States and in Canada.

www.ingramcontent.com/pod-product-compliance
Lightning Source LLC
LaVergne TN
LVHW050922080826
845145LV00001B/169

* 9 7 8 0 9 8 3 8 4 1 2 1 0 *